10656166

Luc watching box-sets of TV shows. She loves reading and she loves to bake. Writing is such an integral part of Lucy's inner being that she often dreams in Technicolor®, waking up in the morning and frantically trying to write down as much as she can remember. You can find Lucy on Facebook and Twitter. Stop by and say g'day!

WITHDRAWN

Also by Lucy Clark

A Child to Bind Them
Still Married to Her Ex!

Outback Surgeons miniseries

English Rose in the Outback
A Family for Chloe

The Lewis Doctors miniseries

Reunited with His Runaway Doc
The Family She's Longed For

Sydney Surgeons miniseries

Falling for the Pregnant GP
One Week to Win His Heart

Discover more at millsandboon.co.uk.

FALLING FOR THE PREGNANT GP

&

ONE WEEK TO WIN HIS HEART

LUCY CLARK

MILLS & BOON

All rights reserved including the right of reproduction
in whole or in part in any form. This edition is published
by arrangement with Harlequin Books S.A.

This is a work of fiction. Names, characters, places, locations
and incidents are purely fictional and bear no relationship to
any real life individuals, living or dead, or to any actual places,
business establishments, locations, events or incidents.
Any resemblance is entirely coincidental.

This book is sold subject to the condition that it shall not,
by way of trade or otherwise, be lent, resold, hired out
or otherwise circulated without the prior consent of the publisher
in any form of binding or cover other than that in which it is published
and without a similar condition including this condition
being imposed on the subsequent purchaser.

® and TM are trademarks owned and used by the trademark owner
and/or its licensee. Trademarks marked with ® are registered with the
United Kingdom Patent Office and/or the Office for Harmonisation
in the Internal Market and in other countries.

First Published in Great Britain 2018
by Mills & Boon, an imprint of HarperCollins*Publishers*
1 London Bridge Street, London, SE1 9GF

Falling for the Pregnant GP © 2018 by Anne Clark

One Week to Win His Heart © 2018 by Anne Clark

ISBN: 978-0-263-93348-2

MIX
Paper from
responsible sources
FSC® C007454

This book is produced from independently certified FSC™ paper
to ensure responsible forest management.
For more information visit www.harpercollins.co.uk/green.

Printed and bound in Spain
by CPI, Barcelona

FALLING FOR THE PREGNANT GP

LUCY CLARK

MILLS & BOON

To dearest Aunty Rae,
the road ahead might get bumpy
but at least we have each other to lean on.

Eph 3:12

CHAPTER ONE

CLAUDIA-JEAN NICHOLLS STOOD on tiptoe, stretching as high as she could to the top shelf. 'Nope.' She relaxed back with a sigh and rubbed the large baby bump. 'It may help, little one, if you didn't continue to stab me with your elbows. Hmm? How about giving Mummy a break?' She stepped back to look at the item she wanted with longing. 'Why didn't I wear my platform shoes?'

'Do they make platform shoes that high?'

CJ turned to look at the owner of the deep voice but all she saw was a firm chest beneath a navy polo shirt. She lifted her chin to meet the man's gaze and saw a small grin on his lips. 'Are you teasing me about my height?' she asked, her tone light and jovial. When you lived in a small country town, it was almost second nature to have a chat with anyone you met, even if they were a stranger.

He shook his head, his grin widening. 'Not at all. Merely posing a question.'

'Well, to answer your question, no, I don't think they do.' Her own smile increased and she pointed to the item on the shelf that was out of reach. 'Would you mind help-ing me, please? Coffee beans. The red bag.' She placed a hand on her belly. 'There are a few at the back but how they expect me to get them in my condition is beyond me. I should demand a step stool for every aisle.'

'Or enlist the help of a tall friend every time you want to

go shopping,' he offered. 'A safer option to platform shoes and step stools, especially in your condition.' He quickly obliged, obtaining the coffee for her. 'How tall *are* you?'

'Five feet, two inches tall and thirty-five weeks wide.' CJ chuckled at her own joke as she placed the coffee beans into her disorganised grocery trolley. 'Thank you for your help.'

'You're more than welcome.'

With another smile in his direction, she pushed her trolley a little further down the aisle, looking for the next item on her list. She could feel him still watching her and when she looked over her shoulder, almost hitting herself in the face with one of her blonde pigtails, she saw him frowning and looking down the otherwise empty aisle. 'Something wrong?'

'Er...no.' He looked up at the sign above them. 'This is aisle eight.'

'I know.'

'It's just I was told by the store manager that I'd find Dr CJ Nicholls in aisle eight.'

'And you did.' CJ spread her arms wide. 'And then you helped her get coffee beans from a high shelf.'

The man did a double take. *'You're CJ Nicholls?'*

'I am.'

'But...but...you're...er...too young.' At her arched eyebrow, he quickly continued. 'What I mean is...you look about eighteen years old.' He shook his head, his wide grin returning. 'You're having a laugh, right?'

'You think I look eighteen? How very flattering but add at least another twelve years to that and you'll be right on the money.'

'You're thirty!' The incredulity in his tone should have been flattering.

'I guess wearing my hair in pigtails doesn't help the argument that I am indeed a qualified general practitioner.

It's just that wearing my hair up gives me headaches, keeping it loose makes me hot, and I really don't want to cut it so…' She allowed her sentence to trail off as she held out her hand. 'Claudia-Jean Nicholls. *Dr* Claudia-Jean Nicholls. I went to medical school and everything.' Her smile was wide, bright and absolutely dazzling. Her green eyes twinkling with merriment.

'Uh… Ethan Janeway.'

'Oh, you're Ethan.' She shook his hand enthusiastically, ignoring the small wave of heat that spread up her arm at the touch. 'I wasn't expecting you until this evening.' She gestured to her shopping trolley. 'Hence the reason for this last-minute shop. There's nothing in the cupboards.' Why, all of a sudden, did she feel so self-conscious? Perhaps it was because she was faced with a very tall, very dark and *very* handsome stranger who had the most amazing blue eyes she'd ever seen. A stirring of something foreign sizzled in her tummy and it definitely wasn't indigestion! He frowned and she flicked her pigtails back over her shoulders. 'Problem?'

'Why should it matter if there's nothing in the cupboards?'

CJ shrugged and glanced at her watch. 'Whoa, look at the time.' She started pushing the trolley and was pleased when he fell into step beside her. 'I guess I like to eat food when I get home from work,' she remarked, answering his previous question. 'I naturally presumed you would, too.'

'I don't follow. Why should you be concerned with where and when I eat?'

'Your lodgings, while you're in town, are at my house.'

'They're…what now?'

'I thought you knew. It was in the paperwork I sent through. We share a kitchen, laundry and lounge room.'

'The paperwork stated that accommodation was provided with the job. It's why I'm here.' He indicated their present surroundings. 'I went to the clinic to pick up the key for my lodgings, only to be directed here and told to find you.' His gaze rested momentarily on her pregnancy. 'I'm the locum to cover...maternity leave.' He spoke the last two words slowly, as though finally realising that she was the person he was locum for.

'That's right. I'm going on maternity leave as soon as we've got you settled, although why Donna doesn't think I can work up until—' She stopped. She and Donna had had several discussions about this maternity leave, namely that CJ didn't think she needed to take leave at all. Decreasing her workload to part time would have worked just fine but Donna had stood her ground and insisted CJ employ a locum. CJ had finally agreed to find someone for three months, Donna had insisted upon six months. 'Never mind. Any other questions?'

'Er...do we share a bathroom?' He glanced once more at her pregnant belly.

'No.' Her smile broadened. 'Which is just as well because, with Junior jumping up and down on my bladder all night, I need a clear path.'

'And that's why you're shopping? Because I'll be living with you?'

'Sharing a house,' she corrected. 'The bedrooms, with en suites, are at opposite ends of the house. We only finished the renovations last week.'

'You and your husband?' A small frown puckered his brow. 'Or partner?'

CJ dropped her gaze to her ringless fingers. 'My husband passed away. It's just me and the baby now.' She flicked a pigtail over her shoulder.

'I'm sorry. I didn't mean to be...indelicate.'

'You weren't to know and, besides, Pridham is a very small town. I'm sure you'll know all there is to know about me from the patients by the end of your first week.' She grinned. 'At any rate, the "we" I was referring to was myself and Brett, the builder.' She turned into the next aisle and checked her list again, then looked at the shelves and lifted a hand dejectedly.

'Why is everything on the top shelf today? I swear it's a conspiracy to stop pregnant women from getting what they want. Ethan, would you mind getting that jar of pickles down, please?'

'Cravings?'

She grinned again. 'Oh, yeah. Pickles and bananas are high on the list at the moment.'

'Your body must be low in sodium and potassium.'

'Excellent deduction, Dr Janeway. If I hadn't already been impressed with your extensive résumé, I am now.' She chuckled as she added a few more things to the trolley, checked her list and nodded. 'That's it…unless there's something you'd really like or need?'

He scanned the contents of the trolley before shrugging. 'I can come back tomorrow if need be.'

'OK.' She headed for the checkout.

'Ah, I see you found her,' Idris, the store manager, said as CJ started to unload the contents of the trolley.

'In aisle eight, just like you said.' Ethan quickly took over unloading the trolley, especially when she picked up a large tub of ice cream and almost dropped it. 'Allow me,' he stated.

'It's OK. I can manage.'

'I have no doubt but still, this one time, allow me.' Ethan continued to put the groceries onto the checkout conveyer belt. 'I thought, as you're almost to term, that you would have given up work a while ago.'

'Ah…the life of working in a small town. It's definitely a vocational calling because it's all work and no play. Plus, it's usually very difficult to get locums to agree to come this far away from a major city for any extended period of time.'

'I did.'

'Which means you're rare and valuable.' She smiled at him as he finished emptying the trolley. 'Thank you. It's also nice to meet a true gentleman.'

'Do you mean because I helped a pregnant woman?' He shook his head. 'That's not what makes me a gentleman because in my opinion *anyone*, male or female, should help a pregnant woman, especially one in her last trimester.' There was a slight vehemence to his words that CJ admired. When her phone rang, she pulled it from her pocket. 'Dr Nicholls.' Her words were absentminded, still thinking about what Ethan had said, but her mind quickly cleared as her practice manager's voice came down the line.

'Just a heads up, CJ. Ethan Janeway's arrived. He came to the clinic to collect the key to the house and I told him you were at the supermarket. Did he find you?'

'Yes. Yes, he found me. We'll head back to the house so I can put the shopping away and then come over to the clinic. Nothing urgent?'

'No. Just wanted to make sure you'd met our new locum.'

'OK. See you soon.' CJ disconnected the call and paid for her groceries, watching Ethan put the bags into the trolley and begin to push it outside. He was definitely considerate. Hopefully that was a good sign that he would fit well into the town, the medical practice and the shared accommodation.

'Where's your car?'

'Over there.' She pointed to the silver Mercedes.

'Nice wheels.'

She shrugged. 'Not really my kind of car. It was my husband's,' she explained. 'It gets me from here to there and, at the moment that's all that counts.' They unloaded the shopping...well, Ethan unloaded the shopping, glaring harshly at her when she attempted to lift a bag. 'I used to walk most places but now...' she rubbed the heel of her hand over a part of her abdomen, pushing gently on the little foot that was underneath her ribs '...it's kind of impossible.' She took her keys out of her handbag. 'Did you walk or drive here?'

'Drove.'

'OK. Follow me in your car and we'll take this stuff back to the house.'

'Then to the clinic.' He nodded. 'I heard your conversation.' With that, he headed towards a red car parked opposite hers. The car immediately drew her attention. It was vintage with a soft top and leather seats.

'Wow! This is yours?'

'It is.'

CJ headed over to the vintage car and ran her fingertips lovingly over the rim of the door. The soft top was down, which gave her a complete view of the leather upholstered seats and wooden panelled dash board. 'It's in great condition.'

'I've had it restored.'

'Did you do it?'

'Most of it but my brother's a mechanic so I let him help.'

'Big of you.' She grinned and continued to walk around the car as she spoke, inspecting and admiring it as she went. 'May I have a quick look at the engine?' She'd come to stand before him, her green eyes glazed with an honest passion that Ethan found intriguing.

'Of course.' He lifted the concertina hood and stood back.

'Nice cams.'

* * *

Ethan was momentarily taken aback by her knowledge. He'd yet to meet a woman who understood cars. Now it appeared he'd met one—a pregnant one at that. 'Uh, thanks.' He scratched his head. 'How do you know so much about cars?'

'My dad. He used to restore them when I was a kid.' She shrugged one shoulder. 'I helped.' Her smile was still wide with delight. 'I think I should let you know that I *will* be begging for a ride or two while you're here.'

'Of course,' he said again. He lowered the hood and when she didn't say anything else, he gestured to her car. 'Shall we get going?'

'Yes. The ice cream's already started melting. Lucky it's not the height of summer.' He watched as she walked back to her car. What a unique woman. He shook his head as though to clear it from thoughts of CJ Nicholls—*Dr* CJ Nicholls, he corrected, who he'd discovered didn't look a day over eighteen, was heavily pregnant and had a passion for vintage cars. Definitely *not* the type of woman he was usually interested in, but she was definitely intriguing.

It wasn't the fact that she was pregnant that was presently bothering him, but the fact that they'd be sharing a house. Being around pregnant women wasn't his thing. He didn't shy away from them, and he'd proved that when his brother and sister-in-law had had their second child. He'd been the dutiful uncle, visiting in hospital, cooing and making all the right noises, but at the end of the day he'd returned to the peace and quiet of his apartment.

Living, for the next six months, in the same house with the temporarily pregnant CJ Nicholls and soon-to-be newborn baby wasn't what he'd signed up for. He wished he'd known the intricate particulars prior to his arrival because if he had, he wouldn't have come. Perhaps there was a hotel he could stay at, or an apartment he could rent, but both of those would take time to organise and would be exceptionally expensive.

He was still annoyed he'd been forced to take a sabbatical from the excessively busy hospital where he'd worked non-stop for the past six years. When he'd ranted and raved to his sister, Melody, rhetorically asking her what he was supposed to do with his time, especially as he'd finished working on his research project, she'd pitched the idea of being a locum in a quiet country town.

'It's four hours' drive from Sydney. You'll be able to breathe in fresh air, rather than city smog. You'll be able to handle the work of a general practice with your eyes closed, and on weekends you can go for long drives in your car,' Melody had told him.

Ethan had to admit that the drive from Sydney to Pridham today had indeed been a relaxing one...at least after he'd managed to leave the city outskirts behind. Melody would be pleased he was trying to relax. His family had been worried about him, especially after he'd suffered a mild heart attack. 'A warning shot across the bows,' his cardiologist had told him. At least he was being proactive. At least he was trying to change by taking a break from his stressful job.

All of these thoughts went through his head as he followed CJ Nicholls's car back to her house...the house he was supposed to live in for six months. She drove carefully and responsibly, indicating with enough time for him to follow, and eventually she pulled into a driveway—with a double garage—across the road from the medical clinic and local district hospital. At least everything was nice and close.

Ethan helped her to unpack the car and carried the groceries into the kitchen, telling her to sit down and just point to where things went. CJ poured herself a glass of water and did as he suggested, lifting her feet to rest them on one of the other chairs at the table. He needed to gather more information, to find out whether there was anywhere else he could stay. Once the shopping was put away, he leaned against the bench and watched as she sipped her water.

'Ah. That's nice and cool.' She shifted slightly, rubbing her stomach. 'I could just curl up and sleep for a few hours.' Closing her eyes, she tilted her head back, exposing a long expanse of neck. Ethan swallowed, his gaze drawn to it. It looked soft and smooth and—

He forced himself to look away and cleared his throat. What on earth was wrong with him? He didn't do relationships, not since... He stopped the thought. Now was not the time to think about his past. 'Uh...so the house. Does it belong to you or...does the clinic own it...or...are there other places I could stay...or...' He let his words trail off and looked out the window next to the kitchen sink.

'You don't want to stay here?' Her eyebrows hit her hairline in surprise.

'Uh... I was just asking. I don't want to impose.' He indicated her pregnant belly. 'You're going to have your hands full very soon. Do you really want a stranger living here, cramping your style?'

CJ's answer was to take another sip of her water, clearly thinking over her words before she spoke. 'I have no objection to sharing the house. It's certainly big enough and I sincerely doubt you'll hear the baby crying all the way from your end. The walls are well insulated.'

'Part of your remodelling?'

'Yes. It's an old house but over the years I think I've gutted almost every room and redone it.'

'You like renovating?'

'I do. Houses. Cars. I like taking something old and making it new and functional, whilst at the same time still maintaining the essential character of the object.'

He nodded. He knew exactly what she was talking about

because that's the way he'd felt about his car. 'You've lived here a long time?'

CJ nodded. 'The house was originally attached to the medical practice. The part you're in was the consulting area with a small emergency area out the back. The rest of the house was where we lived.'

'We? You and your husband?'

'No. My dad, my sister and me. I was thirteen when we moved in.' She grinned and he had to admit that when she did, it lit up her face. 'It was an old place but one we filled with love.' CJ rubbed her stomach, her words nostalgic and melancholy. 'We moved here after Mum had passed away. This town was our new beginning and that's exactly what we got.' She sipped her water. 'Five years later, the clinic across the road was built but Dad kept that part of the house...' she pointed in the direction of what would be his living area '...for his study, and the little surgery at the back became his bedroom.'

'Has he passed away?'

CJ nodded. 'Last year, after a three-year battle with Alzheimer's. He stayed here as long as he could before my sister found a great care facility in Sydney close to where she lives, and I stayed here to continue running the practice.'

'Is that what you wanted?'

'That had always been the plan.'

'Your plan, or his?'

'Both.' Her smile was natural and instant. 'I love this house, I love the town, I love the people.'

'And your husband? Was he also a local boy, too?'

'No.' CJ finished her drink, then stood and took her glass to the dishwasher. 'We should get over to the clinic.'

'I didn't mean to pry.'

'You didn't,' she said with a shrug before walking out of the house, not bothering to lock the door behind her.

'Uh...do we need to lock up?'

She shook her head. 'Crime is low in the town but if locking the doors makes you feel better, then lock away.' She didn't stop walking as she spoke, only gesturing back to the door. Her bright, jovial tone had disappeared completely and her words were flat. He really hadn't meant to pry, especially as she'd been quite happy to chat about her family. At least he now knew the topic of her husband was off limits.

As CJ opened the door to the clinic and headed inside, she couldn't help but notice the way Tania's eyes turned all dreamy at the sight of Ethan.

'Hi, handsome. Good to see you back,' Tania openly flirted.

'Any patients for me this afternoon?' CJ asked, trying to shift the receptionist's gaze from Ethan to herself.

Tania snapped out of it. 'Just two.'

'How many does Donna have?'

'She told me not to tell you. Just see your two patients, do your ward round and go home to rest. You know that's what you want to do, CJ.'

She sighed. 'I guess. When's my first patient?'

'Five minutes.'

'Good.' She walked down the small corridor into her consulting room, pleased that Ethan had followed. 'Did you meet Donna when you came in earlier? She's my partner.'

'No.'

'OK. Then I guess you haven't been shown around so I'll do that once I'm finished with the patients. You may as well sit in, start to learn the ropes.'

'Agreed.'

CJ sank down into the chair and sighed. 'I am getting more tired than normal and that frustrates me.'

'You're so used to being busy?' He could certainly relate to that.

'Yes. Come Monday, you'll be taking over my consulting work. I'll be doing house calls with you this weekend... and maybe the odd one here and there over the next few weeks if it's OK with you. I just don't want to get bored and I know I will.'

'Was it Donna who insisted you get a locum to cover your maternity leave?'

'Donna, Tania, the nurses, the patients and the majority of the town. Yes.' CJ couldn't help the sad sigh that escaped her. 'I feel so useless and it makes me think back to when my father's health began deteriorating. *I* was the one trying to pick up the slack and take over from him without him realising it, but of course he did and—' She stopped talking and sighed again. 'I just feel big and useless and...fat.'

'You're not fat. You're having a baby,' Ethan calmly pointed out. 'And you're not useless. Your body is growing a human being! You studied anatomy, you know how difficult that is—to grow a human being. *I* can't do it. You can, so how about, as my first act as locum to this practice, I advise you not to be so hard on yourself and your temporary limitations.'

His warm, smooth words washed over her in such a relaxing fashion that she felt her earlier tension begin to melt away. 'I suppose you're right.'

'I *know* I'm right.'

She smiled at that. 'Well, I'll accept the advice, even though you don't officially start consulting until Monday.'

'That's very big of you, Dr Nicholls.'

'I thought so.' The phone on the desk rang and she picked it up. 'Yes?'

'Jed's here,' Tania said down the line.

'OK. Send him in,' CJ replied before hanging up. Then she pointed to the phone. 'This is an internal line—usually Tania or Donna—and these two lights are your outside lines.'

'Always good to know. So, who are we seeing first?' Ethan stood and came closer, leaning over and pressing a button on the computer, pleased when Jed's file came up. 'Good. The same computer programme I'm used to.'

'Great. Sometimes it's the little things that can trip us up.' Like the way his spicy scent seemed to wind its way around her senses. It was nice. She liked it. She momentarily closed her eyes and gave herself a mental shake. That was the hormones speaking. Spices smelled more vibrant to her and she liked it. As Ethan moved back to his chair, ready for the consultation, CJ reset her mind where her new colleague was concerned.

Sure, he might be good looking and, yes, he smelled wonderful and had gorgeous eyes...and was tall enough to help her out when she needed it, but he was just a locum... just a man who would be out of her life in six months' time. She shouldn't get attached.

When Jed came into her consulting room, CJ smiled brightly and introduced Ethan. The two men shook hands and when Ethan closed the door behind Jed, CJ smiled her thanks then focused on her patient.

After the consult, she quickly typed up her notes about Jed's treatment on the computer.

'Do you usually go out to the waiting room and call the patients through?' Ethan asked.

'Usually, but at the moment, getting up and down is difficult so Tania rings through when the patients have arrived and I tell her when to send them in.' The phone on the desk rang, the light for an internal call blinking.

'I'll go,' he stated. 'What's the patient's name?'

'Chandra.' And before she could say another word, Ethan had disappeared to the waiting room, returning a moment later with four-year-old Chandra and her mother. His actions, although well meant, only made CJ feel like an expectant whale once more. She knew it wasn't for ever and she knew that part of the way she was feeling was due to her overactive hormones but…she still didn't like it.

Once Chandra and her mother had left, Ethan watched as CJ quickly typed the notes into the computer. Before she could finish, though, a sharp pain gripped her abdomen and she moaned, feeling very uncomfortable.

'What is it?' Ethan was instantly by her side, his gaze roving over her, visually checking for signs of labour.

CJ shoved away from the desk and stood up, walking back and forth as she rubbed the side of her belly. 'It's nothing. Just a swift kick from junior to mother. Ugh. I swear this kid is going to be a footballer.' She rubbed her stomach again and when the baby responded, without thinking she reached for Ethan's hand and pressed it to her stomach. 'See? Feel that? As a fellow doctor, you have to agree that that's one strong kick!'

When he didn't answer, she looked up. Their gazes locked and the atmosphere around them seemed to zing with newly charged electrons. Even deep inside her she felt them explode and she sucked in a ragged breath. It was unusual, it was unexpected and it was most certainly unwanted.

Ethan was stunned by the sensation. Not only was he alarmed by feeling her baby kick, a sensation he hadn't felt for quite a number of years, but also he hadn't expected the jolt that had travelled up his arm and ripped through his body. He was attracted to this woman! How was that possible? There was no way an attraction to anyone was paramount at the present time.

It took a few moments for him to realise she'd released her hold on his wrist. Still, he left his hand on her stomach for a fraction longer before jerking away and walking briskly from the room.

CHAPTER TWO

ETHAN OPENED HIS eyes and stared at the ceiling, furious with himself for not being able to sleep. Why had she put his hand on her belly? Feeling an in utero baby kick had been the last thing he'd wanted to do. It was also the last thing he wanted to think about right now.

He sat up, swinging his legs to the floor, then slowly looked around the room, lit by veiled moonlight. The wardrobe had sufficient coat hangers at one end and ample drawer and shelf space at the other. There were also several fluffy bath towels on one of the shelves.

In the corner of the room was an Australian jarrah desk, with a comfortable chair pushed beneath. The desk was functional but also kept with the decorated theme of the room, which, he had to admit, was very masculine. Well, CJ had mentioned that this part of the house had originally been her father's. Ethan looked more closely at the three framed pictures on the wall, which were all of vintage cars. Nice cars, too. Were they her father's pictures? Was that her father's old desk? If so, it leant a more personal touch to the room and he felt privileged she had chosen to have her memories on display for others to share. Perhaps seeing her father's things around also helped her to cope with the loss.

He hadn't done that. When he'd suffered great loss, he'd arranged for movers to come to his house and pack everything into boxes before delivering it to a storage locker… a storage locker he still paid for six years later. Then he'd sold the house and bought a sterile apartment near St. Aloysius Hospital. If he hadn't been forced to take time off, he'd be there right now, working and forgetting his past.

Sighing, Ethan raked both hands through his hair, keeping his thoughts on a tight leash. He *was* here, which was far better than lying on some beach, being bored for six months. As he took another look at the pictures, peering closely at the detail of the cars, he had to admit that CJ had gone to a great effort to make him comfortable, but what type of woman liked vintage cars?

He supposed a lot of women did but he'd never come across them before. It was a refreshing change. The restoration of his car had been a bone of contention between himself and Abigail. She'd accused him of spending more time with the car than with her.

'I don't mind you being at the hospital until all hours, Ethan. That's your job, I get it. But when you're home, I want you to spend that time with *me*, not your car.'

He stood and started pacing around the room. He still felt uncomfortable about sharing accommodation with CJ. He wasn't used to living with anyone and he wasn't sure he wanted to adjust. He liked his life the way it was…or the way it had been before his imposed exile from the hospital.

Why had his body betrayed him like that? A prime candidate for a major heart attack? The medical tests had to be incorrect—even though he'd insisted the results be repeated. He exercised. He ate right. Sure, he was stressed but everyone else he knew was also stressed and they hadn't been told by the CEO to take a six-month sabbatical and de-stress. Why had it been—?

His thoughts halted as he heard a sound nearby. A door being opened and then closed? He strained, listening for more sounds. Quiet footsteps. Was there someone in the house? He shook his head, reminding himself that he was now *sharing* a house with someone else. Was CJ up or was there someone at the front door? An emergency? Did she need help?

He quickly pulled on a T-shirt, his legs already covered by a pair of pyjama pants. Deciding this was still too informal to greet a possible intruder, he grabbed his robe, belting it loosely before opening his bedroom door. When another sound came, he decided to go and investigate, his entire body alert. He crept into the hallway, keeping to the shadows as he made his way towards the kitchen. Peering around the doorway, all the tension left him as he saw CJ standing in front of the open fridge door, peering inside.

'Couldn't sleep?' he asked, walking into the room.

She jumped sky high and spun to face him.

'For heaven's sake, don't go creeping up on me like that.' CJ placed one hand over her heart and the other on the baby. She grinned at him and flicked her loose, golden hair over her shoulder. 'Although, if I do go over my due date, you could always scare me into labour.' She returned her attention back to the fridge and pulled out the pickles and bananas. As she moved, Ethan took stock of what she was wearing. She was dressed in an oversized nightshirt, her robe open and hanging down her back, and pink fluffy slippers on her feet.

'Baby won't settle,' she offered by way of explanation as she put the food onto the table. 'Would you mind getting the chocolate spread down from that cupboard, please?' She pointed in the direction of one of the high kitchen cupboards before turning back to the fridge. 'Want anything?' She pulled out a large bottle of ginger beer.

'No.' He put the chocolate spread on the table. Her silky hair was cascading smoothly over her shoulders and the urge to run his fingers through it surprised him. It had been a long time since he'd had such an urge, and he instantly quashed it. He'd met his first love at university, sweet Abigail. He ignored the surge of guilt that always came whenever he thought about her. Why, oh, why hadn't she let him help her? He clenched his jaw. Nothing could be done to change the past. He was done with love. Over. Gone. Finished.

Living here wasn't what he wanted. He didn't want to be around people, having to deal with emotions. He didn't want to be attracted to anyone. He didn't want to make compromises in his private life and if he'd had any doubts before, seeing his pregnant colleague shift around the kitchen only emphasised that he needed to live somewhere else.

'Keep me company,' CJ suggested, as she put a plate and knife on the table before easing herself down into the chair. 'Whew. I tell you, just getting up and down now is such an effort. I'll be glad when this is all over.'

'You'll still have to get up and down to the baby,' he pointed out, as he pulled out a chair at the opposite end of the table and sat down.

'Sure but at least I won't be lugging him or her around with me twenty-four hours a day, seven days a week. The baby can sleep in the cot and I can enjoy having my body back to myself.'

'Except for feedings.'

'True.' She sighed. 'Donna told me the other day that so many women spend so much time focusing on the pregnancy that they give little thought to what happens afterwards. The feeding, the nappies, the constant alertness even when you're exhausted.' She took a sip of her drink, then remarked, 'I think I'll be good at the last bit. Being a doctor, I'm used to the odd hours and the constant demand for my time.' She reached for a pickle, before proffering the jar to him. 'Are you sure you won't join me?' Before he could answer, she smeared the pickle with chocolate spread and held it out to him. 'It's oddly delicious. Want to try?'

A bubble of laughter escaped before he could damp it down. 'Thanks, but, no, thanks. You go right ahead.' His new colleague really was like no other woman he'd met before. She was open, honest and sometimes he wondered if she filtered her thoughts before speaking them out loud. Still, it was a refreshing quality to be around. It was as though she was more than comfortable with who she was and she didn't care who knew it. Abigail had always been so conscious of adhering to the dictates of society that sometimes he'd been worried at her lack of confidence in exerting her own opinions and thoughts. Where his wife had never wanted to rock the boat, it appeared CJ was more than happy to jump overboard and splash around in the water.

Ethan rubbed his chin and sighed. It was wrong of him to compare the two women as they'd clearly had very different upbringings. Why he was comparing them at all, he had no clue. What he was conscious of, however, was the salty and sweet scents of what CJ was eating and within the next moment his stomach growled, betraying him.

CJ chuckled. 'Grab some food. Shut that growling stomach up.'

'It's OK. I don't like to eat between meals.'

'Between meals? Ethan, it's…what…?' CJ glanced at the clock on the wall. 'It's three o'clock in the morning and clearly you were wide awake, as I'm pretty sure I wasn't *that* noisy. Perhaps you couldn't sleep because you were hungry.' She waved another chocolate-smeared pickle in his direction. 'If this doesn't tempt you, grab an apple or whatever takes your fancy. Go on. Live on the edge. Eat something *between* scheduled mealtimes.'

Ethan listened to her, his smile increasing as she chatted away, teasing him with light-hearted banter. 'Does everyone in this town talk the way you do?'

Her answer was to shrug as she chewed her mouthful, then swallowed. 'You'll have to figure that out for yourself. As far as I'm concerned, we only live our lives by the restrictions we force upon ourselves.'

'And do you *have* any restrictions?' His stomach growled again and he was rewarded with another light tinkling chuckle from the woman opposite.

'I guess you'll have to figure that out, too.'

He had to admit she had a nice laugh. It was a lovely sound and as it washed over him, he breathed in deeply and relaxed a little. 'Perhaps I will have a piece of fruit.' With that, he stood and went to the fridge. 'You keep bananas in the fridge?' he asked a second later and again she chuckled.

'Why not? It stops them from ripening as fast.'

'Is that true?'

CJ swallowed her mouthful. 'I have no idea but it sounds as though it could be true. And speaking of bananas...' She reached for the one in front of her and began to peel it, pleased she'd managed to break through his defences. After he'd stalked out of her consulting room, she'd sat there confused. She wasn't sure where he'd gone, but as she'd had to go over to the hospital after finishing her measly clinic, she'd found him there, in a deep discussion with the Clinical Nurse Consultant. Together the three of them had done a round of the ward, with Bonnie, the CNC, introducing Ethan to the rest of the staff.

She watched as he polished the apple on his robe before taking a bite, walking back to the chair he'd recently vacated. 'You have a nice smile,' she stated, and he paused, apple poised for another bite, and glared at her. 'Sorry. I didn't mean to blurt that out but it's true. I hope I didn't make you uncomfortable.'

CJ shook her head as she watched him take another bite of his apple. 'My dad used to say that I had no filter, that what I thought was what I said. Sometimes he said it was very refreshing and other times quite annoying.' She chuckled and took another bite of her banana. Life was what you made it and as far as CJ was concerned, she didn't have time for double talk and silly games.

'So…how do *you* handle it when someone just blurts out the truth, perhaps saying something you don't want to hear?'

'Huh.' She laughed without humour. 'My husband used to say a lot of things I didn't want to hear.'

Ethan nodded. 'I think that happens in most relationships.' At least, it had for him. There were things he'd regretted saying to Abigail and things he regretted *not* saying to Abigail. She, however, had preferred to keep quiet, had preferred not to tell him what was really going on in her life…even though he had kept asking her if something was wrong. She'd been so secretive. And too late he'd understood why. He slammed the door shut on his thoughts yet again.

'Well, in my marriage…' She hesitated for a moment, then continued. 'I may as well tell you because you'll no doubt hear my sad tale from the gossips in town.'

'You don't have to.'

'I'd rather you hear it from me, without the added embellishments. You see, my husband was having affairs. I, of course, was the last to know.'

'That…er…would have been…devastating.' Ethan shifted uncomfortably in his chair and took another bite of his apple.

'I guess I'd known our marriage wasn't working for some time as we rarely spent time together.'

Ethan's gaze momentarily dropped to look at her pregnant belly before meeting her eyes again, the lift of his eyebrows stating he believed otherwise.

'Well…clearly we spent *some* time together, but it was the *last* time as well.' CJ suddenly realised she was full and put the lids back on the food jars in front of her, just like she'd put the lid on her marriage, and shoved those memories back onto the shelf.

'You're very open, very trusting,' Ethan blurted. 'I've never met anyone like you before, CJ.' He put the apple down. 'I'm practically a stranger to you and yet I'm living in your home. Did you do any background checks on me? Did you research me?'

'Of course I did. I may try my best to be open and honest, as I find it avoids confusion, but I'm not naive, Ethan. I checked out your references and spoke to a few mutual acquaintances.'

'What? Who do we know in common?'

'I have several colleagues and friends at St. Aloysius Hospital.'

'Really?'

'Yes. I did my training there.'

'Huh.' He picked up his apple and took another bite. 'I didn't know that but, then, I know less about you then you clearly know about me. So, who do we know in common?'

'Carol Blacheffski. Steve Smith. Patrick Janoa. Melody Janeway.' She raised her eyebrows as she said the last name.

'You know my sister?'

She nodded. 'I know her well enough to ensure you weren't an axe-wielding homicidal maniac.'

Ethan sat up a little straighter in his chair. 'Wait a second. You know her? She told me she found the job in the classified section of a medical journal.'

'She did. I advertised for the locum then, as she knew me, she called me and we talked.'

'About me?'

CJ laughed and slowly started to ease herself up out of the chair. 'Clearly.'

'You both set me up!' He put the half-eaten apple onto the table and glared at her.

'How is this a set-up?' She spread her arms wide, as though she had no earthly idea what he was on about. 'I need a locum.' CJ gestured to her pregnant frame. 'The fact I was able to get a brilliant surgeon to come and cover my leave was a godsend. Trying to get a GP out here, in a small tourist town, for any length of time is bad enough as all the newly qualified doctors want to get their foot in the door at the big city practices and start earning the big bucks. You, on the other hand, needed some respite and to downsize your workload. Melody thought it was just what the doctor ordered.' CJ grinned at the pun.

'So you were organising me.'

'*I* wasn't. Your sister, on the hand, might have been. She sounded very worried about you.'

'And you didn't think to mention this to me earlier, that you knew Mel?'

'I thought you knew!' CJ spread her arms wide again before sighing heavily. 'It wasn't some big conspiracy and why does it matter *how* things transpired? The point is, you're here now and I'm very grateful.' Clearly Ethan was upset at this news but right now, with a small foot shifting awkwardly across her abdomen, she wasn't in the mood to have an in-depth conversation on the matter. She rubbed the baby, trying to ease the little one into a more comfortable position.

'Wait. Did my sister know I'd be sharing accommodation with you?'

'Uh…' CJ thought back to the conversation but her forgetful pregnancy brain made it difficult. 'I think so.' She shook her head and smothered a yawn. 'I honestly can't remember, Ethan, and I'm tired now so I think I'll go brush my teeth again and head back to bed. Gotta be up in another three hours.'

'Actually, before you go, there's something I need to say.'

When she looked at him, it was to find him standing rigid in the middle of the kitchen, arms crossed over his chest. 'What's that?'

'Uh… I think it's best if I find somewhere else to live.'

'You don't like it here?'

'I don't like sharing.'

She pondered his words. 'That would have been interesting for you and your siblings while you were growing up.' It also rang some alarm bells in the back of her mind that she needed to watch her step where Ethan was concerned. Quinten, her husband, hadn't liked sharing things, except his bed. Quinten had also become overbearing and controlling. Was Ethan really like that or was that just the image he liked to convey so that people didn't question him too deeply? Either way, she had no room in her life right now for a drama king.

'That's not what I meant.'

'I know what you meant. You're not used to sharing accommodation. I get it.' CJ smothered another yawn. 'I don't think you'll find a furnished apartment in town available for the length of your stay. Most of the bed-and-breakfast places around here are booked up for the weekends and school holidays.' She rubbed her belly. 'However, you're more than welcome to try. If you're uncomfortable here and you feel that's what you need to do, then I guess that's what you need to do.'

'Just like that? You're OK if I go, even after you went to so much trouble to remodel your house?'

CJ hooted with laughter. 'I didn't remodel it for *you*.'

She put the banana peel in the bin and stacked the dishes in the dishwasher.

'Uh...of course not,' he said. 'But is it OK if I stay here until I can arrange something else?'

'Of course.' After she'd finished tidying up, she headed to the door that led to her part of the house, but paused and turned to look at him. 'I'm guessing you're not used to being sociable and chummy with your work colleagues?'

'Did Melody tell you that?' He was annoyed with his sister and didn't disguise it.

'No. Your manner does.'

'Is that so?'

'Yes. It tells me that you're used to being respected, to not having your decisions questioned and that you don't particularly like interacting with subordinates.'

If he'd been uncomfortable before with the way she just blurted out her thoughts, it was nothing compared to now, and it was mainly because she'd hit the nail right on the head. In a matter of hours of their first meeting, CJ Nicholls had seen right through to the heart of him and it completely unnerved him.

'Ethan, if it makes you feel better, stay somewhere else and only interact with the staff and patients when absolutely necessary. So long as my practice is in one piece when I get back from maternity leave, I don't care what else happens.'

'I've upset you,' he stated.

'No.' She shook her head sadly. 'I'm not angry or annoyed, Ethan. I feel sorry for you. I thought we could be friends, but it's OK if that's not the case.'

'Look, Dr Nicholls, all I want for the next six months is to get out of bed, do my job and spend my evenings in peace.'

She stared at him for a long moment before nodding. 'OK. If that's the way you want it, that's fine.' There was no anger in her tone, no girlish outrage, but there was definitely a hint of pity, which was the last thing he wanted. 'Goodnight, Ethan. I hope you're able to sleep.' With that, she headed through the door that led to her part of the house.

Ethan stood in the kitchen for a while longer, pondering their conversation. He'd survived pity before. He'd been the source of gossip, people whispering in the corner, stopping whenever he walked by, then starting up again the instant he left. He'd locked himself away, just as he'd locked his belongings away and it had been working... until he'd met CJ Nicholls.

It really did leave him with one major question—should he stay, or should he go?

CHAPTER THREE

WHEN SHE WOKE on Saturday morning, CJ felt as though she'd been put through the wringer. She turned on her side, swung her legs over the edge of the bed and slowly pushed herself upright, keeping her eyes closed in an effort to stop the spinning sensation.

Gradually opening her eyes, she tried to focus but it was no good and a wave of nausea hit with force. She clamped a hand over her mouth and rushed to her bathroom. Once her early morning dash was over, she showered and dressed, beginning to feel much better, even though she was already exhausted.

'No one said the last trimester was easy,' she mumbled as she shuffled into the kitchen.

'Feeling better?'

She stopped. Ethan was sitting at the kitchen table dressed in a pair of casual trousers and navy cotton shirt, eating a stack of pancakes drowned in maple syrup. She sniffed appreciatively and smiled as she walked over to the stove.

'Yes, thank you. I guess baby didn't want the pickles, chocolate spread and bananas after all. These, however, smell delicious.'

'You still want to eat after...being sick?' There was concern in his tone.

'I do. Once the morning sickness has passed, I'm usually fine—' She chuckled. 'That is until the next time I eat something baby doesn't appreciate.' CJ peered at the pancake batter in the jug. 'So does this mean you know how to cook?'

'It does. Please, help yourself.'

CJ did just that and soon was sitting down with one pancake, drowning her own in real maple syrup. 'Mmm. These are heavenly, and if you decide that you do want to stay here for the next six months, feel free to make these any time.'

By now, Ethan had finished his breakfast and was stacking the dishwasher. 'Are you usually sick in the morning?' His tone was one of doctorly concern.

'No. Not really. I mean it depends on what I've snacked on around three o'clock in the morning.'

'That's your usual middle-of-the-night routine?'

'At the moment, but some advice I was given regarding children is that just when you think you've got them into a routine, they change it. So I'm not holding out because Junior here changes his, or her, mind almost as much as I do.'

'You don't know the baby's sex?'

She shook her head. 'I'm more than happy to be surprised.'

'And you've spoken to your obstetrician about your morning sickness?'

CJ angled her head to the side, surprised to hear the hint of real concern in his tone. 'You're concerned about me?'

'Naturally. You're a pregnant woman, I'm a doctor. It's part and parcel of who I am.'

She chuckled at that. 'I hear you wholeheartedly. I can't go to a restaurant without silently diagnosing the people sitting around me.'

'OK, then you understand that I'm only asking these questions because I'm professionally concerned?'

'I do.' She nodded. 'And although I know all the ins and

outs of pregnancy and giving birth from a doctorly perspective, going through the process is giving me a whole new perspective.' She took a mouthful of pancakes, savouring the flavours. After swallowing, she continued. 'I've come to realise that my pregnancy doesn't run parallel to many of the medical texts but then, as Donna has said, each pregnancy is different and with mine, morning sickness has been sporadic throughout, not just in the first trimester. Even now, with only a few weeks to go, my appetite is as hearty as it's always been.' She smiled.

'And just to appease your concern, my blood pressure is fine, my ankles aren't swollen and I'll continue to see Donna weekly until the baby decides to make an appearance.'

'The obstetrician won't be here?'

'If she's here, then well and good but both Donna and I hold diplomas in obstetrics.' CJ forked in another mouthful.

'So you're happy for Donna, your friend and colleague, to deliver your baby?'

'Women in country towns usually rely on a friend or a grandmother or an old aunt to help them through deliveries, especially if it takes for ever for the doctor to arrive. Why is this any different? Except in my case, my experienced friend is also a well-trained doctor.'

'What about midwives? Are there any in the district?'

She shook her head. 'It would be good, though. We have two part-time district nurses, one from each hospital, but a midwife would definitely be helpful. However, the government believes that with two district hospitals and two GPs this area is well provided for…and I guess we're much better off than some other districts.'

He pondered her words as he fixed himself a coffee. 'Can I get you a drink? I see you have some decaffeinated coffee here. Or would you like some herbal tea?'

CJ shook her head. 'I'm fine for now, but thank you.' As she continued to eat, he hunted around the kitchen for the sugar and took the milk from the fridge.

He was glad she was receiving regular check-ups with Donna. With everything that had happened to Abigail, it had made his doctorly instincts almost over-cautious with all pregnant women. He would also need to get used to not working with the latest equipment and specialists on demand. He'd had no idea that Pridham would only have visiting specialists who came this way once a month, sometimes less, leaving the overworked GPs to pick up any slack. Perhaps this job was going to be more interesting than he'd thought.

Ethan glanced across at her, watching her devour those pancakes, secretly delighted that she was enjoying his cooking. He usually had little time to prepare balanced meals, preferring to grab something relatively healthy from the hospital cafeteria. Now that he was in Pridham, he would have the time to exercise more, do more cooking and drive his car. Sure, he'd be working but the stress would be different. Consulting in clinics and doing house calls would be very different from all-day operating lists, overbooked outpatient appointments, departmental administration work and research projects.

As he sat down to drink his coffee, he thought more about the conversation they'd had earlier that morning. It had unnerved him a little to discover that CJ knew Melody. Had Mel told CJ about Ethan's mild heart attack? Had she told CJ the reason *why* he'd almost worked himself into an early grave? He sipped his coffee, glancing at her over the rim of his cup. Even if Melody hadn't said anything to CJ, had any of the other people she'd spoken to revealed gossip about Abigail? About the baby?

If she knew all about him, perhaps he should learn more about her? He'd called her trusting to take a stranger into her home but, likewise, he'd accepted a job and accommodation and had, for all intents and purposes, spent last night in a stranger's home.

What did he really know about the pregnant woman opposite him? She was a local in Pridham, ran a busy practice, held a diploma in obstetrics and was a pregnant widow. It made him wonder about her, made him want to ask more questions, to get to know her better, and that, in itself, was uncommon for him. He usually wanted to know as little about his colleagues as possible, other than they were competent and skilled enough to do their work.

Clearing his throat, he put his cup down on the table. 'Uh… CJ, if you don't mind me asking, how did your husband die?'

'Quinten died in a car crash almost nine months ago. It was six weeks after he'd passed away that I found out I was pregnant.' CJ sighed, shaking her head sadly. 'Quinten had never wanted children, anyway, so, regardless of the situation, I would have been raising this child on my own.'

'He would have left you in the lurch?' Clearly, from what she'd told him last night, her marriage hadn't been a happy one—at least near the end of it. He could relate to that far more than she probably realised. He and Abigail had been very happy in the beginning, but near the end…

She shrugged one shoulder. 'Who's to say? Perhaps he would have done the right thing and at least financially provided for the baby.' CJ put her knife and fork together on her plate, then leaned back and rubbed a hand over her stomach, smiling at her baby bump. 'Did you enjoy that, my sweetheart? Because Mummy certainly did.'

'How long were you married?'

'Five years, but we'd grown apart, as I mentioned last night.' She shrugged the words off with feigned nonchalance. 'That was my old life. I now have a new one I need to concentrate on.' She smiled brightly—a little too brightly, he thought as she levered herself up. 'Thanks so much for breakfast. Donna's doing morning clinic so we don't need to bother with that, although you will be rostered on once a fortnight to work a Saturday morning.'

Ethan nodded. 'I re-read all the paperwork last night.'

'Right, well, how about I slip on some shoes and then we can head off to Whitecorn District Hospital.'

'That's the other district hospital where I'll be doing a clinic once a month?'

'Correct.' She cleaned up the mess she'd made, wiping down the benches before heading into her part of the house. When she returned, she'd tied her hair back into low pigtails and added a scarf. 'Mind if we take your car?' She batted her eyelashes at him pleadingly and smiled sweetly. He couldn't help but grin at her efforts.

'Subtle.' They headed outside into the April sunshine.

'Well, I did warn you that I'd beg a ride.'

'Yes, yes, you did.' Ethan held the passenger door open for her.

'There'll be more traffic on the road today, being a weekend.'

'Tourists?'

'In droves, but it's great for the area.'

'Bad for the doctors?'

'No. We're only called in when necessary and poor Donna's been covering any emergencies for the past few weekends anyway. I told her it was no trouble for me to be rostered on but she likes to mother me.' CJ sank down into the comfortable, upholstered leather. 'Nice.' She drawled the word out on a sigh. 'Oh, this is *very* nice. How much of the internal restoration did you do yourself?'

'I didn't do the seats or the dash but I certainly banged out a lot of dints and hunted through old junk yards until I found just the thing I needed.'

CJ nodded. 'You've got to take your time. Restoring a car isn't something to be rushed.'

'I completely agree.' Ethan was astonished to hear the words coming out of her mouth as they were the same words he'd said to Abigail. However, his wife really hadn't understood his passion, much as he would have liked her to. 'You're the first woman I've ever known to enthuse to the point of obsession over a car.'

'What do you mean, to the *point* of obsession? I *am* obsessed. Just as you are.' She laughed and closed her eyes, enjoying the feel of the wind on her face. As they drove along, Ethan once again found himself breathing a little more deeply than before. His cardiologist would be pleased.

'You're not filling your lungs all the way,' Leo had told him when Ethan had insisted the results of his physical examination be repeated. 'You need to slow down and—'

'If you say *smell the roses*, I'll punch you in the nose, mate.'

Leo's answer had been to laugh. 'Ethan, we've known each other for decades. I respect you as a medical professional *and* as a friend, and it's because you're my friend that these test results concern me so much.' Leo had shaken his head.

'It's just a hiccup. I'll slow down. I promise.'

'But you won't. I know you and this "hiccup", as you call it, may have been a mild heart attack but it means others will follow if you *don't* change your lifestyle. To lose you to a massive heart attack that could easily be prevented—it's a no-brainer. My recommendation to the CEO that you take an imposed sabbatical for six months stands. Smell those blooming roses. Breathe the fresh air. Get out of the city. Get out of your comfort zone. Meet new people and learn to appreciate life again.'

'I appreciate life,' he'd growled, completely furious with his friend. 'It's why I'm a surgeon.'

'Appreciate *your* life,' Leo had clarified. 'Fill your lungs—all the way. Breathe as deeply as you can and enjoy the exhalations as your stress ebbs away.' And for some reason, since his arrival in CJ Nicholls's life, Ethan had breathed more deeply than he had during the past six years.

Perhaps he was jumping the gun a bit, saying he wanted to look around for somewhere else to stay? He decided to put a mental pin in the thought and just see what else unfolded. For the moment, the drive through the beautiful countryside, surrounded by the early changing of the autumn leaves on the rows of grapevines, was very relaxing.

'How does the tourism impact the hospitals and clinics?' he asked CJ after he'd negotiated the car out of the main road of town.

She lifted her head and glanced across at him, her sunglasses in place, a scarf covering her hair. She looked very…nineteen-twenties chic. 'We have the odd emergency—burst appendix, perforated ulcers, that sort of thing. Food poisoning pops up every now and then. Of course there are coughs and colds and general ailments people don't think of during the week because they're so busy running around. Then they go away for the weekend, their bodies start to relax from the daily grind and they pick up the slightest bug or virus.

'Sometimes we have people involved in car accidents, primarily because they've been stupid enough to drink and drive, but thankfully we haven't had anything for a few years.' She pointed to the road ahead. 'Go left at the T-intersection. The hospital's just down the road there.'

As he indicated to turn, he saw the Whitecorn District Hospital and soon they were pulling into the car park. When he brought the car to a stop, she turned and grinned wildly at him, slowly removing the scarf and sunglasses.

'That was…exhilarating. Thank you.' Her smile was so genuine, as though she didn't have a care in the world. How could she be like that when she was heavily pregnant and facing single parenthood? He stared at her for a long moment, astonished how her smile seemed to light up the darkness around his heart. He didn't want to be moved by her. It was one of the reasons he not only *wanted* to keep his distance but seemed to *need* it as well. CJ Nicholls was…an enigma and one he didn't want to discover—or so he told himself.

Ethan opened his door and climbed from the car before walking around to help her out. He took both her hands in his and after she'd swung her legs around, she carefully eased herself from the convertible. 'Getting in is much more graceful than getting out.' She laughed, staring up into his eyes. And it was there, in that moment, that it felt as though the earth had stopped rotating, that time seemed to freeze, locking the two of them in a strange bubble of awareness.

Was it the curve of her lips or the brightness of her eyes that was capturing his attention? He still held her hands, and they felt small and vulnerable inside his own. How was she going to give birth and raise a child alone? Didn't she know that so many things could go wrong? He knew. He'd experienced all those things and the pain had been acute. For that split second he wanted to haul her into his arms, to offer protection, to let her know that she had to be sensible, to formulate a plan and account for all possibilities. Why he felt so determined to protect her, he had absolutely no clue.

He glanced at her lips, his gaze hovering there for a long moment…long enough for her lips to part, allowing pent-up air to escape. What was this…thing, this…awareness that seemed to encompass them? Her lips were so perfectly sculpted, as though they'd been made for him…

just for him. How was this possible? How could he be so drawn to a woman who, up until a month ago, he hadn't even known existed?

'Are you all right, Ethan?' Her words were soft and filled with concern and he immediately flicked his gaze back up to meet hers. He saw her look down at their hands and it was only then he realised his grip on her hands had tightened.

'Sorry.' He let go and took a step back, shoving his hands into his pockets. He didn't want to have any emotions, protective, caring or otherwise, towards his colleague. She was worried about *him*? 'I'm fine. Just…er… wanted to make sure you were steady on your feet.'

'I'm good.' CJ gestured to the main entrance of the hospital. 'Shall we?' As she walked on unsteady legs towards the hospital, leaving him to secure the car, CJ tried to understand what had just happened. Apart from being completely mesmerised by his spicy scent and having tingles of delight shooting up her arms from where he'd held her hands, she'd also seen a powerful emotion cross Ethan's face—one of primal protection.

Why would Ethan—a man who barely knew her—want to protect her? Want to keep her safe? It wasn't just his protective instincts she'd sensed. The way he'd stared at her mouth had caused the tingles already flooding her body to re-ignite and burst into a thousand stars of awareness. There was no denying that Ethan Janeway was an exceptionally good-looking man but the fact remained that they were colleagues. Besides, this was hardly the most opportune time in her life to be considering any sort of romantic involvement. The only person she needed to fall in love with was her unborn child. No one else.

With her pep talk done, CJ pulled on an air of professionalism and introduced Ethan to the hospital staff. She introduced him to everyone they came across, even the domestic staff, which was something he found a little strange. In a large hospital, it was impossible to find the time to get to know *everyone*, yet here it appeared CJ not only knew everyone, she knew what was going on in their lives—and they in hers. He shook his head. The intimacies of small, rural towns were not for him.

'Was I right?' she asked Toby, one of the male cleaners, who was swinging a polisher over the floors. They had finally finished a very long tour of the twenty-six-bed hospital, CJ bringing Ethan up to date on every single patient, and were on their way out.

'Yes, you were, CJ. Molly bought some of that manuka honey you suggested, swirled it around her gums and, sure enough, the ulcers started disappearing.'

'I'm glad.'

Toby turned the polisher off, then pressed his hand to her stomach. 'How's our baby doing?'

CJ grinned widely. 'Just fine.'

'Not long now.'

'No. Not long now.' She waited patiently for him to remove his hand before continuing down the corridor. At the main entrance, Andrea, the clinical nurse consultant who had accompanied them on the round, met them.

'Now, you go get off your feet. I don't want those ankles swelling,' Andrea instructed sternly, then she turned her attention to Ethan. 'Make sure she rests.'

'I will.'

'Oh, no,' CJ groaned. 'Have you joined the over-protection brigade as well?' she asked Ethan.

'Leave him alone. We're all here to look after you,' Andrea stated. 'That's what family do.'

'OK.' CJ smiled and waved. 'I'll see you tomorrow,' she threw over her shoulder as she headed towards the door.

'Tomorrow!' Andrea's tone made CJ stop. 'Claudia-

Jean Nicholls, you are *not* picking grapes in your condition. Does Donna know?'

'That I'm planning to go, like I do every year? Yes.'

'This year's a little different, CJ. You're in no condition to pick grapes.' Andrea waggled a finger at her.

'I doubt there's any risk of me overdoing things. I have so many of you watchdogs around, guarding my every move.' She compassed Ethan in her words and Andrea nodded.

'True.' Then Andrea placed a hand on CJ's baby. 'I'm positive it's a boy.'

'Donna has a betting pool under way. Make sure you register your vote. Date, time, gender and weight.' CJ yawned, then waved. 'See you tomorrow,' she said again, before heading out to Ethan's car. She secured her scarf and sunglasses and gratefully accepted his help with buckling the seat belt. It wasn't until they were on the main road heading back to her house that he started asking questions.

'You're going grape picking tomorrow?'

'Sure. Have you ever done it before?'

He shook his head. 'Can't say that I have. I prefer to drink the wine from a bottle once the entire process has been finished.'

'Leaving it up to the experts?'

'Something like that.'

'Doesn't take an expert to snip off a bunch of grapes. Besides, it can actually be a lot of fun. I think you'll enjoy it.'

'Pardon?'

'I said I think you'll—'

'I heard what you said, but why did you say it?'

'Because you're invited.'

'To where?'

'To the vineyard tomorrow.'

'What vineyard?'

'Donna and her husband have a few acres of vines. Quite small, compared to the large companies around here. Every year we all go and help pick the grapes.'

'Isn't it a bit late? It's April. I thought the grapes were usually picked in February and March?'

'It depends on the vintage, when it was planted, the weather—lots of things. The grapes on Donna's property are ready now.'

'They don't have machines?'

'No. It's not set up for machines, so we pick by hand.' CJ yawned again. 'It'll be fun…and a good way for you to get to know Donna away from the practice. I was sure you wouldn't mind but if you really don't want to come…' Another yawn, her words starting to get more sluggish as exhaustion began to set in. 'And want to look around for other accommodation, then that's fine, too.' She paused before saying softly, 'I guess.'

Was it his imagination or had she sounded a little disappointed if he decided not to come and help with the grape picking? She did make a valid point, though. Networking in a less formal atmosphere would help him to build relationships with his new colleagues. Donna was a partner in the medical practice and it sounded as though several of the staff from both hospitals would be there. Ethan knew the importance of networking and reluctantly admitted CJ had been right to suggest he attend.

When he glanced over at her, it was to discover she was asleep. Her head was at a slight angle but they weren't too far from her house. He drove a little more carefully, ensuring he didn't take the corners too quickly.

'We're here,' he announced after he'd stopped the car in her driveway. He gently placed a hand on her shoulder to wake her but he couldn't. 'CJ?' Nothing. 'Claudia-Jean?' Still nothing. She was out for the count. He climbed from the car and opened the door to the house with the keys she'd given him yesterday. There was no way he could let her sleep in such an uncomfortable position because it wouldn't do her or the baby any good.

Ethan slowly and carefully helped her from the car but still she didn't wake up completely. He placed an arm about her shoulders to help, but when she sagged against him, he did the only thing possible—he swung her into his arms.

She was surprisingly light, and placed a lethargic arm about his neck before snuggling in. 'You smell nice,' she murmured sleepily.

He carried her through her part of the house and into her room, placing her on top of the bed. There, she pulled off the sunglasses and scarf before snuggling into the pillows. 'Thank you.' The words were hardly audible but he appreciated them all the same.

He stood there, watching her sleep. She still looked about eighteen years old and he smiled to himself. Her hair had come loose from one of the pigtails and was half over her face. Ethan reached out and smoothed it back behind her ear, then jerked his hand away as though unsure why he'd even performed the action. What was wrong with him?

She was beautiful, no doubt about that. There was something different about her...something unique that was drawing him in, making him want to spend time with her. Relaxing. That was it. He found being in her presence very relaxing and once again, as he breathed in, he was able to fill his lungs. It felt good...and at the same time confusing. Why was it he found her so compelling?

He raked a hand through his hair, exhaling slowly. She liked vintage cars, she liked driving in them, she liked chatting with people and being a part of a community. He could see some similarities. When restoring a car, you needed to take your time, to choose wisely. Was that how CJ lived her life? Taking her time to make long and lasting friendships? If today was any indication, he would say that was a resounding 'yes'. Did he?

As soon as the thought came, Ethan pushed it away. He had a life—a life in Sydney that he would return to in six months' time. He would be cleared to go back to work and that would be that. He had close relationships with his sister, his brother and his parents...at least, he *used* to have a close relationship with them. The past six years had blurred from one day to the next and on each of those days, work had been his only constant.

'Make new friendships,' both Leo and Melody had told him. 'Take your time with things. Live in the moment. Try new experiences.' Wasn't that what he was doing? What he'd done today? What he was planning to do tomorrow? He could feel the world of CJ Nicholls starting to envelop him and he wasn't sure whether it was good or bad.

'Hmm... Ethan.' The word was whispered from CJ's lips as she sighed and shifted slightly on the pillows.

His eyes widened at the sound. Why was she moaning his name in such a way? And why did he like it so much? He riffled his fingers through his hair again and forced himself to leave her room...immediately.

This woman was dangerous. She was making him feel things he didn't want to, and it was starting to get to him.

CHAPTER FOUR

ETHAN HEARD CJ wake during the night but he stayed in his room. There was no way he was going through a repeat of the previous early morning rendezvous when CJ had made him smile, had made him relax his guard. He was still trying to understand his reaction to his new colleague, still trying to figure out whether he should move out of her home or…

'Or what?' He whispered the words into the quiet room, lacing his fingers behind his head as he stared at the ceiling. 'Stay around and help her when she has the baby?' It wasn't as though she didn't have a lot of help being proffered from her friends and colleagues. Everyone he'd met since arriving in the district seemed to accept CJ's unborn child as part of their family. In the beginning it had confused him a little but he had to admit it was definite testament to CJ's easy-going personality. She was both respected and loved by the people of this little town. In fact, he'd never seen such loyalty before.

'That's because you locked yourself away. Your heart and your emotions.' He sat up, swinging his legs over the side of the bed as he said the words. They weren't his words, they were his sister's, his brother's and his parents'. His family had been worried about him after Abigail's death, after the baby's death. They'd done what he'd asked—they'd given him time, but when they'd thought that time was up, that he should be talking about his feelings, he'd pushed them all away. The only problem with his family was that they hadn't allowed it.

'If you don't want to talk about it, fine,' Melody had countered one night after she'd tried everything she could to get him to go and see a psychologist. 'But don't think you can push me away. I'm your sister. I love you. I care about you. Deal with it.' And she'd been right. He was fortunate his family loved him and now he was starting to realise how horribly he'd treated them, especially during those first few years after the tragedy.

Being out of Sydney, away from the frantic pace of life he'd forced himself to live, was really giving him time to think. He didn't like to admit it, but he was also coming to realise that he'd ignored his pain for so long that it had actually affected his health.

'I don't want to die,' he'd told Melody the night he'd returned home from hospital. After his 'hiccup', he'd been hospitalised for a few nights as a precaution and when he'd been released, Melody had insisted on staying that first night at his apartment with him. 'I miss her. I miss the baby, even though I was only a father for less than a day.' Ethan had shaken his head. 'I don't want to talk about it and I don't want to think about it, but neither do I want to die.'

And it was then his sister had voiced the plan of coming here, of getting away, of doing something productive but relaxing with his imposed six-month break. The fact that he'd managed to breathe more easily in the past forty-eight hours than he had in the last six years was clear proof that being here was the right thing.

But was being near CJ the right thing? Why was he so concerned with her? With her unborn child? Why had he felt that overwhelming urge to protect her and her child? Was it just because she was pregnant and looked the picture of radiant health? Her blonde hair, her smiling eyes, her mouth that would easily quirk at the corners, a smile always at the ready.

Ethan breathed in deeply, then out again as he thought about her.

Being with her, hearing the sound of her voice, enjoying the small memories of her father that were scattered around the house, the openness of this woman was encompassing him and helping him to slowly unwind.

He opened the curtains and gazed out at the night sky, the half-moon providing slivers of light. Ethan lay back down in the bed, propping his head up on some pillows, staring out at the stars. He reflected on how CJ had worn the scarf around her hair in the car, about how she'd fallen asleep on the way back and how she'd sleepily murmured his name. Even though he wasn't sure why she had, he couldn't hide his delight that she'd been thinking of him as she'd drifted off to sleep. Why he'd been delighted, he wasn't one hundred percent sure, only that…it had been a long, long time since any woman had sighed his name in such a way and it gave a much-needed boost to his ego.

At six o'clock, he was astonished when his alarm woke him up. He'd slept and, apart from the slight crick in his neck, he felt fairly well rested. As he headed to the bathroom to shower, the hot water helping to soothe his neck, he felt determined to try and enjoy the day CJ had planned for him. Networking was good. Networking was necessary if he wanted to break into the tight-knit community of the town, and this would be the way to do it. The last thing he needed was to be ready to help out in the clinic but have no patients booked in to see him because they didn't trust him.

Walking into the kitchen, he was surprised to find CJ sitting at the table eating a bowl of cereal. 'Have you been up all night?'

She looked up at him and smiled that sweet and lovely smile he hadn't been able to stop thinking about. She shook her head as she chewed her mouthful of food. He had to admit that she looked glowing, in a pale green knit top with three-quarter–length sleeves, the colour making her eyes more vibrant. Her blonde locks were once again in pigtails, making her look vulnerable and…adorable. She swallowed, her smile widening.

'No. Not *all* night. Junior let me get some sleep because…today is grape picking day!'

'Do you really plan on picking grapes or are you going to sit and put your feet up and let everyone else do the hard work?'

CJ laughed, the sound settling over him like sunshine. 'Not you, too. You're starting to sound like every other over-protective person in this town. I might help out a bit but only with the vines at chest height. My brain hasn't completely turned to mush.'

'Glad to hear it.' He took the cereal down from the cupboard.

'You don't need to eat. Breakfast is provided and it's a lavish spread.'

He put the cereal away and looked at her bowl.

'Junior was hungry.' She grinned and carried her bowl to the sink. The black skirt she wore swished around her legs and she adjusted the hem of her top so it wasn't crinkled over her stomach. 'So, does the fact that you're up and ready to shake, rattle and roll mean you're coming grape picking with me?'

'Someone's got to keep an eye on you.'

'Ha. Trust me, Ethan. Everyone there today will be keeping an eye on me.'

'They really are protective of you?'

'Yes.'

'Because your husband died?' He knew he was probing

but what she'd said about her husband yesterday had only stirred up more questions. She hesitated before nodding. 'Were they protective of you *before* your husband's death?'

'Of course they were.' She looked away and gestured towards her room. 'I'll just grab my handbag, then I need to stop off at the clinic to pack my medical bag and then we can go.' She effectively changed the subject by walking out of the room.

Ethan frowned, his dislike for her husband continuing to grow, which was ludicrous. The man had done nothing to him and up until a few days ago he hadn't even known of Quinten's existence. Still, every time he mentioned her husband, sadness came into CJ's eyes—a haunting sadness that indicated her marriage hadn't been a happy one.

When she returned, she was her bright, happy self and they went outside. 'I won't be a moment,' she said, heading over to the clinic. 'You can wait in the car if you'd prefer.'

Ethan walked beside her. 'Expecting some emergencies today?'

She shrugged. 'I know Donna will have a well-stocked emergency kit but I still like to have a bag packed, just in case. Besides, there's the usual ailments—cuts, scrapes, mosquito bites.'

'Mosquitoes?'

'Yes. Because the vines are constantly drip-watered, it makes shallow puddles that are an ideal breeding ground for—'

'Mozzies,' they said together.

She packed her bag, going over the check list twice before locking up the clinic and walking back to her house. 'Can we take your car again? It's a dream to ride in.'

'Of course.' He held the door for her before heading round to the driver's seat. 'If you weren't pregnant, I'd even let you have a drive, but the seats don't adjust all that well.'

'I'll hold you to that once the baby's born.' Once her

scarf and sunglasses were in place, she gave him directions to Donna's house.

'What is that smell?' he asked, as they neared Donna's house. 'It's like…alcohol and…' He sniffed again, unable to pinpoint the smell.

'Manure,' she supplied.

'Exactly.' He turned into the driveway and followed it up the winding path.

'The vineyard owners have to save water where they can, so it's recycled into "grey water". Sometimes it can give off a bad aroma but it's worse after the grapes have been crushed.'

'And this is supposed to be fun,' he stated dryly.

CJ laughed as Donna's house came into view. 'Yes.' She waggled a finger at him. 'So make sure you enjoy it.'

The house was surrounded with cars parked at all sorts of angles and Ethan managed to find a space not too far from where the festivities were taking place. He came around and helped CJ out of the car, his fingers lingering a moment longer than necessary. It was enough to make her pulse jump into the next gear and start racing with anticipation.

'Thank you.' The words came out on a breathless whisper. She glanced down at the ground and cleared her throat before meeting his gaze once more and smiling shyly up at him. 'I'm not used to playing the damsel in distress but there's no way I can get out of the car without help—at the moment.' She tried to laugh off the feelings he was evoking, telling herself she was silly for even experiencing them in the first place. Look at her, for heaven's sake. What man would find her attractive now?

'I don't think you're a damsel in distress.' His blue eyes were intense with sincerity, his deep voice slightly husky and filled with promise. 'I think you're a radiant mother-to-be.'

She swallowed, unable to look away. They were standing closer than she'd realised and she could still smell the fresh scent of his shower. Everything around them became a blur as they continued to focus solely on each other. Desire—surprising yet very real—raced through him at an alarming rate and he forced himself to take a step away.

As he closed the car door behind her, CJ was thankful for the momentary reprieve as she tried to squash the emotions he was forcing to the surface. She cleared her throat. 'I'd better go find Donna. Would you mind passing me my bags, please?'

Once she had them in her hot little hands, she took off so fast he was surprised. The only time he'd seen a pregnant woman walk that quickly was when she needed to go to the bathroom! Perhaps that's where CJ was headed...or perhaps she wanted to get away from him.

Either way, he was very glad there was a growing physical distance between them. 'Just do your job and get back to your life,' he muttered to himself as he followed the direction CJ had taken towards the house.

'Yoo-hoo! Dr Janeway.' He turned at the sound of his name being called. He was just about to head up the few steps to the front door when Tania, the receptionist from the clinic, came around the side of the house. 'We're all out the back. Here.' She linked her arm through his. 'I'll show you.'

Ethan forced himself to smile as he allowed himself to be led by Tania. 'Look who's here,' Tania chattered as they came around the house to the rear entertaining area where about twenty-five people were gathered. There were introductions all around and before he knew it, an empty plate was being thrust into his hands and he was being guided towards a rustic table laden with food. There were cold meats, cheese, salads and loads of fresh fruit.

He was greeted warmly by Donna and her husband, as

well as many others, and all the while he made polite conversation he kept an eye out for CJ. Was she all right? Was she inside with her feet up? He wanted her to rest but he also wanted to be around her. She was his anchor in this strange new place and he was a little miffed that she'd deserted him so quickly upon arrival.

Had she felt it, too? That tug? That stirring of desire that he'd experienced yesterday at Whitecorn Hospital but which he had brushed off as 'ridiculous'? Today, though, when he'd held her hand, when he'd stood close to her, when he'd breathed her in, he could have sworn she'd been just as mesmerised by him as he'd been by her. How was that possible? They barely knew each other.

'Try the olives,' she told him, suddenly appearing by his side, plate in hand. 'They're grown on the property, too.'

'You're hungry again?'

'Eating for two,' she stated, loading up her plate. When she went to sit down, he was pleased she'd left room for him to sit next to her. The conversations flowed naturally and after a while of feeling like an outsider, Ethan began to relax. These were nice, genuine people and they were accepting him as easily as CJ had.

Two hours later, the grape-picking had well and truly begun. Once he'd been shown what to do, Ethan worked quickly and efficiently. He was by no means a stranger to hard work and found the task both enjoyable and, oddly, relaxing.

'Having fun?' She pulled on one glove to protect both her hand and the grapes.

'Yes. I am.'

'You sound surprised.' CJ used her pair of snips and cut off a bunch of grapes, putting it into his bucket.

'I am.'

'Are you always surprised when you try something new and it turns out to be fun?'

He nodded. 'Leaving Sydney. Coming to a new town. Meeting new people.' He listed them. 'I didn't think any of them would be fun but it hasn't been as bad as I'd thought.'

'And what about sharing a house with another person?' she added, then looked at him questioningly. 'Are you going to stay?'

Ethan pondered her words for a moment. 'There's no denying that your place is practical. It's close to the clinic and hospital. That's a bonus. There's somewhere for me to garage my car. That's good, too.'

'You've heard me having morning sickness, seen me sleeping in your car and shared night-time snacks with me.' She ticked the things off on her fingers. 'I'm thinking that any other awkward moments we might share would pale in comparison to those.'

Ethan couldn't help but laugh at her words. He found her openness completely refreshing as Abigail had rarely said what she'd been thinking. That had been part of their problem. He'd allowed himself to think she was fine and... He focused his thoughts on the woman before him, rather than his past. 'You really are the most unique woman I've ever met.'

'I'm going to take that as a compliment.'

'You should.'

And there it was again. They were looking at each other with a strange sort of awareness, as though an invisible bond was forming between them. His gaze dipped down to encompass her mouth and watched as the smile disappeared, her tongue slipping out to wet her lips.

'Thank you,' she said quietly.

'For...?'

'For saying nice things like that—and meaning them.'

'You're not used to receiving compliments?' He waved

an arm around at the various people who were picking grapes. 'Everyone I've met in this town simply adores you.'

She chuckled. 'But most of them have known me since I was a young girl.' She went back to snipping grapes and so did Ethan. 'When I first started working in the practice with Dad, I used to think the respect I was given was by association. They respected my father, so they were giving me the benefit of the doubt.'

'And now?' Ethan crouched down to snip the lower bunches of grapes.

'I know they respect me because I'm a good doctor and also because of the way I loved and respected my dad.' CJ gestured to where some other people were cutting grapes a few rows away. 'Take Robert, for example. He knew my dad, helped him restore cars, played darts with him and it wasn't until my dad's funeral that Robert told me how proud he was of me. Proud that I'd become a great doctor, like my dad. Proud because as my father's health had deteriorated, I'd treated Dad with respect.' CJ sniffed as tears sprang to her eyes. 'It was nice to hear.'

'You clearly still miss your dad very much.'

'I do. Every day.' She smiled and snipped another bunch of grapes. 'I know the people of this town love me, which is one of the reasons I always refused to leave whenever Quinten voiced the idea.'

'He didn't like it here?' Ethan asked cautiously. He was willing to listen to CJ talk about her husband but he didn't want her getting upset. She'd already been standing on her feet for quite a while and although it wasn't summer, it was a warmish kind of day.

'He did at first. He came here from Sydney to start afresh after a bad business deal. We'd met, dated and were married within the year.'

'That's fast.' He thought about he and Abigail, being

friends throughout university and eventually taking their relationship to the next level many years later.

'That's what everyone said but I was determined, and so was he. And things were great for the first few years. I think he had some notion that wherever he went with his work, I would follow. A business deal came up in Sydney and he was all gung-ho, ready to just up and leave.'

'But you couldn't. You're a country doctor with a busy practice,' he stated.

'Exactly. Dad's health had deteriorated, I was working round the clock at the practice and helping my sister move Dad to Sydney.'

'Perhaps Quinten thought you wanted to be closer to him?'

'That was one of the arguments he put forward. Quinten was very good at manipulating situations to his own advantage. Yet where he was planning on living in Sydney would have been a two-hour drive in peak traffic from where my father was.'

'It sounds as though—' Ethan stopped and shook his head. 'Never mind.'

'It's OK, I know what you're going to say and you're not the first person to say it. Quinten didn't respect me. Not as a woman, or as a doctor.'

'It does sound that way.'

'It's true. He told me that my refusal to leave and move to Sydney was what had ended our marriage for him.'

'Did he leave?'

She shook her head. 'The business deal fell through, which he blamed me for. He was always looking for that "get rich quick" scheme, and I eventually discovered the truth behind his initial move to Pridham in the first place. He'd lost a fortune on the stock market. Of course, at the time he told me it was something else, someone else's fault—never his. It was just lie after lie, and I was too

naïve, as far as men went, and believed everything.' CJ
snipped a large bunch of grapes with extra force. 'I'm not
now. When you learn lessons the hard way, they tend to
stick.'

'You're a strong, independent woman.' It was a statement and CJ nodded firmly.

'Damn straight.' She held her snips in her gloved hand
and rubbed her belly protectively. 'I've got to be strong.
The baby needs me.'

Ethan straightened and smiled. 'Good to hear.'

'Thanks for listening to me ramble.' She moved her
hand around to her back and began rubbing in the arch.

'Thank you for trusting me.' He looked down at their
bucket. 'I think that's full enough. Shall we take it in?'

CJ nodded and removed the glove from her hand. Then,
as they walked back down the row of vines towards the
house, she linked her arm through his, as though it was the
most natural thing in the world. When Tania had done the
same thing earlier, he'd been slightly uncomfortable. Now,
though, when CJ did it, he found nothing uncomfortable
about her touch, neither did he see anything in her expres-
sive eyes other than happiness.

Had they just become friends? He wasn't used to making new friends this fast but perhaps that was because
he usually held everyone at bay. Since Abigail's death,
he hadn't let anyone new get close to him and yet as CJ
had been talking he'd felt the urge to share his own story
with her, to tell her of his own disastrous marriage so
CJ would know she wasn't the only one who had felt so
broken-hearted.

'CJ!' The urgent call came through the house.

'What's wrong, Tania?'

'Robert's been stung by a wasp and he's not feeling
too good.'

'What?' Ethan was surprised. 'There are wasps around

here?' They all headed for the door. CJ headed into the kitchen and rummaged around in Donna's cupboards.

'What are you doing?' Ethan demanded.

'Getting some pure honey. Grab my medical bag, will you? It's over near the table.' He did as she asked and once she'd found the honey they headed out.

'So why are there wasps?'

'When the birds peck the fruit, it makes them nice and sweet.'

'Perfect for bees and wasps.'

'There aren't too many about, wasps, I mean. Where's Donna?' she asked Tania as the receptionist led the way to where Robert had been picking grapes.

'She forgot the bratwurst so she's gone to the shops.' Tania led the way but when Ethan saw Robert, lying on the ground, his body beginning to shake, he ran ahead.

'He's going into shock.' Ethan felt for Robert's pulse and checked his breathing. 'Someone get a blanket and call the ambulance. Robert? Robert, can you hear me? It's Ethan.' The response he received was a whimpered cry. 'Did you know he was allergic?' Ethan asked CJ.

'No.' CJ was working quickly, drawing up a shot of adrenaline before handing it to Ethan. As he was crouched down near Robert, it was easier for him to administer it.

'Oh, Robert…' His wife, Amanda, dithered and CJ quickly comforted her.

'He'll be fine. I'm going to treat the stings and the adrenaline Ethan's administered will help settle things down.'

'Will he need to go to hospital?'

'I'd like to keep him in overnight just so we can keep an eye on him.' CJ slowly knelt on Robert's other side and opened the honey.

'Oh.'

'He'll be fine,' CJ reiterated.

'What? What are you doing?' Ethan asked as CJ glopped some honey onto the sting sites.

'The honey soothes the skin. It also helps reduce swelling and any painful sensations. How's Robert's pulse rate now?' She waited while Ethan placed his fingers to Robert's carotid pulse.

'Better.'

'There's a portable blood-pressure monitor in my bag.'

'Great.' He hauled it out and wrapped the cuff around Robert's arm before pumping it up to check his BP. 'It's low but the adrenaline should bring it back up soon.'

'How are you feeling now, Robert?' CJ asked gently.

'Sleepy.'

'OK, but I need you to stay awake, just for a bit longer. We're going to get you to hospital where you'll be pampered like a prince.'

'Whitecorn?' The question from Robert was weak.

'No. Pridham, that way you'll be nice and close to Amanda.'

'Amanda?'

'I'm here, darling.'

CJ watched as Amanda knelt down and bent to kiss her husband's cheek. Even at their age, they were still there for each other. CJ rubbed a hand over her stomach, making a silent promise that she'd always be there for her child— no matter what. She glanced up and was startled to find Ethan watching her. They shared a brief moment when they seemed to connect on such a personal level, then he returned his attention back to their patient.

CJ followed suit and concentrated on the stings. 'The swelling seems to be reducing,' she told Robert. 'Does it still hurt a lot?'

'I've had worse.'

Amanda's concerned laugh helped lift the mood. 'That's the spirit.'

'Ambulance is here,' Tania called.

Just before they shifted Robert onto the stretcher, Ethan took his blood pressure again and was happy to report it had improved dramatically.

'Told you you'd be fine,' CJ reassured Robert as the stretcher was manoeuvred into the rear of the ambulance.

Donna arrived home from the shops and was quickly being brought up to date on the situation.

'I'll travel in the ambulance with him,' Amanda said. 'Could someone bring my car to the hospital?'

'I'll arrange it,' replied Donna. 'CJ, you and Ethan go get Robert settled in and, Ethan—' Donna fixed him with a determined look '—afterwards I want you to take CJ home and make sure *she* has a rest.'

'Good call.'

'Here are your bags, CJ,' Tania said as she came running out from the house. She smiled at Ethan. 'See *you* tomorrow.'

Ethan escorted CJ back to his car after thanking Donna for a wonderful morning.

'I can drop you home first.'

'Pardon?'

'I can drop you at home first and then go to the hospital to see Robert settled.'

'It's all right. Robert might get worried about me if I don't turn up.'

'I'll tell him you're having a rest. It's what pregnant mothers do.'

'Still, I don't want to worry him. He likes to fuss over me as his own grandchildren live too far away.'

'It appears most of the town of Pridham—and Whitecorn, for that matter—love to fuss over you.'

'Yes. It's nice.'

He could imagine it would be for her. She wouldn't take it for granted either. Instead, it was obvious she appreciated every single person's protective attitude towards her and her unborn child.

It didn't take them long to get Robert settled and once CJ was satisfied with her patient's vital signs, Ethan took her home.

'Off to bed, sleepyhead.'

'OK.' She stifled a yawn and shuffled off towards her bedroom. 'Wake me if anything exciting happens.'

That was the last Ethan saw of her for the rest of the day. He knew she'd wake up an hour or so later and specifically made sure he was out of the house. He went for a drive, enjoying the scenery and the ambience of the area. It was relaxing, colourful and a million miles from the hustle and bustle of Sydney.

When he returned it was night-time and again there was no sign of her. He went to his room and got ready for bed. He had clinic tomorrow morning and house calls in the afternoon. Although the pace was different from Sydney, the patients still had real complaints and he owed it to them to be alert.

He glanced over at the clock. It was only nine-thirty and here he was, tucked up in bed. If his colleagues could see him now, they'd laugh. Perhaps it was the manual labour he'd done that morning that was making him feel so exhausted. 'Or maybe it's the way you can't seem to get CJ out of your head,' he muttered, and buried his head beneath the pillow, forcing his thoughts in a completely different direction.

CHAPTER FIVE

FOUR-FIFTEEN. The digital clock had to be wrong. He'd been tossing and turning for hours. *Surely* it was almost morning! He flung the covers back, climbed from the bed and pulled on his robe. He needed a drink, and not just water from the bathroom tap.

Ethan headed out to the kitchen, stopping in the doorway to check that the coast was clear. Had CJ been up already? He glanced around the darkened room. There were no signs that anyone had been in the kitchen. No jars of chocolate spread left out, no dishes in the sink. Perhaps she'd packed everything away in the dishwasher.

Regardless, the kitchen was empty now. Ethan hurried over to the sink and filled the kettle with water then switched it on. While he was waiting, he looked through the herbal teas CJ had in the cupboard, and decided on Sleepy Baby tea, as it prescribed a relaxing outcome.

Herbal teas had been a more recent addition to his 'new lifestyle' campaign. Melody had suggested it, saying that it often helped her to get a good night's sleep. 'You need at least six hours of REM sleep, Ethan.'

'I get six hours of sleep,' he'd argued.

'In one block?' Her questions had been pointed. 'Didn't Leo suggest you cut down on your caffeine? How many cups do you usually have?'

Ethan had shrugged. Most days he lost count but even

he knew it was too much. He did what he needed to do in order to get through his day, being as effective as possible, and he said as much to his sister.

'But you're not being effective.' Melody had reached out and taken his hand in hers. 'Don't you see that? You may be keeping up to date with your paperwork, your research projects, and being a brilliant surgeon to your patients, but at the end of the day you're being ineffective to your own health.'

'I don't care,' he'd told her, the soft, caring tone doing more to damage his self-control than anything else.

'About your own life?' Tears had instantly sprung to Melody's eyes and it was then, seeing his sister's worry and concern, that Ethan had started to actually listen to her biggest fears for his health. He'd tried to change, tried to cut down on the caffeine, but about four weeks after that conversation his body had decided to take control of things by having a mild heart attack.

'Morning.' CJ's soft, cheery greeting startled him, and it was only then he realised that the memories had brought tears to his own eyes. Ethan quickly sniffed and turned his attention to finding a cup and putting the teabag into it. 'Junior's doing the morning exercise routine a little later today. Maybe there's hope.'

'For what?' Ethan glanced over his shoulder at her, noting she looked absolutely adorable with her hair all messed up and stuck out at funny angles. Her robe was hanging open and her feet were in those ridiculous fluffy slippers. She looked…good enough to eat. Ethan cleared his throat, willing the kettle to hurry up and boil.

'That Junior's going to grow out of being an early riser,' she answered.

Ethan's lips quirked slightly. 'Wishful thinking?'

She crossed both her fingers and held up her hands, making him smile even more. 'Something like that. What are you drinking?' She peered into his mug on her way past him to the fridge.

'Herbal tea.'

'Mmm. Sounds good.'

Without saying another word, Ethan took another cup down and added another teabag. 'Sugar or honey?'

'Honey, please.' She took some cheese out of the fridge and headed over to the bread bin where she retrieved a small baguette. 'Hungry?'

'No, thanks.'

She closed the bread bin, picked up a knife and a plate before seating herself at the table. 'So why can't you sleep?' She spread some cheese onto the bread.

Ethan looked at her, his mind filtering through several different things he could say. Thankfully, the kettle switched itself off and he almost pounced on it, pouring water into the waiting cups. 'Adjusting to a different place.'

She swallowed her mouthful. 'Miss your own bed?'

'Something like that,' he murmured. When the tea was ready he took hers to the table before walking towards the door with his own mug. 'See you later in the morning.'

'You're not going to stay and keep me company?'

She'd asked him that before and he'd stayed. Because he'd stayed, he'd become better acquainted with her. After their time picking grapes together, he would now say that they were becoming friends and if that was so, wouldn't that mean she'd want him to talk about his own life? Part of him did want to tell her about Abigail, to open up and be free from his self-imposed exile, but the other part— the logical part—wanted to leave the kitchen and find a way to return their relationship to one of strict work colleagues. However, it was *because* she was an open, honest, giving person, that he knew if he didn't stay, at least for a few minutes while he drank his tea, and keep her company, she might be offended.

'Sure.' He turned back to the table and sat a few seats away from her.

CJ blew on the hot tea. 'So, I called through to the hospital to check on Robert. He's sleeping soundly. All vital signs are fine.'

'Good.'

'I'm glad you were there to help.'

'You would have been able to handle everything with your hands tied behind your back,' he commented.

'Thank you. That's nice of you to say, but I have to tell you, in my present condition, I definitely can't move as fast as you. It's frustrating.'

'I'm sure it is. Soon, though, it will all be over—'

'And I'll be frustrated for a different reason,' she finished with a wry grimace.

'I thought you were looking forward to it.'

'I am. I'm getting desperate to meet my child. To hold it in my arms, to smother it with kisses, but the fact remains that being a single mother is not going to be an easy trick. Then there's the clinic and what if I need time off after you leave and we can't get another locum? What if something goes wrong with the birth? I'm happy with my level of medical care, don't get me wrong, but I just have all these thoughts constantly running through my head and I can't seem to stop them.

'What if I go over my due date and I have to be induced? What if I have a reaction to the medication? What if it's so painful I can't cope? What if Donna's at another emergency and I have to deliver the baby myself? What if something's wrong with the baby? Am I going to be a good mother?' Her voice had risen to a crescendo and she buried her head in her hands, her shoulders shaking as she started to cry.

Ethan was horrified. Not at what she'd said but how concerned she was about everything. He'd had no idea her stress levels were this high and the doctor side of him kicked in, knowing such stress could seriously affect her blood pressure.

'I was trying to call Donna to talk to her about all of this but she's actually out at an emergency at Whitecorn Hospital and I also don't want to bother her every time I have a moment of neurotic weakness. And...and...all of those questions are only the tip of the iceberg because once my anxieties start to warm up, they really get going.' She sniffed and raised her head again. 'What if I can't cope with the baby and can't return to work—ever? What if I have postnatal depression? What if I can't do this by myself?'

'Borrowing trouble won't get you anywhere.' He tried to placate her, wondering if he should leave a message for Donna to stop by after the emergency. For the moment, the best thing he could do was to let CJ talk, let her get her frustrations out, because he'd come to realise that she wasn't the sort of person to bottle things up...unlike him. If she could talk things out, cry a little and release the pressure from her anxious thoughts, then she soon might be able to get some rest.

Tears continued to trickle down her cheeks and she patted the pockets of her dressing gown for a handkerchief. Trying not to feel helpless but also wanting to be helpful, Ethan quickly took the box of tissues from the window ledge and brought them over to her.

'Thanks.'

He sat down beside her and took her small hand in his. The instant he did that, he realised his mistake. His intention had been to talk to her like any other patient, to reassure her, but all he could now concentrate on was that her skin was so incredibly soft. Ethan rubbed his free hand over his forehead, trying to jump-start his mind. When he spoke, his voice was lower, more intimate than he'd intended. 'It's natural to have doubts, CJ. Very natural.'

'I know, but what if some of them come true?'

'Then you'll deal with them.' His words were direct and filled with hope. 'One by one. You'll formulate a plan, you'll find the help you need, and you'll get on with things. You're very well supported in this town. Everyone—and I mean *everyone*, from the cleaner at Whitecorn Hospital to the store manager at the grocery store—is supporting you.' He shook his head in amazement. 'I know I've said this before but it really does astound me because I've never met anyone who was so well respected and so adored by those around her. You're a genuinely nice person, CJ.'

'Wow.' Fresh tears trickled down her cheeks, but they were tears for a different reason. 'That is such a lovely thing to say, Ethan. Thank you. You're a good friend.' She withdrew her hand from his and blew her nose.

Ethan closed his eyes, remembering a very similar conversation with Abigail. She'd been stressing and he'd placated her, thinking he was comforting her, but he'd been wrong. Her worries had been well founded and he hadn't done enough to help, because she had kept so much from him, and he hadn't seen the danger till it had been too late. It was one of the things that ate him up at night and even though the specialists had told him there was nothing he could have done for either his wife or his child, deep in his psyche he couldn't stop feeling that hadn't been the case.

Well, he wasn't about to let history repeat itself. He'd managed to verbally reassure CJ but actions often spoke louder than words. 'Well, then, friend, why don't I organise an ultrasound for you? It'll help put your mind at ease. You'll be able to see that the baby is OK and I'm sure Donna can arrange a urine test if that will also help alleviate any concerns you might have.'

'Yeah. OK.' Another bout of tears leaked from her eyes

and he couldn't help but smile at her overactive emotions. 'I hate being at the mercy of my crazy pregnancy emotions. I cried at a commercial on television last week but it was a commercial for *soup*!' She blew her nose again and looked at him imploringly. 'You don't think I'm overreacting, do you?'

'Not at all.'

'Thank you, Ethan. Thank you for not making me feel silly and for being so supportive and calming me down.' It was her turn to reach out and take his hand in hers, holding it tightly, worry and fear still lurking at the back of her mind.

'That's my job. Er...not as your doctor,' he added quickly, 'but as your friend.' He was doing his best to ignore her touch, to ignore the way it was creating havoc with his senses. He ignored the tightening in his gut, and at the way his heart was thawing a little more every time she touched him, or stared into his eyes, or mesmerised him with her scent or her laugh or—

'Aw. How sweet. Thank you for being my friend.' Fresh tears sprang to her eyes and she gave his hand another squeeze before letting it go so she could blow her nose again. Ethan chuckled at her crazy emotions, then shifted back in his chair and sipped his tea. CJ had already broken through several of his defences and now *he* was the one feeling vulnerable.

He was pleased he'd been able to allay her fears, to help her out. Helping people. It was one of the things that had driven him, especially these past six years since Abigail's death. He hadn't been able to help his own wife so he'd developed the insane notion that it was his job to help everyone else. Help them—but still keep his emotional distance. Detached. That was the word his sister had used to describe him.

'You do good, Ethan, but you're so detached from reality, from real emotions and situations that you can't see how badly it's affecting you. It's not healthy to go through this life all alone, not connecting with other people.' His sister's words echoed in his mind. Melody had been right. He took another sip of his tea, belatedly becoming aware that CJ was watching him—concern in her eyes.

'Ethan, are *you* OK?' she asked softly.

'What makes you ask?'

'Well, you've alleviated my concerns, I've released some emotions and now my brain can function again, and what I can't figure out is why you're awake at this time in the morning?'

'I told you, I'm…not used to my surroundings.'

'But I'll bet that when you were an intern, you would have been able to sleep anywhere. All interns do because the hours and work are so long and hard.'

'And I was considerably younger and less set in my ways.' He smiled, hoping the attempt would stop her from asking more questions. Whilst he'd had the urge to share things with CJ, it didn't mean he actually had to do it. He reminded himself that he liked his life segregated, that work and friendship didn't mix.

'So, what's your place like?'

'My place?' He frowned.

'Where you usually live in Sydney.' She held out a hand before he could speak. 'Wait. Let me guess. You have a lovely four- or five-bedroom house located in an inner-city suburb so the commute to the hospital doesn't take too long. There'll be enough garage space for not only your play car, which is presently parked in my garage, but also a more sensible, probably dual-fuel car for driving around town.' Her eyes were alive with merriment as she continued to guess where he lived. 'Also, the furnishings inside your house would be stylish yet practical and the art hanging on the walls would consist of carefully chosen pieces, some prints by Impressionist painters, and some by local artists because their work really captures your moods.' CJ nodded. 'I'm right, aren't I?'

Ethan sipped his tea, astonished she was actually quite close, describing the house where he'd lived with his wife. Sadly, he shook his head. 'Not any more. I actually live in a two-bedroom, inner-city apartment located one block from the hospital. I have the bare minimum of furniture and no pictures on the walls.'

'What do you mean, "Not any more"?'

'I used to live in the place you described but I don't now.' How had they ended up on this topic? Why had he even answered the way he had? All he'd had to do was say she'd been wrong...but he hadn't.

'Why?'

'The commute time was too long. I wanted to be closer to my patients.'

'How long have you lived in the city?'

'Er...' He cleared his throat and sipped his tea. 'Six years.'

'Oh.' There'd been a defensive thread in his tone and he could tell she wondered if she'd said something wrong.

'Why is it important where I live?'

'It's not important. I was just trying to figure out why you couldn't sleep here. Now I realise Pridham is probably too quiet for you.'

'That's probably it.'

'Probably? You mean you don't *know* why you're not sleeping?'

Ethan was instantly on guard. 'Why are you so concerned?'

'Because I don't want my patients being seen by a doctor who suffers from insomnia.'

'I do not have insomnia.'

'Really?'

He frowned. 'Are you intent on questioning me because of something my sister told you?'

'Melody?' She seemed genuinely surprised with the question. 'Why would she tell me anything?'

'You said you spoke to her, spoke to other people at St Aloysius Hospital before I came to work here. What did they tell you?'

'They told me you were a brilliant surgeon.'

'They didn't tell you the rest of the gossip?'

'What are you talking about? What gossip?' she asked, clearly perplexed.

Ethan closed his eyes and slowly shook his head. His own paranoia had been his undoing. 'I'm sorry, CJ. I didn't mean to snap just now. 'I...uh...' He hesitated. 'Things happened to me and, uh...'

'I wasn't prying, Ethan, and I know what it's like to work in a big hospital where people love to gossip. Believe me, working in a small country town is just as bad.' She smiled, hoping it might settle him. 'I was just concerned that you weren't sleeping. That's all.'

'So you don't know why I'm here? Why I've taken the job as your locum?'

'Because you wanted a break from the rigours of Sydney life. At least, that's what you wrote in the email you sent me with the application. However, given the conversation we've just had, I'm thinking there's more to it.'

Ethan toyed with his half-full cup on the table before wiping his sweaty palms on his robe. 'I...uh...' He paused and took a moment to concentrate on his breathing. 'I had a mild heart attack. It was just a warning,' he added quickly. 'I'm on a forced sabbatical from the hospital.'

'Oh, Ethan.' CJ shook her head sadly. 'I didn't know. Honestly. No one I spoke to said a word about that. They only told me how brilliant you were. No confidences were betrayed, just as I won't betray this one.' She placed one hand on her heart, her gaze filled with genuine concern. For a man who, only a few days ago, had told her he liked to keep his colleagues as colleagues and nothing more, she deeply appreciated him sharing such a personal piece of information about himself. 'Thank you for telling me. I appreciate your confidence.' They both took a sip of their teas, CJ mulling over everything he'd told her. 'So being here is supposed to be a change in pace for you?'

'Something like that.'

'I know you've only been here a few days, but how are you feeling so far?'

He breathed in deeply, filling his lungs. 'No tightness of chest.'

'You were having chest pains? For how long?' Her tone was inquisitive but professional, as though she was speaking to one of her patients.

'Professional concern?'

She shrugged one shoulder. 'I'm a doctor. I diagnose everyone—as do you. It's a habit.' When he didn't immediately answer her question, she prompted, 'How long have you been having these pains, Ethan?'

'Increasing in severity for the past six years.' His words were quiet yet matter-of-fact.

'Six years!' CJ gaped at him. 'What happened six years ago?'

'I moved to the city. I took up the position of Director of General Surgery. I began back-to-back research projects, which finally ended two months ago.'

'As well as heavy clinics, admin and operating lists?'

'Yes.'

'That's quite a workload.' CJ finished her tea and placed her cup on the table, her thoughts racing. 'No wonder your health has suffered but I'm also glad you're heeding the warnings, that you're not ignoring them.' She continued to think, voicing her thoughts out loud. 'So when you moved to the city, that was from the suburbs?'

'Yes.'

'From the house I described? The one with the nice furniture and big garage?'

'Yes.'

'You moved from that to a small city apartment?' Her brow was puckered in a frown as she tried to add two and two, but wasn't coming up with four as the answer. 'You said the commute was too much?'

'I'd taken up the directorship. I needed to put in longer hours.'

'But why take the directorship in the first place if you knew it would take you longer to comm—' She stopped, the frown disappearing, only to be replaced by a dawning realisation. 'You were in a relationship.'

'Yes. I was married.'

'The marriage ended, you moved from the suburbs, took up the directorship and lived a block away from the hospital. You threw yourself into your work, almost literally.'

'Yes.' Ethan stood and picked up both their cups, taking them to the sink.

'I understand marriage break-ups. Mine was no picnic and if Quinten hadn't passed away, we would most definitely be discussing our separation and divorce right now.'

He turned from the sink, shoving his hands into the pockets of his robe. 'My marriage didn't break up because my wife and I got divorced, CJ. My wife, Abigail— that was her name... Abigail...' He clenched his jaw and looked down at the floor before raising his gaze to meet hers. 'Abby died.'

Time seemed to stand still, the sound of the clock's second hand becoming duller as she stared at him with a mixture of compassion and pain. 'That's the reason I left the suburbs and threw myself into my work. To forget the pain, to forget the anguish, to just…forget.'

With that, he turned on his heel and headed to the door that led to his part of the house. A moment later, he was gone, only the sound of the ticking clock filling the silence as CJ sat there, absorbing everything he'd told her.

He was a widower who was still very much in love with the memory of his wife.

CHAPTER SIX

WHY THIS SHOULD matter so much, she wasn't sure. As CJ shuffled back to her room, brushing her teeth and emptying her bladder in the hope of getting a few decent hours of sleep, she thought back to those moments of awareness she'd experienced since Ethan Janeway had entered her life. Even tonight, holding his hand and feeling the strong, protective reassurance he exuded, had left a residual warmth deep down inside.

He'd stared at her yesterday, when they'd arrived at Whitecorn Hospital, as though he'd wanted to press his lips to hers. She'd been too busy reeling from the fact that she'd actually wanted him to follow through with that urge to even contemplate *why* he'd looked at her in such a way.

Why had he?' It made no sense. Was he simply looking for female companionship? If that was the case, why on earth would he consider a heavily pregnant woman? She was uncomfortable all the time and slept in a bed with a plethora of pillows. None of her sexy lingerie fitted her and probably wouldn't for some time, and soon she would be even more exhausted as the sole parent to a helpless baby. What on earth was attractive about any of that?

When Ethan woke the next morning, he was surprised he'd actually managed to sleep—again. 'This might actually become a habit,' he mumbled after he'd dressed for his first day on the job. Heading into the kitchen, he was pleased to have it to himself. While he ate breakfast, he kept glancing at the door through which CJ might walk through at any moment. Indeed, any little sound had him tensing with anticipation.

He still couldn't believe he'd not only told her about his heart attack but also about Abigail. Normally, he was a closed book—even with his family. It had taken Melody quite a while to get through to him and he knew his tenacious sister had only kept badgering him because she'd been incredibly worried about him…worries that had been proved correct.

He glanced once more towards CJ's door. Would she want to ask him more questions or would she respect his privacy? 'Probably the latter,' he murmured to himself. Both of them had been through marriages that, from what she'd said about her husband, hadn't been the happiest, and both of them had lost the opportunity to change the outcome. If Abigail had survived, he'd vowed to himself to be a better husband, to be more attentive, to help her, to listen to her more. Ethan sighed heavily. But she hadn't survived. She'd been taken from him and so had—

He stopped the thought. He may be trying to be more open, to be more communicative, especially with the people who mattered most in his life, but dwelling on such heartbreak would not help him at all this morning, especially when he had a clinic to attend to.

He glanced again at the door that led to her part of the house. Perhaps he should just check on her before he left; after all, with the anxiety she'd been exhibiting during their early morning *tête-à-tête*, he wanted to see for himself that she was indeed OK.

'Professional concern,' he muttered to himself as he knocked softly on the door. He'd check on her and then he'd be able to give Donna a report of what had happened, keeping CJ's doctor in the loop as to her patient's emotional state. He listened carefully for a moment but didn't hear anything. Slowly he opened the door and walked quietly towards her room.

The door was open and he heard her steady breathing before he saw her. Good. She was sleeping. Relaxed, sleeping and surrounded by a horde of pillows. He headed back to the kitchen relieved she was doing fine. After discovering his own wife had had pre-eclampsia and had kept it from him, Ethan was more than a little cautious when it came to pregnant women in their last trimester. As far as he was concerned, Abigail's death, and that of his gorgeous little baby girl, would not be in vain. Not on his watch.

CJ woke up in exactly the same position in which she'd gone to sleep, indicating she'd had a great sleep. Checking the clock, she was astonished to find it was after ten in the morning. Her first instinct was to scramble out of bed and rush over to the clinic, before she remembered that Ethan was here.

A smile instantly spread across her lips at the thought of her housemate. Ethan had come to Pridham so that she could rest and look after herself. Where she'd thought she might have been bored, right now, she felt a wave of stress leave her. That was very nice.

She sighed again and stroked her stomach. 'Thank you, sweetheart,' she told her baby, 'for letting Mummy have a good sleep. Do you feel good too, my honey?' Taking her time, CJ showered and dressed, singing in the shower and keeping up a steady dialogue with her unborn child. 'We're going to relax this morning because Ethan's doing the clinic. Then we'll go and visit some people this afternoon so we can introduce him to today's house call list.'

Secretly she hoped they could do the house calls in his awesome car. It was nice they shared the same interest, especially as she and Quinten hadn't really enjoyed the same hobbies or activities. Being able to talk to Ethan about car engines, about the stitching on the leather seats, about sourcing difficult parts that were out of stock—that sort of thing was wonderful. It meant she wasn't having to watch what she said in case she said something to upset him, as she had with Quinten.

Now, though, she realised the reason Quinten had often picked an argument with her had been because he'd felt guilty about wanting to leave her. They'd been a wrong fit right from the start. CJ sighed and headed to the kitchen. Once again the kitchen was tidy and she was thankful Ethan wasn't a messy slob, like Quinten.

Why she was comparing the two men, she had no idea. Perhaps it was because, apart from her father, they were the only other men she'd lived with. Yes, Ethan was showing promising signs of being a great housemate and, hopefully, a great friend, too. She ignored the little voice at the back of her mind that questioned the way that one smouldering look from Ethan could ignite a fire within her such as she'd never experienced before. She didn't want to acknowledge the fire or the spark because if she gave it too much thought, she might end up making another mistake, and where romance and love were concerned, she'd already made her fair share.

Besides, any crazy emotions she felt towards Ethan were no doubt due to her overactive pregnancy hormones and nothing more. Once the baby was born, the crazy feelings would stop and she would return to normal... she hoped.

Added to that was the fact he'd told her about his wife. He was a widower who was still coming to terms with his grief. Perhaps being in Pridham would help him to heal, help him to accept his past and move forward into a less stressful future. CJ hoped she'd be able to support him through that, but as nothing more than a friend.

Her phone buzzed, bringing her thoughts back to the present, and she checked the text message. She was pleasantly surprised to find it was from Ethan, the message stating an ultrasound had been booked for her in two hours' time.

'How sweet. He's so sweet, baby,' she told her child. 'Sweet and thoughtful.' CJ shook her head. 'No. Not sweet, he's being professional and helpful…and thoughtful, but then he *is* a doctor and therefore is supposed to be thoughtful and helpful and professional.' She frowned as she decided what text message to send back but after typing several messages and then deleting them because they either sounded too personal or too sterile, she decided on sending emojis—one of a smiley face and one showing a thumbs-up.

'Why is this so hard? The line between housemate, friend, professional colleague, keeping out of each other's way or helping each other out, and…' She trailed off, sighing once more. 'Well, at any rate, I have time to get a few things done before the scan so up we get.' She rubbed the little foot that was sticking out, urging it back into place. 'Let's wash your new clothes so they're all ready when you arrive. That way, they'll feel all fresh and lovely rather than musty and starchy.' As she hadn't wanted to know the sex of the baby, CJ had stuck with buying pastels and cute outfits that would suit either gender. By the time she was due at the hospital, the outside washing line was filled with the tiny outfits being blown gently by the autumn breeze, and CJ's nesting instinct had been satisfied.

As she walked across the road, she couldn't help the

slight spring in her step and knew it was because she would be seeing Ethan soon. She felt good, she felt happy and it was simply because he'd cared enough to suggest making this scan appointment so her mind would continue to be at ease, especially through the night when her fears usually raised their ugly heads.

Stopping at the clinic first, she was interested to see how Ethan had been coping. As she walked into the waiting room, she found Donna quietly discussing something with Tania, two patients still waiting.

'What are you doing here? I was about to go over and meet you at the hospital,' Donna stated as soon as she saw CJ. 'I hope you've been resting.'

'I can't be resting every minute of the day, Donna,' she countered with a good-natured smile. 'I slept in until ten o'clock, had a leisurely breakfast and managed to get all the baby's clothes washed and on the line.' She paused for a moment. 'Wait—what do you mean, you were going to meet me at the hospital?'

'For the ultrasound,' Donna stated. 'Ethan asked me to make the appointment. He seemed quite concerned about you.' Donna fixed CJ with a worried look. 'You should have told me you had concerns. You know I'm there to support you for whatever you need.'

CJ shrugged. 'I guess with Quinten always saying I made mountains out of molehills, I sometimes feel as though I'm still overreacting—to anything and everything. Besides, the neurotic thoughts I have in the middle of the night often ease during the light of day. And I did try to call you but you were at Whitecorn.'

Donna frowned. 'I didn't know you'd called.'

'Night sister answered your phone.'

'Ah, yes. I'd left it at the nurses' station before treating Mr Bartlett.'

'Oh, no. Mr Bartlett? Is he—?'

Donna held up her hand to stop CJ's questions. 'He's stable.'

She sighed with relief. 'He was another good friend of my dad's. I hope he's able to pull through.'

'You and me both.'

The phone on Tania's desk buzzed and she quickly answered it. 'Yes. I'll tell her,' she replied, then nodded to her colleagues. 'The sonographer is ready for you.'

'Head on over, CJ. I won't be far behind you,' Donna said.

'OK. Thanks.' CJ started to head out the door that led to the hospital but as she did so, Ethan came out of his consulting room with a patient. The patient stopped, grinning brightly at the sight of CJ. Pleasantries were exchanged, the patient placed their hands on the baby bump and gave their prediction as to the gender before heading towards the waiting room. All the while, CJ was highly conscious of Ethan's presence.

He'd looked mildly startled to see her when he'd exited the consulting room and after nodding and smiling politely at her, he'd stepped back and not said a word. After the patient had left, CJ found she couldn't move, found that she wanted to stay where she was and just be near him, despite knowing what she now did about his wife. It was odd.

'How's everything going?' she asked.

'Very well. Everything is set up—the consulting room, the computer system—to work like a well-oiled machine and that's exactly what's been happening.'

'Good. Good.' A moment of uncomfortable silence passed.

'Er...' Ethan gestured towards the direction of the hospital. 'Heading over for the scan?'

'Yes. Yes…thanks for letting Donna know. Sometimes I think I'm being too over-dramatic and other times—'

He held up his hand to stop her. 'You're welcome.' Another moment of strained silence passed. 'Uh… I'd better go call my next patient in.'

'Sure.' She jerked her thumb towards the hospital. 'I'd better have that scan.'

He nodded again, then took a step towards her and said softly, 'Let me know the results.'

CJ held his gaze and there it was again…a zinging of awareness between them, as though there was something happening between them that neither of them had either asked for, or wanted.

'I…uh…had hoped to be there but I have…' He pointed towards the waiting room.

She shook her head and smiled at his words. How sweet of him. 'Oh, it's OK. Of course you're busy and if anyone's going to understand—'

'It's you,' he finished for her. And there it was again, the undercurrent of a conversation they weren't articulating. CJ licked her suddenly dry lips and Ethan's gaze dropped to follow the action with great interest. 'I, uh… checked in on you this morning to ensure you were OK but you were sleeping. Very soundly,' he added as an afterthought, that gorgeous smile of his appearing and creating havoc with her heart.

It took a moment for her to realise what he was saying, and her eyes widened in mortification. 'I was snoring!' She raised her hands to cover her face and was rewarded with a soft chuckle from Ethan. The sound washed over her and filled her with utter delight before she removed her hands and heaved a heavy sigh. 'Well, you've already heard me being ill so let's just add snoring to the list.'

'Were you sick this morning?'

'No. Actually, I wasn't.' It wasn't until he'd asked the question that she realised she hadn't even thought about it.

'Probably because you were able to sleep in and not rush around first thing in the morning.'

'More than likely.' She smiled at him once more. 'And it's all thanks to you.'

He held up his hands but his smile was still in place. 'Hey, I'm just here doing my job. I'm not a hero or a saint.'

'Are you still here?' Donna remarked as she walked towards the two of them. Ethan quickly stepped back, putting distance between himself and CJ.

'I was just checking to see how Ethan was coping,' CJ remarked.

'He's doing fine. Now come on, the sonographer is waiting for you.' Donna put her hand in the middle of CJ's back, urging her forward. 'Let Ethan get back to work. He still has several patients to see before house calls this afternoon.'

'I'll see you then,' CJ said to Ethan over her shoulder as Donna continued to usher her towards the hospital. Ethan knew he shouldn't stand there and watch her go but it was only a second later that she disappeared from view.

'What the heck just happened?' he whispered to himself as he headed to the waiting room to call his next patient through. As he worked his way through the rest of the clinic, he kept his questions at the back of his mind. Why was it that whenever he was within close proximity to CJ he couldn't stop staring at her mouth? He'd told her about his wife, how he was a widower, so clearly she understood that he was a man who hadn't dealt with his grief…didn't she? Perhaps he needed to make it clear that he wasn't interested in a relationship with anyone. He'd told her he wanted to just do his work and when his contract was up he planned to return to his life in Sydney.

But as he wrote up the notes for his last patient, he

couldn't help but compare the life he'd had in that small apartment to the one he now enjoyed here. Although he'd only been in Pridham for less than a week, with the people he'd met, the acceptance he'd received, the support he'd been given, he had to admit he found it quite encompassing. He'd been able to breathe deeply, to fill his lungs completely and without stabbing pains. When he'd checked his own blood pressure, it was to find it at a far more acceptable reading and he was actually sleeping three to four hours per night. How could he be seeing such incredible results in such a short space of time?

Was it down to CJ's easygoing manner? He did like hearing the sound of her voice, he did like seeing her smile and, more importantly, he liked being the one to *make* her smile. He liked the way she smelled, of sunshine and happiness. He liked her gumption, that she accepted her lot in life and was prepared to get on with what needed doing. She wasn't wallowing in a pit of despair, lamenting about being left as a single parent. Naturally she had concerns and he was honoured that she'd felt comfortable enough to share them with him, and that he'd been able to do something to help.

He glanced at the clock on the wall. She should well and truly be done with her ultrasound by now and he wondered what the results were. Was she feeling more relaxed, more at ease? Was her blood pressure stable? Did she have any excess swelling around her ankles? He wanted to remain vigilant, to ensure she didn't fall victim to the same condition that had taken his wife. Granted, the circumstances were different and CJ was definitely looking after herself, but pre-eclampsia could turn to eclampsia far too quickly and then...

At the sound of feminine laughter, laughter that sounded a lot like CJ's tinkling laugh, coming from the direction of the waiting room, Ethan stopped his thoughts from progressing into the dark abyss, and quickly finished his work before heading out to where she was.

Sure enough, CJ was there, sitting in one of the waiting-room chairs, her feet up on a stack of magazines on the coffee table. Donna was leaning against the receptionist counter and Tania was twirling a pen between her fingers. His gaze settled back on CJ, pleased to see her resting.

'How did everything go?' He wasn't going to beat around the bush. She was his colleague and he was worried about her.

'Good.' She smiled brightly and rubbed her belly.

'Blood pressure is down, swelling is within normal parameters and the baby's head is engaged. I've also done a urine test—all clear, no protein.' Donna was the one to give him the medical report and he smiled at her before taking a closer look at CJ's ankles for himself. Yes, they were good. The tension started to leave him now that he knew she really was OK.

'Are you all right?' CJ asked him softly as the telephone rang. Tania answered it and told Donna it was for her. Donna headed off to her consulting room and Tania went to the bathroom. It wasn't until they were alone that she reiterated the question.

'Yes, I'm fine. It's you I've been concerned about.'

'You have?'

'Of course.' He sat down in the chair opposite her, the coffee table between them.

'Why?'

'Why? Because, as I'm sure you know, a lot of things can go wrong in the last trimester. It's better to be safe than sorry.'

CJ smiled. 'Are you always this adamant with the patients? Don't get me wrong,' she continued before he could respond, 'it's a good thing, especially in general practice.'

'Not all surgeons are scalpel happy,' he replied. 'Some

of us actually do care about our patients.' Even as he said the words, he knew he hadn't been as concerned about some of his patients as he should have been. It was simply because he hadn't wanted to engage with the personal aspect, preferring to leave that up to his registrars. Getting personally involved with people would have required the wall he'd built around his heart to be broken down and he hadn't been ready for that. He wasn't sure if he was ready for it now but whether he wanted that wall to come down or not, it was happening and it was all because of the woman opposite him.

'Ready for house calls?' she asked, lifting her feet from the table and shifting in her chair, preparing to lever herself up. Ethan was quickly at her side, holding out his hands to help her up. 'Thank you.' As she stood, he once again found himself in close proximity to her hypnotic gaze and encompassing scent.

Neither of them moved; neither of them seemed to be breathing. The world around them had come to a standstill, as though they'd somehow been able to press the pause button in order to concentrate on exactly what was flowing between them.

'You smell really good.' Her words were barely audible and he couldn't help but stare at her perfectly shaped mouth, wondering if it would taste as good as it looked.

'So do you,' he returned.

'Stop looking at me like that.' CJ's gaze was flicking between his eyes and his mouth and he realised in that one split moment that whatever it was he was feeling towards her—something that had no name and no real substance—was reciprocated. She could feel it, too.

'I can't seem to help myself.'

'None of this makes any sense.' Again her words were so softly spoken it was as though they were communicating telepathically.

'I know.'

'But it's there. We're not imagining this?'

'If we are, then we're both sharing the same dream.'

'I want you to kiss me but if you do, I don't know what it will mean and that just confuses me further.'

There it was again, that complete and utter sense of open honesty that summed up CJ's entire personality. All her words did was to fan the fire deep within him, the fire that he hadn't even realised had been reignited, the fire of desire, of passion, of need. How was it possible for his world to have been tipped upside down so fast?

'I *want* to kiss you.' He kept his gaze trained on her mouth as he spoke, shaking his head slowly from side to side. 'I know it's wrong and stupid and impulsive and confusing but the desire is there. I don't know how or why...' He breathed slowly as he closed the small distance between them, drawn to her as though it was the most natural thing in the world. He was still holding her hands, still touching her, and whether it was that combined with the pheromones surrounding them that propelled him to within the close proximity of her mouth, there didn't seem to be any force there to stop him.

'This is lunacy,' she managed to whisper, right before his lips brushed a feather-light kiss to hers.

CHAPTER SEVEN

THE MOMENT SEEMED to last for an eternity, yet in reality it was no longer than a split second. Ethan pulled back, unable to compute the different thoughts surging through his mind. He'd just kissed another woman. That alone was enough to help him ease back, to stare into her half-closed eyes and resist the dreamy message she was silently sending him to repeat the action. He wanted to do it again, to continue to explore the sweet secrets her mouth offered, but the fact remained that he'd kissed a woman who wasn't Abigail and the realisation caused his gut to knot with guilt.

Dropping her hands as though burnt, he took a giant step back, almost tripping over the coffee table and knocking several magazines to the floor. To aid in covering his confusion and panic at what had just happened, he immediately bent down to retrieve the magazines, putting them back onto the table and taking another step away from her.

'I'll…uh…' He pointed towards the door. 'I'll go get the car ready.' With that, he gave her a wide berth before exiting through the front door. As he walked out, he heard Tania come back into the waiting room and realised how close they'd come to having their kiss witnessed.

What on earth had he been thinking? He hadn't. That was the answer. He hadn't been thinking. He'd allowed himself to get sidetracked, to relax, to let his guard down. 'This is what happens when you don't keep focused, when

you listen to others and start to interact with the world.'
Ethan continued to mutter to himself as he walked across
the road to CJ's garage and unlocked the outer door.

His car. His beauty of a car. It had always been able to
relax his stress. He glanced over to the workbench in the
corner and saw a container of polishing cloths. Without
further thought, he grabbed a cloth and began to rub it
gently over the car's body, as though wiping away his turbulent thoughts and re-setting his mind to exhibit a more
professional demeanour.

He was here to do a job. He was here to look after the
patients until CJ's maternity leave finished. Where he'd
been looking forward to spending time with her doing
house calls this afternoon, he now longed for the time
when he could do the house calls on his own. She would
be at home, looking after her baby, and he would be either
stuck in the consulting room or his bedroom, not daring
to engage with her lest she should once again capture his
attention with her dreamy green eyes and luscious smile.

'I'm sorry, Abigail,' he remarked as he threw the cloth
back into the container and pulled the keys from his pocket.
Yet as he slipped behind the wheel of the car, all he could
think about was how much his wife had loathed the vehicle.
She'd been angry about the time he'd spent with the car,
calling herself a restoration widow. It had been an escape
for him when their problems had become insurmountable.
If he'd known how much she'd been suffering, would he
have spent more time with her? And would it have made
a difference?

He shook his head slowly as he buckled his seat belt
and started the engine. He wondered if Abigail would be
happy he'd kissed another woman, that he hadn't been able
to stop thinking about another woman, that he was eager
to spend time with another woman? He really hoped so.
But she'd probably be annoyed that he still loved the car.

He loved to polish it, to tinker with the engine and to feel his tension decrease as he went on long drives.

As he reversed the car to the front of the clinic, he saw CJ come out, a medical treatment bag in her hands. Leaving the engine idling, he quickly climbed from the car and took the bag from her, placing it securely on the small back seat. Then he held her door and helped her into the car, clenching his jaw and doing his best to ignore the powerful surge of awareness that spread from his hands and up his arms, before entering his bloodstream.

She thanked him for his help and once they were both buckled in, he waited for directions. CJ provided them whilst tying a scarf around her hair and slipping her sunglasses into place. After that, they drove along in silence and apart from the occasional 'Turn left at the next T-intersection,' and other navigational instructions, they both seemed quite content to absorb the serenity of the drive.

When they finally arrived at their first patient's house, Ethan stopped the car and turned the key to cut the ignition. The silence enveloped them but neither of them moved. CJ breathed deeply, then slipped off her scarf and sunglasses.

'It really is an incredible machine.' She stroked the dashboard. 'Thank you for the relaxing drive,' she told the car, then undid her seat belt and turned to look at Ethan. 'And thank you for doing the steering part.'

His smile was instant and she felt the earlier tension that had surrounded them begin to abate. He'd brushed a kiss to her lips. It wasn't as though he'd been making a pass at her but rather openly acknowledging that there were high levels of awareness pulsing between them. For CJ, that acknowledgement, that she wasn't the only one experiencing those sensations, was enough…for now. Her focus needed to be elsewhere, especially after today's ultrasound. The baby's head was engaged, and could be born at any point within the next week.

'Who's first on the list?' Ethan asked as he climbed from the car, quickly coming around to help her out.

'Thanks. I'm looking forward to the day when I can get in and out of a car without such a hassle.' He let go of her hand the instant she was standing and steady on her feet. Her smile faded and she glanced at him from beneath her lashes as he retrieved her bag. She needed to remain focused and professional so CJ cleared her throat and answered his question. 'Molly Leighton. She's almost sixty-two and she's been suffering badly from stress. She's been the manager of one of the larger vineyards for the past forty years. I keep suggesting she retire but she won't hear it. She's had high blood pressure, chest pain and a spate of mouth ulcers but—oh, you met her husband the other day. Toby—the cleaner. The one swinging the floor polisher at Whitecorn District.'

He nodded. 'Manuka honey?'

'Correct. Molly needs to slow down and smell the roses but instead she works herself into a frenzy. She almost didn't speak to me again when I prescribed four weeks off work.' CJ shook her head. 'What that woman needs are some grandchildren to help her unwind but there's no chance of that on the horizon.'

'Let me guess. You're going to let her help you with yours.'

'And why not? I need help, Molly needs to slow down. It's a win-win situation.'

'And what about your child?'

'It wins as well because it will be smothered with love.' CJ shook her hair free in the wind, running her hands through the locks. He glanced across, instantly mesmerised by the way her hair was flowing gently in the breeze, the golden locks glinting in the sun, her long neck exposed in the autumn sunshine. Had she no idea how incredibly beautiful she was?

'Shall we go in?' Without waiting for him to answer, she walked up the front path and knocked on the door. It was flung open almost immediately by a woman dressed in a casual suit with her dark hair immaculate and her make-up perfect.

'Come in, CJ. Oh, and you've brought the new Dr Janeway, too. Toby told me about meeting you.' Molly ushered them both inside. 'Tea? Coffee? I've made some fresh scones.'

'That would be lovely,' CJ responded at the same time Ethan refused. 'Now, Ethan, you *must* try one of Molly's scones, especially when they're fresh from the oven. They are mouthwatering.'

She'd turned to face him as she spoke, so her back was to Molly. Her eyes conveyed an urgency that she wanted him to accept Molly's offer. He smiled at their patient. 'In that case, how could I possibly say no?'

Molly literally beamed. CJ hadn't seen her smile like that in a very long time. As Molly headed to the kitchen, Ethan spread his hands wide, as though silently asking why she'd made him accept. 'Cooking is the only thing that seems to be taking Molly's mind off the fact that she's not working. Besides, part of the reason for house calls is to provide a holistic approach to general practice medicine. Everywhere we go today, we'll be force-fed food and drink, which…' she rubbed her belly '…is good for the baby but bad for my bladder.' CJ chuckled at her own joke but as Molly came back into the room, carrying a tray of scones and drinks, she quickly stopped.

They sat in the 'good' lounge room on plastic-covered sofa chairs, CJ willing Molly to relax. Molly's recent tests had shown her mouth wasn't the only place where an ulcer might be brewing.

'Have all my test results come back?' Molly asked, getting straight to the point.

'Not yet but I'm fairly certain you do have an ulcer in your stomach.'

'Might the manuka honey help that, too? After all, it's worked extremely well for my mouth ulcers.'

'Yes, so Toby was telling me. That's great news.'

'When can I go back to work? I've baked all the recipes in one book and am about to start on the next book. Toby's complaining he's starting to put on too much weight.'

'I'm sorry, Molly, but if you return to work too soon, it might cause more problems. The last thing we want is for the ulcer to perforate. First, we need to start treatment for the ulcer and I can't do that until the tests are confirmed.'

Molly crossed her arms and sighed huffily, clenching her jaw and shaking her head. Every muscle seemed to be clenched and CJ's concern for the other woman's blood pressure increased.

'CJ, you were right.' Ethan's deep voice broke through the tension of Molly's demeanour. 'These scones are incredible. Molly, you're a marvel in the kitchen.' He smiled at their patient and CJ watched as the other woman instantly relaxed, a slight blush colouring her cheeks. Did he have this effect on *all* women?

'Right. Let's take your blood pressure and have a look at your mouth and throat. I'll ring the path lab in Sydney to see how much longer those results will be.'

'I can do that,' Ethan offered. 'I have contacts at the lab and might be able to put a rush on the results.'

Molly looked at him as though he'd hung the moon and when CJ took Molly's blood pressure, she was pleasantly surprised at the lower BP rate. 'Good. Much, much better. Whatever you're doing is working.'

'Looks as though I'll be starting on savoury baking treats tomorrow,' Molly sighed.

'Well, if you ever find you have too many treats…' CJ rubbed her belly '…the baby's been quite famished of late so send them my way.'

Molly nodded. 'I'll make sure I do that.'

It wasn't much longer before they took their leave and once they were back in the car and CJ had given Ethan directions, she thanked him for his help.

'You were like a de-stressing machine for her. I think it's mainly thanks to you that we'll be getting delicious food from Molly.' She put her scarf and sunglasses back on but as the clouds above were starting to darken a little, Ethan decided to put the soft top up just in case.

'It's good to see you still have a healthy appetite,' he remarked. 'Many women don't eat that much during their last few weeks of pregnancy.'

CJ chuckled. 'No such luck with me. Baby is definitely hungry all the time.'

He smiled. 'Every pregnancy is different.' He turned the key in the ignition and the engine purred to life. 'Where to next?' CJ gave him directions to the next house call, which was a good fifteen-minute drive away. 'I don't mind,' he stated as he started the engine once more. This time, with the soft top up, it was easier for them to hear each other speak. 'Getting to drive around these roads with the incredible scenery is one perk of the job I'm definitely enjoying.'

'I'm pleased to hear it,' she responded, now curious to discover what he thought might be other perks of the job. Was kissing her one of them? She cleared her thoughts and focused on their next patient. 'This next case is concerning but also interesting. Margaret is thirty-two weeks pregnant and, from the tests I've run, I'm fairly sure the baby has foetal alcohol syndrome.'

'Really?' The tone in his voice instantly changed, and

as he spoke, his words were clipped and direct. 'I've had some experience with this.'

'You have?' She was surprised. 'You've had a patient with foetal alcohol syndrome? Huh.'

'She wasn't a patient,' he remarked quickly. 'Do you have a copy of the test results here?'

CJ nodded. 'I've got all the files on the patients we're seeing today on my tablet computer.' She tried to reach into the back to the medical bag and eventually succeeded, pulling out the device and turning it on. As they drove along, she read out Margaret's most recent test results. 'Again, I'm waiting to hear back on the last round of tests, which will hopefully confirm my suspicions.'

'What's her background?'

'Margaret works at her parents' winery, and has been drinking wine since she was about thirteen. Not excessively back then, and always under her parents' control.'

'Do they drink?'

'Yes. Again, not excessively but constantly.'

'Clearly you think the baby's in danger?'

'I'm not sure. I only know what I've read in the information published and that's still not conclusive. If we could figure out a way to get Margaret to cut down the drinking, it would help. She says she's not drinking as much as before but I'm concerned.'

'Is she married?'

'Yes, but her parents and husband have insisted she quit work for the moment and concentrate on the baby. She had a lot of bleeding early on in the pregnancy,' CJ added by way of explanation. 'They didn't want her to miscarry but now I'm concerned that they've wrapped Margaret so tight in the proverbial cotton wool that the poor woman isn't able to do anything now.'

'Very over-protective?'

'Yes, and I think the solitude might be driving her crazy

at the moment because of picking season. Both her husband and her parents are working longer hours than usual.

'I've been monitoring Margaret in between her visits to the obstetrician, and as you're helping with my list, that job will now fall to you, hence why it's important you meet her.'

'Have you raised your concerns with the obstetrician?'

'Of course, and between the two of us we're monitoring the situation closely. However, I would really value your opinion, too.' She pointed. 'Go left up here.'

He turned the car into a long, rambling driveway that was lined with trees. At the end of the driveway was a large, architecturally designed modern homestead, with all sorts of different angles here and there. 'Interesting.'

'It may look odd from out here but inside every room affords an exceptional view of the vineyard.'

'This is Margaret's house?' He brought the car to a halt in the curved gravel drive and quickly went around to help CJ out.

'Her *family's* house. Margaret and her husband live in the west wing of the house and her parents in the east wing.'

'Let's see what we're faced with,' he muttered, after he'd grabbed the medical bag and they'd headed up the curved steps to the front door, CJ hanging onto the handrail to assist her ascent.

'Dr Nicholls,' Margaret said with forced joviality upon opening the door. 'What an unpleasant surprise.'

CJ glanced briefly at Ethan and then back at their patient. Margaret leaned heavily on the door before letting go and staggering slightly away from them. This wasn't good.

'Come to check up on me, no doubt. See that I'm doing the right thing. You shouldn't have worried. I have my husband, my parents, my in-laws *all* checking up on me.' Margaret had gone into the living room and sat down on the leather lounge. There was half a glass of wine on the small table in front of her. CJ sighed and followed, opening the medical bag and taking out the blood-pressure monitor.

'Let me take your blood pressure, Margaret.'

'If it'll make you happy,' she slurred, and held out her arm. As CJ took her BP, Margaret glared at Ethan. 'Brought a little friend with you.'

'This is my colleague, Dr Ethan Janeway. He'll be filling in for me while I'm on maternity leave.'

'No doubt sticking his nose into everyone's business, just like you. Giving advice where it's not wanted. That's all you doctors are good for.'

'We're also here to help you,' CJ said.

'You sound like my mother.' Margaret cleared her throat and mimicked in a nagging voice, 'Call the doctor if you have any pain. Just put your feet up. That's our grandchild you need to look after. Don't do anything.' She growled the last. 'Just lie there all day, be a vegetable and provide nourishment for the baby. Baby, baby, baby. I wish Doug had never talked me into having this baby.'

'You don't mean that, Margaret. It's just the drink talking,' CJ soothed as she reported Margaret's BP to Ethan. Both of them shared a concerned look.

'It is not. I didn't want this child in the first place.'

'How much have you had?' It was the first time Ethan had spoken and Margaret glared at him.

'Don't you presume to come in here with your high and mighty ways. I don't have to answer any of your questions.'

'How much have you had?' Ethan's tone was firmer and more insistent than before.

'How dare you question me?' Margaret's voice was becoming shrill.

Ethan glanced around the room and then stalked off through a doorway.

'How dare you take such liberties? This isn't your

house.' Margaret went to stand but it was too difficult. CJ put a hand on her shoulder but the other woman shrugged it off. Ethan stalked back in with two empty red wine bottles and one that had just been opened.

'Call the ambulance. I want her admitted.'

CJ pulled out her cellphone and made the call.

'Y-you can't do this. You can't just d-drag me off to hospital,' Margaret stammered.

'We can if we think either you or the baby is in danger,' Ethan told her.

'The baby. There it is again. Ruining my life.'

'You're doing an excellent job of ruining *its* life as well,' he replied firmly. 'CJ, pack her some clothes and call her husband.' He offered CJ his hand to help her to her feet.

'Leave Doug out of this. He has nothing to do with this.' Margaret was defiant as CJ left the room.

'He is the father of your child. He has a right to know where his wife and child are.'

'I'm staying right here. You can't make me go to hospital and the baby is fine. It kicked me all last night and the only time it really stops is when I have a glass of wine.' Her words had started out tough but ended on a sob.

Ethan could see the emotional anguish Margaret was in but knew he needed to keep the firm line if he was going to get through to her at all.

'It's ruined my life,' Margaret's slurring words continued. '*I* was important before I got pregnant. I helped my father, I ran the business, *I* was important and now…now I'm just an incubator. They won't let me do anything. They won't let me even look at the paperwork.' Tears started falling but Ethan still kept his distance.

He walked over to the hallway where CJ had disappeared and called to her. 'Margaret needs you,' he said when CJ returned. She walked into the room to find Margaret sitting on the lounge, rocking slightly backwards and forwards, her hands covering her face as the tears poured out. She rushed over and placed her arm about the other woman, reaching into her pocket for a clean tissue.

'Here.' Margaret took it, turning slightly in CJ's direction, and cried.

'*You* know how hard it is,' Margaret wailed.

'Yes, I do.'

'But at least you could keep on working. At least you haven't been told the only thing you're good for is providing for the baby. I can't even blow my nose without them worrying about the baby.'

'I know,' CJ soothed. 'They stopped worrying about you, didn't they?'

Margaret cried harder. The next time CJ looked up, Ethan had gone. She wasn't sure where but she didn't see him again until the ambulance arrived.

'Margaret.' CJ gently shook the other woman's shoulder. She'd cried herself dry before dozing off. 'Margaret. The ambulance is here.'

'Huh? Why do I need to go?'

'So we can check that you and the baby are all right. Your blood pressure is lower than it should be and you have some swelling around your ankles.'

'Is that bad?' Margaret now looked concerned.

'It's not good. Come on,' CJ urged. Thankfully, the fight seemed to have been knocked out of Margaret and she was a compliant patient during the transfer to Pridham District Hospital. Ethan and CJ drove behind the ambulance and once they'd arrived they settled Margaret into a room.

Ethan filled out the paperwork for the tests he wanted Margaret to have. 'We'll need to keep you in overnight, which is why Dr Nicholls packed a bag for you.'

'Yeah, yeah.' Margaret closed her eyes. 'Just go away and let me sleep.'

'Probably a good idea,' CJ said as they went out of the

room. Margaret needed to sleep off the alcohol and here she could do it where they could also monitor her condition. 'I'll be around later tonight to check on her,' she told Bonnie, the CNC.

'No. *I'll* be around later tonight,' Ethan contradicted. 'CJ will be at home, resting.'

Bonnie nodded in agreement. 'Glad to see *someone* can make her rest. See you this evening, Dr Janeway.'

'Were there any other house calls for today or can they wait until tomorrow?' Ethan asked CJ.

CJ checked the list on her computer. 'None that are urgent. I'll have Tania put them onto Wednesday's house call list.'

'Good. What else do you need to do now?' he asked as he escorted her out of the hospital.

'Write up notes for the patients we've seen today and then email them to the surgery.'

'Right. You head back home, I'll do the paperwork and put my car in the garage.' He looked pointedly at CJ. 'Put your feet up and rest.'

'But I'm hungry. I was going to cook dinner and—'

'I'll cook dinner. If I get home and find you standing...' He let his words trail off and shook his head. There was something about his stance, the abruptness in his voice that made her concerned.

'Ethan, are you all right?'

'I just need you to rest, to put your feet up, to ensure that you and the baby are OK.' He clenched his jaw and CJ decided she'd simply do as he asked, especially as she was rather exhausted. As she headed across the road, leaving Ethan to do the work, CJ admitted that seeing Margaret behave in such a way had indeed been upsetting.

CJ's pregnancy hadn't been planned. In fact, when Quinten had told her he was leaving her, that he didn't love her, CJ had never thought they'd share one last night...one night when she'd foolishly thought she'd be able to change his mind, to show him that she was as adventurous in the bedroom as the next woman. Quinten hadn't seen it that way at all. Instead, after what she'd thought was a rekindling of their love, he'd kissed her forehead, told her she'd been great but that he couldn't stay here, living with her in this pokey little town where nothing ever happened.

Then, still lying in their bed, she'd watched him pull an already packed suitcase from the cupboard and head for the door. He'd had it packed even before they'd started to make love? In stunned disbelief, she'd put the question to him. 'Why did you even bother? If you'd already made up your mind to leave, why even bother?'

'Hey. I'm a red-blooded male and you were fantastic, sweetheart, but... I've had better.' He'd started out of the room.

'Wait.' CJ had grabbed her dressing gown and followed him as he'd walked to the front door. 'So this is it? We're done? Just like that?'

Quinten's answer had been to sigh tiredly. 'CJ, we've been over for years now. You know it. I know it.' He'd picked up his car keys, then turned to give her a once-over. 'Let's not pretend any more. You and I, we don't...fit.'

With that, he'd walked out the door, walked to his car and driven away, the tyres squealing on the bitumen road. She'd wanted to shout at him, to slam the door, to release the hurt and pain he'd inflicted on her with his horrible words, but that wasn't what she'd done.

Now, as she sat at the kitchen table, pickles, chocolate spread and bananas in front of her, CJ spoke softly to her baby. 'I came inside, little one. I pulled the sheets off the bed and I washed them. I wanted to wash every aspect of him out of my life that night.'

'Who...are you talking about?' Ethan's deep voice sounded behind her and it was only then that CJ realised she'd been sitting at the table for quite some time. He walked into the kitchen, smiling softly when he saw the food in front of her, and sat down nearby. 'Is everything all right?'

CJ sighed slowly. 'I was just thinking about how Margaret's pregnancy was planned, and look how it's turned out. Yet my pregnancy wasn't planned, and I just can't wait for this baby to come and complete my life.' She picked up a chocolate-smothered pickle and chewed thoughtfully. 'It's sad how things work out, never as you thought they might. I really hope Margaret is able to stop drinking, to see that the baby isn't her enemy. It just so sad,' she repeated.

Ethan was quiet for a moment before picking up one of the slices of banana and eating it. CJ was more than happy to share her food with him and a small thread of happiness made its way through her melancholy aura. 'Were you talking about your husband?'

She nodded. 'I was thinking about the night he left. I thought we were reconciling, that we were going to be able to fix the problems he'd already raised, but that wasn't the case. Instead, he used me and discarded me. I just needed to wash him out of my life, to pack up everything he'd left behind that reminded me of him and get rid of it, but after washing the sheets, exhaustion set in. I slept that night in my dad's room, the room that's now yours, wrapped up in blankets and curled into a tight little ball, feeling so small and so little.'

'You didn't pack everything away?'

'Four hours after Quinten drove off, the police knocked on my door to tell me he'd been killed. He'd driven from here, picked up the woman he'd been having an affair with, who lived in Whitecorn, and then taken a turn too fast on the road and ploughed his car into a tree, killing them both outright. After that, I felt… I don't know what I felt, except numb. Packing his things away felt too much like erasing him from existence and… I thought I owed him… I don't know… I owed him *something* but…' CJ shook her head.

Ethan reached over and took her hand in his. 'You owe him nothing.'

'Don't I owe the baby at least some memory of who their father was? Sure, Quinten didn't know about the baby— neither did I—but—'

'All you owe this baby is love and you're already providing that. You're looking after yourself, you're asking for help, you're eating strange foods but you're resting.' He smiled as he spoke. 'You're doing all the right things and that's what counts.'

CJ looked at their hands, their fingers seeming to intertwine so naturally. His touch made her feel wonderful, reassured, confident about the tasks that awaited her. Still, she noted the sadness behind his eyes, a sadness that shielded repressed pain.

'Ethan,' she began softly, 'when your wife died…' At her words she felt his hand go limp and he tried to pull back but she held on for a moment longer. 'How did she die?'

He jerked his hand back and this time she let go. 'Why do you ask?'

CJ shrugged one shoulder. 'You mentioned you'd had experience with foetal alcohol syndrome and that it wasn't via a patient. Then, when you were talking to Margaret, I just had a…feeling. You just seemed overly concerned for her—which is good, I want you to be overly concerned with the patients—but I just sensed there might be more to it than you're letting on. And with me,' she continued, before he could get a word in edgeways, 'you're very concerned about me, that I don't overdo things, that I take it easy, that I rest and relax and do what's right for the baby. I don't mind. Everyone else in the district fusses over me and the baby but with you it seems…deeper. As though you're almost desperate to ensure both the baby and I are OK.'

'I thought that was the role of the GP, to ensure their patients have the right treatment.'

'I'm not your patient,' she pointed out.

'No. You're my new friend, and as I've been a confirmed workaholic for years and rarely have the time to *make* new friends, is it any wonder I'm concerned about your health?' He stood and walked to the kitchen bench, his back to her for a long moment before he turned to face her, his arms crossed, his expression closed.

'You're avoiding answering the question, Ethan, and I think I might have guessed why. I think I know how your wife died and I think it was due to complications with a pregnancy. That's why you're so worried about *me*. You're determined to make sure the same thing doesn't happen to me.'

As CJ spoke the words, she watched the blood drain from Ethan's face, and she knew she was right.

CHAPTER EIGHT

'YOUR WIFE DIED in childbirth?' She went to stand but he quickly held up a hand to stop her.

'You need to rest. You need to be off your feet. You need to ensure you don't...' He stopped, closing his eyes before saying with choked emotion, 'That you don't get pre-eclampsia.'

'Oh, Ethan.' CJ didn't care whether she was on her feet or not, she wanted to be near him, to comfort him, to be there for him as he'd been there for her the whole time he'd been in town, but he clearly didn't want that comfort, not at the moment. 'What happened?'

Ethan leaned against the bench, needing to keep the distance between them. He shouldn't be surprised that she'd figured it out. CJ Nicholls was a smart woman. However, the only reason she'd been able to figure it out was because he'd let down his guard—something he'd sworn to himself he would never do. He hadn't planned to let anyone inside the wall he'd built around his heart and somehow, without him fully realising it, mortar had broken down and bricks had crumbled, releasing light into the cavern...a light in the guise of the woman before him.

He knew she was waiting for him to speak but first he had to deal with that nagging voice from deep within, telling him to just walk out the door, to leave, to snub her. The more he looked at her, seeing the genuine concern in her eyes, hearing the compassion in her tone, he knew if he was ever going to open up to anyone about his past, it would be this woman. She'd been through so much herself, she'd been honest with him from the very beginning and he instinctively knew that whatever he told her, it would be held in the strictest confidence.

'Abigail was always so organised, so in control. I was working day and night at the hospital and she resented that. At some point we stopped talking and I couldn't get through to her, so when I wasn't at the hospital, I was out in the garage with the car.' He shook his head sadly. 'She'd always tell me off for spending more time with the car than with her but…' He swallowed and chose his words carefully. There was no point in hiding from the truth any longer. 'Restoring the car relaxed me. She didn't.' Ethan spread his arms wide, then let them fall back to his sides. 'I was a bad husband. A bad father to my unborn child.'

'I doubt you neglected her completely, Ethan.' CJ's tone was reassuring.

'Of course not. I loved her. I loved the thought of her having our child, our little girl. I couldn't wait to be a dad, to have a family. That's why I wanted to get the car all done and sorted out so that when the baby came, I would have more free time to spend with both of them.'

'Tell me more about Abigail.'

His smile was natural. 'Abigail, as I said, was very self-sufficient, very directed. When we met at university, we became friends for a few years and then…things progressed into more than friends. Abby went into organisation mode. She had everything planned. How long it would take for us to save up and get our first house, where we should get married, when we would start having children. It was all in her clearly thought-out plan—sometimes even with colour-coded charts.'

CJ grinned at that. 'I admire people like that but that's

probably because I'm so disorganised... Or, as my father used to term it, "creatively chaotic".'

Ethan walked over and pulled out a chair, sitting down and sighing. 'And that was my major mistake with Abby. I let her organise, I was happy to be organised. I thought that if she had worries or concerns, especially about the pregnancy, that she would tell me but she didn't. When she was getting angry with me for always being in the garage when I wasn't at the hospital, *that* was her cry for help. She didn't come out and say directly, *I'm scared, I'm worried, I don't feel well.* Instead, she just read book after book, scouring the internet, looking up different symptoms and trying to figure things out herself.'

'She wasn't a doctor?'

Ethan shook his head. 'No. Abigail did one year of nursing at university and changed majors to accounting.'

'That's a big change.'

'She was an academic at heart. Did her honours, her master's degree and finished her doctorate during the pregnancy. I was so proud of her. Order. Structure. Purpose.'

'You clearly loved her very much.'

'I did. I do. I always will.' Ethan tilted his head back and closed his eyes. 'But she's not here. She had swelling at the ankles, her blood pressure was up. She didn't want to worry me. That's what she said to me when we were in the ambulance, heading to the hospital. "I didn't want to worry you as I know you've been hectic at work." I felt so guilty. I still do.' He dragged in a deep breath, then opened his eyes and looked at CJ. 'Why didn't she tell me? I could have helped her. Why was she so scared that she couldn't tell me?'

'Ethan, you can't blame yourself. Even in today's world, with all the medical advancements we've made, things still go wrong.' CJ reached out her hand to him but he didn't take it. Couldn't. There was still something he had to tell her, something he hadn't told anyone, something only he and the staff in the room at the hospital where his baby girl had been born knew. He clenched his jaw and sniffed as he felt tears begin to threaten. Not only were they tears of grief but also tears of anger.

'Babies sometimes don't make it through childbirth, especially with something like eclampsia,' CJ continued.

'And birth defects.' The words were out before he could stop them and he sniffed once more.

'What?' The word was barely audible and she sat back up, her hand sliding from the table to rest protectively on her own child.

'My little girl…' No sooner were the words out of his mouth than the tears started to trickle down his cheeks. 'Ellie—my little Ellie—she was…she had…' He pursed his lips and accepted the clean tissue CJ fished from the pocket of her dressing gown. He dabbed at his eyes, then blew his nose.

'Abigail had been drinking. I'd had no idea. None whatsoever. She'd been so stressed from her studies, with the pregnancy, with me not being there, and she couldn't tell me any of that. She hid it all from me and then, when it was too late, when the eclampsia had taken hold, there was nothing to do but try and save the baby, but even then it was too late.' Another tear ran down his cheek and before he knew it, CJ had somehow shifted her chair around so she was closer to him. She put her arms around him and he let her. She held him close and he let her.

'Ellie lived for almost twenty-two hours. I changed her nappy, I held her, I told her… I… I loved her.' The grief, the pain, the despair of losing his daughter came to the fore and he cried like he'd never cried before. CJ did nothing but hold him, support him. She didn't ask questions. Instead, she cried along with him, sharing in his loss.

Eventually, he was able to ease back, looking around

for more tissues. He spied the box on the kitchen bench and eased himself from CJ's arms, before bringing the box back to the table and sitting down again. His legs weren't strong enough to support him; every muscle in his body ached yet the relief at having finally told someone else about Abigail's deception and the resulting consequences was overwhelming.

'I gave Ellie a bottle and she wrapped her tiny fingers around one of mine.' He blew his nose again and exhaled a calming breath. 'I took photos of her but I've never shown them to anyone, I've never looked at them again.'

'I'm so glad you took some pictures of her. She deserves that, she deserves to be remembered and loved by you for ever.' As CJ spoke, a fresh bout of tears flowed down her own cheeks. 'You're an amazing man, Ethan, and you would have made an amazing dad.'

'How could you possibly know that?'

'Because of the way you talk about Ellie.' She gave him a watery smile. 'You use the same tone my father used to use when he was talking about how much he loved me and my sister, and my dad was a great dad.'

He absorbed her words for a moment, then asked again, 'Do you really think I would have been a good daddy?'

Her smile was bright and she nodded. 'I know it. The way you look after me, the way you make me rest—it all makes sense now.' It also explained the veiled anger and desperation she'd seen him convey towards Margaret. 'I'm not going to do anything to jeopardise the health of this baby or myself. That's why I brought you in, why I eventually agreed to hire a locum.'

'I know.' He reached out and brushed a few strands of hair from her eyes, tucking them behind her ear. 'You're willing to ask for help. You're open and honest about your limitations. I like that about you.' Whereas Abigail had hidden everything from him. She'd been drinking for months—he'd never known why—and whilst he carried his fair share of the blame in the situation, he'd also come to realise that Abby also bore that blame and had paid for it with her life.

Now, with CJ, it was as though a new world was being opened for him. A world with laughter and a tinge of hope on the horizon. Was it possible he didn't have to keep punishing himself by working day and night, staring down the barrel of an early grave? He stared into CJ's dazzling green eyes and cupped her cheek with his hand before leaning a little closer, the atmosphere between them changing from one of support to one of heightened awareness.

He couldn't stop looking at her mouth and she couldn't stop looking at his. It was as though leaning forward, bringing herself closer to him, to within kissing distance, was the most natural thing in the world.

'CJ.' He whispered her name, the sound soft, delicate and intimate. As he neared, their breath began to mingle, the pheromones blending to form a heady combination. When she licked her lips in anticipation, he exhaled slowly but continued to decrease the space between his mouth and hers.

Before she knew it, Ethan's lips were pressed to hers, much the same as they'd been before, but this time there was more pressure, with the heightened need to figure out exactly what existed between them. She breathed in a deep, shaky breath before sighing into the kiss.

Bringing his other hand up to fully cup her face, he took his time exploring the tastes and flavours she exuded. She was sweeter than anything he'd ever experienced. She filled his senses completely. He could feel himself going under, wanting more, needing more, and she didn't disappoint.

He'd thought that one kiss might get her out of his system. That one kiss might help him to sleep at night. That one kiss would be all he would ever need from her. He was wrong. Groaning, he leaned closer, sifting his fingers through her loose hair, the silkiness of the tendrils only adding fuel to the fire that was already burning wildly through him.

How was it possible to barely know someone yet feel such an undeniable attraction? How was it possible to trust someone, to experience the primal need to take everything being offered? And it was being offered, on both sides. Both of them were one hundred percent involved in the moment, in the heat and delight. What it meant, CJ had no clue but while the exquisite torture continued, she was going to ensure she savoured every moment.

This was passion as she'd never felt it before. How could he stir such incredible longing with a few teasing and exploratory kisses? It was incredible and she felt as though she were floating…lifted up on the wings of desire—desire she was thrilled to discover was mutual.

As though he wanted to continue the slow discovery of every part of her mouth and the secrets contained therein, he sighed with delight, his mouth moving over hers in a sensual caress—a lover's caress. She wasn't sure how she was supposed to cope. She had thought she was on fire before with his testing kisses but now…now the flame had been fanned into something more—a fire that was taking her senses up on an internal climb so high, she felt as though she'd erupt like bright fireworks. Fire-stars, she'd called them as a child and now the term seemed appropriate to describe how he was making her feel. Fire-stars bursting brightly, one after the other as his mouth moved carefully and meticulously over hers.

It was as though he had to memorise every part of her. You do, he told himself, because this moment in time needs to last you for ever. Now that he'd done it, now that he'd given in to the urge to kiss her, he wanted it to be thorough.

The way she responded, not holding back a thing, had him losing his head completely. It was just like her to be so honest with her emotions and he had a glimpse of the love and promises she would have offered to her husband. The man had hurt her, broken her, used her and discarded her. At that thought, Ethan's hands slipped from her hair to her shoulders, somehow wanting to convey the information that he wasn't that sort of man, that he wasn't callous and calculating. If she'd offered him such a gift, he would do everything in his power to cherish it.

That thought was enough to break the hold the delightful taste of her had evoked upon his senses. He broke his mouth free and pressed kisses to her face. He shifted his chair, bringing it closer to hers before nuzzling her earlobe. Was that what she was offering? Was she offering herself to him? He wasn't sure. He didn't have a clear read on the situation. All he knew was that her hair was soft and silky to his touch as he brushed it out of the way so he could rain kisses on the sensitive hollow of her neck.

'Mmm…' she moaned, and shivered slightly as goosebumps broke out over her skin. It was torture, sheer, sweet, torture, and she never wanted it to stop. With an impatience she couldn't control she willed his lips to stop the pleasurable torment and return to her mouth. 'Kiss me,' she whispered, the words hardly audible, but he heard them.

Her words made him smile and helped those unwanted questions to be pushed to the back of his mind once more. It had been far too long since he'd felt this sort of desire, this sort of need, this sort of promise. Whatever this was, she was in it with him, side by side, clearly enjoying the ride as much as he. He pressed another round of kisses to the other side of her neck, enjoying the way she moaned and shivered beneath his touch. Finally, when he couldn't stand it any longer either, he brought his mouth back to hers.

They both relaxed into the kiss, their lips eager to become reacquainted, eager to continue with the journey into the unknown, unexplored desire that had been building between them since that first day in the supermarket. Even though it was all still new, he felt as though he'd been kissing her mouth for ever. The taste of her was genuine and her scent was a powerful, natural aphrodisiac.

Never had he expected such a gamut of emotions when he'd given in to the urge to kiss her. Her tongue lightly outlined his lips and he heard himself groan, amazed again at how this woman could override all his warning signals, his brick walls, and shoot him straight through the heart.

The heart?

The thought was enough to make him pull back. He cupped her face in his hands and stared down into her eyes, both of them breathing heavily. Her green eyes were glazed with pent-up frustrations and desire. Her lips were slightly swollen and pink—irresistible. Just gazing at her now had him wanting her all over again.

He wanted to give in but knew if he did, there was no way he'd have the willpower to stop things from taking their natural course. They kept gazing at each other as their heart rates gradually returned to normal. Her eyelids started to close and she rested her head on his shoulder, sighing contentedly.

'Sleepy,' she murmured, and couldn't help the yawn that escaped. She stayed where she was for a while, Ethan feeling her head become more heavier than usual. Eventually, he eased back, once more cupping her face in his hands as he looked down into her exhausted face.

'Go to sleep,' he murmured, and couldn't resist kissing the tip of her nose. He'd wanted to kiss her mouth again, to press promises to her luscious and addictive lips, but thought better of it. Losing control once was something he could live with. Repeating the action again and again would just be asking for trouble.

'Mmm…' Her eyes remained closed and she smiled at his words. 'I'll just clean up and—'

'Go to bed, CJ. I'll take care of things.'

'You always do that. You always say you'll take care of things.' As she spoke, she opened her eyes and looked at him. 'But you also need to take care of yourself.' Raising a tired hand to his face, she caressed his cheek. 'You've locked yourself away for so long, you've been filled with so many different emotions—anger, pain, disappointment.' CJ yawned again. 'Be kind to yourself, too.' Then she put her hands on the table in order to lever herself from the chair. Ethan quickly stood and helped her up.

'Sleep. I'll make some food and leave it in the fridge for you, ready for your early morning snack.'

'You don't have to—' She broke off as another yawn claimed her.

'Go lie down.'

'All right, Dr Bossy, I'm going.'

He heard her chuckle as she shuffled from the room and disappeared down to her end of the house. He sat there, listening to the sounds as she went to the bathroom before getting into her bed. How could his hearing be so acute, so in tune with every move she made? More to the point, how could he have given in to the urges he'd been doing his best to resist ever since he'd entered CJ Nicholls's world? He'd kissed her! He'd kissed his colleague…his *pregnant* colleague. What had he been thinking?

He hadn't.

Plain and simple—he hadn't.

The strange thing was, he expected to feel a world of guilt descend upon him again because he'd been unfaithful to Abigail's memory, but it didn't. If there was one thing kissing CJ had helped him to realise, it was that he had a right to be angry with Abigail. He hadn't wanted to before. He hadn't wanted to tarnish her memory, not when he'd been grieving the loss of both her and Ellie. His sister and brother had stood by him, his parents, too. They'd done everything they could to support him, none of them realising why he'd just shut everything out, why he'd moved into the apartment and why he'd never wanted to talk about it.

Lo and behold, six years later it was a caring and honest woman who had helped him to see the truth. Yes, he'd failed Abigail by not realising she'd found it so hard to talk to him when she'd started drinking. Yes, he'd failed their marriage by not paying more attention to her. Yes, he'd been so consumed with his own ideals of what his life should entail, namely career success and a stable home life. At the time, he'd had neither, so he'd thrown himself into achieving the former once he'd lost the latter.

CJ had helped him realise these things. Even if she hadn't known it she'd been chipping away at the walls surrounding him; just by being open and honest and accepting, she'd provided him with the tools he'd needed to chip away at those walls from the inside.

Ethan dragged in a deep breath, realising he wasn't able to completely fill his lungs. He frowned but rationalised it was understandable tonight. He'd stepped from the darkness into the light but even as he stood and began preparing a simple meal CJ could easily reheat later on, he felt imaginary shackles from his past start to fall away. The problem was that as they released him from their holds, new questions arose. If he wasn't locking himself away, hiding from the past, it meant it was time to face his future—whatever that was.

As he put a container of food in the fridge for CJ then quickly tidied up the kitchen, he glanced towards her door. Was CJ part of his future?

'No.' The word escaped his lips almost as instantly as

the thought had come. His world didn't involve Pridham. His life was in Sydney, being a surgeon and saving lives. Wasn't it? After everything he'd endured, he wasn't the type of man to enjoy uncertainty but of one thing he was certain—there would be no more kissing the alluring CJ. She wasn't the answer to his problems and he would be wrong to include her. She had her own issues to deal with and massive changes were about to impact her life. The last thing she needed was to be saddled with his baggage.

CHAPTER NINE

'THIS IS THE third time you've been here in under a week, CJ,' Donna said when CJ dropped around to see her on Friday evening. 'How are you feeling tonight?'

'Bit of back pain but a wheat bag will help with that. It's as though baby's running out of room in the front so is starting to expand towards my spine.' She chuckled 'Or that's how it feels.'

'Come and see me tomorrow morning and we'll do a check-up.'

'OK.' She nodded. 'I just wanted to give you an update on the patient I saw today.'

'I thought Ethan had taken over most of the house calls.'

'I've done a few.' CJ sighed, a frown furrowing her brow. 'Ethan's so determined to ensure I'm resting, I don't think he wants me to do *anything*.' Every time she'd seen him during the past week, all he'd expressed had been his concern for the baby and that she needed to rest. There had been no mention of their kiss, of what he'd shared about his past, about anything that had occurred that night, and all it had done was to confuse CJ even more.

He'd taken to being out of the house early and when he was home in the evenings, he worked in his room. Oddly enough, he still kept cooking food for her, although he'd do it either when she was in the shower or having a snooze. Yet every time she went to the kitchen to find something to snack on, there in the fridge was a balanced and nutritious meal that she could heat in the microwave. Considerate and confusing. That was Ethan.

'Is that why you keep coming around? To show him you're not completely useless?'

'No. I come here because I need to tell you about the patients. Keep up, Donna.' CJ snapped her fingers at her friend, then smiled. 'And also because I miss our chats. When you go from being crazy busy and talking to people all day long to just lying around with your feet up, doing nothing but dozing, it's surprising how quickly you become bored.'

'So you decided to still drop in on patients?' Donna checked.

CJ shrugged one shoulder. 'Old habits…but I do it mainly to satisfy myself that my patients are OK. I saw Margaret today.'

Donna nodded. 'She's one we're all worried about. How was she?'

CJ made the so-so gesture with her hand. 'She's not drinking, at least, not that she's admitting, but she's very depressed. Those two nights she spent in hospital made her realise that her situation is extremely serious.' CJ shook her head.

'Should Margaret and Doug get counselling? Should we hospitalise Margaret for the duration of her pregnancy?'

'I've tried the counselling route at the moment as Margaret does seem to like being at home but given she still has about another six weeks to go, perhaps we should consider hospitalisation.'

'What does Ethan think of the situation?'

Margaret was the one patient they'd discussed yesterday when CJ had been in the lounge room with her feet up when he'd arrived home from clinic. 'He said it doesn't look good. Margaret may still miscarry at any stage.'

Donna sighed. 'Has Ethan seen this type of thing before? Foetal Alcohol Syndrome?'

CJ thought back to what he'd confessed about his wife. 'He has, as a matter of fact, and because of that, he's done a lot of research into it.'

'Good.'

'The main problem Margaret faces is that if she doesn't stop drinking now, the likelihood that the baby will be born with some sort of deformity will increase. I've been reading up on it, too, but even now it might be too late and the baby might not even survive.'

'Does Margaret know this?'

'I've told her the facts. Ethan's told her the facts. I know the social worker came and saw her when she was in hospital and talked to her about the possibility of birth defects. We're doing all we can and we're not trying to scare her but rather inform her.' CJ sighed with exasperation. 'In the end, though—'

'It's up to Margaret.'

'Exactly.'

'I'll get Ethan to discuss the idea of prolonged hospitalisation with Margaret's obstetrician.'

'OK.'

'Or…you could tell him.'

'Me? Ask Ethan to talk to Margaret's obstetrician?'

'Yes. You live in the same house as him. It's not like you don't talk at all.'

CJ shook her head quickly. 'No. No. It's much better coming from you.'

Donna eyed her carefully. 'Does Ethan know you've seen Margaret?'

'Ethan isn't the boss of me,' CJ stated, lifting her chin a little.

'He told me he's been insisting you rest.'

'Insisting is a mild word. He won't let me do anything!

Just because—' CJ stopped. Although she wanted to tell Donna what Ethan had shared with her, had told her about his wife and his unborn child, she didn't want to break his confidence. 'Because I'm pregnant, he thinks I'm useless.'

'You sound very indignant about it.' Donna was looking at her as though she was sure CJ was hiding something. 'Yet when I tell you to rest, you don't sound nearly so put out.' A smile started to form on Donna's lips. 'I think you're a little bit attracted to our new locum. At least, that's the sense I got last week when you were standing in the waiting room about to kiss him!'

CJ gasped. 'You saw us!'

'It was purely by accident. I came out of my consulting room to check something with Tania but saw the two of you and quickly retreated.' Donna shifted forward in her seat. 'So? What was it like?'

CJ thought back to that day and slowly shook her head. 'It wasn't really a *kiss* per se.' Not compared to the ones they'd shared later on. 'More like a moment when we brushed lips.'

'A moment?'

'Half a moment. It was very brief, very light, very...' CJ trailed off, sighing softly before adding, 'Very nice.'

'So you *are* avoiding him. That's why you're out most nights. Visiting me, visiting Tania, visiting a plethora of other people.'

'What? Do you hold regular meetings to discuss my whereabouts?'

Donna laughed. 'Are you avoiding Ethan because of the way he makes you feel?'

CJ straightened her back and flicked her pigtails over her shoulder, determined to deny her friend's words, but the instant she opened her mouth, she slouched and covered her face with her hands. It was no use. 'He's so nice and wonderful and caring, as well as frustrating, infuriating and…sexy.' She dropped her hands. 'I like the way he smells. I like the way he walks. I like the way he talks. I really like him and that scares the living daylights out of me.'

'What's the problem?'

'Problem? Where do I start?' She spread her hands wide. 'How about the fact that his life is in Sydney and mine is here? How about the fact that I've already been burned by one man, that I'm not about to throw myself back into the fire. And the last reason why it just wouldn't work.' She pointed to her belly. 'I'm about to have a baby! All my time and attention and care is about to be completely focused on figuring out how to be a parent.' With her emotions in overdrive, while she'd been talking, tears had sprung to her eyes and she reached for a tissue and blew her nose. A moment later she closed her eyes and said softly, 'Here I am, on the brink of having Quinten's baby, and all I can think about is Ethan Janeway. I mean, what man in his right mind would be attracted to me? Look at me! I'm huge!'

'You're pregnant and you're all baby. You've watched your weight carefully and have hardly put any extra on, even with all your late night pickle and chocolate spread snacking.'

CJ gasped. 'He told you about that!'

'It's hardly a secret, CJ, but it wasn't Ethan, it was Idris at the grocery store.'

'Oh.'

'Once the baby's born, it won't take you long to get your figure back. You'll be your normal size again and everything will feel better.'

CJ dabbed at her eyes before blowing her nose. 'I know. It's all silly, it's all emotional but…' She sighed. 'It was *so* nice to think that he might be attracted to me, especially when I'm huge like this. Do you have any idea what that did for my self-esteem?'

'I can imagine. What's your plan, then? To go out visiting people at night until the baby's born?'

'Sounds good to me.'

'Does Ethan know where you are?'

She shook her head. 'I don't think so but I don't answer to him.'

'That doesn't sound like you.'

'Quinten needed to know where I was at all times and I often thought that was so sweet, that he was interested in me, and yet the truth of the matter was that he only wanted to know where I was so I wouldn't catch him having one of his many affairs.'

'Ethan isn't Quinten,' Donna pointed out softly.

CJ huffed and shrugged. 'I know but I still don't need to tell him where I am at every moment of the day. I don't ask where he goes. He gets up early and is out of the house before I've woken up, so I've taken to visiting people in the evening to give him some time to work, instead of hibernating in my bedroom.'

'That's very considerate of you.'

'If I didn't, then he'd probably go out and he's got nowhere to go.'

'True. Or here's a thought—you could just try talking to him.'

'I do talk to him but there's only so much we can say about our patients.'

Donna chuckled. 'Listen, once the baby is born, you'll feel better. Your life will settle down into a nice, easy rhythm and Ethan Janeway will return to Sydney and all will be forgotten.'

'It could be my hormones that are telling me I'm attracted to him when I'm really not.' She closed her eyes and shook her head. 'Man, that sounds silly when I say it out loud.'

'But why don't we blame those troublesome hormones at the moment?'

'Yes. Yes, I think you're right.'

'And after all he's the only good-looking, single man of your age in the vicinity.'

'True. Very true.'

'So there you go. Opportunity and motive, all of which you had absolutely no control over. You are not to blame.'

'Excellent.' CJ shifted out of the chair and stood. 'Thanks, Donna. I'm glad I came over tonight.'

'So am I. Go home, have a snack, get a wheat bag warmed up and lie down with a good book.'

'Sounds like the perfect prescription.' CJ hugged her friend, then said, 'I might just use your bathroom first. Junior's jumping on my bladder again.'

Ethan stared out the window at the dark and empty street. There weren't as many streetlights here as there were surrounding his apartment in Sydney. The night sky seemed darker, the stars seemed brighter, and he could swear there were more stars here than there were in Sydney.

Where was she?

'Ethan? Are you still there?'

'Yeah. Sorry, Melody. What were you saying?'

'That things are crazy at work. The director's resigned.'

'Oh, yeah. So who's going to take over being Director of Orthopaedics?' He turned away from the window and began to pace around the lounge room, returning a moment later to look out the window again when he thought he'd heard a noise. He'd spoken to his sister more in this past week than he had in the past year, finally managing to tell her the truth about Abigail and Ellie.

After they'd discussed things for a while, Melody had asked, 'Why are you able to talk about it now? Not that I'm complaining, it's just…you know, six years, Ethan, and *now* you can discuss things? You've changed—for the better—and I think it all has to do with the different pace of life in Pridham. You've been forced to re-evaluate your life, to slow down, to breathe, to—'

Ethan had cut her off, not wanting to discuss *every* aspect of his life with his sister. However, since then, Melody had taken to calling him, wanting to chat, wanting to share things in her life with him, and he was pleased she'd taken the initiative. It made him realise just how far he'd distanced himself from his family but, thankfully, they hadn't let him disappear completely. He owed them for that, and he owed CJ for helping him to realise all this.

It was crazy how his housemate had come to mean so much to him so quickly. He'd never thought, when he'd made the decision to come to Pridham, that this sort of thing would happen, that he'd be able to open up and talk about his pain with those who cared about him. He also hadn't expected to be attracted to his new colleague and end up being desperate to kiss her. Yet that's exactly what he'd done. It was ridiculous, though, because his life wasn't here in Pridham. His life was in Sydney, with his patients, his surgery, his department. He liked working in Sydney, he liked operating and was missing it here in Pridham. Granted, the pace of life here was much slower and, as far as his health went, it was doing him the world of good.

Except for this past week. Ever since he'd kissed CJ, he hadn't managed to get any proper sleep. It was little wonder, especially as his thoughts had been constantly churning about what the kisses might mean.

Why did they need to mean anything? That had been his main argument. Perhaps those kisses had just been a means of him releasing the anguish he'd kept locked away for so many years, a way of thanking CJ for helping him to realise he still had a lot to offer the world. However, it was his desire to press his mouth to hers every other time he'd seen her that was starting to do his head in. Where he'd thought the attraction for her would begin to wane, it had, instead, intensified. He'd wanted to kiss her even more, to further explore the sensations only she'd been able to evoke, which was the reason why he'd woken up very early the morning after those exquisite kisses and ensured he had been out of the house before she'd got up.

Since then, he'd done his best to give her a wide berth, not wanting to become a complication in her life. She had enough to contend with and although both districts of Pridham and Whitecorn were watching over her, pledging their support once the baby was born, the desire to gather her into his arms and keep her safe, to protect both CJ and her unborn child, was something Ethan was constantly fighting. *He* wanted to protect her. *He* wanted to keep her and the baby safe. But *why*? Was he merely trying to appease his subconscious? To save CJ and her child, when he'd been unable to save Abigail and Ellie?

Upon hearing another sound from outside, he went to the front door, opening it, but it wasn't her. He checked that the sensor lights were working so that whenever she finally did come home, she wouldn't be navigating her way to the door in the dark.

'Are you listening to me at all?' Melody asked again.

'I am. You're telling me the shortlist for the director of orthopaedics.' Ethan went back inside. 'Hey, isn't your department supposed to be getting a visiting professor or something like that soon?'

'In another few months. Hopefully, the new director will be installed by the time that happens.'

'You could do it.'

'Me? Be the director of orthopaedics?' Melody laughed at him. 'No, thank you. I do not want to play nursemaid to a visiting professor, no matter how brilliant he is. That is not my idea of fun.'

Ethan half listened to Melody as she kept talking, still feeling guilty about driving CJ from her own home. He knew she left because of him. He felt it. If she stayed home, she would hibernate in her bedroom and if she was getting up for her usual three a.m. snacks, he wasn't hearing her.

When she was out this late, he found it almost impossible to work until she was safe at home. He was conscious of her whenever she walked into the house, regardless of whether or not he was in the same room. It didn't matter where she was, he *felt* her and it was driving him insane.

Where was she? He stared out the window and when a set of headlights flashed as they turned into the driveway, he quickly stepped back into the shadows, his whole body relaxing with relief. She was back. She was safe. She was home.

Home?

He brushed the thought from his mind as he quickly headed into his part of the house, not wanting to be in her way. He listened, though, as she opened and closed the front door before making her way into the kitchen. He'd left a meal for her in the fridge and soon he heard the microwave going. Another ten minutes later and everything fell silent. She was safely down her end of the house and he was in his. His sister had hung up, giving up on him not carrying his end of the conversation.

Instead, Ethan sat down at the desk in his room and began to get some work done. Now that CJ was safe at home, he could concentrate.

CJ finished eating the lovely food Ethan had cooked and put the dish on her bedside table, lying back in her bed and patting her baby. 'There you go. All fed for now.' Part of her had wanted him to be in the kitchen when she'd arrived home so that she could tell him about her conversation with Donna regarding Margaret. She'd also wanted to see Ethan for more than two minutes together so they could have an open and honest conversation about what on earth was happening between them.

CJ shuffled off the bed, the pain in her back beginning to intensify. She took her dishes quietly out to the kitchen, moving slowly and carefully, constantly on alert in case she should bump into him. The problem was that even if he came out, even if she asked the questions, she doubted whether either of them would have any answers. She certainly didn't and that's why she was happy to live in avoidance land for a bit longer.

Returning to her part of the house, she continued to rub the pain that was still niggling at her back. 'Did I eat too fast?' she asked the baby, wondering if she was getting referred indigestion pain, but that made no sense. The next moment she stopped in the middle of the hallway, leaning on the wall, as a sharp spasm gripped her lower abdomen. CJ gasped in shock and waited desperately for the pain to subside.

'Ow.' She rubbed her back and her abdomen. 'What was that for? Do you want some chocolate spread?' CJ headed to the stash of food she'd taken to keeping in her room. That way, she hadn't risked waking Ethan when she needed an early morning snack.

Before she could pull the chocolate spread from the bag, another pain gripped her, marginally worse than before. She sat down on the chair and felt instant discomfort, so stood once more, rubbing her belly until the pain eased. 'Just excessive back pain and Braxton-Hicks,' she told herself calmly. It meant things were definitely moving in the right direction. She would brush her teeth, then re-check her hospital bag was packed and call Donna. Although CJ was a doctor, although she'd assisted with many a delivery, reading about a contraction and experiencing one were two very different things. If this was just false labour, at least Donna would be able to put her mind at ease. As she walked to her en suite, another spasm hit.

It was then she felt a loosening sensation before a trickle of water slid down her leg. Her eyes widened in alarm as she rushed to the bathroom and stepped into the shower.

'What?' She wasn't sure what to do so she just stood there, waiting for the liquid to stop running down her legs. 'Oh, my gosh,' she whispered. 'This isn't a false alarm. This is *it*!' She was in labour.

Trembling, she thumped on the wall. 'Ethan! Ethan!' She waited, not knowing whether he could hear her. The trickle was slowing down and she started to relax a little. 'Ethan!' she called again, and thumped some more on the wall, concern in her tone.

'CJ?'

She breathed a sigh of relief. He'd heard her. 'Ethan.' He knocked on her bedroom door, which she thought was cute. 'Come in. Come in. I'm in the bathroom.' A moment later, he stood in the doorway.

'What's wrong? Why are you standing in the shower fully clothed?'

'My water —' She broke off on a gasp as another spasm hit. She closed her eyes and clenched her teeth, bracing one hand on the shower wall and the other on her abdomen.

'You're in labour?' When she looked at him, it was to find him staring at her in stunned disbelief.

CHAPTER TEN

'ARE YOU SURE? You still have a few weeks to go.'

'Tell that to the baby.' She would have laughed if she could. As it was, she concentrated on the pain, which seemed to be getting stronger as well as longer. Finally, it subsided and she relaxed against the shower wall, opening her eyes to look at him.

'I'll call Donna and the hospital and, uh…let them know we'll be over soon.' He reached into his pocket for his smartphone. 'Has it stopped?'

'Yes.'

He pressed some buttons on the phone. 'Let's see how far apart your contractions are.' He stayed with her, quickly calling Donna and then the hospital to give them the latest update. 'No doubt,' he stated after ending the call, 'the entire district will know you're in labour before we even make it across the road to the hospital.' She was still standing in the shower, her eyes closed as she rested her head against the tiles. 'Has the next contraction started?'

'No.' The instant the word left her lips the pain returned. 'I'll change my answer—yes!'

'Just over three minutes.' He waited with her until he thought the pain had subsided. 'Settling down?'

Her eyes snapped open and she glared at him.

'Ah… I'll take that as a no.' He waited until she was

finished, starting his watch again. 'I'll help you through the house and into the car.'

'No car. Can't sit down. I'll walk.'

'You want to walk to the hospital?'

'It's across the road. The car will take longer.'

'I don't know if it's a good idea.'

'Then I'll be having it here because I *can't sit down*!' she shouted.

'All right. Sure. We'll walk.' He held out his hand to her and when she didn't take it he levelled her with a warning glare. 'Accept my help, CJ. I want to give it and, more importantly, you need it.'

'Fine.'

He laughed, the rich sound washing over her in waves of happiness. How was it possible that she could feel so happy and so cross with him at the same time? She knew the thought wasn't worth dwelling on, so placed her hand in his as he helped her from the shower cubicle.

'I know you'd probably feel better if you change but let's get you over the road first. Someone can come back for clothes and things like that later.'

'My bag is packed,' she said, and motioned to the small suitcase by her bed. 'Just pick it up.' She waved her hand impatiently in the direction of the bag. 'Oh, and grab my food bag, too. It's next to it.'

'Food bag?' Ethan grabbed the bags she was pointing to and quickly peered inside the second one. 'Chocolate spread, pickles and bananas. No wonder I haven't heard you in the kitchen.'

'I didn't want to wake you.'

'Hmm.'

'What's that supposed to mean?' she asked angrily as they headed out the front door.

'Nothing.' He knew better than to start a discussion with

a woman who was in this much pain. 'Whatever makes things easier for you.'

'Oh, how magnanimous of you,' she retorted, and Ethan chuckled.

'It doesn't matter what I say at the moment, you're going to bite my head off and that's perfectly fine.'

CJ started to whimper but it ended up being a silly sort of chuckle. 'I'm sorry, I'm just—'

'You don't need to apologise, or explain.' They went slowly, taking small but steady steps, out the front door and across the lawn. They'd just crossed the road when the next contraction hit.

'Right on time,' Ethan announced. CJ gripped his arm tightly as she closed her eyes and concentrated through the pain. Neither of them moved until it was over. 'The duration of the contraction is increasing.'

'Tell me about it.'

He let go of her hand and flexed his fingers. 'Just getting the blood flowing again, ready for next time.'

CJ laughed, then was overcome by a sense of gratitude. 'Thank you, Ethan. Thank you for helping me.'

'Hey, no problem.' He took her hand once more, the other still carrying her bags. 'The ground's a bit uneven here.' They started off again, little baby steps, slowly getting closer to the hospital. Not far from the front door she gripped his hand and leaned in closer. Ethan put the bags down and rubbed her back with his other hand, hoping it did something to bring her relief. He felt utterly helpless and wasn't really sure what he should or shouldn't be doing, but as she wasn't yelling at him, he took this as a good sign.

The night CNC came rushing out with a wheelchair. Ethan shook his head. 'CJ prefers to walk.'

'I don't *prefer* it,' she snapped as the contraction eased. 'I *can't* sit down.'

'Walking will help speed up the labour,' Bonnie told her, as she took the bags from Ethan.

'I think it's moving along pretty fast all by itself.'

'Good. Donna's on her way. Let's get you inside and see what's happening.'

They made a stop-start procession up the corridor, with CJ having another contraction in the middle. She leaned her head against Ethan's shoulder and he rubbed her back soothingly. When it passed, the sister led her into the delivery room. The bed had a floral, frilly spread on it with several throw cushions, making it seem more homely.

CJ had delivered several babies in this room, had walked passed it several times and had always thought it looked very pretty. Now…she wanted to hurl the cushions at the window and rake the feminine cover from the bed. She was in pain and the last thing she wanted was pretty, relaxing things around her.

Where were the drugs?

Oh, it was wonderful that Donna was on her way, that Ethan and the night CNC were being ever so attentive, but where was the anaesthetist? He was the one who could give her some pain relief, an epidural—anything.

'Charlie. Ring Charlie,' she said.

'I've already called him. He's on his way.'

CJ glared at Bonnie. 'Go and get him *now*.'

'I'll settle her in,' Ethan remarked, noticing the surprised look on Bonnie's face.

'I don't need *anyone* to settle me,' CJ added. 'I'm fine. Women have babies all the time and now it's my turn and I'm *fine*!'

'Yes, you are,' Ethan pacified as he tossed the cushions off the bed onto a chair and pulled the bedspread back. CJ smirked in a self-satisfied way at the inanimate objects, glad of his rough treatment of them. He wound the bed down so it was easier for her to get on but she found she couldn't.

'Can't lie down either.' She looked at him, her eyes beginning to fill with tears. 'I can't sit down, I can't lie down and my legs are aching and tired.'

'I know. I know,' he soothed. 'Lean on me.' He gathered her near so her head was resting on his shoulder.

'I'm sorry if I'm being horrible.'

He laughed. 'You're not.'

'Liar.'

He laughed again. 'Probably.'

She pulled back to look at him, her terrified green eyes meeting his sympathetic blue ones. 'Thank you,' she whispered.

Ethan felt a knot of tension, need and anger churn in his gut. Tension because he was fighting as hard as he could against the attraction. Need because it was becoming impossible *not* to give in and kiss her, and anger against her husband for leaving her to cope with this experience all alone.

She was an amazing woman and his feelings for her were intensifying with every moment he spent in her company. It wasn't right. He knew that, but he also knew the wrong thing could sometimes feel so right.

He swallowed over all his thoughts and emotions and bent down to kiss her forehead. 'You'll be fine.' He felt her body tense and knew another contraction was on the way. He helped her through it, his eyes closed as they leaned against each other, both concentrating on what was happening. When he opened his eyes, it was to find Donna standing in the doorway, watching them.

'Good evening. You look as though you're having loads of fun.' She came in and patted CJ lightly on the shoulder. 'Right. Has anyone checked the baby yet?'

Ethan waited for CJ to answer but when she didn't, he shook his head.

'Can you get up on the bed?'

'Too uncomfortable,' she mumbled.

'OK. Stay where you are, I'll work around you.' For the next ten minutes there were people in and out of the room, the baby's heartbeat was checked and found to be perfect. CJ was given a once-over by Donna and pronounced to be almost nine centimetres dilated.

'That's very quick. Hang on, your sister had quick labours with her children, didn't she?'

'Four hours for the first and two hours for the second,' CJ said softly between contractions. 'Looks as though you might break her record.' Donna chuckled. 'I was in labour for over fifteen hours and that was with my last one.'

'Where's Charlie?'

'I'll go check.' Donna headed out, leaving CJ leaning on Ethan, closing her eyes as she tried to rest between contractions. It was a good half an hour later before Charlie walked in the door and by that time CJ was fully dilated.

'Where have you been?' she growled at the anaesthetist when he gave her a cheery greeting.

'It's always nice to feel so appreciated,' Charlie joked as he read CJ's chart, checking that both mother and baby were doing well. 'OK. You have no allergies so let me go get you some—'

Before Charlie could finish his sentence, CJ had another contraction but this one gripped her abdomen even tighter and, quite involuntarily, she gave a push.

'Was that a push?' Donna asked. They all waited and when CJ involuntarily pushed again, Charlie chuckled.

'Well, you don't need me any more,' he joked.

'Yes. Yes, I do.' CJ grabbed him by the front of his shirt and dragged his face closer. 'Give me something. Anything!'

'I can't, CJ. You know that.'

'The window has closed?'

'The window has closed,' Charlie confirmed.

'Open a door,' she whimpered, and let go of his shirt.

'CJ.' Charlie smoothed a comforting hand over her forehead. 'You'll be fine. The baby's fine. There seems to be an abundance of people in here, so I'll be in the kitchen if you need me.'

CJ reached out a hand but he was gone. Her window was shut and so was the door. Why couldn't he open it again? She stuck out her lower lip. 'I don't want to do this any more.'

Donna laughed. 'You're doing a great job and the fact that you're saying you want to go home proves that everything is moving along nicely.' When the next contraction gripped, CJ pushed again. She rested her head on Ethan's shoulder between contractions and closed her eyes, conserving what energy she had.

It seemed to take for ever but three hours later Donna told her to give one more push and the head was finally out. The cord wasn't around the neck and they waited while the shoulders rotated. CJ had managed to get comfortable on a beanbag as her legs had eventually given up supporting her.

Ethan held her hand tightly, dabbing her forehead with a damp cloth. She hadn't wanted him to go and he'd made no move to leave. Now…they were almost finished and she could hardly believe the man she'd known for only a few weeks had stayed to help her through this.

CJ knew it was ridiculous but…she loved him. Whether it was the love of a lifetime or a love of utter gratitude, she had no way of knowing. Perhaps it was the hormones or the intimacy of their present situation but her feelings would not be repressed. The next contraction started to grip and she squeezed his hand once more.

'That's it. Good girl. Keep going, CJ,' Donna coached. 'Snatch a breath—one more push and—'

CJ felt the baby leave her and was amazed at the immediate sense of loss. The intimacy only *she* could share with her child was over. Everything was silent for a second or two and she didn't even realise that Ethan had let go of her hand to quickly assist Donna—and then it came. The most glorious sound in the entire world—the cry of a newborn babe.

Donna placed the child into CJ's waiting arms. 'You have a daughter.'

The loss she'd just felt vanished into thin air as she held her little girl for the very first time, kissing the soft, downy head.

'Oh, baby.' Her eyes filled with tears that spilled over. 'Baby, you're here.'

'What are you going to call her?' The question came from Ethan, his voice not quite so steady. CJ looked up to see his own eyes glistening with tears. She reached out a hand to him, which he took, drawing him closer.

'Ethan…' Her throat was scratchy and sore and with the swell of emotion she felt, it was no wonder it was hard to speak.

'Really? I think you can think of a prettier name than that,' he whispered with a soft chuckle.

She laughed and swallowed. 'Will you help me?'

'Name her?' When she nodded, he smiled. 'I'd be delighted and honoured.'

The child in her arms slept, their gazes held and slowly but surely he moved in closer. The kiss he pressed on her lips was the most natural thing he'd ever done. The feeling of coming home was the most natural feeling he'd ever felt.

And he was at a loss to explain why neither terrified him.

'Have you come up with any more names?' Donna asked as she came around to check on CJ. CJ was sitting in bed, propped up by pillows, feeding her beautiful daughter. 'Everyone's on tenterhooks to find out what you'll call her, and discover who has won the competition.'

'Who picked the right date?'

'Idris at the supermarket. Robert chose the correct time of birth so now we're just waiting on the name.'

CJ chuckled. 'I love the way they all get involved.'

'I can't believe she's two days old and you still haven't even thought of a name.'

'I want to find one that suits her. I liked Susan yesterday but...' She trailed off and shook her head.

'Has Ethan been in this morning?'

'Not yet but we're expecting him soon.' The baby had finished feeding and CJ sat her up to burp her. 'Aren't we a beautiful girl. We're expecting Ethan really soon. Yes, we are. Oh, you're so precious.' CJ kissed her daughter's head, breathing in the scent and filing the memory away for later. Once the baby had released her wind, CJ rewrapped the gorgeous girl in a blanket. 'I like the name Joy. Are you a Joy?' She smiled. 'Yes. Yes you are a joy, an absolute joy.'

'Joy?' Ethan queried as he strode into the room. 'Joy Nicholls. Has a ring to it. I gather you've given up Susan?'

'Yes. I don't think she looks like a Susan any more.'

'What about... Elizabeth?'

CJ watched as he scooped the baby up into his arms as though it were the most natural thing in the world. He kissed her head and rubbed his cheek against her softness, breathing that gorgeous baby scent in the same way CJ had.

'Elizabeth. Elizabeth Nicholls.' She mulled it over. 'I quite like it. Elizabeth. Does she look like an Elizabeth, Ethan?'

He studied the little girl who was going to sleep in his arms. 'You know, I think she does. And also I like Lizzie, for when she's cheeky and mischievous.'

'Where did you get Elizabeth from?' Donna asked.

'It was my great-grandmother's name,' Ethan stated.

'It's very pretty.'

'We need something that goes with Elizabeth,' Ethan continued, rocking the baby gently from side to side. CJ liked watching him hold the baby, liked the way he looked with the little girl in his arms, liked the way he'd just *loved* her so unconditionally. She'd been worried that being at the birth, helping her, holding the baby—all of it would have brought back horrible memories for him but, in fact, it was the opposite. It was as though Elizabeth's birth had helped him to heal. Still, CJ was cautious. There were still too many questions in the air surrounding Ethan, herself and the baby, but for now, naming the gorgeous girl was enough to deal with.

They all thought. 'What about Janice?' Donna asked.

CJ pondered, then shook her head.

'What about Jean?' Ethan suggested. 'After you, Claudia-Jean. You could hyphenate her name, too.'

'EJ and CJ? Well, the Jean part of my name was after my mother so that way Elizabeth would be named after both of us.' She laughed.

'And she deserves to carry the family name—your name,' he continued. 'You did an amazing job, bringing her into this world.' He looked at the baby. 'Elizabeth-Jean Nicholls.'

'It's pretty,' Donna remarked. She looked from one to the other. 'Decided?'

CJ smiled at Ethan. 'Decided. Elizabeth-Jean she is.'

'This calls for a celebration,' Donna said, and headed off to tell the rest of the staff. After Donna had left the room, CJ peered at her daughter.

'Is she asleep?'

'Yes.'

'Do you want to put her down?'

'No.' He smiled sheepishly and sat down on the bed next to CJ. 'I like holding her.'

'Me too. I was supposed to put her in her cot last night but I just didn't want to let her go so I slept with her in my arms all night long. Snuggled together.' Her smile was bright and she sighed with happiness.

'So how are you feeling today?'

'Better.'

Ethan angled Elizabeth up in his arms so they could both look at the baby's sleeping face. 'She's beautiful, CJ. Simply beautiful.'

'She is, isn't she,' CJ whispered rhetorically, brushing her finger lightly over Elizabeth's cheek. 'I can't believe how perfectly I love her. I didn't know she was missing from my life until she was here.' She chuckled and looked at him. 'I don't know if that makes any sense at all.'

'It does.' He turned his head and returned her gaze. 'Perfect sense.' As they continued to look at each other, the atmosphere in the room intensified, the awareness between them growing with every passing second they spent together. Where prior to Elizabeth's birth they'd been able to keep their distance, the experience they'd shared—the miracle of life—seemed to have made the bond even stronger. CJ's lips parted and her breathing increased as she continued to gaze into Ethan's eyes. He made her feel so wonderful, so cherished, so strong and she wanted desperately to kiss him, to show him how much she appreciated his care and support.

Without a word spoken, he leaned forward and placed his lips on hers as though it were the most natural thing in the world. It was like the first kiss they'd shared, featherlight and very brief, then he shifted back slightly and cleared his throat. As she looked at him for a moment longer, she could clearly see his concern, his questions and his confusion. She didn't blame him as she felt the same way. Now, however, was not the time for such a discussion and they both knew it, hence she also understood why he hadn't made the effort to deepen the kiss.

'Er…the nurses mentioned that you're planning to discharge yourself and Elizabeth tomorrow.' He looked down at the baby as he spoke and the moment of repressed need and desire vanished.

'Yes. I'd like to get home and settled into a routine. I'm not far from the hospital, both you and Donna will be across the road at the clinic during the day should we need anything, and you'll be in the house in the evening. I don't see any reason to stay and take up a hospital bed.'

'I'm not criticising you, I'm merely making a statement. The reason I made the statement is that I was also told about the hospital's custom.'

'Custom?'

'Well, it can't be a very good one if their own GP doesn't know about it.'

'Which one?'

'The one where the new mother is taken out to dinner for a few hours the night before she returns home. A celebration for her hard labour.' He raised his eyebrows on the pun.

'Oh. *That* custom.' CJ had forgotten about it, simply because she had no one to take her out. Was Ethan suggesting that *he* was going to take her out? Tingles of excitement buzzed through her. 'Why do you…er…mention it?' Maybe he was offering to look after Elizabeth while she went out to dinner by herself or with some of her friends.

'Because I want to take you to dinner. You deserve it.'

'Dinner?' she repeated. 'Uh…where were you thinking of going?'

'I hadn't actually thought that far. Do you have any suggestions? Favourite places? Or would you like to be surprised?'

'Um…' She couldn't think. She hadn't been out to dinner in such a very long time she wasn't sure what to say. 'Surprise me.'

'OK. Surprise it is.' His smile was wide and encompassing.

'Are you looking forward to this more than me?' As she asked the question, she saw a hint of sadness creep into Ethan's gaze. He looked down at Elizabeth for a moment, brushing a kiss to the baby's head.

'It's also my way of thanking you for allowing me to be a part of your miracle.'

Tears instantly sprang to CJ's eyes and she placed her hand on his arm. 'If the experiences of the last few days have helped bring you some level of healing for your past pain, then I'm very happy.'

Ethan raised his gaze to meet hers briefly and he nodded, then looked at the clock on the wall. 'I have to go or I'll be late for clinic.' He handed her the baby, their arms and hands touching briefly—but it was enough for them both to stop, stare at each other, then mumble muffled apologies. 'Enjoy your steady stream of visitors.'

'We will. They'll all be even more thrilled now that she has a name.'

'See you at seven tonight.'

CJ watched him go, then looked at her sleeping babe. She shuffled down in the bed, discarding pillows as she went until finally she and Elizabeth were snuggled up together. 'I love you, Lizzie-Jean,' she whispered, and kissed the downy forehead. People may come and go from her life, like her parents and her husband—and even Ethan, who would one day return to Sydney. Now, though, she had someone of her own, filling a void in her life she hadn't known existed. Whatever happened or didn't happen between her and Ethan, CJ vowed to be the best mother ever, to always love her little girl.

But it would be wonderful if the man who, she was

sure, loved Elizabeth as much as she did could find it in his heart to love her, too.

'That would be perfect,' she whispered to her daughter, before drifting off to sleep.

CHAPTER ELEVEN

'NO DINNER FOR you tonight,' Donna remarked as she waltzed into CJ's room carrying a garment bag.

'Pardon?' For one heart-stopping moment, CJ thought Ethan had cancelled.

'From the hospital kitchen, I mean.'

'Whew!' She placed her hand over her heart. 'Don't *do* that to me.'

Donna laughed. 'Sorry. Here. I brought you a surprise.' She held out the garment bag. 'It's my present to you.'

CJ unzipped the bag and gasped as she took out a breath-taking black dress. It was simple, elegant, and one that she'd admired at an online boutique for months. She looked from the dress to Donna. 'How did you do it? Ethan only asked me this morning to go out to dinner.'

'I called the online shop and had them express deliver it.'

'What! You shouldn't have gone to so much bother.'

'Nonsense. You deserve this night.'

CJ could feel the tears brimming in her eyes. She put the dress on the bed and rushed to hug her friend. 'Thank you. Thank you so much.'

'Hey, don't start crying now. Ethan's going to be here in half an hour and we don't want your face all blotchy.'

CJ sniffed and smiled. 'You're right.' She picked up the dress and held it against her before turning to Elizabeth, who was sleeping in the hospital cot. 'Look, princess. Does Mummy look pretty?'

'Mummy looks sickeningly good,' Donna said. 'I wish my figure had sprung back as quickly as yours. I don't know. You have an easy and quick labour and a few days later you're almost back to what you were before you became pregnant. It's just not fair.'

CJ laughed. 'I can't help it.'

'No. Although I would like to add that when you get pregnant again—some time in the future—we keep a close eye on you when you go into labour because, boy, oh, boy, do you go quickly. You'll be lucky to make it across the road to the hospital with the next one.'

'What *next one*?' she scoffed, but didn't dwell on it. 'I want to enjoy the baby I have because before I know it she'll be on her way to university.'

'Don't I know it!' Donna laughed. 'All right. Ethan's going to be here soon so let's get you organised.' She pulled out a large bag with cosmetics, a hairdryer, curler and hair spray, and a pair of stockings. 'I stopped by your house earlier to pick up a pair of shoes for you but the back door was locked.'

'Ethan.' CJ shrugged and shook her head. 'He's a stickler for locking the doors.'

'I figured as much. You get changed and I'll pop over and get a pair now. He should be home but give me your keys in case he's still at the clinic.'

When she'd gone, CJ slipped out of her pyjamas and pulled on the dress. The straps were two inches wide in a zig-zag pattern with a row of diamantés in the middle. The neckline also had a zig-zag pattern that came across the top of the bust, glittering diamantés again highlighting the unusual cut. It came to mid-thigh and showed off her legs to perfection.

Thankfully, Donna had bought the next size up from

what CJ usually wore so when she zipped it up, it didn't pull across her bust. She'd already expressed milk after the last feed just in case Elizabeth should wake up hungry while she was gone.

She looked down at her sleeping daughter. 'Oh, baby. You are so beautiful. Sleep well while I'm gone. I'll be back. I promise. I will *never* leave you and I will *love* you for ever.'

Donna rushed back into the room, stopping still as she gazed at CJ. She shook her head. 'Even without the hair and make-up, you look incredible. He isn't going to know what hit him!'

They set to work, piling CJ's hair on top of her head and curling the ends slightly, leaving a few loose tendrils coming down. 'I have another surprise,' Donna announced after she'd finished CJ's make-up. She pulled out a jeweller's box. 'I wore these on my wedding day and they've never been worn since.' Donna handed it to CJ, who opened it slowly. A row of diamonds winked back at her. The necklace was a classically simple strand with matching bracelet and a pair of studded earrings.

'Oh! I can't.'

'You owe it to the jewels. They deserve to be seen and they match the dress perfectly. Now, no more fuss. Turn around so I can fasten these in place.'

CJ did what Donna told her to do, as her hair and make-up were completed. When she stood and looked in the half-mirror of the hospital bathroom, she barely recognised herself.

'You really do look like a princess,' Donna stated. 'Please, have a great time.'

'I feel so spoilt.'

'You deserve it. You've given so much to this town, it's time we all gave something back.'

CJ smoothed a hand down the dress and smiled brightly

at her reflection. Tonight, she decided, was a night of hope and she determined to enjoy *everything* it offered.

Ethan drove his car to the hospital, furious with himself for being late.

He'd called Bonnie to let her know the clinic had run late and to pass on a message to CJ. It was almost seven-thirty! He parked the car, cut the engine and rushed into the hospital. When he arrived at CJ's room, it was to find her dressed in a robe, sitting up in bed, feeding Elizabeth. He stopped and stared, their gazes meeting.

Her hair was on top of her head in a pile of curls, her face had make-up on it and diamonds seem to twinkle around her neck and ears. She looked…sexy! Wholesome, and irresistibly sexy. He swallowed over the dryness of his throat.

'Sorry. She woke up and was hungry, so I thought it would be best to feed her before we go. Will this affect your plans for this evening?'

He gulped as he took a few steps into the room, then stopped. The urge to crush her to him and plunder her mouth was almost too great for him to control. He swallowed again.

'No. I've called the restaurant to let them know but they understand how it is and will hold the table for as long as we need.'

'Good. She's almost finished.'

The room was plunged into silence again and CJ began to feel a little uncomfortable. Why didn't he come into the room? Sit down? Say something? She glanced up at him, only to find him intently watching them. When Elizabeth had finished her feed, CJ closed her robe and handed him the baby.

'Here's a towel. Would you mind burping her while I go and get changed?'

'Sure.' He walked to the bed and sat on the end, glad CJ was leaving the room for a moment. Hopefully, he'd be able to get himself under control again. 'You're worse than your mother,' he muttered to Elizabeth as he rubbed her back soothingly. 'Irresistible and highly kissable.' He pressed his lips to her head. Once she'd finished, he wrapped her up and tucked her into the cot. Then he concentrated on taking some deep, calming breaths. He was determined to be in control of his faculties when Elizabeth's mother returned.

'Ready?'

Ethan spun around and simply stared at the woman who stood in the doorway. Where had *she* come from? CJ felt as if he'd never seen her before. Dressed in the most stunning of black dresses, with diamonds everywhere and long, luscious legs. His jaw dropped open and he felt paralysed with desire.

'Claudia-Jean…you are *stunning*,' he breathed, and, finally able to move his legs, he walked to her side. 'Ready?' He crooked his arm for her to take.

'Thank you.' She smiled up at him and he almost capitulated. The urge to sweep her into his arms and carry her back to their house was increasing at an alarming rate.

'Ready to go?' It was Bonnie who broke the spell as she walked down the corridor towards them.

CJ cleared her throat and looked away first. 'Yes. She's fed, burped, clean nappy and sleeping like a baby.' Bonnie wheeled the cot down to the nurses' station as the two of them walked behind. CJ blew her girl a kiss. 'Sleep sweet, princess.'

Ethan led her out to the car and for once she was glad he'd put up the soft top. 'Are you going to be warm enough?'

'Yes. From the hospital to the car, to the restaurant, to the car, to the hospital. I should be fine.' He walked her around to the passenger side and held the door for her. 'Thank you.'

'Where are we going?' she asked as they drove along, the scent of his aftershave winding itself around her.

'Chateau Cregg.'

'Oh, they have a lovely restaurant there, or so I've heard.'

'Never been?'

'No.'

He smiled. 'I'm delighted tonight is the first time.'

They were met at the door by the maître d' then shown to their table. She smiled across the table at him, determined to enjoy every moment they had together. They talked on a variety of topics while they ate. Ethan told her a few stories from his childhood and the silly things he, his brother and sister had done. She was able to counter a few of them with crazy tales about herself and her sister. After dessert, they made their way back to the car.

'It's been a lovely evening.' CJ sighed wistfully as Ethan pulled away from the restaurant. 'Thank you, Ethan. You can't know how much a night out like this means to me. In fact, I can't recall ever having been out on a night like tonight.'

'I'm really glad to hear that. I had a good time, too.'

'How long is it since *you've* been out on night like this?'

Ethan slowly shook his head. 'Far too long to even remember.'

He changed gear and indicated to turn. 'If I hadn't had a mild heart attack, I would never have come here. I would never have met the people of these districts, seen the way they all seem to look after each other.' He glanced across at her for a quick moment. 'I never would have met you and I never would have been privileged to experience Elizabeth's birth. To see her so…complete.' He nodded. 'It's how it should be.'

'Yes. She is rather awesome.' It was then that CJ looked out the car window and realised they weren't headed back to the hospital. 'Where are we going?'

'To the lookout.'

'Oh?'

'Donna mentioned it today and as I haven't managed to get here yet, and as it's sort of on the way back to the hospital, I thought you wouldn't mind stopping and taking in the sight with me.'

'No, I don't mind. It really is beautiful, especially on a clear night like tonight.'

'And we have an almost full moon.'

CJ grinned. 'So we do. A full moon. A clear night. If I was working in a city hospital emergency department, I'd be worried.' They both chuckled at her words. 'Out here, the same night holds a different purpose.'

'And what purpose is that?'

'That anything can happen.'

Ethan nodded, then drove up a small hill and parked in the car park before coming around to her side to help her out.

'I'm not pregnant any more, Ethan. I can get out of the car by myself.'

'I know…but a gentleman always escorts his date.'

'Is that what I am tonight? Your date?'

'Absolutely, m'lady.'

CJ giggled as he led her over the low stone wall that ringed the car park. 'I think the last time I went on an actual date was…probably high school.'

'Well, tonight you're with me and that's all I care about.'

'Is it?'

He looked down into her face. 'Right now, yes.' He brushed his fingertips across her cheek. 'You really do look extraordinarily beautiful tonight, Claudia-Jean.'

'Thank you.' She dipped her head slightly, hoping he

wouldn't see how much his words had pleased her. 'You don't scrub up too badly yourself.'

'You've seen me in a suit lots of times.'

'Yes, but tonight you're looking… I don't know…different. Handsome different.'

Ethan quirked an eyebrow. 'I don't look handsome at other times?'

She laughed. 'That's not what I meant and you know it. There's something…different about you tonight. I think it might be more in your eyes, rather than what you're wearing.'

His gaze was intense. 'I don't want to hurt you,' he said softly, and CJ's heart was pierced by his tenderness. Again, he brushed her cheek with his hand before cupping her face and drawing it closer to his own. When his lips met hers, CJ sighed into the kiss.

His mouth was soft, gentle, as though she'd break if he exerted any more force. He made her feel precious, treasured and…loved. Was she insane to hope that one day Ethan would come to care for her as deeply as she cared for him?

After a moment, he gently pulled away and gazed at her before gathering her closer in his arms. When he felt the coolness of her skin he pulled back, took his jacket off and draped it over her shoulders. 'Not that I want to cover up your exquisite dress but neither do I want you to get sick. Bonnie, not to mention Donna, would have my hide.'

CJ nodded but was unable to speak. The emotions he evoked in her were so overpowering, so overwhelming she wasn't quite sure how to cope with them. Instead, she took delight in being drawn into his embrace, of resting her head against his chest and savouring the scent of him. She closed her eyes, memorising everything she could, filing it away to take out one day in the future when her life might not be so perfect as it was at this moment.

'The stars in Sydney don't shine as brightly as here.'

'Yet they're the same stars,' she murmured, opening her eyes and shifting away a little. She couldn't look at him. She didn't want to think about Sydney, or the fact that he had a life there—a life without her.

He must have sensed a change in her mood because he whispered, 'I don't want to hurt you, CJ.'

'So you've said.' She pulled back and stepped from his embrace, tugging the edges of his jacket around her. She turned her back to him and tilted her head back to look at the stars. Ethan left her for a moment, desperate to get his own thoughts and emotions under control. Where he never thought he'd come to care so deeply for another woman, here he was, desperate to throw everything away just to stay with her and Elizabeth. He *wanted* to be in their lives, he *wanted* to do whatever it took to ensure both of them remained happy and healthy for the rest of their days. Even the realisation of the thoughts he'd been doing his best to hold at bay was enough to scare him.

He had a life in Sydney, a career. Was that enough for him now? He didn't know. All he was certain of was that Claudia-Jean Nicholls had become incredibly special to him in a matter of weeks! It was impossible, yet here he was, experiencing these emotions.

His only rationalisation was that because he'd shut his heart away for so long, because he'd denied himself the ability to truly interact with other people, the first time he'd stepped back into the light he'd fallen hard for a woman who was so different from every other woman he'd ever known. She'd been open and honest with him, listening to him, sharing her life with him. Not only was she exquisitely stunning, she was generous and kind.

'CJ.' At her name, she turned and glanced at him. He closed the distance between them and placed his hands on her shoulders, both of them staring at the stars for a moment before she slowly turned in his arms to look up at him. She was so brave. She'd overcome so much in her life and was still willing to face the future head on, regardless of what it held. He lowered his mouth to hers, intent on showing her that he cared.

He kept the kisses soft, caressing her mouth with his, wanting to convey just how much he cherished her. When she responded to him, giving herself to him, something deep inside seemed to surge to the surface and he wrapped his arms around her, needing her as close as possible. He wanted this woman. The desire was so powerful, so strong he had no idea how to control it, which was definitely a first for him. He seemed to be experiencing a lot of 'firsts' with CJ and the sensations were knocking him off balance far more than he liked. Still, there was nothing he could do about it—especially when he was holding her so close.

Her scent had wrapped itself around him, in much the same way as his arms were wrapped around her. How could this feel so right when, for a multitude of logical reasons, it was so wrong? They were locked together in an electrifying embrace, one so hot he was sure they'd sizzle and steam if the heavens opened up and poured rain on them.

Still, she matched the intensity of his kisses, as though she was desperate to show him she wanted this as much as he did. Never in her life had she felt this way. Her appetite for him appeared to be voracious and uncontrollable. How in the world was she supposed to let this man go? She knew it was inevitable, she knew the day would come when he would walk away from her. She wouldn't think about that now, not when his mouth was hot on hers, not when her heart was pounding with unbelievable joy. She needed to enjoy this moment in time. This was what she'd craved almost since the first moment she'd laid eyes on him.

He shifted slightly and brought first one arm, then the

other beneath the jacket on her shoulders, ensuring it didn't fall off with the movement. He groaned as he slowly slid his hands around her waist, his thumbs gently caressing the underside of her breasts before continuing around to draw little circles at the base of her spine. Now there was only one barrier separating him from the touch of her skin and for the moment he could live with that.

He broke free, just for a second, both of them breathing heavily, their hearts beating in a wild and unsteady rhythm. He pressed small butterfly kisses to her cheek, down to her ear, where he nibbled for a brief moment before continuing down to her neck.

She arched back slightly, giving him access to what he'd been coveting for weeks. Even the necklace she wore didn't deter him, even though he wished it were gone. She laced her fingers into his hair, revelling in the fact that she was finally allowed to touch him in this familiar way, to feel the soft strands of his dark, brown locks smooth against her fingertips. His head dipped lower still, the kisses warm against the cool air that circulated around them, as he made his way to the top of her chest.

Up and down, along the zig-zag of her dress, he tenderly placed his lips, his hands now spanning her midriff, his thumbs repeating the action they'd performed earlier. She gasped as her body responded, heat burning right through her—and then she felt it. That strange, new sensation that happened to breastfeeding mothers.

'Whoa!' She quickly took two steps away, severing the embrace. 'Stop.'

'What?' He looked at her with dazed confusion. 'Are you all right? I didn't hurt you?' He took a step closer and reached out a hand to her. CJ melted at his concern and smiled, putting her hand in his.

'I'm fine. Really, I'm fine.' She sucked in air, trying to steady her heart rate, but she was feeling the cold without his body there to shield her. 'It's just that…' She took a steadying breath. 'I'm…' Oh, this was so embarrassing. 'I'm…leaking.'

She watched as his eyes flicked to her breasts in alarm before meeting her gaze once more. A smile started to twitch at the corner of his lips as he squeezed her hand.

'Yes. Um…sorry.'

She watched him carefully, unsure *what* he was apologising for. 'Don't apologise. I guess I'm just not used to… well…everything.'

'I think we both got a little carried away.' He raked his free hand through his hair where her own fingers had been only moments ago.

CJ laughed. 'This is certainly a memorable end to the evening.'

'Yes.' When he saw her shiver, he escorted her to the car. 'Pumpkin time.'

'Yes,' she agreed, glad of the car's instant warmth from the wind. He walked around to the driver's side and climbed in. He started the engine, switching on the heater, but didn't make any move to drive.

'It really is beautiful up here.'

'It's one of my favourite spots.'

'I can see why. The whole area, what I've seen of it, is charming.'

'But…?'

'But it's not my home.'

'I know.'

'I don't want you to think I'm taking advantage of you because that's not my intention.'

'I know that, too. The attraction between us is real and sometimes…' she shrugged '…uncontrollable.'

'You can say that again,' he mumbled, and shook his head. 'I guess what I'm trying, very inarticulately, to say is that I don't want to hurt you…but I know I am.'

'Yes,' she stated. 'And I'm hurting you.'

'It can't work.'

'I know. You have your life. I have mine.' A small smile touched her lips. 'I have Elizabeth to consider now. She must come first in all my decisions. Not only that but I have my home, my work and my friends. In time, the way you make me feel will fade and I'll be fine. And you'll be fine. This...' she indicated the wonderful scenery before them '...was just a pleasant interlude.'

Ethan opened his mouth to say something, then thought better of it. Instead, he buckled up his seat belt, waiting until she followed suit, then started the engine. He manoeuvred the car out the exit and down the hill to the town below. Both were silent on the five-minute drive and thankfully, not a minute too soon, soon they were pulling up outside the hospital.

CJ opened her door and climbed out before he could come around to help her. She needed to do things for herself, to be completely independent. She was a mother now. She needed to be strong, determined and focused. When he stood before her, she smiled. 'Thank you again for such an amazing evening. It's one I'll never forget.'

'Nor I.' Then Ethan leaned forward and brushed his lips across hers for one final kiss. They stared at each other for a long moment, their hearts and minds so full with words neither of them would say. CJ broke eye contact first, swallowing over the lump in her throat.

'I'd better go check on Elizabeth.'

He nodded. 'Of course.'

Forcing her legs to move, she turned and walked into the hospital, determined not to look back. The pain she felt in her chest, which coursed throughout her entire body, was evidence that her heart was breaking and now there was no reason to hold back the tears.

CHAPTER TWELVE

'HI.' CJ OPENED the door to let Donna in. 'We were going to come across to the clinic later today for the check-up. I even rang to make an appointment with Tania and she told me I was being ridiculous.'

Donna laughed as she came in and sat down at CJ's kitchen table. 'She told me. You should know by now that you don't need to make an appointment in your own practice.'

'Well, I thought I should do things by the book. You know, no preferential treatment.'

Donna laughed again. 'You really haven't been getting much sleep, have you? That's the only reason I can come up with as to why your brain's gone soft. Preferential treatment, indeed. Who else *should* get it?'

CJ gazed down at Elizabeth, sleeping peacefully in the bassinet. 'I'm actually getting more sleep now than I was before I had her.'

'Good.'

'Have you got time for a cuppa?'

'That would be lovely.'

'Busy clinic?'

Donna nodded. 'Ethan's doing the afternoon clinic and I'll do the house calls. I came across not only to check on how you were both doing but to ask if you'd like to come along.'

CJ found it hard to curb her disappointment. 'Of course,' she said softly, and forced a smile. 'We'd love to come.' She turned away and concentrated on filling the kettle and switching it on. Why did she feel like crying?

'Things still aren't going well between you and Ethan?'

CJ looked at her friend. 'No, but, then, it's no more than I expected.'

'Expected? What do you mean? I thought the night he took you out to dinner was a positive step forward. Now it seems as though you're avoiding each other again.'

'Not so much avoiding but…' She shrugged. 'Well, yes, I guess you could say avoiding.'

'What about Elizabeth?'

CJ smiled and looked at her daughter. 'He'd never ignore her. She wouldn't let him. He's happy to hold her, look after her, especially if I need to have a shower or if I'm on the phone with a patient. The other night I was sitting in the lounge, feeding her, and he came in and sat with us.'

'That's promising.'

CJ shook her head. 'He asked polite, medical questions about how she was doing, feeding and that sort of thing. When she was finished he offered to burp her and when she dozed off he checked her over—even got his stethoscope and listened to her heart—and then, when he was satisfied, he left.'

Donna's lips formed another circle. 'Oh.' The kettle boiled and switched itself off but neither of them moved. 'So what's next?'

She shrugged. 'I'm just taking things one day at a time.'

'He's here for another five months, CJ.'

'I know and I've been thinking about that. I mean, we could talk to him and see if he wants to alter his contract. He doesn't have to stay the full six months we initially agreed on.'

'You're not ready to come back to work. I won't allow it.'

'Not full time but definitely part time or even three-quarter time.'

'Three-quarter time? Will you listen to yourself? Your daughter is only two weeks old.'

'Yes, and she's a good baby. She sleeps well, she feeds well and she's no trouble at all.'

'What about breastfeeding, if you come back to work too early?'

'I've thought of that. Why couldn't I bring Elizabeth in to work with me? She can sleep in the reception area with Tania and when she needs feeding, I can sit down and feed her. Trust me,' she went on quickly, noticing the look of scepticism on Donna's face, 'the patients won't mind waiting if Elizabeth needs feeding. They all adore her and that way everyone can see her when they come to the clinic.'

'What if she needs changing? Or she's sick? Tania can't look after her. Besides, it's a medical clinic, CJ, not a childcare centre.'

'All right. How about I find someone to look after her here at home? A nanny. I'm only working across the road so I can pop home whenever I'm needed, for feeding and stuff like that.'

Donna shook her head and said softly, 'Is it really *that bad* with Ethan around? This time you have now with Elizabeth won't come again. She'll never be this little again, CJ, and I don't want you to miss it because it does go quickly. My kids are at university, living their own lives and occasionally calling their mother, yet it seems like only yesterday I was changing their nappies!'

CJ slumped forward onto the table in defeat. 'I have to find my life—my life without Ethan—and the only way I can see that happening is if he leaves. I know he's as uncomfortable with things as I am and, to be honest, I can't take any more of his extreme politeness.' She lifted her head. 'If he stays for the next five months, I'll definitely be in love with the man and then...when he goes I'll be in even worse shape than now.'

Donna watched her for a moment before getting up and switching the kettle on again. 'OK. We'll have a cuppa, talk through all possibilities and come up with a workable plan—one Ethan needs to agree to as well.'

CJ sighed with relief. 'Good. Let's do this. Let's move forward.'

The next night, when Ethan came home from the clinic, he found CJ nursing Elizabeth in the lounge room.

'Hi.'

She looked up from the child and smiled sleepily at him. 'Hi, yourself. How was clinic?'

Ethan clenched his hands into fists to stop himself from walking to her side and pressing a firm kiss to her lips. Didn't she have any idea just how wonderful she looked, all sleepy and tousled and dressed in her old robe with fluffy slippers? It was definitely not chic but it was comfortable and homey and...very CJ.

'Clinic was long,' he answered, then came further into the room and sat in the chair opposite her. There was quite a bit of distance between them, for which he was grateful. 'Uh...there's something I need to talk to you about.'

'Really? Because there's something I need to talk to you about.'

'Oh. OK. Do you want me to go first?' He'd been going over things in his head for most of the afternoon.

'Sure.'

'Well...uh...' He sighed. 'I don't think I should live here any more. I think I'll get a place somewhere else for the duration of my contract.'

'Oh.' CJ frowned and looked down at Elizabeth, who had fallen asleep, her tummy clearly full. She rearranged her clothing and shifted Elizabeth onto her shoulder so she could rub the little girl's back to help release any wind.

'I mean, it was great I was here when you went into labour so I could help, and also for these first few weeks. I've enjoyed being able to look after Elizabeth when you needed me to, like when you have a shower, but...' He stopped and bowed his head, trying to gather his thoughts into a logical order. 'Basically, I'm too attracted to you to stay here.'

'Wow. That's...very honest.'

'You've taught me it's the best way.'

'I have? Well, then...uh... I was going to ask you if you actually wanted to change your contract so that you finish sooner rather than later. That way, you don't have to worry about looking around for accommodation, you're not trapped here and you can return to Sydney and do whatever it is that you want to do there.' She shrugged one shoulder. 'I'm sure there are several research projects that require your expertise, or even new projects you'd like to get off the ground. You did mention when we went out to dinner that you had several prospects you were thinking about.'

'If I finish my contract early, who will cover your patients?'

'I will.'

'What about Elizabeth?'

'I'm going to hire a nanny. I've already spoken to Molly. As she's only going back to work part time, now that her stomach ulcer is clearing up nicely, she's more than happy to come and look after Elizabeth here for a few days a week. I'll just be across the road so I can come home for feeds. We'll cut my clinic down from five days to two and a half. Donna will pick up any urgent patients and I'll do the house calls where, for the most part, I can take Elizabeth with me.'

He listened intently to what she was saying, feeling obsolete and unwanted. 'You have been busy.'

CJ realised Elizabeth was sound asleep and stood to put the baby in her nearby crib. One of her patients had made it for her and had even put wheels on the base so she could easily wheel it from room to room.

'Do you want me leave?' Ethan asked. 'Really want me to go?'

'Do you want to go?' She shook her head. 'I don't want you to feel as though you're stuck here. You've pointed out before that Pridham isn't your home, that being here is just a temporary interlude for you.' And she couldn't be the romantic lead in that interlude. It didn't work that way. 'You've told me you miss surgery.'

'Even if I return to Sydney, I won't be allowed to practise at the hospital. I'm on an enforced sabbatical, remember.'

'Oh, yeah.' She frowned. 'The last thing we need is for your stress level to go through the roof again.'

'Then me moving out of your home is the most obvious solution to our present dilemma.' He stood and looked down at the sleeping babe, knowing he would miss her a lot. It was quite incredible the way that holding the baby in his arms had not only helped to keep his stress level under control but had also helped him become reconciled with the loss of his own child. Seeing Elizabeth laugh and cry and pull all sorts of other funny faces had helped him to imagine what Ellie *might* have been like if she'd had the chance. But where Elizabeth de-stressed him, being so near to, so close to her mother had a completely different effect.

'Is being near Elizabeth too difficult for you?' CJ asked.

'No. Not Elizabeth.'

'Ah. Being near *me* is difficult.'

'Well, of course it is, CJ.' He raked a hand through his hair in total frustration. 'I can't be in the same room as you without wanting to drag you into my arms. I want to talk to you, spend time with you, see more of the countryside with you. Then reality sets in and I realise this isn't where I belong. I have work, CJ, important work back in Sydney.'

'That's your existence, Ethan. Where's your real life? The happiness?'

He turned and looked out the window into the dark night. He was silent for so long she didn't think he was going to answer. She was just about to leave when he said softly, 'I don't know.'

The emotions she felt for him rose up and overflowed. Slowly, she walked towards him and wrapped her arms around his waist. He tensed but when she didn't move, he shifted slightly so they were facing each other. They held each other, both content just to be. Ethan had never felt comfort like this before, never felt so calm and peaceful.

How long they stood there neither of them were sure but in the end CJ's yawn broke the moment.

'I'll think about whether I want to break the contract,' he stated softly. 'I'm just not sure.'

'OK. If you want to move out, I completely understand. You were never really comfortable here in the first place.'

'I like it here.' He looked down into her face, gazing at her lips. 'I like it too much. That's now the problem.'

'I know.' She waited for a moment, watching him intently. 'It's crazy, isn't it…this thing between us?'

'Yes.' Ethan pulled superhuman strength from somewhere and gently released her from his arms. 'It's so… real. So powerful and intense.'

'Yes—but we can't, Ethan. *I* can't.'

He shook his head. 'Wait—why can't we, CJ? Tell me why?'

'Why? Because soon you'll be gone, Ethan. At the end of your time here, you'll head back to Sydney to your work. I'm not in that picture, and although I'd love nothing better than to be with you, it wouldn't work out—for many reasons.'

'This isn't just about me leaving, CJ. I know it's going to be hard for you to trust someone after Quinten and that's quite normal but I had hoped…that somehow I'd be able to show you not all men are lying cheats.'

'I understand that, Ethan, but—'

'Have I shown you that? Do you think that you could trust me?'

Ethan stood at the door to the lounge room, facing her—like a showdown at high noon. CJ didn't need this kind of questioning, didn't want to be put on the spot, and she certainly wasn't sure she could give him a direct answer. She glanced down at the floor before slowly returning to meet his gaze.

'Yes,' she said softly. 'Yes I think…in time… I could trust you, Ethan, and that fact alone scares me to death.' She bit her lip as it quivered, her eyes as wide as saucers—wearing her heart on her sleeve. 'I could trust you, I *do* trust you—to a certain extent, and even that has surprised me. I trust you one hundred percent in a professional capacity, I trust you with Elizabeth…' She smiled as she said her daughter's name. 'You're so good with her, so natural.'

'And do you trust me with *you*?'

The smile slipped away and CJ felt the tears threatening behind her eyes, felt her throat constrict as she desperately tried to swallow. 'I don't know if I'm strong enough to do that,' she whispered—a tear escaping and sliding slowly down her cheek. 'If I take the risk, if I give you my heart then I… I…' She shook her head, unable to continue.

'It's all right.' He wanted to go to her. He wanted it so badly and he could tell she wanted him to hold her but both of them stood their ground. 'It was a foolish question to have asked in the first place. Goodnight. I'll let you get some sleep while Elizabeth's sleeping.'

Ethan turned and stalked to the bathroom, stripping off his clothes. He turned on the taps and stepped beneath the spray, willing the water to soothe his aching muscles. At least he could do something about the physical aches he was feeling.

Why had it cut him straight to the heart when she'd been unable to answer that question? She was right! He was leaving in five months' time to return to his life in Sydney and the uncontrollable chemistry that existed between them would wither and die when he left.

He scrubbed shampoo into his hair and rinsed it. Things between the two of them had gone too far, too fast and now they were both thoroughly confused. He wrenched off the taps and towelled himself dry.

Once he was dressed, he swallowed some paracetamol and settled down to work. Even though it was close to three o'clock in the morning, there was no way he'd be able to sleep now.

It was a few hours later that Ethan heard Elizabeth's cries come through the house. The little girl certainly had a good set of lungs. A moment later she was quiet and he knew CJ would be feeding her.

It brought back visions of CJ holding the baby tenderly in her arms, her manner natural and relaxed as Elizabeth fed greedily at first and then slowed down to a more sedate pace as her little tummy was filled. It was a sight that had touched him very deeply inside, in a secret place of longing he hadn't known existed.

The fact that he was in love with Elizabeth was of little doubt. 'And what about her mother?' he whispered into the dark.

The next day, CJ headed to the clinic to pick up her medical bag and the list of patients from Tania. Ethan came out to the waiting room while she was there.

'What are you doing here?' He looked around her. 'Where's Elizabeth?'

'At home with Molly. She's going to look after Lizzie while I do a few house calls.' CJ smiled politely at Ethan, picked up the medical bag and headed out the door, leaving him to watch her walk away. This has to be done, she kept reminding herself. She couldn't rely on him, not for anything. Although they'd talked, no firm decisions had been made and CJ needed to move forward, albeit slowly.

As she drove herself around the countryside, her anxiety at whether she was making the right choices started to wane. The scenery really was beautiful out here and after she'd seen three of her patients, she headed to Margaret's house to see how she was progressing.

CJ climbed the stairs and rang the doorbell. No answer. 'Margaret?' she called. 'It's CJ.' She rang the doorbell a few more times then headed around the large house to the back gate. Margaret's car was there but Doug's wasn't. At the back gate CJ was met by a large, barking dog but when she stepped through, the dog sniffing her and clearly recognising her, it started running off, almost stopping and waiting for her to follow. CJ's senses started tingling as apprehension washed over her. She headed around to the large glass back door, which, when she tried to slide the door open, she was pleased to find unlocked. The dog bounded inside and into the front lounge room. As CJ followed, she saw Margaret lying on the floor. Putting her bag down, she rushed to Margaret's side and pulled her phone from her pocket at the same time.

'Ambulance,' she stated as soon as the call was answered. She checked Margaret's pulse. It was there. 'Margaret! Margaret!' she called, but received no answer. CJ finished speaking to the ambulance service then called the clinic, alerting Ethan to the situation.

'I'll notify the hospital. How much has she had to drink?'

'I have no idea.'

'We'll need to do a blood alcohol test so we know what we're dealing with.'

'Can you organise the police?'

'Yes.'

'I'll call you from the ambulance,' she said. 'Can you have Tania notify Doug, please?'

'What about Margaret's parents?' Ethan asked.

'Let's just find Doug first.' When CJ ended the call, she continued to monitor Margaret's situation, her heart filled with concern not only for the woman but for the unborn child. As CJ did an assessment on Margaret's condition, constantly calling to the woman, trying to rouse her, she realised Margaret's jeans were wet…very wet. Her waters had broken.

By the time the ambulance arrived, CJ had managed to rouse Margaret once or twice, as well as find far too many empty wine bottles nearby. When the ambulance pulled up at the hospital, Ethan opened the back doors.

'Doug's on his way in,' he confirmed, as they wheeled Margaret through to the treatment room and transferred her to the hospital bed. Ethan was giving orders left and right.

'I want a blood test taken. Test for blood alcohol level and liver damage. Urine test as well to check for protein. How's her BP?' Bonnie and several of the nurses were carrying out the requests. Ethan strapped a foetal heart monitor to Margaret's abdomen in order to monitor the baby more closely.

Bonnie finished taking Margaret's blood pressure. 'Two hundred over one-ten.'

'Pregnancy-induced hypertension?' CJ checked and Ethan nodded. Margaret's blood pressure was high because she was in labour. She turned to Bonnie. 'Call Charlie and have him come in to assess her. I don't know if he can give her an epidural until we know her blood alcohol level so get a rush on that. Ethan, status on the baby?'

'Heart rate is still low but holding steady for the moment.'

'Good.'

The police arrived soon after and took statements from CJ, as well as doing their own blood alcohol test.

'Has she had any contractions?' Ethan asked.

'Not that I know of,' CJ answered.

'The alcohol might be acting as an anaesthetic so she may not be feeling them,' Ethan added. 'We're going to need to monitor that closely as well.'

CJ nodded and walked to the nurses' station, unable to believe how bad things had gone for Margaret. She closed her eyes for a moment and sighed, wondering if there couldn't have been more done for Margaret and the baby, but apart from forcing her to be hospitalised CJ wasn't sure Margaret had wanted their help.

'Are you OK?' Ethan's soft voice washed over her and she shook her head.

'GPs need to be better informed,' she said softly. 'We need to know what to look for, we need more seminars on these sorts of things—especially for those of us in rural or country areas. We're the first point of contact and we're the ones who usually look after the patients on a day-to-day basis.' She opened her eyes and turned to face him. 'We need to be better informed.'

Ethan listened to what she had to say. She was right. There was a lot of information in hospitals and city centres but they needed to broaden their horizons. 'You've raised a good point, CJ.' He'd been looking for a new research project and although it wasn't strictly his speciality, he knew several colleagues who could help him out. 'I'll see what I can do. In the meantime, don't go beating yourself up over Margaret.'

'Easier said than done. I've known her for years and although we've never been close friends, she was still a patient of mine and I'll always feel like I failed her.'

Ethan wanted to go to her, to stop her pain, to stop her hurting, but he knew he couldn't. To touch CJ, even in a gesture of comfort, wouldn't get them anywhere. He'd hold her and he'd want to keep her there. He'd want to kiss her, to let her know that he was there and that he really did care.

'I feel your frustration.'

She nodded as she remembered that this couldn't be at all easy for him either, given what had happened with his wife. 'I know you do.' Her smile encompassed him and immediately his heart, which had started to feel tight and constricted again, began to relax. What was it about her that enabled him to let go of his stress so easily?

'How's Elizabeth?'

'When I last checked with Molly, she was sleeping soundly.'

'Good.' He jerked his thumb over his shoulder. 'I'm going to go check on Margaret again. I think we need to get her transferred to the labour room.'

'OK. I'll wait here for Doug and bring him through. He shouldn't be too much longer.' Ethan nodded at her words, then headed off to oversee Margaret's transfer.

Three hours later, Margaret's blood alcohol level was reasonable enough for Charlie to attempt an epidural. She had started to feel the contractions, which was a good sign, but Ethan wasn't happy with the baby's present situation.

'Deceleration on the CTG. The baby's going into distress.' They shared a look and with a nod CJ turned to Charlie.

'Give me an epidural block, stat.'

The anaesthetist nodded and set to work.

'Bonnie,' CJ said, 'prep her for an emergency C-section and get the theatre ready.'

'What? What's going on?' Doug asked.

'The baby's not coping,' CJ explained.

'Not coping with what?'

'With everything. First of all, Margaret's blood alcohol level when she came in was point one five. That's three times the state limit for driving.'

'But she's been drinking wine all her life. She can handle it.'

'*She* might be able to but the baby can't. Alcohol in the mother's blood crosses over to the baby through the placenta so the baby has the same blood alcohol level as Margaret. We've been over this several times with you, Doug!' CJ was feeling incredibly frustrated.

'What…what needs to happen now?'

'The baby is in distress, Doug. We need to get the baby out as soon as possible and Margaret's blood pressure keeps climbing. Both are in danger of losing their lives if we don't act immediately.'

He paled at her words. While she'd been talking, they'd been getting Margaret ready to move to the theatre. Once everything was ready, they wheeled her bed down, the machines and monitors she was hooked up to coming along beside the bed.

Soon Margaret was settled on the operating table with a screen erected around her shoulders to shield her from the operation. Ethan talked over the procedure with CJ while they scrubbed.

'Are you happy to take the lead?' she asked him.

'It's been a while since I've done a C-section but I did read up on it a few weeks ago to refresh my memory, just in case this eventuality presented itself.'

She nodded. 'And I've been reading up on what to do with the baby, just in case.'

'So have I.'

'Good. Then between the two of us we should be fine.'

Once Charlie had given Margaret the block, CJ and Ethan stepped up to the table. It wasn't long after making the incision that they were able to get the baby out.

'Congratulations,' CJ said, holding the baby up so Margaret and Doug could see.

'A boy!' Doug whooped. Margaret merely closed her eyes as though in pain. 'We're going to call him Joshua. Joshua Douglas,' Doug continued, a bright smile beaming across his face.

'That's a lovely name,' CJ replied.

Ethan was standing beside her, waiting with a warmed, sterile nappy in which to wrap the premature baby. CJ placed the little boy into Ethan's waiting hands. 'Forceps,' she said, and clamped the cord off with two sets of forceps, cutting the cord in between.

Ethan took the baby to the neonate section trolley, Bonnie working beside him. CJ delivered the placenta before starting to suture. 'How's it going?' she asked.

Ethan was rubbing the baby with one hand, stimulating blood flow. 'Heart rate is low, breathing isn't too good. Bonnie, suction.'

Bonnie did as he asked while he checked the baby's reflexes and colour. 'Still quite blue. Come on, little man, come on,' he urged. He shook his head. 'We'll need to intubate. Facial features are indicative of FAS. Flat mid-face, low nasal bridge, indistinct philtrum and thin upper lip.'

'One minute,' Bonnie said.

'Apgar score is five,' Ethan remarked.

'What…what's going on?' Doug asked.

'The baby's not responding too well,' CJ said quietly. 'How are you doing, Margaret?'

There was no reply. CJ looked over the screen at her patient and saw tears running down the woman's cheeks.

'Blood pressure has stabilised,' Charlie reported, and CJ nodded.

'Colour is mildly improving,' Ethan called. 'Still clinical evidence of neurological dysfunction.'

'What does that mean?' Doug asked, looking worried.

'His reflexes aren't responding well,' CJ interpreted as he sutured Margaret's wound closed. Everyone was waiting.

'Five minutes,' Bonnie said.

'Apgar score is four,' CJ reported.

'What is this Ap thing?' Doug asked frantically.

'It's a score we use to assess the state of well-being in newborn babies.' CJ said.

'What's it out of?'

'Ten.'

'So...so four isn't good?'

'No.' Now was not the time to lie to them, to tell them everything would be all right—because it probably wouldn't. CJ's heart turned over with sympathy and pain for the new parents and she couldn't help her eyes misting with tears. She blinked them away and concentrated on her work.

'Arrange transfer for both Margaret and Joshua to Royal Sydney Children's Hospital,' Ethan said. He continued to monitor the baby and Margaret continued not to say anything. CJ could almost *feel* the guilt radiating from her patient and wished there was something she could do to help.

When it was time to transfer them, Ethan insisted on going with them.

'I can call in favours, get them the best care,' he told her.

CJ nodded. 'Keep me informed,' she said, watching him climb into the Royal Flying Doctor Service plane.

'I will,' he said, then disappeared from her view. She had no idea when he'd be able to return to Pridham, or even if he would. Once he was back in Sydney, perhaps he'd stay for a while. She didn't know. They hadn't had time to talk, to discuss things because she'd been busy trying to be independent and solve all her problems by herself.

If she'd just talked to him, been open and honest as she'd always prided herself on being, then perhaps she wouldn't be faced with so many questions. She headed home to Elizabeth, the house uncommonly quiet once Molly had left. CJ sat in the chair as she nursed her child, tears falling silently down her cheeks as she finally admitted the truth of the situation to herself.

She was in love with Ethan. Hopelessly, one hundred percent in love with him. And now he was gone.

CHAPTER THIRTEEN

THAT EVENING, by the time he'd handed over Margaret and baby Joshua's care to his colleagues, some of whom having been there during his own darkest hours, Ethan decided it was better for him to stay the night in Sydney. He took a taxi to St Aloysius Hospital and called CJ to give her an update. She must have been on another call as he ended up getting her voicemail.

'It's late, so I'll stay the night at my apartment in Sydney and will give you an update on the patients in the morning. I've asked the hospital to call me should there be any complications tonight, but when I left, things were stable. Joshua still isn't doing too well but at least they've managed to stabilise him, giving Margaret and Doug a bit more time with him. Er…yeah. So that's about it.'

Once he'd made that call, the next one he made was to Melody. She answered on the third ring.

'Dr Janeway.'

'Hello, Dr Janeway, this is the other Dr Janeway.'

'Ethan. How are things?'

'A bit crazy.' He raised his hand and knocked on an office door.

'Why? Oh, hang on a second,' Melody said. 'There's someone at my door.' She opened it and nearly screamed with delight when she saw him standing there. He disconnected the call and put his phone back in his pocket as his sister threw her arms around him. 'What are you doing here?'

Ethan quickly explained the situation and also that he needed the spare set of keys she had to his apartment. Melody instantly took them off her key-ring and handed them to him.

'How do you feel?'

'About?'

'About seeing another baby with FAS. Did it bring back memories of Ellie?'

'Everything brings back memories of Ellie. Every baby I see, every morning when I get up and feel that something is missing from my life.' He thought about the past few weeks, when he'd been able to wake in the mornings and hold Elizabeth in his arms. The sense of completion, of healing he'd had from having that little baby close to him had been a therapy he'd never anticipated.

'What are you thinking about now?'

'Elizabeth.' His smile was natural as he spoke the baby's name.

'CJ's daughter?'

'Yes.'

'You don't talk much about CJ,' Melody pointed out. 'I have a theory about that.'

He raised an eyebrow in her direction. 'Really? I can't wait to hear this one.'

'I think you're secretly infatuated with CJ because she's been able to help you get closure on your past.'

'Uh-huh. Anything else, Dr Freud?'

'Yes. I think Elizabeth has filled a void in your life and that's as clear as anything when you speak of her. Your face lights up and your entire demeanour changes. Your muscles relax and your eyes twinkle and you're…happy. I haven't seen you happy in so long, big brother, and the thing that scares me is what will happen when you leave Pridham and return to Sydney at the end of your contract. What happens when you've spent the past five and a half months becoming attached to a gorgeous little girl who doesn't belong to you?'

She wasn't saying anything he hadn't already asked himself, but at the moment he didn't have any answers.

'That little baby tonight—Joshua is his name—did bring back memories of Ellie, but this time, when I thought of her, I imagined her differently. I imagined her smiling at me and giggling and—' Ethan shook his head and tried again. 'It was as though I was imagining what she *would* have been like if she'd been born healthy.'

'Like Elizabeth?'

'Yes.'

'And Abigail? Have you been able to let go of your guilt?'

He nodded slowly. 'I think I'm getting there.' Ethan reached over and took his sister's hand in his. 'Thank you, Mel, for insisting I take a sabbatical, that I take the locum post in Pridham. You said it would be good for me to unwind, to unplug from the stress of the city, and you were right. I'm not saying there aren't stresses in Pridham, of course there are, but…taking a step back from the life I'd been living and being able to see how someone else lives their life has been a privilege.'

'You're talking about CJ's life?'

'Yes.' He smiled as he thought of her and breathed in deeply, filling his lungs completely. 'She relaxes me.'

'I see. CJ and Elizabeth relax you.'

'They do. They really do.'

'And what about the rest of Pridham?'

'It's very picturesque. Great to drive around in my car. CJ loves it.'

'She likes your car?'

He chuckled at that. 'She's a vintage car enthusiast herself.'

'Well…that is surprising. Clearly you two have a lot in common.'

'We do.'

Melody's phone rang and she quickly answered it, sighing heavily as she listened to her registrar. 'Sorry, Ethan,' she stated after disconnecting the call. 'Emergency. I've gotta go.'

'That's fine.' He stood and hugged her close. 'Hey, what's happening with the directorship for Orthopaedics?'

Melody bit her lip, then pointed to herself. Ethan's eyes widened with surprise. 'You're taking it?'

'Acting Head of Orthopaedics at your service.' She gave a little bow. 'Don't know how I got talked into it, but it'll only be temporary, I tell you that much.' They stepped outside her office and she locked the door. 'Anyway, how long are you planning on being in Sydney?'

'I'm not sure. It depends on Joshua. Probably a day or two.'

'OK. So I can see you before you head back to the country?'

'Sure.' He walked her down to the emergency department, being stopped by several people on the way to shake hands and say hello, but then they were off again, busy, busy, busy. After Melody had left, Ethan looked around the ED. People everywhere, everyone hectic and overworked. It was as though he felt the stress the place exuded and when he tried to take a breath, it was odd that he couldn't quite fill his lungs.

He closed his eyes, thought of CJ's smile and the way Elizabeth felt snuggled into his arms. Then he breathed in again, all the way, and felt the stress of his past life melt away as he exhaled.

Returning to his apartment, he was shocked at the stark contrast of the minimalist furnishings compared to CJ's comfortable and homely house. Here there were no pictures on the walls of cars or people, no solid jarrah desks in the corner or comfortable bed linen on beds. Everything here was utilitarian and practical. That was the state his life had been in prior to heading to Pridham, prior to meeting CJ.

He took out his phone and went to call her again but on checking the time he realised it was too late. He didn't have anything to report on their patients and if she'd managed to get Elizabeth to sleep, there was no way he was going to disturb any shut-eye she might actually get.

Where did he live? CJ had asked him that question and he hadn't been able to answer her. Now, looking around his apartment, he at least had part of the answer to that question. 'I don't live here any more.'

By the time he flew back to Pridham and managed to arrange for someone to pick him up from the airstrip and drive him into town, it was well into the evening. He'd ended up being in Sydney for three days, monitoring the conditions of Margaret and Joshua, talking to several people about the possibility of a new research project with FAS, and having lunch with his sister.

When he headed to the back door of the house, he once again found it unlocked and shook his head. Didn't CJ realise she was a mother now, that she needed to lock the doors in order to protect both herself and Elizabeth from harm? Of course, CJ would just counter anything he said with her statistics that Pridham had practically no crime and that if people were going to get into the house, they might smash a window, which would cause more injury and damage than an unlocked door. Her argument was a valid one and a part of him was pleased that she did live in a place where crime was low and Elizabeth could grow up enjoying being part of a close-knit community.

As he went through the house, he listened for sounds of CJ and Elizabeth, unable to believe just how much he'd missed the two of them. They were so vitally important to him and he'd come back to tell CJ as much. To share with her the decisions he'd made and to ask her opinion. He valued her opinions, he valued *her*. Would she be able to value him?

'Hello?' he called softly as he headed into the lounge room. It was empty. He went towards CJ's part of the house and knocked softly on the door. 'Hello?' he called again, and pushed open the door. 'CJ?' He'd tried calling her from the airstrip to let her know he was back but again his call had gone through to her voicemail. Had she got the message?

'Ethan? Is that you? Because if it's not and you're a robber, there's absolutely nothing of value in the house. Just boring memorabilia, which won't fetch you any money if you sell it on the internet.'

He grinned at her words, following the sound of her voice to the bedroom. The door was open and he stopped on the threshold, looking at her standing over Elizabeth's crib, the baby sound asleep. She was dressed in a pair of pyjamas with her robe belted firmly around her waist. He glanced down at her feet and wasn't surprised to see those fluffy slippers she loved so much. At first he'd thought they were ridiculous, but now he realised they suited her. They reflected her personality—warm, soft and comfortable. She probably wouldn't like to hear herself being described that way—what woman would? But Ethan had never felt as comfortable in his life as he did when he was with CJ.

'You're back,' she whispered with a sigh of relief.

'I did leave you a message.' He pointed to her phone, which was on her bedside table.

She nodded. 'I got it. So... Joshua's finally picked up?' She bit her lip and shook her head as tears began to well in her eyes.

'A little,' he confirmed. 'Margaret and Doug have a very long road ahead of them, one that will take years to adjust to. The full extent of Joshua's brain damage is unknown as yet but he'll need to be in hospital for at least the next six months.' He broke off and shook his head. 'Margaret's already talking about selling their share of the vineyard and moving to Sydney.'

'She is?'

Ethan nodded. 'She says she, Doug and Joshua need a new start, one away from her parents.'

'Huh. Good for Margaret.'

'Sometimes when we face our worst fears, we become stronger,' he said as he crossed the room to stare down into Elizabeth's crib, putting his arm around CJ's waist. 'I'm glad Joshua didn't die because the death of a child is...heart-breaking and soul-destroying. It can take years of therapy, of working through things, of having a complete change of scenery, before something clicks and life starts making sense again.'

She knew he was talking about himself, as well as the very long road forward that both Doug and Margaret would face.

'You faced your fears when you were left alone and pregnant and now...' He gestured to Elizabeth. 'Look at that gorgeous girl.'

'She's stolen my heart.' As CJ spoke, her emotions welled and tears pricked at her eyes.

'Mine, too.'

'I love her so much, Ethan. I never knew I could love

someone that much before. I certainly never loved Quinten like this.'

'It's a mother's love.'

'It's a parent's love,' she said as she leaned into him further. 'And I'm still scared. I'm scared I'm going to let her down in the future, I'm scared I'm going to make mistakes, I'm scared that there are so many things that can go wrong. I don't want her to skin her knee falling off her bike. I don't want her to be teased in school. I don't want her have her heart broken when she's older. I want only the best.' CJ's emotions bubbled up and over.

'Oh, CJ.' He ground out her name and in an instant he'd gathered her closer to him. He knew her emotions were that of a person who desperately cared about her patients, not only their medical issues but their personal ones as well. Added to that was the fact that she'd not long given birth herself. He knew she'd be thinking about how she would feel should something terrible happen to Elizabeth. Even as the thought passed through his mind, he felt a surge of empowered protectiveness fill him completely. Elizabeth was vitally important to him, she'd become a part of him and he loved her. If anything were to happen to her…

CJ pulled back slightly, sniffing and rummaging in her robe pocket for a tissue. She blew her nose and looked up at him, overcome with love when she saw tears glistening in his eyes.

'I couldn't bear it if anything happened to our Lizzie… or to you.' He shook his head. 'I missed you both, so much.'

'Missed us?'

'In Sydney. I slept in a sterile, bland apartment. I chatted with people in the hospital corridors for all of thirty seconds because they were always busy going somewhere or doing something, having no time for real discussions or connections. My world there is…empty, and it's empty because *you* and our gorgeous Elizabeth aren't in it.'

She couldn't believe what she was hearing. It was what she'd been dreaming about, desperate to hear him say that he wanted to stay, that he wanted to be with her. She knew he'd suffered terrible pain but surely he could see that he was just the type of man who deserved to be loved? She loved him. Loved him desperately and she wanted him to know that, to understand that she would do everything she could to make him happy, to make his heart smile once more, to shine her whacky brand of sunshine into his life—for ever. She wanted to tell him, she was bursting to tell him, but would he…could he…really feel the same? Was she hoping for too much? There was only one thing to do—she needed to ask him.

'But here?' The words were soft yet held the strongest thread of hope. 'In Pridham? H-how does your world look here?' Even after she'd spoken, she tried not to hold her breath. This was the moment. What he said now might make her the happiest woman in the world…or… No. She wouldn't even contemplate what that 'or' might mean. Swallowing over the nervous lump in her throat, it seemed for ever before he spoke.

Ethan's smile was bright and filled with hope. 'Here…' He gazed into her eyes and her heart turned over with a new wave of love for this incredible and wonderful man. 'Here, my life is in technicolor.'

'Really?' Hope flared higher.

'Yes. It's so vibrant and alive that I need to wear sunglasses.'

CJ laughed joyously at his words. Ethan loved being here…with her.

'You once asked me where my life was and at the time I didn't know.' His gaze hovered momentarily on her mouth, her lips parted and quivering with anticipation. 'I do now. I know where my life is, CJ.' He looked deeply into her eyes before he continued, his words filled with absolute certainty, 'My life…is with *you*. You and Elizabeth. You're my everything.'

A flood of delighted tingles spread throughout CJ's entire body, giving the hope wings that soared to its fullest glory. 'Oh, Ethan,' she breathed, her voice catching on the words. Elation and utter happiness continued to tingle their way around her.

'I know this may seem sudden or crazy or both but…' He stopped and forced himself to slow down. 'I know you've been hurt so badly in the past but I promise I will accept you for the incredibly intelligent, vivacious, honest and hard-working person you are. I trust you, CJ, I trust you with my heart. I give it to you, now and for ever.' He took a deep breath and then slowly exhaled. 'I love you, Claudia-Jean.'

'You… You…' She couldn't get the words out. Her mind was trying desperately to compute everything he'd been saying and the whole time he'd been talking her heart had been singing with delight.

'I love you,' he said for her, and placed a firm kiss on her mouth, as though desperate to prove his point. The kiss instantly turned hard, possessive and urgent. He was a man dying of thirst in the desert and finally finding water. He pulled back and tenderly caressed her cheek. 'I love you,' he stated again, then chuckled. 'I can't believe how many times I'm saying it. I can't seem to stop.'

'Don't ever stop,' she instructed. 'Always reassure me that you love me.' As she said the words, he heard the quiver in her voice, saw the pain, the hurts, the betrayals of the past. She was scared but he knew he could fix it.

'I promise to tell you every day—even if we're having an open and honest disagreement—that I love you. I could *never* want another woman, CJ, because you're all I need. Well…you and Elizabeth.' He laughed. 'The two of you have brought me back to life and I can never thank you enough for opening your life and letting me in. I know you're scared and you have every right to be but you must feel how different things are this time.'

'Yes. It's *very* different. Before you went to Sydney, I wasn't sure if I could trust you with my heart but when you weren't here, not only was the house so dark and lonely, my life was dark and lonely.' She pulled back to look at him. 'You're right. I'm scared. I'm scared to take another chance at love, at marriage—especially as I have Elizabeth to think about this time—but I'm even *more* scared to live my life without you.' Her lower lip trembled. 'Oh, Ethan. I need you so much.'

Ethan couldn't stand it any more. He crushed her to him once again and pressed his mouth to hers. She was his— and he was *never* letting her go. She and Elizabeth were his family. His heart had known it for a while but his mind had taken a little while to catch up.

Eventually, he released her and she smiled up at him. 'I still can't believe you're really here.'

'I am and I'm never leaving you again. I must have been mad.'

'You're really staying? Here? In Pridham?'

'If you'll marry me.'

'Married? Are you sure?'

'One hundred percent. My life is…meaningless without you.' He paused and stared into her eyes, showing her every aspect of his vulnerabilities. 'Please, CJ? Marry me. Be my partner for life. We'll love our Lizzie and we'll love any other children we might have.'

'You want more children?'

'I do. I really do. I want to fill this house with fun and laughter and noise.' He paused, sadness creeping into his words. 'I'll always love Ellie, and Abigail, but they were my past. *You* are my future. You and Lizzie-Jean. I love you. Will you? Will you marry me?'

CJ's heart overflowed with love for the man before her. 'Yes. Oh, yes, yes, yes. I need you, Ethan Janeway. I need you and I trust you.' She placed her hand on his cheek. 'In fact, I adore you.' She kissed him again, then drew back with a gasp. 'But what about your job in Sydney? What will you do here?'

'Firstly, I've resigned from the hospital.'

'What?'

'Secondly, I've decided to set up a private practice here, in Pridham. A permanent general surgeon for the Pridham and Whitecorn district hospitals. Also, I've started negotiations for my next research project, which will be a collaboration with a few of my colleagues at the Royal Sydney Children's Hospital.'

'FAS?'

'Yes, and no doubt we'll be wanting your input, too.'

'Really? I get to have my name on a published paper?' She giggled. 'This really is a night of dreams coming true.' CJ sighed, content and happy and amazed that she could feel this good.

Elizabeth shifted beneath her covers, sniffling a little before starting to cry. Ethan released CJ and bent to pick the baby up. 'That cry doesn't sound good. Is she all right?'

'She's been a little unsettled for the past few days.'

'What?' He picked her up and kissed her forehead. 'Are you all right, my darling?'

CJ's heart melted at the way he genuinely loved their Lizzie. 'She'll be fine...now.'

'Now?'

'We've both been a little unsettled for the past few days. We've been fretting.'

'Fretting?'

'Over you.'

His concerned look disappeared as he held out his other arm to CJ. 'Come here.' He held her close. 'You'll never have to fret again. Either of you. We're a family and we'll be sticking together for ever.' Then Ethan kissed her in such an intense and passionate way that she knew their love *would* last for ever.

The baby slept on.

EPILOGUE

THE WEDDING WAS the most glorious day of her life. The night before she'd insisted on spending the night at Donna's place while Ethan had stayed at her home—*their* home now. They'd made plans to alter the renovations that CJ had not long finished but as both of them enjoyed renovating and restoring old things, it would be a challenge they could do together.

Ethan, as well as covering CJ's clinics, had already started his own general surgical practice. Consulting at both Pridham and Whitecorn hospitals, his clinics booking up so fast he thought he might need to add an extra day in the future. For now, though, he was more than happy playing Mr Mum while CJ eased herself back into part-time consulting. They both enjoyed their days at home with Lizzie-Jean and doing things together as a family at weekends.

'Are you sure you're happy?' CJ had asked Ethan a few days ago.

'I'll be happier when you're legally my wife.' He'd hauled her close and kissed her soundly. 'I love you so much, CJ.' He'd laughed with such carefree abandon that any minor concerns she'd harboured had vanished. 'I can't believe how incredible I feel being here, with you and our Lizzie-Jean and the people of the community.' Ethan had shaken his head in bemusement. 'I never thought I'd say it but... I'm glad I had that minor heart attack.'

CJ had shuddered at the mention of it. 'I'm not.'

'If I hadn't, I wouldn't have re-evaluated my life, I wouldn't have come here, I wouldn't have found you, I wouldn't be blessed with another family to love and cherish, for ever and ever, until death us do part.'

'Practising your vows?'

'I don't need to practise them. They're tattooed on my heart.'

And so when the time came for CJ to marry her beloved Ethan, the ceremony being held at Donna's small vineyard, her heart had been sure and confident. Ethan loved her. Ethan loved Lizzie-Jean. She loved Ethan and Lizzie-Jean...well, Lizzie-Jean seemed to love whoever was cuddling her. The little girl was a delight and one that had only enhanced the happiness CJ had thought she'd never feel.

As she stood facing Ethan, holding his hands and gazing into his eyes, while Lizzie-Jean slept on nearby in Aunty Melody's arms, CJ couldn't help but laugh.

'What's so funny?' Ethan stared at her and slowly shook his head, his own lips beginning to twitch. 'You're supposed to be saying your vows, not laughing.'

'But I'm just *so* happy.' She giggled again. '*You* make me so happy, Ethan. You came into my life when I needed you most—and then stayed. You stayed. I want you to know that I will always be here for you, that I will do my very best to always communicate with you, to share my thoughts, my feelings and my concerns with you. Good and bad. Happy and sad... But here's hoping it's mostly happy. I think we've both had enough sadness.'

'And I promise to do everything I can to keep that smile on your face, to keep that giggle bubbling up and your eyes shining with delight. I adore you, Claudia-Jean. I love you.

My heart is yours for ever…except for the part we share with Lizzie-Jean—'

'And any other children we might have.'

Ethan nodded. 'We'll build a home filled with thoughtfulness, kindness, love, patience and—'

'And a thousand other good things,' she interjected once more.

'Will you let me finish?' he demanded, and a chuckle rippled through the crowd that was gathered around them, helping them celebrate this wonderful union.

'In a minute.' She leaned forward and kissed him firmly on the mouth.

'Uh… I haven't got to that bit yet,' the celebrant said, but no one seemed to mind.

CJ pulled back and looked at her beloved. 'I love you, Ethan Janeway.'

'I love you back,' he responded, then, after kissing her once more, he settled her a small way from him, his hands still firmly holding hers, and turned to the celebrant.

'OK. Get to the part where you pronounce us a family—because we've got some serious celebrating to do!'

The celebrant chuckled but did as she was bidden and a short while later CJ was officially Ethan's wife and Ethan was officially CJ's husband. And both of them were officially ready to start their new life together.

For ever.

* * * * *

ONE WEEK TO WIN HIS HEART

LUCY CLARK

MILLS & BOON

Miss Melanie Mischief Maker—how are you 21?!!
Love you to Voyager and back.

Pr 20:7

CHAPTER ONE

Dr Melody Janeway brushed her hands apprehensively down her calf-length blue skirt and ensured her embroidered white blouse was tucked neatly into the waistband. Next, she smoothed a hand over her unruly auburn curls, ensuring her hair was still secured in the clip at the nape of her neck. She was ready to meet the dignitary.

Melody started to pace in front of her desk, taking deep breaths. 'Cool, calm and collected.' She whispered her mantra in an effort to calm her nerves. When the intercom on her desk buzzed, she almost hit the roof with fright. She pressed the button. 'Yes, Rick?'

'The delegation is here.'

'Show them in, thank you.' She closed her eyes for a millisecond. How had she ever let herself be talked into this job? Acting head of the orthopaedic department? It was ridiculous. Not that she minded the administrative side, but many other aspects of the job, such as lecturing and playing host to delegates, weren't her cup of tea. She was a doctor, not a tour guide!

Melody opened her eyes at the sound of her office door opening. Should she be sitting behind her desk? Would that look more official? Oh, well. It was too late to move so instead she stood like a statue in the middle of the large office with a fake smile pasted onto her face.

The smile, however, became genuine when she found

herself staring up at a man with the most gorgeous brown eyes she'd ever seen. He was tall—a lot taller than she'd expected. Probably about six feet three inches. His hair was a rich dark brown, militarily short and starting to grey at the temples.

'I'm George Wilmont.' He extended his hand as he walked towards her.

'Welcome, Professor Wilmont.' She quickly recovered her composure, pleased with herself for not openly gaping at the man. 'I'm Melody Janeway.' She placed her hand in his, the touch sending a jolt of electrifying tingles up her arm. His fingers gripped her hand firmly, warming not only her hand but the rest of her as well.

She'd been unprepared for such a reaction to this stranger, especially as he held her hand for a fraction of a second longer than was necessary. Melody felt something wild and untamed pass between them. His gaze locked with hers and she saw a flicker of surprise register in his eyes before they both dropped their hands and took a small step backwards.

Whoa! What on earth was that? According to the dossier she had on him as part of the preparation information for this tour, he was a married man. Melody cleared her throat, desperately trying to regain her composure. 'Uh... welcome to St Aloysius Hospital, Professor Wilmont.'

He cleared his throat. 'Please, call me George.'

She nodded. 'I'm Melody, and if you want to make any jokes about singing or asking if I can carry a tune, the answer is yes. I sing very well and often in key.'

George smiled at her attempt at humour, a real smile, not a polite *I'm a professional* type of smile. The effect was real as she noted his eyes spark with a glint of merriment. They stared at each other for what seemed like an eternity, the hours ticking by, yet in reality it was no more than five seconds. Still, it was enough to make her feel highly self-conscious. The smile slid from George's lips and he shifted back again, as though needing to put even more distance between them.

'Melody Janeway, allow me to introduce you to the rest of my staff.' George introduced the people who were responsible for helping him keep to the strict timetable he lived by. As a visiting orthopaedic surgeon, George had been touring the world for almost twelve months and had now returned to his homeland of Australia. He had two administrative assistants, one research assistant, one technical consultant and a personal aide.

Melody's own PA, Rick, was hovering by the door. She beckoned him in and introduced him. 'Rick and I are both at your service this week. If there's anything you need to know or can't find, please don't hesitate to ask.' Melody addressed the group as she spoke but her gaze kept returning to George.

'Thank you,' he responded, smiling politely as their gazes held once more. Melody gave herself a mental shake and checked her watch. 'I guess we should make a start. Have there been any changes to the agreed agenda?'

For the past few months, information had been emailed back and forth between Professor Wilmont's organisers and Rick, ensuring operating theatres and lecture halls were booked, as well as confirming catering arrangements and restaurant reservations. Throughout this week, Melody's job was to be the official representative for St Aloysius Hospital, to be the master of ceremonies at some events, or to simply be there to field questions and introduce Professor Wilmont where necessary. It would be a long, arduous week and if there had been any changes to the agenda, it was best to find out now, rather than at the last minute.

Professor Wilmont's delegation had been organising these types of events in hospitals around the globe since the beginning of the tour in January, so they were very experienced at what they did. That was another reason why it was important for Melody and Rick to ensure St Aloysius measured up to the standards of professionalism the professor would have received from other medical institutions.

'Not that I'm aware of.' George answered Melody's question but turned and raised an inquisitive eyebrow at his personal aide. 'Carmel? Any changes?'

Carmel consulted the leather-bound book in her hands, then shook her head. 'No.' She was a small, thin woman who wore very high-heeled shoes and a tailored business suit, with her almost jet-black hair pulled back in a tight chignon. The consummate professional.

'Excellent.' Melody nodded. 'Well, then, we'd better get started to make sure we don't fall behind schedule.'

'Carmel would never let that happen,' George remarked as Melody walked towards the door and held it open. 'She's a hard taskmaster but a necessary one.' His words were spoken with affection and joviality. Carmel's answer was to provide a polite smile in their direction. 'I'd have been lost without her during this tour.'

George was the last person to exit, apart from her, and Melody inclined her head towards the door. 'After you, Professor Wilmont.' She gestured, indicating he should precede her.

'Ladies first,' he insisted, and the smile he aimed in her direction was one that turned her insides to mush.

She was knocked off guard by the sensation, so mumbled a 'Thank you,' as she went through the door before him.

As they headed towards the operating theatres, Melody pointed out different areas of the hospital, trying to regain her inner composure. It had been quite some time since she'd reacted like this to a man's charming personality, and the outcome of that experience had been one of heartbreak. If she was focusing on playing host, on being professional and imparting information, then her mind couldn't dwell on the unexpected way she was responding to Professor Wilmont.

Once in Theatres, they did a tour of the operating room George would be using when he taught. It had a viewing gallery positioned on a mezzanine floor surrounding the operating table so that students, interns, nursing staff and doctors could easily see what was happening.

'It's also equipped with microphones and miniature cameras. There are two television monitors in the viewing gallery and, as would be expected, we'll be recording the procedures for further study of your techniques.'

'An impressive facility,' George murmured.

'I'm delighted to hear that. I'll pass your comments onto the CEO,' she responded, before they continued with their tour. They headed down yet another long corridor and it was only when George spoke that she realised how close he was to her.

'This is the one characteristic all big hospitals have— long corridors.' His soft, deep tones washed over her and Melody smiled, pleased to find he had a sense of humour.

'And this one has lovely paintings to glance at as people stride by in a rush,' she pointed out.

'True.' There was a wistful note in his tone. 'It's the same in every hospital we've visited. Busy people, rushing here and there and never really stopping to…gaze at the art.' He pointed to a painting of native Australian animals, his pace slowing marginally as he spoke.

'I presume life has been very hectic on your tour?'

'Yes. On the go, non-stop, busy, busy, busy.'

'Have you had any time off during the tour?' she asked as they walked along together.

'We had a month off in June. It was needed by then because we'd all been living in each other's pockets for the past five months. Plus, we get every Saturday off—if we're

not flying somewhere, that is. Carmel's very organised.'
There was the slightest hint of sadness in his tone and she
wondered why. Was he sad that the tour was almost at an
end? Would he miss jet-setting around the world, being
adored and praised for his innovative surgical techniques?

'How do you cope with the jet-lag?'

'Stay hydrated and sleep on the plane.' George recited
the phrase as though he'd said it over and over. 'Actually,
the jet-lag hasn't been too bad because we've done small
hops between countries, but when we arrived back in Australia three weeks ago we took a week off to acclimatise
ourselves to the Aussie weather, especially as we landed
in Darwin.'

'Wise decision, and October is still nice and mild compared to summer.'

'I've missed it, though.'

'The Australian summer?' She looked at him as though
he was crazy, given that summer temperatures were usually exceedingly hot.

He laughed. 'Yes. The heat, the people, the accent. You
have no idea how great it was to hear that Aussie twang
at the airport.'

Melody smiled as she pressed the button for the lift.
When he laughed like that, when his smile was full, she
was astonished to discover her knees weakening at the
sound. He really was handsome. When she'd been planning for the visiting orthopaedic surgeon's tour, she hadn't
given a lot of thought to what type of man he might be.
She'd just expected him to be a surgeon who was intent
on explaining his operating techniques and research projects, before moving onto the next hospital to do the same
thing. She hadn't expected him to have a sense of humour
that matched her own. She also hadn't expected to be so
instantly attracted to a married man—something she normally avoided.

Ian had been married. Of course, he hadn't told her that until they'd been dating for three months. She frowned as she thought about the first man to break her heart but when George looked her way, Melody quickly pushed all thoughts of the past from her mind and concentrated on the present.

Professor Wilmont had a lecture to give in twenty minutes and she needed to get him to the venue without mishap. The lift bell dinged and a moment later the doors opened. 'All right, can everyone fit in?' Melody asked as she held the doors open. 'Everyone in?' When she received affirmative murmurs, she allowed the doors to close and pressed the button for the fifth floor. She refused to focus on the way George was standing right behind her, nice and close, the natural warmth from his body causing a wave of tingles to spread over her. She also refused to allow the fresh spicy scent he wore to wind its way about her senses. Why weren't these lifts bigger?

She cleared her throat and forced her mind back into gear. 'The hospital's main lecture facility, which is where you'll be giving most of your lectures, had a complete upgrade last year,' she informed them. 'I've been assured that all the gadgets are in working order but if you find we don't have everything you require, please let me know.'

'Thank you.' George replied, his tone as polite and professional as Melody's, yet she could have sworn she saw a slight smirk touch the corners of his lips. Was she entertaining him? Or had he simply heard similar spiels at different hospitals around the globe? When the lift doors opened, they all exited, again George waiting until Melody had preceded him. She nodded politely before leading the way to the lecture room.

When she pushed open the large double doors, George's team instantly fanned out to check the facilities. One of his assistants headed to the audiovisual desk to connect his computer to the system, another did a sound check. They scuttled back and forth, checking things with each other and ensuring the slides and short snippets of operating techniques were ready to go.

George walked over to the podium, where Carmel gave him several instructions as well as handing him a folder with notes inside. He familiarised himself with where his water glass would be, where to find the laser pointer and how to adjust the lapel microphone.

Melody wandered over to a seat in the front row and sat down, mesmerised by the confidence he exuded—and he wasn't even giving a speech. Lecturing wasn't one of her strong suits so she was always willing to learn. Just by watching him, she knew she could learn a great deal.

Is that the real reason you're watching him? The question crept into the back of her mind before she could stop it. She'd been doing her best to think of him as Professor Wilmont rather than George, as he'd instructed, but as she sat there, gazing at him, she realised she already thought of him as George. He was a very personable man but, then, he'd need to be in order to carry out the duties of the travelling fellowship. She tilted her head to the side, her gaze following his every move. He was classically tall, dark and extremely handsome.

There was no denying to herself that she found George…intriguing, which made him a man to be avoided at all costs. The last man who had 'intrigued' her, Emir, had broken her heart into tiny pieces and discarded her as though she was nothing more than an inconvenient diversion. One broken engagement was more than enough for Melody, so the last thing she should be doing right now was ogling a married man.

Then again, the irrational side of her mind pointed out, there was no harm in looking, right? She closed her eyes to block out the image of George and concentrated on controlling her warring psyche. Professor Wilmont would be gone at the end of the week, finishing the rest of his tour. He'd be gone and she'd be here, still trying to focus on the duties of being acting head of department. Their worlds were miles apart and the only thing they had in common was that they were both orthopaedic surgeons.

Someone sat in the chair next to her, bringing her out of her reverie. Was it time for people to start arriving for George's first lecture already? She opened her eyes, only to find she was face to face with the man himself. 'Sleeping? I'm not boring you already, am I?' George's deep baritone washed over her.

Melody smiled. 'Not sleeping, just thinking.'

'You were right. This is a great lecture room. One of the better ones.'

'I'm glad.'

'When I visited Bangladesh, I did this same talk in a small annexe next to the hospital. Dirt floors, tin roof, more like a lean-to, and everyone who came huddled around my computer to watch the slides and short recordings I showed.' He nodded. 'It was one of my best talks because I was so relaxed.'

'You're not relaxed today?'

He shrugged one shoulder and checked his tie was securely in place. 'I didn't have to wear a suit there either. Far too hot. How anyone can be completely relaxed whilst wearing a suit, I don't know.'

'You don't like wearing a suit?' There was a hint of incredulity in her words. 'Surely, on this tour, you've had to wear one most days.'

'Yep.'

'Then why do the tour in the first place?'

For the first time since she'd met him she saw a hint of sadness in his eyes but he quickly looked away, checking his watch. 'People should start arriving soon.'

'Yes.' A strange awkwardness seemed to settle over them, although Melody had no idea why. She'd asked what she had thought to be a general question and George's whole demeanour had changed from light-hearted to sad to professional. She wanted to ask why, not to pry but because she was genuinely concerned, but, then, the visiting professor's psyche was none of her business. 'Er...you certainly have a great team,' she stated, taking her lead from him and keeping their conversation to a strictly professional line. 'A well-oiled machine.'

'They certainly are. At first it was all rather strange, having people ordering me about every step of the way, but now, after months of travelling and lecturing, I've learned to trust them. They're all extremely good at their jobs, and if we each do our own thing and avoid getting in each other's way, then things generally run smoothly.'

'I guess that's the name of the game when you're on one of these visiting professorships.'

'Absolutely. Besides, in spending so much time together, we've also become friends.' He gestured to where Carmel was discussing something with Diana, one of the administrative assistants. 'Carmel's amazing. How she keeps all the schedules and travel details and names of people correct, I'll never know.'

'It's definitely a skill.' Melody was equally impressed. 'My PA, Rick, has the same knack. Give me a scalpel over a mound of paperwork any day.' She chuckled. People were starting to arrive and take their seats.

'Making friends with your work colleagues can be an advantage. Of course, when you're a small group, it can sometimes be dangerous.' George sighed as he continued to watch Carmel and Diana.

'Dangerous?' She followed his gaze, picking up on the wistfulness of his tone. Was George involved with Carmel or Diana? Relationships were bound to happen in such a small group that spent so much time together.

'Carmel and Diana.' George shrugged one shoulder. 'They've been on and off again for most of the trip, I can't keep up any more.' As the two women smiled warmly at each other, George nodded. 'Definitely on again at the moment.' Carmel finished talking to Diana, then turned and beckoned to George. 'I'm being summoned.'

'Off to work, Professor,' Melody said with a smile, and as George stood, he returned her smile—a bright, happy smile that made her feel all fluttery and feminine. Why? Why would she feel like that because a handsome man smiled at her?

George listened to what Carmel had to say but his thoughts were still with the delightful Melody Janeway. It wasn't often he met people he instantly connected with, so when it happened it took him by surprise. He glanced once more at Melody, who was now talking with Rick.

'George?' Carmel snapped her fingers at him and he immediately returned his attention to his PA. 'Focus.'

'I'm focused, Carmel.' He chuckled at the way she'd snapped her fingers at him. That usually meant she was in organisational mode. 'I like relaxed, chatty Carmel better than Ms Hospital Corners.'

'Tough.' She handed him the laser pointer then walked over to Melody. George watched as Melody chatted with both PAs before standing and heading to the podium. She moved with grace and ease, smoothing a hand down her skirt before adjusting her papers. She held herself perfectly, her back straight, her shoulders square as she read from the notes, glancing up to look at the assembled crowd. Her voice was clear and her words well modulated. He liked listening to her talk.

Before too long, she was turning to face him, smiling at

him, and he realised he hadn't heard a word she'd said. He'd been so captivated by this new acquaintance that he really had drifted off into la-la land. What was wrong with him? It wasn't like him to behave in such a fashion, and especially not when he was standing in front of a large crowd of people—people who were all looking at him expectantly.

He needed to pull on his professionalism, to brush aside any intriguing thoughts he had about Melody Janeway, and do the job he'd been sent to do. He was Professor George Wilmont, orthopaedic surgeon, and widower. He was not a man who experienced an instant attraction towards a colleague, or acted on it.

This time, when he politely shook her hand to thank her for introducing him, he exuded a cool reserve. This time there was no jolt of awareness. This time he was the consummate professional and he was determined to remain so for the rest of his stay in Sydney.

CHAPTER TWO

LUNCH WAS A lavish affair for a 'few' special guests—all fifty of them. Thankfully, as St Aloysius Hospital was situated in the heart of Sydney, there were a plethora of delightful restaurants in the vicinity, and Melody knew Rick had booked several of them for lunches and dinners throughout the week.

When she'd arrived, she'd discovered that she was seated next to George. The scent of his spicy aftershave teased at her senses, making her aware of his nearness. Closing her eyes for a moment, Melody composed herself, needing to remain polite but professional.

She'd never had the greatest luck with men, as her older brothers, David and Ethan, would attest. After her last break-up, one that had fed the hospital gossips for a good six months at least, she'd decided to focus on her career. Two years later, she was now where she wanted to be, but she was also lonely, spending more and more hours at the hospital in order to curtail the emotion.

When would it be her turn to find an honest man? A man who wanted to settle down and start a family? A man who wasn't already married, or who believed in monogamy? Probably when you become brave enough to date again, her head answered her heart. She had been shy, not wanting to put herself out there again, hoping that fate would simply bring the right man to her doorstep.

She glanced at George Wilmont, watching as he chatted animatedly with the doctor seated on the other side of him. She liked the way his lips curved into a smile, the way his deep, rich tones could wash over her and ease away her tensions. No man had ever turned her head, made her laugh and captured her interest as quickly as George Wilmont.

Melody forced herself to look away. She needed to rein in her crazy romantic notions and her desperation to find the man who was her soul mate, because George Wilmont was definitely *not* that man. At the moment she should view him as nothing more than a handsome diversion who would leave at the end of the week.

When the time came for George to say a few words, Melody accepted her notes from Rick, who was really earning the title of 'right-hand man', and headed to the podium. After she'd once again introduced George, he'd thanked her but this time when he'd smiled her way, it hadn't been the polite professional mask he'd had in the lecture theatre. No, this time, while she'd been standing at the podium in a room full of her peers, George had decided to hit her with a one hundred percent, full-watt smile.

The pep-talk she'd just given herself vanished from her mind as she allowed herself to be dazzled by him. She might have even gasped at the sight but her mind hadn't been functioning properly, given his enigmatic presence, so she wasn't certain.

What she *was* certain about, however, was the way her body seemed to be tuning itself to George's frequency without her permission. In fact, once he'd given his short talk and returned to sit beside her, his spicy cologne once more started to wind its way around her, causing a devastating effect on her equilibrium. She didn't want to be so aware of him, yet she was.

She focused on the conversation taking place about the latest medical breakthrough, listening intently to

George's opinion on the subject. During their entrée and main course, George answered many questions. It was a rare opportunity to have access to someone who was travelling the world, hearing and seeing at first-hand new innovations in the ever-changing orthopaedic world, and her colleagues were making the most of it.

Just as their desserts were being brought around, George stood and removed his suit jacket. Melody found her gaze drawn to his movements and she watched from beneath her lashes, mesmerised by the way his triceps flexed beneath the material of his shirt. It almost made her hyperventilate. She took a sip from her water glass, breathing in as she swallowed.

Melody spluttered and started to cough. George patted her on the back and everyone at their table stopped talking and watched her.

'You all right, Melody?' George asked as he sat down again.

His concern was touching and she looked at him with an embarrassed grin. She coughed again and nodded. 'I'm…' another cough '…fine.' She didn't sound fine, even to her own ears, as the word had come out like a tiny squeak. Melody cleared her throat. 'Fine,' she reiterated more strongly. Everyone resumed their conversations and she'd half expected George to continue talking to Carmel. Instead, he leaned over and refilled her water glass.

'Try it again.' He held the glass out to her and she took it, their fingertips touching—just for an instant. It was enough to spread a deep warmth throughout her body, causing her to gasp quietly. She was so aware of him it was ridiculous. Why couldn't she control these sensations?

Her smile faded but she did as he suggested, conscious of the way he watched her actions. Their gazes held and Melody found herself powerless to look away. She rested the glass on her lower lip. As she tilted the liquid towards her mouth, she exhaled slowly, her breath steaming up the glass. She sipped and swallowed, replacing the glass on the table before her trembling fingers dropped it.

'There,' he whispered, but didn't smile. 'All better.' His gorgeous brown eyes were intense. Melody felt momentarily hypnotised. Within an instant George had somehow made her feel...desirable.

'George will know.' Carmel's voice intruded into the little bubble that surrounded them.

George tried desperately to listen to what Carmel was asking, all the while trying to figure out what had just happened with Melody Janeway. He'd been mesmerised by her again. Was it the way her lips had trembled ever so slightly as she'd rested the glass on her lip? Or the way they'd parted to allow the liquid to pass between them. He swallowed convulsively and pushed thoughts of her from his mind, even though he seemed conscious of her every move.

Carmel was still talking and although George could see her lips moving, he was having great difficulty in concentrating. Thankfully, the last few words sank in and he was able to answer the question in an authoritative and controlled manner.

Melody rose to her feet and quietly excused herself. George glanced at her, noticing the way she smoothed her skirt down over her thighs. It wasn't the first time she'd done it and he wondered if it meant she was nervous. Not that he was objecting to the action, for each time she did it, it drew attention to her gorgeous legs.

Why was she nervous? Had she felt that unmistakable pull of attraction between them? Or was she always this jittery? He wouldn't know. He didn't know the woman and yet the sensations he felt when around her had occurred several times during their very short acquaintance. It was like nothing he'd experienced before but he'd assumed the sensations were solely on his side. *Did* she feel it? The question kept reverberating around at the back of his mind as he tried to concentrate on the discussion at their table.

A mouth-watering chocolate dessert was placed before him but he pushed it away, not interested. He'd had enough of food—for the moment.

'Are you all right?' Carmel asked quietly, leaning closer to him to ensure her words didn't carry to the other people around them.

'Fine. Why?'

'Because you can't seem to stop staring at our hostess for this week.'

George was stunned at his friend's words. 'What? I wasn't staring at her,' he whispered vehemently.

'It's OK, George. It just means you're normal and Melody is a very attractive woman, but not my type. Definitely more your type.'

'I don't have a type. I'm in mourning.'

'You can't stay in mourning for ever, George. You and I both know that's not the life Veronique would have wanted for you. Besides,' Carmel continued quickly before he could say anything, 'it's not every day a woman really captures your attention. Melody's the first I've noticed you taking an interest in throughout the entire tour.'

'That doesn't mean to say I'm going to act on it.'

'Aha. You *do* like her. I knew it.'

'Shh.' George glanced around them but no one seemed to be paying them much attention. They would just think that he and Carmel were discussing aspects of the schedule. 'Whether I like her or not is irrelevant. We have a hectic schedule to get through and then we'll be gone at the end of the week.'

'We're off to Perth.'

'Perth, Adelaide or anywhere in between, I don't care. The point is that I have a life waiting for me in Melbourne.'

'What life?'

'I have a house. A job.'

'Things you couldn't wait to leave behind when the fellowship began,' she reminded him.

George pursed his lips, knowing she had a point. When the tour had started, he couldn't wait to leave Melbourne, to leave the grief of his life without Veronique behind. Although he was looking forward to a less hectic pace of life, he wasn't sure Melbourne would hold the same charms for him as it had before. He knew that with everything he'd seen and experienced on this tour, he was a very different man from the one who had left, eager to escape his grief.

Carmel glanced momentarily down at her phone, which had buzzed with a message. 'It's the little things in life that mean the most,' Carmel stated a moment later, a soft smile on her lips.

'Message from Diana?' he asked, gesturing to her phone.

Carmel's smile increased. 'Yes.'

'You've managed to sort things out, then?'

'Yes. Diana was jealous of that redhead we met in Darwin but I've assured her there was nothing going on between us. We just had to work closely together, just like this week I'm working closely with Rick and Melody.'

'I'm glad you're back together. It's more harmonious for the rest of us,' George couldn't help but tease. He was glad Carmel was the one who had come on the tour with him. The fact that she'd been the director for other travelling fellowships and had been helping Veronique to organise this one when tragedy had struck—well—George was glad it was Carmel who had come, especially as she and Veronique had been good friends. Carmel had known his wife, had known how happy the two of them had been together, so to hear her now say that it was OK not to deny his instant connection with Melody Janeway was almost a relief.

Carmel chuckled at his words, then noticed Melody walking back towards their table. 'Finding harmony in your life is a good thing, George.'

George followed Carmel's gaze, his whole being mesmerised by the way Melody walked. She was so graceful, like a dancer, hovering momentarily to talk to someone before continuing her way back to him. 'You haven't been captivated by anyone since Veronique, which definitely means there's something about Melody that has caught your attention.'

Carmel's words floated over him in the background as George noticed that the small auburn curl that had escaped the bonds of the clip was now securely back in place. He wondered if her hair colour was natural. Either way, he knew it suited her and made the green of her eyes seem more intense.

He forced himself to look away as she sat back down, trying his best not to be affected by the allure of the floral scent she wore. He was intrigued by her, interested to get to know her better and the knowledge troubled him. Carmel had been right when she'd said that no other woman had captivated him, not the way Melody Janeway had. What was it about his new colleague that was causing him to behave in such a way?

'Feeling better?' he asked, and she smiled politely in his direction, the smile causing his gut to tighten with a need he'd thought repressed.

'Yes, thank you. It was—um—silly of me to choke on the water like that. Then again,' she said with a small chuckle, 'I'm usually the person who drops their knife on the floor and or spills food on their shirt.'

With that, George's gaze instantly dropped to her shirt to check if she'd done just that. When he realised he was staring at her breasts, he instantly focused his gaze back on her lovely green eyes. 'You're in the clear today.'

'So far,' she remarked jestingly, and he returned her smile.

'Were you clumsy as a child?'

Melody pondered his words for a moment. 'Not clumsy exactly...or at least not that I can recall. I'm sure if you asked my brothers, they'd have a different story.'

'Older brothers?' George was delighted she was talking to him about her personal life. He wanted to know about her, he wanted to know what made her laugh, what thrilled her, what made her sad. Perhaps Carmel was right and he should just accept the little moments of happiness he could experience.

'Yes, but thankfully as we've grown older, they don't treat me like I'm completely useless. Now we're all good friends. How about you?' Melody couldn't stop herself from wanting to know more about him, about things that weren't contained in the professional dossier she'd been sent months ago. 'Any siblings?'

He nodded. 'I have younger twin sisters who still love to stick their noses into my life.'

'My brothers aren't twins, there's eighteen months between them, but as I'm four years younger, the two of them did a lot of things together and I always felt like left out.'

'I'm like that with my sisters. They've always had each other.'

'There you go, then. We're both the odd ones out in our families.' She picked up her glass and held it out to him. He quickly clinked his against hers, and they both sipped. Their gazes held again and she felt her smile begin to fade. That underlying tug of attraction was starting to wind its way around them and she desperately fought for something to say that would break the moment. 'You haven't touched your dessert. Don't you have a sweet tooth?'

'Not really. I used to before I started this tour but I've had so many working dinners and lunches—even breakfasts—that my sweet tooth has definitely disappeared.'

'That's a lot of food.'

'Absolutely.' He smiled. 'But it gives me the opportunity to speak to more people, to get the word out about new advances, new techniques, and that's one of the main aims of visiting professorships.'

'Excuse me, Melody,' Rick interrupted. 'I've just had a call from Mr Okanadu's office.'

'Problem?'

'One of his private patients is having complications.'

'He's gone to Theatre,' Melody stated, and automatically checked her watch. Rick nodded.

'Something wrong?' Carmel asked, her radar ears picking up the conversation.

'Mr Okanadu, the surgeon who was scheduled to assist George in Theatre this afternoon, has called through with an emergency.'

Carmel thought calmly for a moment, then indicated to Melody. 'I'm sure you wouldn't mind stepping into the breach, Melody.'

'Me?' Melody looked from George to Carmel to Rick, then back to Carmel. 'Surely there's someone—'

'You're a qualified orthopaedic surgeon,' Carmel stated. 'And I'm fairly sure, being the thorough professional that you are, you've already read the information packet sent to all host hospitals regarding the techniques George will be teaching.'

'She has,' Rick chimed in. 'And she chose the patient. She was putting Mr Barnes's mind at ease this morning before ward round, telling him he'll have the best surgeon in the world performing the operation.'

'Best surgeon, eh?' George drawled, a glorious smile lighting his face, his brown eyes twinkling with delight.

The effect was mind-numbing and Melody wasn't at all sure she'd be able to keep herself under control while standing opposite him in Theatre. At the moment, she was glad she was still sitting down as she wasn't sure her legs would have continued supporting her. What was it about his smile that seemed to make her body melt and her mind go blank?

'So it's settled,' Carmel stated, then rushed off to tell the rest of the team.

'Where is she going?' Melody asked.

'To make the necessary changes. Every day, an extensive diary is kept about who operated on whom and where and when and everything else. The slides for the presentation will need to be changed, your name inserted instead of Dr Okanadu's...' He trailed off and shrugged. 'That sort of thing.'

'Would you mind quickly going over the procedure again with me? Just talk me through the highlights,' she stated. Although she had read up on the procedure, now that she'd been forced into this, she wanted to do an excellent job.

Before George could answer, someone came over from another table and commandeered his attention, leaving Melody sitting there, trying her best to remember what she'd read.

'You OK, boss?' Rick asked, pulling up a chair beside her.

'No.'

'Oh? What's the problem?'

'I don't want to assist.'

'You'd rather be up in the gallery, squashed in all hot and bothered, telling people to shush so you could hear what was being said?' He paused. 'Now you get to be a part of the action, Melody. It's an honour and a privilege and you'll have the best view in the house.'

'I guess when you put it that way...' The one thing she wasn't looking forward to were the small sensual bursts of tension she seemed to experience whenever George was near. She would have to work extra-hard on her self-control and professionalism in Theatre.

Accepting her fate, Melody reached for her water glass again and drank the contents. That would be her last drink until she came out of Theatre. At least she hadn't choked on this drink. Surely that was a good sign that she wouldn't make a fool of herself. Right?

CHAPTER THREE

'Suction,' George ordered, and Melody complied. They'd been in Theatre for almost four hours now and George looked as fresh as when he'd first walked in. At first Melody had been very conscious of the packed viewing gallery but once the operation had begun, she'd pushed it to the back of her mind. She had a job to do and they owed it to their patient to do just that.

They still had an hour to go on the pelvic reconstruction. George's research in this field had led him to invent a device that made certain aspects of the surgery more manageable. He'd been extensively published in several of the world's leading orthopaedic journals, hence why he'd been chosen for this visiting professorship. And here she was—operating alongside him. She couldn't quite take it in.

'Now we'll start reducing the posterior aspect of the fracture. I'll be fixing one eight-hole, three-and-a-half-millimetre reconstruction plate, securing it in place with two screws at either end.' George spoke in his normal tone, knowing his words would be picked up on the microphone that was situated within the theatre.

When the viewing gallery had been built, the actual operating room had undergone a transformation as well. Small cameras had been installed, enabling everyone to see the procedure being performed. Apart from general teaching, this was the first time the theatre had been used for a visiting specialist.

'I'll need an inter-fragmentary screw as well to keep that acetabular margin firmly in place,' George said once the reconstruction plate had been positioned.

'Swab.' A few moments later, George glanced at Melody and she read the satisfaction in his gaze. The look made her feel as though they were sharing a special secret. 'I'm happy with that,' he stated. 'Check X-ray, please.' While they waited for the radiographer to take the X-ray, George looked up at the viewing gallery and explained some of the finer points of the surgery he'd just performed.

Melody allowed herself a brief glance up, only to see several heads in the gallery bowed as students, interns and registrars alike furiously took notes. Thanks to the cameras, though, it meant a permanent record would be kept of this procedure so anyone who had missed it could view it online through the hospital's link.

Melody had never been so relieved to walk out of theatre and into the changing rooms, leaving George to finish answering questions and the theatre staff to clean up. Operating with him had been a wonderful experience, but during the first few minutes of the procedure she'd been so acutely aware of him that her heart had been beating a wild tattoo against her ribs. Forcing her professionalism to the fore, Melody had pretended he was just like anyone else she'd operated with.

Although she hadn't been the centre of attention, Melody had still felt as though she were trapped like a mouse in a cage. All those people, watching everything they did. 'Relax,' she told herself as she had a quick shower. 'It's over.' Everything had gone fine. There had been no complications, no awkward moments. George had been very explicit in what he'd wanted each member of staff to do and Melody realised he was used to operating with strangers.

As she dried herself and headed to her locker, she knew there was no way she'd ever be able to cope with the pressures of a visiting professorship. She was a good surgeon and that was all she wanted. The opportunity to do further research into micro-surgical techniques of the hand and fingers was definitely enough to keep her occupied for quite some time.

She was just tucking in her shirt when two of the nurses who had been in Theatre with them came in.

'Hot-diggity,' Hilary said, fanning her face. 'He is one gorgeous man. Pity he's married.' Hilary giggled. 'Not that that would stop me.' She covered her mouth. 'Oops. Naughty me.'

'I thought he was a widower.' Evelyn angled her head to the side. 'That's what one of his assistants told me.' Evelyn looked at Melody. 'Have you heard anything, Melody?'

'About what?' Melody started to brush her curls. She hated gossip. When she'd been engaged to Emir, there had been a lot of gossip going on about her. Not only had Emir been cheating on her with several women, one of them had fallen pregnant. If it hadn't been for Evelyn, who had come and told Melody the truth about Emir's infidelities, she would have still been living in cloud cuckoo land.

Before she'd confronted her fiancé, a distraught Melody had asked her brother, Ethan, to make some discreet enquiries. When Ethan had confirmed it, Melody had called off the engagement. Then Emir had told her a German doctor was carrying his child and that the two of them were moving to Germany to raise their family.

That had hurt more than anything. Prior to their engagement, Emir had been adamant that he never wanted to have children. Melody had taken months to come to terms with the fact that she'd never be a mother if she married Emir and eventually she'd accepted that. Then to have him turn around and say he was more than willing to be a father to another woman's child had made Melody realise that Emir simply hadn't wanted to have children with *her*. He hadn't wanted *her*. He hadn't respected *her*. He hadn't truly loved *her*.

'About Professor Wilmont!' Hilary exclaimed, bringing Melody's thoughts back to the present. 'Honestly, Melody, you should get out from behind that desk or operating table or whatever it is you hide behind more often because that man is *so* hot.'

Melody clipped her unruly auburn hair back in its usual style. 'He's a great surgeon. That's what I know about him,' she replied. There was no way she was going to tell them that he set her blood pumping, made her knees go weak and took her breath away all with one smouldering, sexy look. She closed her locker. 'Are you both coming to the dinner tonight?'

'I have another shift,' Evelyn said.

'I couldn't afford it.' Hilary actually pouted. 'And lucky you—you get to sit next to him.'

'Enjoy it,' Evelyn offered with a genuine smile before Melody walked out of the room and headed back to her office. She needed to check her in-tray and make sure everything was up to date. Rick was absent from his desk, so she headed directly into her office and almost jumped in fright when she saw George seated comfortably next to her desk.

'George! I thought you'd gone.' And how had he changed so quickly? Her stomach lurched in delight at the sight of him, and her knees started to weaken. She told herself off for behaving like a ninny and forced her legs to work, walking over to her desk before quickly sitting.

'I wanted to thank you personally for assisting me at such short notice.'

Her smile was instant. 'It should be me who's thanking you for the opportunity. Or should I thank Mr Okanadu's emergency?'

George chuckled and the sound washed over her, warming her even further. 'Either way, it was great to be able to work with you.'

'You made everything easy for me—and the rest of the staff,' she added. She looked at him for a second, tilting her head to the side. 'Are you always so...direct in Theatre or is it just because you have an audience?'

He nodded. 'It's the audience. I've become accustomed to having people watch me.'

'Well, you're certainly very good at what you do.' She idly shifted some paper around before placing her hands palms down on the desk in an effort to control her wayward emotions. How was it that just his close presence was enough to turn her into a jittery, hormonal mess? The intercom buzzed and she was glad of something to do. She pressed the button. 'Yes, Rick?'

'I'm going now, Melody.'

'All right. See you tonight, Rick.'

'Yeah, but only if I can tie that bow-tie thing straight. Who made it a formal dinner, eh?'

'We can blame Carmel,' George called loudly, and Rick chuckled before saying goodbye. 'He's good,' George said. 'How long has he been working with you?'

'No.' Melody shook her head. 'The question you should be asking is how long have I been working with him? He's been the PA to the head of orthopaedics for the past three years. I only started six months ago.'

'How old is he? He looks about seventeen.'

'Shh.' Melody giggled. 'Don't tell him that. He's still trying to fight his cute baby face looks. He's twenty-four and an excellent PA.' Melody pulled her bag out of a drawer before locking her desk. 'When the head of department was taken ill at the beginning of this year, it was Rick who helped me find my feet. Without him, I'd have gone down the gurgler ages ago.'

'So you're not into hospital politics? Administration?'

'Not really.' Melody stood and motioned to the door. 'We'd better make a move or we'll end up being late for dinner.'

'Sure.' George followed her out of her office and waited while she locked it. Melody turned and bumped into him. She hadn't realised he'd been standing so close.

'Sorry,' she mumbled, and quickly took a step to the side. She glanced down at the floor, trying desperately to control the mass of tingles that were now raging rampantly throughout her body. Melody kept her head down as she moved a few steps away before raising her head to look at him. One of her curls managed to escape from its bonds and swung down beside her cheek.

To her astonishment, George reached out a hand towards her, as though he intended to tuck her hair behind her ear. Melody held her breath, her gaze darting erratically from his hand to his face and back to his hand again. Then George swallowed and dropped his hand back to his side, shoving it into his pocket. He clenched his jaw and took a step back, then glanced at her briefly before looking away, the moment slipping by.

'Ah—are you—? I mean—do you—um…?' She stopped and forced herself to take a steadying breath. 'How are you getting back to the hotel? Do you need a lift?'

George nodded, a slow smile forming on his lips. 'That would be great. Thanks.'

'Car park is this way.' Without waiting for further communication from him, Melody headed off down the corridor and turned right at the end. She opened a door and started heading down the stairs. She was acutely aware of George following her and it wasn't until they'd gone down three flights of stairs that she pushed open the door that led to the street.

'I'm parked over here,' she told him as they walked side by side.

'So, the previous head of orthopaedics? You said he was taken ill?'

'Yes, in February. He was working out this year and had planned to retire at the end of it. Now he's retired early.'

'So he's not coming back?'

'No. He's officially resigned from the hospital.'

'Which leaves you in charge?'

'They have to advertise the position. I'm only Acting Head until the end of this year,' she told him as she stopped by her white Jaguar Mark II. She unlocked the door. 'So when you finish your tour, do you want a job?' She chuckled, but even the thought of working closely with George day in, day out filled her with a mass of tingles. She pushed the idea aside.

'*This* is your car?' George frowned in disbelief.

'Yep.' Melody climbed in and reached over to unlock the passenger door. 'One thing about old cars, they don't usually come with the mod-cons like central locking,' she said as George slid onto the comfortable leather seat.

'Wow.'

'I know, right? Such an awesome car. I love it.' She put her seat belt on. 'It was a present from my brothers when I passed my final orthopaedic exams. David's a mechanic,' she added by way of explanation. 'Both he and Ethan like restoring old cars.'

'Are they both mechanics?'

She chuckled as she put the key into the ignition before starting the engine. 'Ethan likes to think he is but he's more a mechanic of people—also known as a general surgeon.'

'Huh. Does he work at St Aloysius as well? I'd like to meet him.'

'He used to.' Melody chatted as she began to exit the car park. 'Ethan used to be Head of General Surgery but earlier this year he had a mild heart attack. He's OK now,' she added, then grinned. 'More than OK, actually, as he recently got married.' Melody sighed romantically. 'It was a wonderful wedding in the lovely wine district, just inland of Sydney.'

'Around Whitecorn?' he asked, and she was surprised.

'Yes. Pridham and Whitecorn hospitals. That's where he now works as a general surgeon.'

'I have friends there. Donna and Philip Spadina. Donna tutored me through medical school.'

'What? Ethan and CJ's wedding was *at* Donna and Philip's small vineyard.'

'Ah… I love being back in Australia,' he sighed. 'Everyone knows someone who knows someone else. Nice and close.'

She chuckled. 'Have you been homesick for Australia?'

'Just a bit.'

'Has it been difficult, jet-setting around the world, showing off your brilliance?' Melody couldn't resist teasing lightly. Oh, my gosh, she thought. I'm flirting with him! George laughed and the sound washed over her with joy. She'd made him laugh. Evelyn's words floated in the back of her mind, stating that she thought George was a widower. Was it true?

'The beginning was difficult, getting into the swing of things, but then it evened out. Now I think this part of the tour is the most…tedious.' He shifted in his chair, turning to face her slightly. 'I don't mean to imply that I don't like being here at St Aloysius—or any other hospital, for that matter.'

'It's OK, George. I understood what you meant. It's not the work, it's the day-to-day grind, especially when the end is so close.'

'Thank you.' He shook his head. 'You get it. Carmel's fretting because she doesn't want it to end.'

'Perhaps she doesn't know what she's going to be doing when this is over.'

'That would bring uncertainty,' he mused, as though he hadn't considered it.

'What about you? What happens after you've written up all your reports and caught up with your friends?'

George sighed. 'I'll go back to my job at Melbourne General, I guess.'

'You guess?'

He chuckled. 'I don't know what I'm going to feel like doing. It's as though my life's in limbo but it's where I need to start in order to figure out what to do next.' George slowly shook his head, then changed the subject, turning the spotlight on her. 'And what about you? Are you going to apply for the job you're doing now?'

Melody tried to focus her thoughts. 'Probably not.'

'You *really* don't like the administration?'

'Not particularly. How about you?'

'It doesn't bother me. Especially after this year.'

'I guess you don't get much time to relax.'

'Not really. Depending on where we are or what we're doing, I sometimes get a bit of free time.' George shrugged, as though he didn't really care one way or the other.

Melody didn't envy him at all. For a moment she wasn't sure what to say and the silence began to stretch. *Say something*, she told herself. Anything to break the awkwardness that was enveloping both of them. 'So I guess the VOS definitely cuts into your family time.'

He glanced at her and frowned. Oops. Had she overstepped the mark?

She was just about to apologise for her statement when he said, 'It's not too bad. I managed to see one of my sisters when I was in New Zealand so that was a bonus.'

It was Melody's turn to frown as she pulled into the entrance of the hotel. The fact that he hadn't mentioned his wife made her wonder if Evelyn's assumption was correct. George glanced her way and saw the frown.

'Something wrong?' he asked.

Melody instantly smiled. 'Everything's fine.' She wanted to blurt out her question, to ask him about his wife, to know one way or the other whether the feelings she was having for him should be quashed or—or what? Was she planning on throwing herself at the handsome surgeon if he turned out to be single? Or was she going to be professional and remain detached? Still, the question seemed to be going round and round in her head like a broken record. Did George have a wife waiting for him in Melbourne or was she—? Melody shook her head and sighed. 'I guess I'll see you a bit later at the dinner.'

'As the dinner is in my honour, you can count on it.' He gave a playful wink as he climbed from the car and shut the door.

Melody drove to her apartment, even more confused than before. Why had he winked? That wink had caused a new wave of tingles to flood her body, had made her heart beat faster and encouraged her to hope that he was, indeed, not married. She wasn't the type of girl to go after a married man, not after Ian. She wasn't the type of girl to suffer from instant infatuation, or at least that's what she'd believed this morning.

Now, after meeting George Wilmont and spending so much time with him today, she knew that if the right man came along, she was definitely prone to instant attraction because that's exactly what she felt for George!

CHAPTER FOUR

GEORGE SCANNED THE crowded outer room that was starting to fill up. When he'd first started on the VOS tour, he'd been astounded at the number of dinners he needed to attend. Now, though, he was an expert at them. At least in his medical lecturing he'd been able to write new lectures, sharing information he'd garnered throughout the tour.

His gaze scanned the room as people started making their way through to the ballroom. He checked his watch. Five minutes over time already. Carmel would become agitated soon. Where was Melody? They couldn't start without her. She was the MC.

He looked around again and realised he'd been unconsciously searching for her the entire time. Someone came up, introduced themselves and shook hands with him. George listened to the questions being asked of him and gave the usual replies, all the while allowing his gaze to flick to the door every few seconds.

'Excuse me.' Carmel politely interrupted his conversation, drawing him to one side. 'It's time to begin.'

'Melody's not here yet,' George pointed out.

'If we wait any longer, we'll be getting to bed after midnight.'

'We'll be getting to bed after midnight anyway.' He smiled wryly at his friend, his eyes pleading. 'We can wait for her, right?'

'Ah...so you *do* like her.' Carmel's tone changed to one of delight. 'I knew it.'

'She's nice. Everyone likes her,' George felt compelled to point out.

'It's OK to like someone, George.' Carmel's words were soft and encouraging. 'You're not meant to spend the rest of your life alone, you know.'

George shrugged a shoulder at his friend's words because he wasn't sure how to respond. He wasn't used to having these sorts of feelings, especially when he carried the memory of his wife with him wherever he went.

Carmel glanced at her phone to check the time. 'We can give her another five minutes and I'm only acquiescing this once because it's great to see you taking a chance to move forward.'

'But I'm not.'

'Lie to me, George, but don't lie to yourself.' She fixed him with a firm stare before heading off.

George exhaled harshly and ran a finger around the collar of his shirt. The room was becoming too stuffy and he sneaked out the door, heading towards the lobby. Was Carmel right? Was he lying to himself? It was true that ever since meeting Melody Janeway that morning, he'd had a difficult time removing her from his thoughts. She was beautiful, intelligent and funny. What a lethal combination!

He checked his watch again. Ten minutes late. Was she lost? Was she at the wrong hotel? Why was she late? Veronique had been three hours late and he'd been telling himself back then not to worry. Yet all the time she'd been— He stopped his train of thought. This was no time to be thinking about Veronique.

As soon as he saw Rick enter the hotel, he almost pounced on him. 'Where's Melody?'

'She's not here yet?' Rick asked in surprise, immediately pulling out his phone.

'No.'

'It's gone straight to voice mail. She's probably at the hospital. I'll ring the ward.'

'Thanks.' George started to relax. At least Melody hadn't been involved in an accident.

'She's just left?' Rick said into the receiver. 'Good. Thanks.' He disconnected the call. 'She left the hospital five minutes ago so she shouldn't be long now. She's a great doctor.' Rick grinned, then shook his head mockingly. 'Pathetic head of department but a great doctor.'

'I guess that's what's important.' George smiled, feeling more at ease. 'Why don't you go and tell Carmel what's happening?' he suggested. 'I'll wait here for Melody.'

'You just don't want to face Carmel,' Rick stated with a knowing nod, and George laughed.

'Caught me out.' As he watched Rick go, he knew that wasn't the reason he didn't want to go in. He wanted to see Melody with his own eyes. To make sure she was OK. There were still other people trickling in so she wasn't all *that* late, even though his aide would disagree. George walked over to the wall and looked unseeingly at a painting. Why? Why was he so anxious to see Melody?

On the drive from the hospital to the hotel, he'd been happy in her company, chatting and getting to know her. With the schedule he'd maintained throughout the tour, he'd rarely had the opportunity to get to know the people he'd worked alongside. Every week it was somewhere new, every week it was giving the same information to a different group of faces. He'd met some lovely people, some overly academic professionals, and some people with no sense of humour whatsoever.

Yet from the moment he'd shaken hands with Melody Janeway, experiencing that instant jolt of awareness, he'd been captivated by her. Her twinkling green eyes, her unruly auburn hair with the odd curl that didn't seem to want to do as it was told. He liked her laugh, he liked the sound of her voice and he liked her intelligence. Never in his life had been so instantly drawn to someone. Was it wrong to want to know her better, or was it foolish not to? As Carmel had said, he wasn't meant to live the rest of his life alone.

'George?'

At the sound of her voice, he spun on his heel and gazed at her. There it was again, that instant jolt of awareness.

'What are you doing out here? I thought you were supposed to have started by now.'

George felt as though he'd just been slugged in the solar plexus. She looked…stunning. Wearing an off-the-shoulder, black beaded dress that shimmered when she walked, Melody was a vision of loveliness. The dress was expertly cut, falling to mid-calf, and moulded superbly to her shape. Her auburn tresses had been wound on top of her head with a few loose tendrils springing down. She wore a necklace with a small square-cut diamond pendant and matching diamond studs in her ears.

'I wanted to wait for you.' His tone was thick with desire. 'I'm glad I did. You look…breath-taking.'

His words were sincere and the way he was looking at her made her feel light-headed. George really thought she was breath-taking? She took a small step closer, her gaze never leaving his. 'Thank you, George. That's a lovely thing to say.'

'And I mean it.'

She smiled brightly, still trying to come to terms with how incredible he looked in his black tuxedo, white shirt and bow-tie. When she'd walked in and seen him, her knees had almost given way and as she was wearing three-inch heels, the result would have been disastrous. Thankfully, she'd been able to hold onto a vestige of control.

George cleared his throat and pasted on a polite smile, crooking his elbow towards her. 'Shall we?'

They headed towards the ballroom and as they headed towards the top table, several people stopped George to ask questions or shake his hand. Melody walked ahead of him and George realised her dress had a split at the back, revealing a generous amount of her legs. Her shapely calves, the indentations of the backs of her knees and a brief glimpse of her thighs.

He swallowed and forced himself to look away, concentrating on the carpet, but once he reached the table, he couldn't help but sneak one last glance at her sexy legs. A few minutes later Melody was at the podium, apologising for the delay as she'd been called to the ward. She spoke so naturally, so confidently and looked so exquisite that afterwards he couldn't remember a word she'd actually said.

Once she'd finished her introduction, George stood and thanked her, pulling his professionalism from thin air so he could concentrate on what he needed to say, rather than on the woman whose floral scent was winding its way around him, creating havoc with his senses.

As he spoke, commanding the attention of the two hundred or so people gathered tonight, Melody began to relax, enjoying listening to his deep, melodious voice. She admired the way he threw in little anecdotes, working his way through his speech without the prompting of notes.

'You didn't do too badly,' Rick later commented, as he crouched by her chair.

'I could say the same thing for your bow-tie. How long did it take you to do that?'

'Ages. I only arrived a few minutes before you and I didn't even have the excuse of having stopping by the hospital.'

Melody raised her eyebrows. 'Checking up on me?' She took a sip from her water glass.

'George was concerned,' Rick told her with a shrug, and pointed to her glass. 'Not drinking tonight?'

She shook her head. 'The patient I saw in the ward may need surgery later.'

'Oh, yeah, you doctors have *all* the fun.' He glanced over to where one particular nurse had caught his attention. 'Er—I'll catch up with you later.' He straightened his bow-tie. 'There are a few nurses I want to impress while I'm dressed like this.'

Melody chuckled as he headed off but his words stayed with her. George had been concerned about her? She sneaked a glance at him as he spoke to someone. Had he really been worried about her, or the dinner starting on time?

Melody's head was starting to spin. She needed some space. She picked up her clutch purse and stood.

George watched Melody walk away from the table, his gaze drawn to the sway of her hips and her gorgeous legs. Why was she so captivating? He forced himself to look away, returning his attention to Carmel, only to realise his aide was watching Melody as well.

In fact, all the men at the table were watching her. 'Wow!' one of them remarked. 'Melody looks—'

'Like a woman,' one of the other men finished, and they all laughed.

George felt his hackles begin to rise. 'Problem?'

'This is the first time Melody's worn a dress to an official departmental function,' someone told him. 'So it's the first opportunity we've had to see her in anything other than business clothes.'

'She sure looks different. If being head of department means Melody dresses like that, she has my support for the job.'

'She's also a colleague of yours.' George's tone was clipped, disgusted by their chauvinism. 'An intellectual woman who is a brilliant surgeon. Please provide her with the respect she deserves.' He knew his tone sounded pompous and arrogant but he didn't care. Women had to work twice as hard as men in this world and Melody had done just that. What she needed was to be respected for that, not for what she chose to wear. 'You were saying, Carmel?' George turned his attention to his aide.

He still found it hard to concentrate on what Carmel was saying, his thoughts caught up with Melody and the fact that she wasn't beside him. He was astonished how much he felt her absence, given that when he'd woken up this morning he hadn't even met her! When she returned, he immediately stood and held the chair for her as she sat.

'Thank you.' She smiled at him and again he felt his gut tighten. Clearing his throat, he included her in the conversation with Carmel, valuing her opinion. Ten minutes later, Melody's phone rang.

'Excuse me.' She fished it from her purse. George was aware of her quiet voice as she spoke and moments later she ended the call. 'It looks as though I'll have to pass on coffee,' she told everyone at the table.

'Emergency?' George asked.

'Yes.' At the interested glances she received, she elaborated. 'Fractured olecranon, radius and ulna. My registrar says the patient is showing signs of compartment syndrome.'

'Can't your registrar deal with it?' Carmel asked hopefully. 'You are the MC, after all.'

'Sorry, but it's a private patient,' Melody explained as she picked up her bag.

'I think she's fulfilled her MC duties for the night,' George told his aide.

When she stood, all the men rose to their feet. 'Oh, please, sit down,' she said with a smile, before turning to George. 'Sorry to run out on your welcome dinner but these things can't be helped.'

George remained standing. 'No need to apologise. Besides, we're almost done.' They shook hands and again Melody felt that warm buzz of excitement spread up her arm. She nodded politely before dropping his hand and walking away from the table. She was stopped a few times on her way out but as the room was filled with people linked to the medical profession, they all understood when she said she had an emergency.

She took the lift down to the ground floor, and while waiting for the valet to collect her car she fought for self control. In less than twenty-four hours she'd met a man who affected her like no one else ever had, and she was having difficulty getting him out of her mind. She drove carefully to the hospital, heading straight for the emergency theatres. She changed into theatre clothes and went in search of her registrar.

'Nice hairdo,' Andy, her registrar, teased, and she laughed.

'How's Mr Potter?'

'Coping well. I've explained what's happening to him and he's signed the consent form. The instruments and theatre are ready. We're just waiting on the all-clear from the anaesthetist.'

'Excellent.' Melody went to see her patient and have a word with the anaesthetist before checking the notes Andy had taken during the evening. When everything was organised, they started to scrub.

Once in Theatre, Melody had her mind in gear and off George Wilmont. She focused her attention on Mr Potter's arm, which he'd injured while playing tennis.

Both she and Andy concentrated on what they were doing but, as always, enjoyed a bit of conversation while performing their duties. 'Glad the VOS is finally under way?' Andy asked.

'Most definitely. One day down, four more to go.' Andy had known she hadn't wanted to act as host for the VOS and had tolerated her mounting apprehensiveness with a cool, calm and collected attitude.

'I take it the dinner went well.'

'Yes.' Melody frowned.

'The VOS seems like a nice guy.'

'Did you manage to get to the viewing gallery this afternoon?'

'I came in late. Couldn't see much. You, on the other hand, certainly had a bird's eye view. How did that happen?'

Melody chuckled and told him about Mr Okanadu's cancellation while she inserted a drain into Mr Potter's arm, which would hopefully ensure against further recurrence of compartment syndrome.

'What was it like? I mean, operating with one of the greats?'

She heard the door to her theatre open but thought nothing of it. 'What was it like? It was scary, that's what it was like.' Melody paused for a moment. 'Not scary assisting George, that part was fine, but having all those people watching? No, thank you.'

'George, eh?' Andy teased. 'On a first-name basis already?'

'What do you expect me to call him? Professor? His Excellency? Brilliant Surgeon?'

The sexiest man alive? She kept that last one to herself but smiled beneath her mask. She heard someone slowly walk around the table and come to stand behind Andy.

Melody frowned and raised her gaze to look just past Andy's shoulder. Her eyes widened in surprise as she looked directly into George's deep brown eyes.

'I'd settle for the last one,' he said in that deep voice she was becoming accustomed to.

Melody quickly put a dampener on the frisson of awareness his close proximity caused her. For a second she thought she'd spoken her last description out loud and lowered her gaze, forcing herself to concentrate on her work. She was almost ready to close.

'George,' she said, hoping her voice didn't betray the surprise, elation and confusion she felt at his unannounced presence. 'What brings you here?'

'Curiosity.'

'For compartment syndrome?'

He chuckled at her words and she momentarily allowed the sound to wash over her.

'Introduce us,' Andy whispered, and Melody cleared her throat.

'George, this is my registrar, Dr Andy Thompson, who is going to help me to close up Mr Potter's arm so we can get out of here.'

'Nice to meet you, Andy,' George remarked. Although he was wearing full theatre garb, George remained on the outer perimeter of the operating table.

'Likewise, sir.'

'Shouldn't that be "Sir Brilliant Surgeon"?' she teased Andy, as she started suturing.

'No. That was what *you* were supposed to call him,' Andy replied.

She glanced over at George. 'I take it coffee was served without a hitch?'

'Yes.'

'Good.' There was silence for a while as Melody and Andy continued with their work.

'It must have been a good night,' Andy said. 'At least, judging from Melody's flash hairstyle that's now hidden beneath her theatre cap.'

'It was,' George replied, his gaze meeting with Melody's for a few seconds.

'Right. We're done,' Melody announced, forcing herself to look away. She nodded to the anaesthetist before heading out of Theatre. She de-gowned and took a deep breath. George followed her, removing his own theatre garb as well. 'So why did you really come down here?' she asked as she headed into the doctors' tea room so she could write up the operation notes. When he didn't reply, she stopped and turned around, unsure whether he was still there. He collided with her, his hands instinctively resting on her waist to control his balance.

'Sorry,' she mumbled, and lifted her chin to gaze up at him. They were standing just inside the door to the empty tea room and Melody didn't know whether she wanted it to fill up or stay deserted. 'I wasn't sure if you were…still…' Her voice trailed off. Aware that George hadn't removed his hands from her body, his touch burned through the green cotton of her theatre scrubs, making her intensely aware of their close proximity.

She felt a smouldering fire within her come to life. Her breathing became shallow, her lips parting to allow the air to escape. Her knees started to weaken as his thumb started moving in tiny circles, fanning the blaze.

His brown eyes were clouded with desire, his breathing as uneven as her own. 'Why did I really come?' he asked. They were close, so close that his breath fanned her cheek as he spoke. He smelled good—too good—and the scent of him only exacerbated the weakness of her knees. She knew she had to be careful, knew she had to keep control of her habit of jumping into the fire before assessing the risks. She'd been badly burned in relationships before and knew her inherent optimism of wanting to always see the best in people could get her into trouble. Was George Wilmont trouble? Was he married? Was he a widower? She still had no clue, and if it was the former then she wanted nothing to do with him, other than being the professional host the VOS required her to be.

'Melody, I…uh…' He paused and shook his head. 'I

really didn't think this through,' he muttered, as he took a step away.

'Think what through?' She held her breath, her body zinging with anticipation. George was rattled and she secretly hoped it was *her* that had rattled him and even then, only because *he* had rattled her.

'Coming here. Walking into your theatre. Jabbering at you now.' He pushed a hand through his hair and shook his head. 'Sorry. This was a mistake.' He went to leave but turned when she called his name.

'Now that you're here, there is a question I want to ask you.'

'Oh?'

It was Melody's turn to feel awkward and unsure but after a moment of reflection she forged ahead. 'I'm sorry if this seems forward or overly personal but—are you married?'

He raised his eyebrows at the question. 'Married? No.'

A bubble of laughter rose in her and she momentarily covered her mouth. He wasn't married. This was a good thing, right? It meant that the feelings she was developing towards him weren't wrong, that she didn't need to feel any guilt at being attracted to him. 'Oh. It's in your dossier.'

'Really? You must have received an old copy of the information.' He glanced down at the floor for a moment before meeting her gaze once more. 'I'm a widower. My wife passed away eighteen months ago.'

'I'm sorry, George.' Her words were heartfelt.

'It wasn't your fault.'

'No, but losing someone close to you is never easy.'

He nodded. 'You'd think, seeing death as often as we do, that we'd have better coping mechanisms in place.'

'You'd think so, but it's rarely that cut and dried. It can take many years to get over a loved one's passing.'

'See?' He held one hand out towards her. 'That's exactly how I think. You...*get* me.' He sighed. 'Many people don't.'

'They expect you to move on with your life?'

He nodded. 'I know I'll have to—eventually—but...' He stopped.

'When you're ready, it'll happen.' Her words were soft. 'I haven't lost a spouse, but I have lost close friends and family. Grief takes time and that time is different for everyone.'

'Yes.' He raked a hand through his hair. 'And then you meet someone new and that person makes you...feel.'

'Feel what?'

'Just *feel*.' George shook his head. 'You made me *feel* today, Melody. That's what I've come here to tell you because I don't understand it and I didn't ask for it and... I just wanted to be open and honest and clear.'

'Clear? About what?' Feeling emboldened by their frank discussion, Melody took it one step further. 'That we're attracted to each other?'

'You feel it, too?' His words were soft, deep and filled with a mixture of confusion and longing.

'Yes.'

'Well... OK. Uh—I guess the next question is, do we do anything about it?'

'That *is* the question, and I don't know the answer.' She shrugged her shoulders.

George leaned against the bench and the two of them stared at each other. 'Neither do I.'

CHAPTER FIVE

LATER, AS MELODY drove home from the hospital, she reflected on the way she and George had just stared at each other, neither of them sure what to do or say next. They were attracted to each other and she was relieved they'd actually discussed this openly. Her past relationships had been riddled with lies.

So many lies. So many deceptions. So many mistakes. That's what her adult dating life had consisted of, which made George Wilmont's open frankness all the more appealing. It ran true to form that the next man to make her heart pound would be another unobtainable man, although thankfully not for the same cheating reasons as before.

George was single. George was devastatingly handsome. George lived over nine hundred kilometres away from her.

'It's just your luck in men,' she told herself as she opened the door to her apartment. She headed to her room and changed from the expensive evening gown into her comfortable pyjamas. It had been a long and hectic day, a day that would be seared in her memory for the rest of her life as it was the day she'd met George. She could clearly remember her father saying, 'Most days just run one into the other and then, out of nowhere, comes a day that can change your life for ever.'

'Oh, Dad,' Melody whispered. 'You were so right.' Her

mind was full of mixed emotions—happiness, confusion, excitement and anticipation. What on earth would happen tomorrow? In order to wind her mind down from the hectic and tumultuous day, Melody headed to bed and pulled out the copy of her latest medical journal. She opened it to the paper she'd read the night before—a paper by Professor George Wilmont. Now that she'd met the man, when she re-read the paper she could hear his voice coming through the words on the page. That deep, sensual, melodious voice of his that was soothing and divine and…and that mouth as it moved to form words and…

When she almost dropped the journal on her face, Melody realised she was falling asleep. Putting the journal down beside her, she switched off the light and snuggled down, all too clearly recalling the way he could stand in front of a packed lecture room and enthral his audience. With visions of him in her head, she drifted off to sleep, a small smile on her lips.

The smile was still there the next morning as she awoke to her alarm with thoughts of George Wilmont still dancing around the edge of her dreams. She opened her eyes and stared at the ceiling. 'I dreamed about George.' She closed her eyes and turned off her alarm. How could she dream about a man she hardly knew? He was only here for another four days.

'Four days!' she told herself as she shoved the bed covers aside and headed to the bathroom. Turning on the shower taps, Melody allowed the spray of the hot water to calm her thoughts. 'You can do this,' she told her reflection as she dried her hair. 'You're a professional. Just go to the hospital, smile politely at him, do your work and just—just concentrate on—on…' She desperately thought of something else to think about before the answer hit. 'Your research.'

How had he managed to do it? Ever since Emir had broken her heart, ditching her for a life with another woman, Melody had focused solely on her work. True, being acting head of department was enough to keep her busy and she'd been grateful for that, but it still raised questions about her future.

Would she ever be a bride and not just a bridesmaid? Would she ever be a mother and not just an aunt? When would it be her turn? Would it *ever* be her turn? Had she missed her window? She wasn't getting any younger and her biological clock was definitely starting to tick. Was she just going to let two bad apples ruin what might be her opportunity to find a good apple? Could she risk her heart once again? Should she allow her fancy to have free rein or would George break her heart? If he did, where would she be then? Three times defeated by love!

Her thoughts continued to war as she finished getting ready for work, eating a light breakfast of juice and toast before driving to work. When she arrived, she made sure her cool, calm and collected professional façade was in place as she walked to her office. 'Good morning, Rick,' she said as she breezed in through the door.

'Well, hello. Aren't you looking like the consummate professional today?' her PA teased. She'd dressed in one of her power suits. Navy trousers and jacket and white silk shirt. Her hair was clipped back at her nape in the hope that her unruly curls would behave themselves.

'Thank you,' she replied as she quickly flicked through her in-tray. She had five minutes before she needed to head to the ward, so she dealt with some paperwork before returning the papers to Rick so he could process them.

'Gee, thanks,' he muttered, and she smiled sweetly at him. 'Off to ward round?'

'Yes.'

'Nervous?'

'Who, me?' she joked, and reached for her stethoscope.

'There's nothing else I have to do this morning? No more speeches? Introductions?'

'No. As far as George's schedule is concerned, he's accompanying you on the ward round and then he's back off to the lecture theatre. You're in clinic while he's lecturing to the fourth- and sixth-year medical students. Dinner this evening is at the hotel George is staying at.'

'Great. Thanks,' she said, then headed towards the ward. With every step she took, she did her best to calm her increasing nerves. She was going to see George again. Would she feel the same immediate connection as yesterday? Would it be stronger?

When she entered the ward, she felt as though she was going to be physically sick, her stomach was churning so much. It was ridiculous that simply the thought of seeing George was making her feel so nervous. Still, she took a deep breath and pushed open the door to the discussion room, where everyone congregated for the ward round meetings, only to find George and his team weren't there.

'Huh.' She couldn't help the deflation she felt. Why wasn't he here? Where was he? Were they still coming for her ward round?

Several medical students, interns, physiotherapists and nurses turned to look at her expectantly. Some murmured good morning, and Melody politely returned the greeting. There were more people than usual and she frowned, knowing it was due to George. Everyone wanted to learn, watch and absorb everything he did during his time there, and rightly so. It wasn't every day that visiting professors came to the hospital. It would make for a slower ward round, but it couldn't be helped. After all, this was a teaching hospital.

'There you are, Melody,' the CNC said as she came bustling in. 'I've just received a call from Rick, who wanted

you to know Professor Wilmont and his team are stuck
in traffic.'

Melody took a deep breath and let it out slowly, thinking fast. She was glad George and his team were OK and
that nothing bad had happened to them. 'Thank you.' But
what should she do now? Should she wait to see if George
arrived within the next ten minutes or should she start the
round without them? As a general rule, ward round started
on time, regardless of who was or wasn't there. If ward
round was late, it meant the catering and cleaning staff
would be inconvenienced as it would interfere with their
routines, the nursing staff would be running late all day
and it also wasn't fair to the patients.

Melody followed the clinical nurse consultant back to
her desk and reached for the phone. 'Rick?' she said a moment later. 'More information, please.'

'There's a car crash on Frost Road that's blocking traffic. Are you going to wait for them?'

'I'm not sure. Did Carmel give any more details?'

'She said they could be five minutes or five hours. She
was sounding pretty stressed.'

'OK. We can't keep everyone waiting, and if George
misses the entire ward round, he can just join tomorrow's,
can't he?'

'Who are you trying to convince?' Rick laughed.

'Keep me informed of the situation.'

'Will do.'

Melody replaced the receiver. 'Thank you,' she said to
the CNC. 'I'll be starting the ward round on time, Sister.'

'Of course, Doctor,' the CNC replied with a nod. Melody returned to the discussion room, where people were
talking quite animatedly about the turn of events. She was
swamped with questions as soon as she walked through
the door.

'Is Professor Wilmont coming today or not?' one nurse asked.

'I have no idea. He's stuck in traffic. We'll be starting the round on time, though.'

'But you can't,' another complained.

'Yeah. This is my day off and I've specifically come in to watch him.'

'So have I.'

'I've cancelled a meeting,' someone else said.

'Well, I can't control peak-hour traffic any more than Professor Wilmont can,' Melody stated. This was not a good beginning to the day. 'We'll be starting the ward round in…' she glanced at her watch '…three minutes. Thank you.'

She walked out and headed to the ward kitchen. She needed coffee—and fast. She made herself half a cup and drank it down before returning to the discussion room to start the round. As they went from patient to patient, Melody kept checking the doorway, hoping George and his team would arrive.

They were halfway through the round when she looked up, straight into a pair of brown eyes that instantly melted her insides. George! His silent arrival threw her off guard and she faltered for a second but quickly managed to recover.

As they moved on to the next patient, Melody took the opportunity of announcing his presence. 'Glad you could finally make it, Professor Wilmont.' Several people turned to look at him. He merely nodded, not a smile in sight. 'I take it this morning's traffic jam will ensure you don't forget Sydney in a hurry,' she said lightly, and a few people chuckled. 'And now we come to Mrs Hammond. How are you this morning?' she asked her patient.

'Not bad, not bad, dearie. Got a bigger crowd than usual, I see.'

'Yes.' Melody smiled back and started her spiel on Mrs Hammond's injuries. Melody's stomach was knotted up again and she worked hard to control her involuntary emotional response to seeing George again. Yesterday hadn't been imagined. Her attraction to him was real. Very real.

After they'd finished the round, they returned to the discussion room, where Melody usually answered questions, as well as asking a few herself. She wasn't at all surprised when many people asked their questions of George and she was pleased when he checked with her before answering them.

Mindful of George's tight schedule, Melody checked her watch and called for a final three questions. He shot her a grateful look. Almost a minute later Carmel appeared in the doorway, ready to wrap things up.

As people starting filing out of the room, Carmel came up to her. 'I need to speak to you,' she said, her tone carrying a hint of annoyance, before she headed over to George. Melody wondered what on earth she'd done to annoy Carmel.

George was still talking to a few people and Melody needed to check on Mr Potter, who was still in the critical care unit under close supervision. 'I need to check on a patient and then I'll be in my office,' she told Carmel.

She nodded then politely interrupted George's conversation. Melody left, trying to figure out what was going on as she headed to CCU. Mr Potter's compartment syndrome was showing no signs of returning and Melody was pleased with his progress. He would need to have his drains taken out in a few days' time. She wrote up her notes, releasing Mr Potter back to the orthopaedic ward before heading to her office. No sooner had she sat in her chair than her door opened and an angry-looking Carmel stormed in.

'I wasn't at all impressed, Melody.'

'With what?' she asked, feeling her hackles begin to rise.

'You started the ward round without George!'

'What was I supposed to do? Wait for him?'

'He is the visiting orthopaedic surgeon,' Carmel pointed out.

'Who just happened to be stuck in a traffic jam. It wasn't my fault, Carmel. Besides, if it means that much to him, he can just come tomorrow.'

'But he was scheduled to come this morning.'

'And he did.'

'You still could have waited.'

'No, Carmel, I couldn't. Firstly, I have patients who are in hospital for treatment. That means physio and OT appointments. It means social workers calling on them. Time for their family and friends to visit. Meals need to be served. Blood tests and X-ray appointments need to be organised. If ward round is late then everything else is thrown off for the rest of the day. Secondly, I was also trying to keep to George's own schedule, which you're so rigid about adhering to.'

Carmel opened her mouth but Melody was all fired up. After all, she was a redhead and once she got going it was hard to stop her. 'Don't you even think of blaming me for this morning. I had no control over George being late, and just because you're angry and frustrated it doesn't mean you can look to me as your scapegoat. Accept the situation, Carmel. Accept that the ward round started without George.'

'But it was down on his schedule that he was to take the ward round.'

'*Take* the ward round? No. Your schedule was wrong. As far as I was concerned, George was merely *joining* my ward round. I'm in charge of that ward, Carmel. Not you, not George. If I'm away, the job falls to my senior registrar, Andy Thompson. As a visiting dignitary, surely

George would realise that he has no real say in the treatment of my patients?'

'I do realise that,' George said from the doorway, and both Melody and Carmel turned to look at him. Neither of them had heard him enter and she wondered how long he'd been standing there. His words made her feel a little better but she was still angry with the way this entire morning had been handled.

'I'm glad to hear it,' she snapped.

'Why are you angry with me?' He spread his arms wide.

'Because you're the VOS. You know how ward rounds and hospitals work and, therefore, you should instruct your team accordingly.'

'You're right.' George crossed the room to stand next to them. 'Carmel, you promised me you'd be calm. Delays happen.'

'I *am* calm.' The words were said between clenched teeth and George couldn't help but smile. He placed a hand on his friend's shoulder. 'Diana was asking for your help in the lecture theatre. The Bluetooth isn't connecting properly today and one of the cables is missing.'

'Ugh!' Carmel growled. 'I *knew* today was going to be one of the bad days.' With that, George's PA stormed from the room.

'You'll have to excuse her. She's really a lovely person deep down inside but she's overly efficient, overly organised and overly obsessive-compulsive when it comes to schedules. A typical type A personality who doesn't know how to relax.'

Melody sighed, her earlier annoyance with Carmel dissipating. 'My brother used to be a type A personality. Then he survived a heart attack and changed his ways, thank goodness.'

He smiled. 'Thank you for understanding. It's been a very strange morning. Carmel had one of her hissy fits when I got out of the car to see if I could help. Thankfully, no one was badly injured so I returned to the car.' He tugged at the knot of his tie. 'Sometimes I wonder why I'm putting myself through this.'

'What? Wearing a tie?' she joked, hoping to lift the serious frown that now creased his brow. He stopped pacing and looked at her, the corners of his mouth twitching up slightly.

'You know what I mean. Just between you, me and the gatepost, I'm sick and tired of being handled all the time. It took a while to get used to and most of the time I can accept it, but on mornings such as these, when things are out of our control, Carmel goes off on one of her tangents.' George raked his hand through his hair and then shook his head. 'I probably shouldn't be talking to you about it. Sorry. I didn't mean to burden you with my problems.'

She didn't comment. She didn't want his confidences—they were too personal, and that was the last thing she needed, but who else did he have to talk to? 'Surely the professionalism between us can also extended to me offering my services as a sounding board?'

'Thank you.' He stared into her green eyes and she was glad she was still seated behind her desk as butterflies seemed to take flight in her stomach, twisting her emotions into nervous knots. How did he evoke such a reaction within her when she hardly knew him?

The tension between them was almost palpable, and it scared her. She didn't want this. She didn't want to become involved with a man who would be gone at the end of the week. Regardless of how he made her feel, he would leave and she would be left in limbo.

'I'd better go,' he said abruptly, breaking eye contact. Melody looked away as well, dragging in a deep breath.

'Yes.'

He walked over to the door and then stopped, turning to look at her. 'Are you coming up to the lecture theatre now?'

'Ah…' She stalled, knowing she should as his lecture was due to start within the next few minutes. 'I'll be along directly,' she told him.

Without another word, he left her office and Melody slumped forward over her desk. 'Why?' How was she supposed to find the strength to get through this week? No. She could do this. 'Pull yourself together,' she demanded. She tried to focus her thoughts on the work in front of her but her mind refused to budge from thoughts of George.

With one hypnotic glance, she was lost. He had a lovely smile, he had a great personality and he made her feel as though she was not only a woman of worth but also a woman of beauty. No man had ever made her feel that way before and that made George Wilmont different. The sensations he evoked were intensified, powerful and dynamic and that was very different from anything she'd felt before—*very* different.

CHAPTER SIX

'MELODY!' RICK'S VOICE made her spring up from her chair and glare at him standing by the door. 'You're supposed to be upstairs at the lecture.'

'How late am I?' How long had she been sitting there, thinking about George?

'It started ten minutes ago and the last thing I need is an angry text coming in from Carmel.'

'Carmel texted you asking where I was?'

'No.' Rick frowned. 'But I'm expecting one. That woman is crazy OCD when it comes to her scheduled events.'

'You can say that again,' Melody remarked as she shrugged into her suit jacket. 'I don't know why it should matter whether I'm a few minutes late. I'm not introducing him today. I'll just sneak in up the back and no one will notice.'

'George will,' Rick pointed out. 'He seems very…attentive towards you.' Her PA's tone was suggestive.

'He's just being a polite professional,' Melody countered.

'Ha! You should have seen him last night, pacing around with concern because you were late.' Rick waggled a finger at her. '*That* was not a polite or professional man.'

Melody sighed and shook her head. 'I don't have time to debate this with you.' As she headed out her office door, she pointed towards his desk. 'Do some…work stuff, will you?'

Rick chuckled and spread his arms wide. 'All done. This department is a well-oiled machine, thanks to me.'

Laughing at her PA's antics, Melody rushed to the lecture theatre, pushing Rick's comments from her thoughts and focusing on how best to sneak in. She didn't want George to think she wasn't interested in what he had to say because she was. When she arrived, he was just walking to the podium and she quickly sat down in one of the back seats. He looked up, his gaze melding with hers, as though he'd instinctively known where she was sitting, and her heart slammed wildly against her ribs.

Taking a breath, he began his talk, his gaze now roving over the audience before him. Melody found herself completely drawn in as he explained and illustrated, with the assistance of a detailed visual presentation, a new technique that could be adapted for both hip and knee arthroplasty. Afterwards, he was again inundated with questions and answered them patiently. He was brilliant. Handsome, successful, brilliant, and lived in a different city.

She should continue to recite that to herself over and over until Friday evening when her time with him would come to an end. George would leave here, just like all the other places, and she would do well not to let her thoughts have flights of fancy.

Melody returned to her office and collected her bag then headed to the restaurant across the street where they'd again be having lunch. This time there were only about thirty people, rather than the hullabaloo of yesterday, which meant they were in a smaller, more intimate function room.

'I didn't think you'd make it in time for the lecture but you did,' George commented as he sat down next to her, the warmth from his body, combined with his spicy after-shave, creating havoc with her senses.

'Sorry about missing the preamble.'

'No need to apologise. I thought an emergency might have come up after I'd left.'

'Nothing so justifiable. Just admin work.'

'Not your favourite, if I recall correctly.'

'I've learned if I keep on top of it, it isn't all that bad.'

'True.'

'Did you have to do a lot of admin work in your job prior to taking on the VOS?' Surely his work at Melbourne General Hospital was a safe topic. That way, she was finding out a bit more about him—but only in a professional capacity. She told herself that the questions she asked him should be the same questions she'd ask of any colleague and not just the colleague who was causing goose-bumps to pepper her skin at his nearness.

'I did. I was head of department, like you, but stepped down for these twelve months.' George leaned in closer to her and said in a conspiratorial whisper, 'And I'm not entirely sure I want to return.'

'Oh?' She tried not to stare at his mouth as he spoke. She tried to comprehend his words, the delicious scent he wore was creating havoc with her thoughts. 'To the hospital? To your job? To Melbourne?'

George stayed where he was for another moment, glancing at her mouth before meeting her gaze, causing another wave of delight to wash over her. Then he eased back in his chair, breathing in and sighing audibly, clearing his throat a little. 'I want to return to Melbourne, of course, and the hospital, but I'm not too sure about usurping the acting head as by all accounts he's doing an excellent job and…' George closed his eyes for a moment and shook his head. 'And I think I just need a break.'

'Understandable. The VOS is intensive and so is being head of a department.'

'Hmm.' He rubbed a hand over his chin, deep in thought. Melody watched him for another long moment, wanting to know his thoughts, wanting to be a sounding board for him, wanting to help him sort out this dilemma, but that wasn't her role. From the corner of her eye she saw that Carmel was headed their way and belatedly realised that while they'd been talking everyone else had taken their seats, the waiting staff already bringing out the entrées.

'Heads up,' she murmured, and George instantly looked towards where Carmel was almost upon them.

'Here's your next speech, George.' Carmel smiled encouragingly as she handed him some papers. 'There's no podium so—'

'Just stand and give it here?' he stated rhetorically and rose to his feet, putting the papers on the table in front of him and buttoning his jacket. As he did so, Melody reached for her water glass.

'Don't choke,' he said softly, giving her a wry smile.

'Funny,' she returned, just as softly, before he started his speech. She was impressed with the way he was able to make each speech sound unique and still provide interesting information on the chosen speciality of orthopaedics. Soon everyone was clapping and the rest of their meal was being served. The person seated to her left was a theatre nurse she'd worked with several times and the two of them talked about a variety of topics.

The entire time, she was acutely aware of George sitting on the other side of her, filling her water glass or offering her a bread roll or passing the butter. He was so attentive and yet everything he did seemed quite ordinary as he would often pass bread or butter to other people as well. Was she reading too much into every little thing? Every little move he made?

A few times she managed to share a moment of conversation with him, or join in the larger conversation going on around the table, but she couldn't shake the feeling that George was wanting to talk to her about something else, to continue their discussion about his position at Melbourne General or— Melody shook her head. She was going round the twist, trying to wrap her thoughts around the verbal and non-verbal conversations she and George were having. What she *was* completely conscious of, though, was the way just being next to him was increasing her awareness of him. How was she supposed to get the man out of her head when her body seemed to be tuning itself to his frequency?

Just as coffee was being served, Melody checked her watch and gasped when she realised the time.

'Something wrong?' George asked, a frown on his face.

'If I don't hustle, I'll be late for clinic.' She took a quick sip of her coffee.

'I'll walk back with you,' he stated.

'That's not necessary.' She drained her cup and stood. 'Besides, it will take you ages to get out of here. Everyone wants to have a word with you.'

'Well, they'll have to wait. I need to have a word with *you.*'

'Oh.' Melody wasn't quite sure what to say. She shifted away from the table and pushed her chair in as the nurse who'd been sitting beside her asked George a question. Melody watched as George turned from her and gave the nurse his attention, but instead of listening intently he actually fobbed the nurse off.

'I'm sorry, I have an important meeting and I'm running late. Will you be at the dinner tonight?'

The nurse nodded.

'How about we catch up then?'

'Sounds great,' the nurse replied, her eyes saying that

she'd like to do more than just talk with him. George, however, seemed oblivious of the nurse's intentions. It made Melody wonder whether George was a bit of a player, like Emir. She had no real reason to believe anything he said. She'd only met the man yesterday and already he'd told her that he was attracted to her. Wasn't that odd? Sure, he'd be gone by the end of the week but perhaps his entire plan was to enjoy a night or two of hot, meaningless sex with her before he left. She had no idea.

As she left the room where they'd had lunch, she saw Carmel noticing George was trying to leave early. Chances were that Carmel would stop him from leaving and if Melody waited, it would make her even later for clinic. She was out of the restaurant and heading towards the pedestrian crossing when George caught up with her.

'I thought I said I'd walk back with you.'

'From the look of things, you were otherwise engaged.'

'What are you talking about?'

'Forget it,' she said, angry with him for not knowing when women were throwing themselves at him. Surely an attractive man of his age knew how to reel in the females? She shook her head. He was no different from Emir. Emir, who'd had affairs with far too many female staff members at the hospital. Emir, who'd had such an easy, charming manner with women and used it to his best advantage. Well, she wasn't going to be taken in by another womaniser.

'So what did you want to talk about?' she asked as the pedestrian light turned green. She headed off across the road with George at her side, both equally as huffy as the other.

'I wanted to talk about what's going on between us.'

'What? Now?' She spread her arms wide as she crossed to the other side of the main road. 'George, we're both a little busy.' She pointed to the restaurant. 'Go back and do your job and leave me to do mine.'

'Wait. Why are you angry with me again?'

Melody opened the side door leading to a staircase that came out near her office. George followed her, their footsteps echoing off the walls. When they came out in the department, she headed up the corridor and went directly into her office. She held the door for him and closed it the instant he was inside.

'What is it that you couldn't wait to tell me?' she asked.

George didn't stop walking and paced restlessly around her office. 'Well, now I feel stupid with what's just happened and how—' He stopped and raked a hand through his hair, then looked at her for a long moment. 'You get in my head, Melody.'

'Huh?'

'Last night at the dinner, today at the lecture, just now at lunch—you get in my head and turn my thoughts to mush, and that's not good.'

'What are you talking about?'

He covered the distance between them with a few easy strides, then slipped his arms around her waist, bringing her closer. 'Do you feel that?'

The heat of his body? The spicy scent surrounding him? The way such a touch could cause her body to come instantly to life, so much so that she forgot all rational thought? 'Y-yeah.'

'That's what I'm talking about. You're in my head and I can't think straight when I'm near you, so I think to myself, Look, George, just keep your distance. Be professional. But then when I'm not around you, I'm thinking—about—you.' As he spoke the last two words, his gaze dipped to once more encompass her mouth. 'I think about kissing you. I think about holding you like this—and so much more.'

Melody closed her eyes against the heady combination

he was presenting. 'I know.' She needed to think clearly, to say what she needed to say. 'But how am I supposed to know you don't give this spiel to every woman you meet in a new town? You'll be gone at the end of the week and I'll probably never see you again.' She opened her eyes after speaking the words, wondering if he was listening to what she was saying or whether he was just intent on following the physical attraction between them.

'And I keep thinking that you might be the sort of woman to bewitch every man you meet. How am I supposed to know that you don't flirt with every new surgeon you meet? Or whether you really do like me for who I am—underneath the pomp and ceremony of the title—because, believe me, I've seen it all.'

'Have you?' Melody eased back slightly and George immediately dropped his arms.

'You'd be surprised.' George slumped down into the chair and sighed heavily. 'I guess for some people sex is just sex. It isn't linked with emotions or consequences, but for me, well, I'm afraid it comes with both.'

'So you never took anyone up on their...offer?' She walked around her desk and sat in her chair.

George met her gaze and slowly shook his head. 'I haven't been interested in anything but work—until yesterday morning when I met you.'

'Oh.' Again, there was that honesty. He was being as open and as forthcoming as he'd been last night when she'd finished in surgery. Both of them were clearly perplexed by this instant and mutual attraction yet both of them also knew it was pointless to give in to their feelings. However, when George held her the way he was, Melody had a difficult time remembering anything to do with rational thinking. 'I guess that does change things.'

'It does, Melody. It really does and I have this overwhelming urge to tell you about my life, to share my thoughts and concerns with you.'

'Such as whether or not to take up your previous position when you return?'

'Well, that and—and I want to tell you about my life, about the things that matter to me, about what movies I like, about what makes me laugh and—and about—my wife.'

'Your wife?' She was surprised at this.

'Yes. You see, the way you make me feel—which I had never expected to feel again—is making me question everything.'

'It is?'

'Yes.' He buried his face in his hands for a moment before standing to pace once more. 'Look, I'll just blurt it out because chances are, as I sneaked away from the lunch without Carmel's permission, she'll be calling me in a minute to tell me I'm late for my next appointment. Also, you have clinic so— Right.' He stopped pacing and shoved his hands into his pockets. 'I'll just come out and say it.'

'OK.'

'My wife, Veronique was her name.' He paused and looked down at the floor, clenching his jaw. A moment later he lifted his head and met her gaze. 'She was my admin assistant for about a year before we were married. It was her idea to apply for the VOS and, in fact, when I was successful in obtaining the post, Veronique was the one who arranged everything.' He clenched his jaw then forced himself to relax before saying softly, 'She died in a road accident six months before the VOS began.'

'She was supposed to be with you on this tour? In Carmel's job?' Melody sighed and nodded, realising how difficult things must have been for him.

'Yes. We were supposed to be experiencing all of this together. She was proud of me and my work and she wanted the world to know about it.' He shoved his hands into his pockets again. 'After she passed away, I felt I owed it to her to do the tour, to carry out her wishes, as it were.' He shook his head sadly. 'Obligation, eh? It makes us do things we don't want to.'

'Your wife was right to be proud of you and to want the rest of the world to know about your techniques and the device you've invented. Obligation or not, the VOS will help so many surgeons to perfect their techniques and, in turn, will help their patients and that, George, is very noble. *You* are noble.'

'No.' He shook his head for emphasis. 'I'm far from it because what man has these sorts of feelings for another woman eighteen months after his wife's death?' He gestured to the two of them. 'That's not noble. That's not respectful. That's not the type of legacy I want to leave to Veronique.'

His words were raw and painfully honest and it allowed Melody see that the man before her was still a man very much in love with his wife. He may have feelings for her but they were clearly feelings he didn't understand and neither did she. Both of them were trying to make some sort of sense of this undeniable instant attraction they felt for each other.

His phone rang and he sighed heavily when he saw the caller.

'Carmel?' she asked.

He nodded and connected the call, not bothering to say hello but just listening before saying, 'I'll be right there.' He disconnected the call and put his phone back into his pocket. 'Duty calls.'

'For both of us,' she added, as she crossed to the coat rack near her door and picked up her white clinic coat. George, the gentleman that he was, took the coat from her and helped her into it before passing her the stethoscope

from her desk. 'Thank you for being honest.' She angled
her head to the side and smiled. 'It's refreshing.'

'Thank *you* for listening to me ramble and I don't mean
to scare you or confuse you any further but I wanted you
to know—' He stopped and raked both hands through his
hair. 'I'm probably not making any sense.'

'Yes. Yes, you are, George. In telling me about Veronique, in sharing what this tour meant to both of you, it
might help us both to put the brakes on these crazy feelings we're having.'

'Exactly.' He shook his head. 'But when you say things
like that, when you *understand* what it is I'm trying to say,
that only makes it worse because it highlights just how well
you seem to know me and that only intensifies the attraction I feel for you, because the last woman who understood
me the way you instinctively do was—'

'Veronique,' she finished for him.

'Yes.' He stared at her for another fifteen seconds then
turned and opened her office door. 'We're both going to be
late if we stand here trying to make any sense out of this.'

'True. Work. Work is always dependable.'

'Work will see you through.' He followed her out of the
office and waited while she locked her door. 'It's what I
told myself after Veronique's death.'

'Yeah. It's what I told myself after my break-ups.' She
smiled sadly at him. 'Have fun at your next meeting.'

'Have fun at clinic,' he stated, then grinned. 'Ah—
clinic. Those were the quiet and uncomplicated days of
my past.'

She laughed, pleased they'd been able to lighten the atmosphere a bit. 'You sound nostalgic.'

'I am.' He pointed to the stairwell door. 'I'm going this
way.'

She pointed towards the direction of clinic. 'And I'm
going this way.'

'Will you be at the dinner tonight?'

'Yes.'

'See you then.'

With that, she turned and walked away from him, proud of herself when she didn't look back. George Wilmont had just provided her with another reason why she needed to keep away from him—the fact that he'd clearly adored his wife. 'And that only makes him more attractive,' she grumbled as she headed into clinic, apologising to the sister for her tardiness.

She did her best to push thoughts of George and everything he'd told her to the back of her mind so she could concentrate on clinic. Thankfully, with the back-to-back patients she hardly had time to draw breath let alone dwell on thoughts relating to George. She managed to finish seeing all her patients just after five-thirty, which was only half an hour late. Melody wrote up the last of the notes as her registrar, Andy, stopped by to let her know he was also finished. 'Are you coming to the dinner tonight?' she asked.

'After missing last night's dinner? I'll definitely be there.'

'See you there.' She returned her attention to the notes but heard Andy's voice in the distance, talking to someone. The nurses had left the instant the last patient had departed so Melody wondered who it might be. Seconds later, she heard footsteps heading towards her consulting room and looked up expectantly at the open doorway.

'Hi,' George said a moment later. 'I hope I'm not disturbing you?'

Melody's heart lurched happily at the sight of him and a shiver of excited anticipation worked its way down her spine. Yes, he was disturbing her—far too much for her liking. 'No. I'm just finishing up.' She motioned to the notes, all the while trying to calm the effect he was having on her.

'Don't let me interrupt,' he said, and looked at some of the posters stuck up on the wall around the clinic room. Melody quickly finished writing the notes and the instant she'd closed the file and put her pen down, the phone on the desk rang.

'Excuse me,' she said, but George merely nodded. 'Dr Janeway.'

'Oh, Melody. Good, I caught you. An emergency has just come in. They're demanding the head of unit,' the triage sister said.

Melody groaned resignedly. 'Details?'

'Right scapula, right Colles' and dislocation of the neck of humerus. Melody, it's Rudy Carlew.'

'Is that name supposed to mean something to me?'

'Honestly, Melody, don't you ever go to the movies?'

'Sure. So?' She glanced at George only to find him watching her.

'Problem?' he asked softly.

'Emergency,' she mouthed, and he nodded.

'Rudy Carlew is the hottest thing in movies,' the triage sister was saying. 'Mr Gorgeous? *Everybody's Hero*? That's the latest superhero movie—surely you've seen that one?'

'Oh, yeah. I've seen that one. Right.' Melody at least had a picture of the actor in her head.

'He's been filming his latest film in several locations around Sydney and today they were doing a stunt, and he fell.'

'OK. I'm on my way.' She hung up the receiver and turned her attention to George.

'What's happening?'

'Rudy Carlew is in the ED.'

'Who?'

Melody laughed. 'I'm glad to see I'm not the only one out of touch. He's a movie star,' she continued as she packed up her desk and headed for the door. Turning out her light, she looked over her shoulder at him. 'Want to accompany me to the ED?'

'Sure.' His enthusiasm was evident.

'I guess most of the operating you've done has been scheduled, right?'

'Exactly. I can't recall the last time I dealt with an emergency.'

Melody pressed the button for the lift and while they waited she tilted her head and eyed him thoughtfully. 'What's the deal with your operating and practising licence? You must have operated in some of the finest facilities in the world.'

'I have. For visiting professorships, the recipient is granted an international operating licence.'

'So you could quite easily operate with me right now if I asked?'

'Yes.' The lift arrived and they rode it to down to the ED. 'Will you?' George asked the question with the delighted anticipation of a child at Christmas. 'Please?'

Melody couldn't help but smile at him. 'I don't know.' She pretended to consider him thoughtfully. 'How's your upper-limb expertise?'

'Pretty rusty,' he confessed. 'But I'd only be assisting,' he was quick to point out.

'Let's see how his injuries present. Chances are he won't require surgery at all.' She told him what the triage sister had said and he nodded, all pretence gone as they walked into the ED. If she'd wanted to get people's attention, she had it—walking in with the visiting orthopaedic surgeon to treat a movie star.

What had started out as a difficult day was turning into one that most definitely had its perks.

CHAPTER SEVEN

THE NOISE COMING from outside was deafening and hospital security was stationed at the front door, as well as the door that led through to the treatment area.

'Oh, there you are, Melody,' the triage sister said, a hint of excitement mixed with exasperation in her voice. 'He's in treatment room two.'

'Thanks.' Melody pointed to where the security guards were standing. 'What's going on?'

'Mr Carlew's fans!'

'Oh.' Melody shrugged and led the way to treatment room two. 'Hello,' she said to the patient lying on the bed. She did indeed recognise the talented Rudy Carlew. 'I'm Dr Janeway, Head of Orthopaedics. This is my colleague, Professor Wilmont.'

Rudy Carlew nodded slightly and then winced in pain.

'Can't you people do something?' the woman standing next to him complained. 'He's in pain.'

Melody accepted the patient chart from one of the nurses and checked his analgesics. 'Are you still experiencing pain, Mr Carlew?'

'Rudy,' he said softly.

'Any pain, Rudy?'

'Minor.'

'You people have got to do something,' the woman shrilled again.

'I don't believe we've been introduced.' Melody politely.

The woman sighed with dramatic exasperation. 'I'm his manager. Now do something.'

'I will,' Melody said. 'Unfortunately, you'll need to wait outside. The sister here will show you where.'

'I'm not leaving him.' The woman grabbed his hand and poor Rudy cried out in pain.

'It's all right, Astrid. I'll be in good hands.'

Astrid looked at him, then back to the doctors. 'He's worth a lot of money to the studio, so fix him.'

'Why don't you appease the fans, Astrid,' Rudy stated.

'Yes. I can do that.' Astrid headed out.

'Now, Rudy.' Melody moved in for a closer look at his injuries. 'Let's see what sort of damage has been done.' She inspected both his arms gently. He had a few cuts and scratches on his legs and upper torso, which had been attended to by the ED staff.

'I think we'll let Radiology enjoy your company next.' Melody smiled as she wrote up the X-ray request forms. 'You've dislocated your shoulder but I don't want to put it back in without it being X-rayed first.'

'Why not?' he asked.

'Because you may have fractured the top of your humerus, which is the upper arm bone. If you have, we'll need to operate in order to fix the pieces of bone together before we can even attempt a relocation.'

'If not?'

'Then I can put it back in.'

'Will it be painful?

Melody smiled. 'We'll make sure you have sufficient analgesics to cover the pain. Your Colles' fracture, which is your wrist, looks straightforward and can probably be fixed with a simple plaster cast.'

'I can't have a cast on my arm,' he stated in a normal voice. 'I'm right in the middle of shooting a movie. The hold-up of waiting for my arm to heal in a cast would cost the studio millions.'

'I'm sure we can arrange for you to have your arm strapped and then in a half-cast for the hours when you're not on camera.' Melody continued calmly. 'There are options.'

'Can I get a second opinion?'

'Of course,' she replied, not at all offended. 'First of all, let's see what the X-rays show and then we'll know exactly what we're dealing with.'

'Right you are, Doc,' he said with a smile. He was a handsome man, Melody thought, but his looks were too... *polished.*

'You handled that well,' George said once Rudy had been wheeled off, with three adoring nurses at his side, towards Radiology.

'Why do you sound so surprised?' She laughed as she led him into the ED tea room. 'Coffee?'

'Thanks,' he said as he took off his suit jacket and loosened his tie.

'Black. No sugar, right?'

'How did you know?'

Melody chuckled. 'Let's see, since you arrived here, I've already had three meals sitting next to you. I simply noticed you didn't add anything into your coffee before you drank it.'

He smiled at her. 'And you have yours with just milk.'

'I do.' Melody quickly fixed them coffee and brought the cups over to the lounge where he was sitting. George took a sip of his coffee, then put the cup on the small table in front of them. He stretched his arms over his head and closed his eyes.

'How long do you think Rudy will be in Radiology?'

Melody knew that George had said something but for the life of her she had no idea what he'd said because her gaze had been drawn to the way his muscles flexed beneath his shirt when he stretched. It should be outlawed. His crisp, white shirt did nothing to hide what lay beneath and Melody's heart rate accelerated.

She quickly looked away, in case he intercepted her gaze. What was she doing, ogling him like that? He was a man in love with another woman. Or, more correctly, the *memory* of another woman. Memories were powerful things to compete with. She stopped her thoughts short. Wait. Compete? Did she *want* to compete for George's attention?

'Melody?' There was concern in his voice when he spoke.

'Sorry.' She forced herself to meet his gaze but she didn't hold it for long. She needed to be careful. She'd been burned too often in the past and perhaps it was necessary for her to remind herself every day that soon George would leave her life just as quickly as he'd entered it. Besides, did she really want to risk a quick fling with a man when she'd vowed to take the next relationship slowly—*very* slowly? She glanced his way again and found him watching her.

'Something wrong?'

'No. No. Nothing's wrong.' She shook her head for emphasis and then eyed him cautiously. 'Why do you ask?'

'No reason,' he stated. 'You just seemed miles away.'

'Hmm.' She tapped the side of her head. 'There's a lot going on up here but nothing I'll burden you with.' She chattered too fast, which indicated how his nearness was starting to affect her. She should stand, she should move, she should put more distance between them as right now the warmth and charm exuding from him was starting to become like an aphrodisiac to her. What was wrong with her? She was behaving like an adolescent with a crush.

It certainly didn't help matters when he shifted closer

and leaned towards her. 'This attraction between us...' he murmured quietly, his gaze holding hers.

'Hmm?' Melody waited, holding her breath to see what he would say next.

'I try to stop myself but then I get near you and...' He paused. 'Are you...seeing anyone at the moment?' He wasn't sure why he was asking. Perhaps it was because her earlier comment about relying on work to help her through after her break-ups had made him think. Although they both knew that nothing should happen between them, he still seemed to have a burning need to know all about her.

'Uh...' That wasn't what she'd expected him to say but the fact that he'd asked her that particular question meant— what? What did it mean? That he was hoping something was going to happen between them? That he was checking—just in case? 'Actually, no. I'm not involved with anyone. My...er...my last relationship didn't end well.'

'I'm sorry to hear that.' And his words were genuine, which surprised her.

'You are?'

He shrugged one shoulder and shifted again, sliding one arm down the back of the lounge, his hand now resting near her back. 'Everyone deserves to find happiness, Melody.'

'True but I—' She shrugged. 'I guess happiness keeps eluding me.'

'Was it serious?'

'We were engaged.'

She'd been engaged? The thought had never crossed his mind. It also drove home just how little he knew about her. 'Does he work here?'

'No. He did, though. Thankfully, he left and moved to Germany.'

'That's a big move.'

'Well—given the doctor he impregnated while cheating

on me lives in Germany, it was logical.' Melody couldn't hide the pain she felt at Emir's betrayal.

'What a fool.'

'To move to Germany?'

'No. To cheat on *you*.'

'Oh.'

'You deserve better than that.'

'I do, don't I?' She met his gaze, her eyes flicking to encompass his very near, very kissable mouth. She closed her eyes, needing to control her increasing attraction to him. 'But it's made me very cautious, George.' She opened her eyes and stared into his.

Neither of them moved. Both were caught in the bubble of sensual awareness that only seemed to intensify every time they were alone.

The tea-room door opened and a nurse poked her head around. George instantly stood and picked up his coffee cup, carrying it to the sink. 'Rudy Carlew's films are available for viewing,' she stated, pointing to the computer in the corner of the room.

'Thanks.' As soon as the door closed, Melody sighed and looked at him. 'Fast moves.'

'I'm too old for this and—I don't want anyone to think there's anything going on between us.'

'There isn't.'

'But the gossips make up their own stories based on little fact.'

'You're worried about the gossips?' She stood and headed over to the computer, entering her code so they could view the X-rays.

'I am.' He shook his head. 'It's not fair to you.'

Wow. Was he really that concerned about her? How incredibly sweet. She smiled warmly and beckoned him over. 'The dislocation of the shoulder looks clean,' she said as he joined her. He wasn't as close as he'd just been and for that she was grateful. She needed to concentrate and she was finding it increasingly difficult to do so with George around. She clicked on the next image. 'Ulna and radius, on the other hand, not so clean. It'll require open reduction and internal fixation.'

'You'll need to reduce and relocate the Colles' as well,' George pointed out. 'What do you think about bandaging and putting his arm in a splint?'

'We just need to keep everything stable,' she agreed with a nod.

'If you insert a few K-wires here…' George pointed up to the fracture site of Rudy Carlew's right wrist '…that will hold the fracture in place.'

'I'd need to restrict him in the length of time he is out of the splint and he'll require a nurse to handle the bandaging.'

'Absolutely.'

'What do you think? An hour a day.'

'At least for the first two weeks. Then once you get the check X-rays done, you may be able to extend that time frame or decrease it, depending on how things look.'

Melody nodded. 'Could be a workable solution. Let's see how we go in Theatre. And speaking of which…' She walked to the phone on the wall and called through to the emergency theatres to see if one could be booked immediately.

'We're in luck,' she told him as she finished putting in the verbal request. Next she headed back to her patient, who was now in one of the isolated rooms at the end of the recovery cubicles.

'It looks as though we may have a solution to your problem,' Melody told Rudy. 'But,' she added at his brilliant smile, 'you'll be under strict instructions as to how much you can do and, please, no more stunts! Use the stuntman next time.'

'Yes, Doctor,' Rudy said with mock remorse.

'I can't make any promises,' Melody reiterated. 'It was Professor Wilmont's idea so if it doesn't work out, you can blame him for dashing your hopes.'

George chuckled. Melody explained the operation to Rudy and once he'd signed the consent form, she headed to Theatre to get everything prepared. 'It's six-thirty now,' Melody said to him. 'Unfortunately, it doesn't look as though you'll have time to help me in Theatre.'

'Why not?'

'George, you have a dinner at eight o'clock. That's only an hour and a half away.'

'I do know how to tell the time,' he said with an admonishing grin.

'Stop teasing.' Melody smiled, enjoying their easy banter. Emir had never clicked with her like this. Perhaps that was why she found George so hard to resist! 'Carmel will come looking for you and then you'll have to leave in the middle of the operation. Actually, I'm surprised she's allowed you a few free hours.'

George chuckled. 'It'll be all right. The operation's going to take— what? Forty-five minutes?'

'More than likely, if we don't run into complications.'

'I seriously doubt it.'

'You have responsibilities.'

'I have an hour and a half. We'll be fine.'

The look he gave her said that she could trust him and for a split second Melody wondered whether he was only talking about the operation or—something more? She decided it was best not to pursue it so she showed him where the changing rooms were and escaped behind the door marked 'Females'.

'You're a cool, calm and collected professional,' she mumbled to herself as she changed. 'You've been through a lot worse than this. It's just an attraction. Nothing is ever going to come of it. He's still carrying a torch for his wife and he's leaving at the end of the week. He has a tour to complete and even after that's done he'll be living in a different state.'

'Talking to yourself again, Melody?' Evelyn asked as she walked in to the changing rooms.

For a second she froze. How much of her mumbling had Evelyn heard? Melody adopted an air of nonchalance and continued to put her hair up.

'So, another opportunity to work with the great Professor Wilmont,' Evelyn squeaked excitedly. 'And assist with an operation on Rudy Carlew. Is this the best job or what?'

Melody couldn't help but laugh. She didn't need to tell Evelyn to make sure she kept herself the information about Rudy Carlew strictly confidential as the nurse had proved herself to Melody in the past to be a woman of integrity and discretion. If it hadn't been for Evelyn's compassion in telling Melody the truth about Emir, perhaps Melody's heartbreak would have been even worse.

'The only downside,' Evelyn continued, 'is that after tonight my contract with the hospital expires.'

'I didn't realise you were doing agency work. You've been here for at least the past twelve months.'

'I've been filling in for a nurse on maternity leave. She's back tomorrow, which means I won't be around to visit Rudy.' They walked out together. 'How did you get Professor Wilmont to agree to operate?'

Evelyn's question made Melody want to throw caution to the wind and say something like it had been her natural charms that had led George away from his busy schedule in search of a more refined amusement but instead she cleared her throat. Not wanting to create hospital gossip, she said, 'Firstly, he's *assisting* me. Secondly...' Melody shrugged '...he asked.'

Melody checked on Rudy to make sure that everything

was going according to plan before she headed for the scrub sink. There was no sign of George but she knew he'd arrive soon. The hairs on the back of her neck and along her arms rose the moment he entered the room and she was amazed at how aware she was of him but tried to hide it as best she could.

As they stood at the scrub sink, he said, 'Everything ready to go?'

'Yes.'

'I called Carmel,' he told her. 'So at least she knows where I am.'

Melody glanced at him and almost gasped. The theatre greens brought out the golden flecks in his brown eyes—eyes that she could willingly drown in. She tried not to dwell on it and scrubbed her hands harder but the scent of his aftershave, the deep melodious sound of his voice, the warmth emanating from his body as he stood beside her made her completely forget what she was doing. She glanced at his large, capable hands as he continued to lather them and his arms. So strong. So masterful. So…sensual.

This will not do! Melody returned her gaze to her own arms and hands, intent on focusing her thoughts on the upcoming operation. Thankfully, by the time the operation began she was back in control of her emotions. George was merely another surgeon assisting her.

They worked well together, relocating the shoulder and performing open reduction and internal fixation on the fractured radius and ulna. The K-wires that needed to be inserted into the wrist were another matter yet together they worked it through with both of them quite satisfied with the result.

'A job well done,' George remarked as he pulled off his mask and theatre cap. Melody looked up at him and he smiled. It was that gorgeous thousand-watt smile that sent her body into meltdown. A flood of tingles swamped her, and her knees turned to jelly.

She turned away from him, desperate to get herself under control. She had to find some way of saving her sanity, at least for the next few days, but the more time she spent with George, the more she was coming to care for him and that in itself was incredibly dangerous.

CHAPTER EIGHT

'MELODY? ARE YOU feeling all right?'

'Yes.' She dared a quick glance up at him while she disposed of her theatre garb. 'I'd better write up the notes,' she mumbled, and quickly headed back to the tea room, thankful George wasn't following her.

She was glad of the momentary reprieve as it gave her a moment to get her racing heart rate under control. She wrote up the notes but discovered she'd made two mistakes. It irked her when her mind wandered into Georgeland. Why *did* it irk her so much? Was it the fact that she was attracted to George? Or the fact that she felt out of control whenever he was around? And what was wrong with feeling a little out of control once in a while?

She knew there could never be anything between them so why shouldn't she enjoy the way he made her pulse race? Or the way her stomach churned in excitement? It was definitely bolstering her bruised ego. George found her desirable. After what Emir had done to her, why shouldn't she be delighted with George's attentions? It could be something she could hold close to her heart, especially when she became all anxious about never finding anyone to truly love and accept her.

'Thought I'd find you here.' George's voice washed over her and Melody momentarily closed her eyes, savouring the sound and the way it made her feel, before opening her eyes and turning to look at him. He was dressed in his suit again, looking more handsome than before, if that was possible. 'I'd better get going.' He stayed in the doorway, not venturing any further.

Melody automatically looked at the clock, gasping as she saw the time. Ten minutes to eight. 'I'd completely forgotten about the dinner.'

He smiled. 'I thought as much. You are still coming?'

'Yes, but it appears I'm going to be a little late. As the dinner is at your hotel, it won't take you anytime at all to change and get to the venue.'

'Whereas you need to go home, shower and change and then drive to the hotel,' he finished for her.

'Yes.'

'I'll save you a seat.'

Melody chuckled. 'That's pretty decent of you—especially as the seating has already been assigned.'

He returned her smile and she melted. 'See you there,' he said, then walked away. Melody sighed, the silly smile still on her face. You're not having much luck, she rationalised. Even though she knew George still carried a torch for his wife, she couldn't blame him. To have loved and then lost would mean that Veronique would be in his heart for ever. The problem was that it only endeared him to her even more. He wasn't about to let his past fade away but would carry those memories with him for ever. But was he looking to move forward? To try new relationships? He said it had been only eighteen months since his wife had died, so was he ready, and did it really have anything to do with her?

'Work,' she said, and stood, pushing thoughts of George Wilmont out of her mind. She headed for Recovery to check on Rudy and when she was satisfied with his condition, she left the nurses to drool over their movie-star patient.

* * *

At home, she took a leisurely shower and dressed with extra care. She'd seen the slightly veiled looks of desire in George's eyes yesterday evening, and tonight she wanted to see it again. He made her feel feminine, delicate and sexy—all at the same time. They were sensations she'd never felt before and she'd discovered, much to her chagrin, that she liked it.

Melody smoothed her hand down the long burgundy silk dress she'd bought two weeks ago specifically for this occasion. Tonight, instead of piling her curls on top of her head, she let them fall loose. Vanilla essence was next and she dabbed some on her wrists and behind her ears. Usually, she wore perfume but tonight she wanted to—what? Leave a lasting impression on George? Have him find her too good to resist?

'Just enjoy it,' she told her reflection. 'Nothing is going to happen and at least you'll have some nice memories to combat the awful ones.' With a firm nod, she collected her bag and keys before heading out the door.

Melody arrived just over an hour later, but when George saw her he knew it had been worth the wait. The same re-action he'd experienced the night before hit him again. She was a vision of loveliness, dressed in a rich burgundy fabric that shimmered when she walked. Her hair was loose and he had the sudden urge to thread his fingers through her glorious mane that shone reddish-gold beneath the artificial lights. He was amazed at how strongly she affected him and although he'd done his best to fight it, he'd found he was losing the battle.

'Hey. Here's Melody,' Andy announced, breaking into George's intimate thoughts. George watched her look their way as Andy called her name and waved. She waved back and said something to the people who had waylaid her before heading in their direction. She walked with such grace and poise, holding her shoulders back. She was one elegant lady.

George waited impatiently for their gazes to meet and when they did he found it hard to disguise the desire he felt. He smiled quickly, hoping she hadn't seen, but he doubted it. Even though he'd only met her yesterday morning, George knew she was a very perceptive woman.

He stood and held the back of the vacant chair next to him. 'Here, have a seat. You must be exhausted.'

'Thank you.'

'How did the operation go?' Andy asked from across the round table.

'Routine,' Melody replied. 'How did you know?'

'George said you'd been called to Theatre. So it was nothing interesting?'

'Not really. Dislocated shoulder, fractured ulna, radius and Colles'.'

'Sports injury?'

'No. Actually, the patient sustained a fall.' As she spoke, George motioned to the waiter, who nodded in understanding and soon brought out a meal for Melody.

'I had the kitchen hold a meal for you. I knew you'd be hungry after being in clinic and then Theatre,' he told her when she looked at him with delighted surprise.

'That's so considerate. Thank you, George.' His thoughtfulness touched her deeply. How was she supposed to resist him when he did such nice things? 'I thought I might have missed out.'

'I knew you'd be hungry,' he told her softly, delighted that he'd impressed her. He felt himself preen like a peacock and couldn't stop it. 'After all, you've been going non-stop since lunchtime.'

'I'm famished,' she agreed, and tucked right in. He was

pleased to see she had a healthy appetite and didn't appear concerned about her figure. Veronique had been the same. In fact, Melody had many of the same qualities as Veronique and in a strange way it comforted him. Perhaps that was the reason he'd been drawn to Melody in the first place.

As far as looks went, they were like chalk and cheese. Veronique had been a bit shorter than Melody, who he guessed to be about five feet eight inches. Where Melody had long auburn hair, Veronique's had been blonde and short. Melody had green eyes, Veronique's had been brown.

Yet a lot of their mannerisms were very similar. The way they walked. The intelligence, which was reflected in their eyes, and the way they could both make him laugh. It was uncanny and nerve-racking at the same time. The main difference he could see was that Melody was a surgeon and, therefore, understood every aspect of his work. That hadn't always been the case with his wife. The simple delight he'd felt standing at the operating table by Melody's side, assisting her with a routine procedure, had surprised him. The knowledge made him feel guilty, as though he was cheating on Veronique because he could share a part of his life with Melody that he hadn't been able to completely share with his wife.

Melody was a giving, caring and open person, just as Veronique had been. It stood to reason that he'd be attracted to a woman with similar qualities, but where his feelings for Veronique had grown over time, his immediate awareness of Melody had caught him completely off guard. He wasn't being fair to himself or to Melody—his guilt for feeling as he did, for even thinking about moving forward with his life, was a huge obstacle between them and, quite frankly, Melody deserved better.

What awaited him on his return was the life he'd left,

the life of a confused, grieving man. He had an empty house, an empty car, an empty life without his wife. All of those possessions, even his job, held no delight for him any more and that's why he wasn't looking forward to the end of the tour.

He shook his head slowly and glanced at Melody, watching her chat animatedly with her registrar. He wasn't that man any more. While the tour had indeed been gruelling, it had helped him find perspective in his grief. He'd been to so many different hospitals, met so many different people from all walks of life. Veronique hadn't wanted this tour to take place in only large teaching hospitals, she'd wanted George to give instruction and hope to surgeons in small hospitals in the developing world where the facilities might not have been state of the art but where the care for patients had been paramount.

He'd done all that. He'd helped people, providing those developing countries not only with new surgical techniques but leaving behind the gift of the device he'd invented, which could cut surgical time in half. He'd done all of those things, provided a lasting legacy for his wife, but what was he supposed to do on his return to Melbourne?

Melody's laughter floated over him and he breathed in a calming breath. That sound, the brightness in her eyes, the way her lips curved—he liked them all. They made him feel alive again, not just a man who was trudging his way through the wilderness. His attraction to Melody may have been instant, it may have knocked him for six, but it had made him *feel* again, and for that he would be grateful for ever.

Still, until he figured out exactly what he wanted to do with his life, he was better off distancing himself. It wasn't fair—to either of them—to trifle with their emotions. He looked at his empty plate, frowning unseeingly at it. He didn't want to stop experiencing these emotions, he liked feeling alive again, but he also knew it was the right thing to do and he prided himself on always being the type of man to do what was right.

'Are you OK?' Melody's soft words cut into his thoughts and he quickly pasted on a smile.

'Yes.'

'You were concentrating so hard on your empty plate that I thought you might be performing a secret male bonding ritual with it.'

George chuckled, feeling instantly better. 'Close but no cigar.'

Melody's mobile phone rang, bringing her back to reality. She quickly connected the call, frowning as she listened to the information. 'I'll be right there,' she replied.

'You don't seem to be able to get through a complete dinner. It's either the beginning or the end,' George jested.

'Anything wrong, Melody?' Andy asked.

'Not really. They want to transfer a patient out of the hospital.'

'Now?' Andy glanced at his watch. 'It's almost midnight.'

'Makes sense,' George replied with a nod. 'They want you to check he's all right to be moved?'

'Yes.'

'Who's the patient?' Andy asked, completely baffled.

'Rudy Carlew,' Melody replied as she stood and collected her bag.

'Rudy Carlew! You operated on Rudy Carlew and you didn't tell me?' Andy asked incredulously.

'Oh, not you too.' Melody laughed. 'Perhaps it's just as well you weren't in Theatre, Andy. We had enough trouble with the theatre nurses drooling over him. I'd better get going. Goodnight,' she said, her gaze encompassing the table in general.

'I'll walk you out,' George offered.

'It's all right, George,' Andy said, quickly gulping his coffee and standing. 'I'll go with her. I'm not going to miss the opportunity of meeting one of my favourite movie stars.'

Melody met George's gaze, a small smile on her lips. He returned the smile and shrugged one shoulder. Again, it appeared they were completely in sync with each other, having an unspoken conversation, but this conversation was one filled with regret at not being able to spend more time together. Even though they knew they shouldn't, what they knew and what was continuing to develop between them were two very different things. 'See you tomorrow, then.'

'Of course.' She took a few steps away, then turned and fixed him with a cheeky stare. 'Uh—will you be there for ward round? I'm just asking—' she hurried on, a teasing glint in her eyes '—so I know whether to start without you.'

George laughed. 'Oh, you're funny. I don't think we're scheduled for ward round but if there's a change, we'll let you know.'

'Just so long as you do it before eight-thirty, otherwise you'll have to join in whenever you get there.' A few of the other people at their table laughed, knowing what had happened that morning.

'We'll do our best,' George responded, and held out his hand to Melody. Deprived of spending a few minutes alone with her, he felt the need to touch her at least. Melody slowly slid her hand into his and held it firmly. Her skin was soft and smooth and George couldn't resist stroking it gently with his thumb.

His gaze met hers and held for a split second. He saw a flash of longing enter her green depths and felt a stirring deep within. Conscious of the people around them, he reluctantly let go of her hand. 'I hope you won't be held up too long at the hospital.'

'You and me both,' she replied, and he was delighted that her tone was a little unsteady, indicating she was as affected by him as he was by her.

'Ready, Melody?' Andy asked, eager to leave.

Melody turned from George, cleared her throat and nodded at her registrar. As they walked out, Andy mumbled, 'I still can't believe you didn't call me to assist you. Rudy Carlew!'

'George was there.'

'George assisted you?'

'Yes. Problem?'

'No.' Andy frowned as they waited for the lift. 'It's just that he's so...*qualified*, and a lower-limb specialist and yet there he was, assisting you.'

'Oh, so I'm not qualified?'

'Come on, Melody. You know what I mean.'

'I do, Andy. George wanted to assist. Think about it. The last time he would have helped out in an emergency situation would have been before he'd started the VOS.'

'I guess a change is as good as a holiday.'

Melody chuckled. 'Something like that.' As they rode the lift down to the ground floor and waited for the valet to retrieve her car, Melody wondered whether her own feelings towards George were because having him around this week was like she was on holiday from her usual schedule. Ordinarily, she'd have clinics, elective surgery, lectures, meetings and the on-call roster to deal with, but this week a lot of things had been postponed to accommodate the VOS schedule. Was that why she was experiencing these emotions towards George? Because it was similar to the sensations of a holiday romance?

Usually, when two people were attracted to each other they would spend an hour here or an hour there, slowly getting to know each other. With George and herself, they'd spent so much time together during the past two days that if she was to proportion out the actual hours, it was as though they'd known each other for at least a month and a half.

The problem was, while she was enjoying the attention, while she was delighted with the way George could make her feel, she knew it couldn't last—but the more time she spent with him, the more she wanted it to. Surely it was good that she was moving forward when it came to her romantic life? That she was willing to accept the attentions of a man and to know that he wasn't out to use or debase her? It was scary, it was mind-blowing and it was…exhilarating.

Once again, Melody had to force thoughts of George from her mind when they arrived at the hospital, especially as it was to find Rudy's manager, Astrid, in a complete tizz. 'Finally! You're here. We need to move him now,' she stormed. 'The fans have all gone home and if we don't do it soon, they'll be back and annoying him again.'

'Isn't that the price of fame?' Melody commented as she started her examination. Andy, who she'd thought might turn into a groupie fan, was the consummate professional.

'You're showing no signs of any complications,' she told Rudy, 'but it's still too early to tell. Where did you say you'd be going?'

'To a hotel,' Astrid answered for him. 'He'll have a private doctor and private nurses to take care of him. So, please, save us all some time and sign him over or he'll just discharge himself.'

Melody clenched her teeth but forced a smile. 'I'll need to talk to the doctor who'll be taking over his treatment,' she said. 'And the nursing staff.'

'Well…we haven't actually employed anyone yet. We just need to get him moved!' Astrid huffed before flipping open her bag and taking out a cigarette. Melody watched her in disbelief.

'Astrid,' Rudy said tiredly, 'put that away. This is a hospital.'

'What? Oh.' Astrid looked at the cigarette in her hand as though she had no idea where it had come from. 'Sorry,' she replied softly, and it was then Melody realised the other woman simply ran on nerves.

'Listen, why don't we sit down and discuss the best course of action for Rudy? He needs to be monitored for the next twenty-four hours at least. I think I might be able to help out in recommending a nurse. As far as a doctor goes, how about Andy...' she gestured to her registrar '...does a house call twice a day? It would only be for the next few days and after that you'll be fine with weekly or fortnightly check-ups.'

Rudy nodded. 'Sounds fair. What do you think, Astrid?'

'As long as it means we can move you now, I don't care.'

'Which hotel will you be staying at?' Melody asked, and wasn't surprised when he named the hotel where George was staying. After all, it was Sydney's finest.

'Hey,' Andy remarked, 'we've just come from there. We had a dinner there this evening. Food was fantastic.'

'Good to hear.' Rudy sighed and closed his eyes. Melody realised he was exhausted—and rightly so.

'Do you have transport organised?'

'It's all ready to go,' Astrid replied, her impatience returning. 'So can we move him now?'

'Let me arrange the nurse first,' Melody replied, and headed to the nurses' station to use the phone. She motioned for Andy to follow her. 'I'd like you to monitor him tonight. Is that all right with you?'

'Sure. Wow! I get to be orthopaedic doctor to Rudy Carlew.'

Melody smiled. 'Quite a feather in your cap, eh?'

'I'll just head over to the residence where I keep a

change of clothes and meet you back here,' he said, already starting out the door.

Melody sat down and called Switchboard. After obtaining Evelyn's home number, she gave her a call.

'Hi, Evelyn. Sorry to wake you,' Melody said.

'I'm not on call,' Evelyn told her with a yawn. 'I don't even work there now. Remember?'

'I know, which is why I called. As you were in Theatre for Rudy Carlew's surgery, and are already familiar with the case, I was wondering if you wouldn't mind being his private nurse for the next few weeks.'

'Did I hear you right? No. I must still be asleep and this is a dream.'

Melody laughed. 'You heard me right, Evelyn. His manager wants him out of the hospital tonight.' Melody gave Evelyn the details of where he was staying. 'We'll be moving him there within the hour.'

'Is Rudy showing any sign of complications?'

'Not yet.'

'Well, you only operated on him a few hours ago so it's too soon to tell,' Evelyn mumbled.

'So will you do it?'

'You'd better believe it,' the nurse replied with a laugh.

'Good. Now, with your nursing agency, you'll need to—'

'I'll take care of it.'

'OK. I'll see you at the hotel.'

Rudy was collected from one of the back entrances to the hospital, after a security sweep by his bodyguards had revealed no fans to be found. Andy rode in the luxurious limousine with Rudy and Astrid, while Melody followed them in her car. At the hotel, Melody met Evelyn by the lifts. 'Oh, good,' Melody said. 'Thanks for doing this at such short notice.'

'Are you kidding?' The nurse giggled. 'This is just the best thing that's ever happened to me. So where is he?'

'Being brought in through the back entrance.' They took the lift up to the fourth floor, which was where a number of fancy suites were located. Astrid had told her the room number but as there were bodyguards standing in the corridor, Melody surmised that they'd beaten Rudy there.

A door marked 'Staff Only' opened and Rudy was brought through in a wheelchair. He was just being taken into the room when a door along the corridor opened. Melody looked around and saw George, dressed in faded denim jeans, a white T-shirt and with damp hair, come through the door.

He stopped when he saw her. 'Melody!'

'George!' Her surprise equalled his. She drank in the sight of him. Dressed in casual clothes and fresh from a shower, the man was even more devastatingly handsome than she'd thought possible. Her heart rate increased and her mouth went dry. The butterflies in her stomach took flight and her knees turned to jelly. Melody leaned against the wall for a moment, feeling slightly dizzy. The man had actually made her swoon!

'Are you all right?' he asked, taking a few steps together her, but one of Rudy's bodyguards intercepted him.

'No. It's all right,' she said quickly, and held up her hand to stop him.

'Ma'am, security has to be kept tight,' the bodyguard replied.

'No. You don't understand. This doctor assisted with Mr Carlew's surgery earlier this evening.'

Astrid came out of the suite. 'What's going on?' she asked, and then spotted George. 'Oh, hi again,' she said. 'It's all right.' Her last comment was directed to the bodyguard. 'Has that other equipment come up yet?'

The 'Staff Only' door opened as she spoke and the

equipment, which had been hired from a private hospital, was wheeled through. 'This way,' Astrid instructed. The bodyguard followed her and waited for Melody.

'Uh… I'll be there in a moment. Tell Andy to get things started,' she ordered, and the bodyguard shut the door behind him.

'Doing a little private consulting?' George asked, his tone husky. He didn't move. They simply stood there, staring at each other. Melody's gaze raked over him again and she realised his feet were bare. He looked so…different out of his suit. Relaxed, gorgeous and dangerously sexy!

CHAPTER NINE

HER HEART HAMMERED wildly against her ribs and she was positive he could hear it. Melody tried to swallow but found her throat completely dry. 'I…um…hope the…um…' She trailed off as he took a small step towards her. Her breathing increased and she parted her lips to allow the air to escape more easily, her gaze never once leaving his.

Again, he moved, slowly closing the distance between them. Melody took an involuntary step backwards, only to encounter the wall once more. He was like a lion stalking his prey—slowly, cautiously. She couldn't move even if she wanted to. She was mesmerised by him.

With a few more steps he was standing before her. In her high-heeled shoes, their gazes were almost level. Her gaze flicked to his lips and saw them part.

'Oh,' she gasped as he raised his hands and placed them on the wall on either side of her head. Her breathing was now so utterly out of control there was no hiding just how much this man affected her. She'd been attracted to other men in the past but never had it been this intense.

She looked up into his eyes, noting the mounting desire in him as George slowly leaned closer. His clean, fresh scent only heightened her awareness of him.

'You were saying?' His deep voice washed over her and Melody's eyelids fluttered closed, savouring the moment. She opened them again and looked longingly at his lips.

'Huh?'

'Didn't you want to…ask me something?'

Did she? She had no idea. Her brain failed her, her only conscious thought being that if George didn't kiss her, she'd go insane. The effect he had on her senses was sending them spiralling out of control. Her body was in tune with his as she silently urged him to come even closer.

How much longer was he going to torture them? If she could get her arms to move, she'd reach out and bring his lips to hers. She was paralysed, no, hypnotised and there was nothing she could do about it, such was the effect George had on her.

'Captivating,' he whispered. Never before had he felt like this. It had to be right—but even if it was wrong there was no denying that the only thing he wanted to do right at this very second was to claim Melody's luscious lips in a mind-shattering kiss. A kiss that would satisfy them both—of that he was absolutely sure.

Closer and closer he came until his breath was mixing with hers. Melody closed her eyes, unable to summon the strength to keep them open. She waited—waited impatiently for his mouth to touch hers while still enjoying the sensations he was evoking throughout her body.

The click of a door being opened, together with Andy's voice saying, 'I'll check with Melody,' penetrated the sensual haze with a jolt.

Melody's eyes snapped open, her limbs came to life and she quickly ducked under George's arm, trying to compose herself. Her legs were like jelly and as she took a step away she stumbled.

'Hey, Melody,' Andy said as he spotted her and then quickly held out a steadying hand. 'You all right?'

Not trusting herself to speak, she nodded.

'George?' Andy looked past her and Melody risked a

glance over her shoulder. He was casually leaning against the wall, his hands in his jeans pockets.

'Andy.'

'Are you staying on this floor?'

'Yes, a few doors down.' He kept his gaze away from Melody's, although the way she'd looked a few seconds ago would now be burned in his memory for ever. Her face had been turned expectantly up towards his, her lips parted, her eyes closed, her skin tinged with a faint pink glow. Beautiful! 'I hear Rudy Carlew's one of my neighbours.' He forced himself to ease away from the wall.

He was determined to ensure Andy didn't pick up on the sexual tension that existed between Melody and himself. He needed to protect her as best he could and if that meant not looking at her then he wouldn't.

'Yeah, and Melody and I are his doctors,' Andy said excitedly. 'Come and say g'day,' he urged, and knocked on the closed hotel door. It was opened by one of the bodyguards and Andy headed in.

Melody hung back, anxious for a look, a word, something from George to reassure her. Instead, he gave her a wide berth and for the first time since she'd met him he went through the door before her.

She felt hurt. Didn't he realise she needed some reassurance? Had Andy not interrupted them, George would have kissed her and there was no way she would have fought him. She'd wanted it just as desperately as he had.

Feeling suddenly cold and bereft, Melody rubbed her arms as the first spark of anger ignited deep within. Why was it she felt as though she'd done something wrong when she knew she hadn't? She surmised it was because both Ian and Emir, whenever things had gone wrong or hadn't gone the way they'd wanted, had always shunned her, shutting her out, making her feel as though everything had been her fault.

Didn't George want her? Was he just playing with her? She shook her head, not wanting to believe it. Her old neuroses were rising to the surface. Emir had told her he hadn't wanted children but his decision to follow his pregnant mistress to Germany had helped Melody realise the truth—namely that Emir hadn't wanted to have children *with her*. He hadn't wanted to marry *her*. Now George was acting the same. Now that he had her dangling from his hook, he wasn't interested in more. Was that the case? Was he only interested in the chase?

She followed him into Rudy's room. How dared he pretend nothing had almost happened between them? Why hadn't he given her a little smile or a yearning look to let her know that they were still in sync, that they could still have these unspoken conversations even when other people were around?

She hated feeling like this, having her thoughts all jumbled when she needed to have clear, calm and collected thoughts. More to the point, why was she allowing him to have such power over her, to affect her in such a way? Her anger grew and it encompassed herself as well as George.

Perhaps she should thank Andy for interrupting them. Perhaps she should consider this a lucky escape. After all, if they had kissed, then she would have had more physical sensations to fight. Perhaps she was better off.

'Would that be right, Melody?' Andy was asking her, and she realised that everyone in the room was looking at her expectantly—except George.

'Uh—well—um…' she stumbled, not at all sure what Andy had asked.

'I think you're spot on, Andy,' George answered. 'Good work.'

'Ah—absolutely,' Melody responded, finally finding her voice. Her hostility towards George diminished a bit as she acknowledged that he'd just rescued her. She needed to get out of there, to sort out her emotions before she made a fool of herself. 'If that's all you need…' she glanced at Rudy and then at Andy, her gaze eluding George's '… I think I'll head home. It's been a very hectic day and tomorrow promises to be no less so. Call me if you need me,' she told Andy as she turned and headed to the door, the burgundy dress swishing around her ankles.

'I'd better be going too,' George announced to the room.

'Aw—come on,' Astrid purred, and Melody watched as the other woman crossed to George's side and linked her arm through his. 'Surely you don't have to go just yet? Now that we've got Rudy settled, we can all relax and have some fun.'

'Ugh,' Melody groaned softly, and continued to the door one of the bodyguards held open for her. 'Relax and have some fun,' she mimicked softly as she stormed over to the lifts. 'That man doesn't know his own charm and probably has every woman he meets falling in love with him.' She assaulted the down button, pressing it repeatedly.

'Mumbling to yourself?' George asked from behind her, and although Melody's body shivered in excitement at the sound of his voice, she didn't turn around. Instead, she pressed the down button again.

'I'll walk you out.'

'There's no need,' she replied between clenched teeth.

George watched as she pressed the button again, muttering something about slow hotel lifts. He frowned, unsure why she was so angry. 'It's no trouble,' he told her.

Melody spun to glare at him. 'I don't care if it's an imposition to you or not, the fact is that I don't want you to walk me out. I'm a big girl, George, and I'm more than capable of riding in the lift, walking to the valet desk and waiting for my car.' She pressed the button. 'That's if this lift ever gets here.'

'Why are you angry with me again?' He spread his arms wide.

'Oh, this is all *my* fault?' Her temper was at boiling point. She was cross with him, cross with herself and cross with the lift. She glanced around for an exit sign and stormed over to the door marked 'Stairs'.

'Melody!' George charged after her, completely baffled as to why she was upset. The concrete stairs were cold beneath his feet but that was the least of his worries. 'Talk to me,' he demanded, his voice echoing. The clip-clop of Melody's shoes reverberated around the stairwell and he was pleased to note she was holding onto the railing. The last thing she needed was a twisted ankle.

'There's nothing to say.' She rounded the bend and started on the next flight. She was grateful that Rudy's suite hadn't been on the twentieth floor but given the way she was feeling she wouldn't have cared how many flights of stairs she had to walk down. All she wanted was to get out of the hotel and away from George.

'Nothing to say? You're being stubborn and irrational.'

Melody stopped and whirled around to look up at him. He stopped too. 'Stubborn? Irrational?'

'Yes.' There were only two steps between them and George slowly moved down one, hoping she wouldn't move. It didn't work.

She whirled around again and started clopping her way down the noisy stairwell. 'So what if I am being irrational? I've got good reason.'

'Then tell me what it is so I can apologise.'

'It's the fact that you don't know you've done anything wrong that's made me angry.' That and her own uncontrollable reaction to him. She had to become stronger. She had to fight the attraction between them with every ounce of her strength.

'Wanting to kiss you was wrong?'

'Oh, you know it was,' she growled. 'And then you want to pretend it didn't happen.'

'But it *didn't* happen,' he returned.

'Not the kiss, that's not what I'm talking about.'

'Then what are you talking about? I'm completely perplexed about why I'm suddenly in the doghouse when, as far as I'm concerned, I've done nothing wrong.'

'Isn't that always the way with you men?' She threw over her shoulder as she continued her descent. 'And then there's Astrid and goodness knows how many other women throwing themselves at you, day and night.'

'That's hardly my fault—and I'm not with Astrid, I'm with you.'

'Because you're hoping to pick up where we left off?' she queried. 'You didn't get to kiss me, so now you'll chase after me in the hope that you'll get what you want in the end?' She clicked her tongue disapprovingly. 'You men really are all the same.'

'You keep saying that,' George argued back. 'Are you really comparing me to the dead-heads you've dated in the past?'

'Dead-heads? They were both qualified doctors and you don't even know them.'

'They broke your heart. That means they were not only stupid but idiotic, and I don't care how many university degrees they held. A qualification doesn't give you licence to treat people badly.' His words were harsh and filled with annoyance. Was he annoyed at her or at the dead-heads she'd dated?

'At any rate, it's none of your business.' She rounded the corner for the final flight of stairs.

'It *is* my business if you're going to tar me with the same brush as them.'

'How can I? I hardly know you, George. You tell me you're attracted to me, that no other woman has made you feel this way since—' She stopped and sighed, not wanting to have a discussion about his wife because she really only knew what George had told her and therefore had no authority to speak about it.

'My wife,' he finished for her. 'Yes, that's true.'

'That's what you *tell* me. You've been travelling for so long, you're bound to get—well—lonely and...'

'So you just think I try and kiss any woman who shows an interest in me, eh?'

'How do I know? You might.' The last thing Melody wanted to think about now was George kissing other women. Jealousy reared its ugly head.

'Even though we've spent such a short time together, Melody, I thought the answer to that question might have been obvious. For all I know, you might be the type of woman who gives in to every guy who makes a pass at you.'

'What?' She stopped walking long enough to turn and glare at him. 'How dare you?'

'Ah, so you don't like either. It's all right for you to accuse me of awful behaviour but not vice-versa.' He came to stand beside her on the step, both of them staring at each other, their emotions rioting. Melody was still annoyed with him for withdrawing from her the way he had, for pretending that almost-kiss hadn't happened and that she—she— He'd made her feel unworthy but she wasn't sure how to voice such a thing given she really had no idea where or if this attraction between them was going anywhere.

Melody looked down at the stairs, trying to control her emotions and her thoughts. Finally, she raised her head to look into his eyes, eyes that had the ability to make her forget all rational thought. 'Look, all I was saying is that you're a very handsome man and I'm sure you've met plenty of women during the VOS who would have been more than willing to indulge in a brief affair while you were in town.'

'And what if there were?'

Melody's eyes widened in surprise. Was he admitting to it? Was he a womaniser? 'Were there?' she asked quietly, trying hard to control her disappointment.

'Yes.'

She felt as though he'd hit her. Her mouth opened in disbelief. She'd been hoping against hope that he wasn't that way and now he was admitting as much. Turning, she started walking down the stairs again, thankful she was almost at the lobby. George, however, was clearly fed up with everything and took the stairs two at a time, passing her and barring her way just before she reached the door that led to the lobby.

'Yes, there have been women who've made passes at me during the VOS, but I didn't take any of them up on their offers. Melody, I've been working through a lot of emotions during this tour and the last thing I needed was... entanglements.' He held out his hand to her. 'Until you.' His tone was soft and endearing, urging her to trust him.

She looked at his hand but didn't take it. He dropped it back to his side and nodded. 'You're the first woman I've wanted to kiss since Veronique. Is it so wrong that I'd follow through on that instinct?'

'Perhaps not, but it was what you did afterwards.'

'What? Protecting you against gossip? Trying not to let Andy see that he'd almost caught us together?' His words were earnest. 'I don't want to leave you with more to deal with after I leave.'

Melody closed her eyes. He'd been trying to protect her? Was that just a line? An excuse for his behaviour? She'd heard so many excuses from Ian and Emir in the past that it was difficult to know whether George was speaking the truth. Opening her eyes, she sidestepped him and stalked through the door into the lobby.

'And as far as the almost-kiss goes,' he continued as he went after her, 'you were quite willing for it to happen, too.'

Melody stopped and turned to face him, glad that, except for the bare minimum of staff, the lobby was deserted. 'I am not having this discussion with you here.'

'Then come back up to my room and we'll discuss it there.'

'Ha. Come back to your room? That should be the last thing I do.'

'Why?'

Melody opened her mouth to speak but couldn't. She wanted to tell him that if she went up to his room, there was no way she'd be able to resist him. He would kiss her and she would willingly let him. She knew it was because she wanted it, more than she wanted anything else right now, but she'd also given in to her wants before and it had ended in heartbreak.

'I'll tell you why,' he continued. 'You don't want to come back to my room because you can't trust yourself.' He lowered his voice and took a step closer. As he did so, he stubbed his toe on a nearby table and grunted in pain.

Melody reached out and steadied the vase of flowers on the table before glancing down at his foot. He'd flexed his ankle to hold the toes upwards and was hobbling towards a chair. She looked into his eyes and saw the pain there.

'Let me look at it,' she said, and reached for his foot.

'No. It's fine. I can take care of it.'

'Stop being such a martyr and let me look at it.' Melody grabbed his heel and lifted it up.

'Is everything all right?' one of the staff asked.

'It's fine.' George glared at Melody as she tweaked his sore toe.

'Sorry.' She continued checking the range of motion. 'Not broken,' she announced, and turned to face the staff member. 'He'll be fine,' she said. 'My prescription is two paracetamol and bed rest. Perhaps you might help Professor Wilmont to the lift so he can get back up to his room?' Melody smiled sweetly, enjoying George's disadvantage.

'I'm fine,' he repeated, and stood to prove it.

'Well, if that's all, I'll be on my way.' Melody handed the staff member her valet ticket and after a brief nod he left them alone again. 'No charge for the examination,' she told George.

'How generous of you.' He frowned and she realised that she'd better not try to push him any further as his mood had changed drastically. Previously, he'd been willing to reason, to discuss things calmly. Now he wasn't in such a good mood and she didn't blame him—stubbed toes were painful.

Melody decided to take pity on him. 'Go and rest. I'll see you tomorrow,' she said, and turned away from him. It was either that or throw herself into his arms. He looked so gorgeous, standing there in his faded denims, his brown eyes telling of his exhaustion. It had been hard to resist but with every step she took away from him, she grew more proud of her success.

'Melody,' he called softly, and she turned around, gazing at him expectantly.

'Thanks.'

'For what?'

'For talking to me.'

Was he trying to make her feel guilty? Emir had often used that tactic and she'd fallen for it every time. His next words, however, made her rethink.

'I know it wasn't easy for you and I appreciate it.' His gaze bored into hers and she felt that familiar stirring sensation in her stomach. 'Drive carefully.' With that, he turned and hobbled over to the lift. Melody watched him, torn between amusement at the sight he made and the urge to assist him.

'Your car is here, ma'am.'

Melody forced herself to look away and walked out of the hotel. George pressed the button for the lift and glanced her way. She was magnificent, and she had become far too important to him, far too quickly.

The lift bell chimed and George hobbled in, recalling the way he'd felt as she'd cradled his foot in her hand. As she'd been angry with him, he'd half expected her to be rough with her examination but, instead, she'd been extremely gentle. Her skin had been soft against his and although she'd touched him in a professional, medical way, George hadn't been able to stop the stirring of excitement that had shot through him.

At the fourth floor, he walked to his door and reached into his back pocket for the key card. Once inside, he opened the curtains and turned off the lights before settling back on the bed, propping his foot up on a few pillows.

He'd come so close to kissing her—so agonisingly close. Ever since they'd met, George had wanted to sample her mouth and the longer he waited, the more urgent the desire grew.

He knew the score. He knew she didn't want to get hurt and he had no desire to hurt her. He raked an unsteady hand though his hair and groaned in confusion. What about Veronique? Would she mind if he kissed another woman? The feelings of betrayal hit him forcefully but it still didn't stop him from making a decision. He'd be leaving at the end of the week and, regardless of the war taking place inside him, he knew one thing for sure.

Despite everything—he needed to kiss Melody.

CHAPTER TEN

MELODY DIDN'T SLEEP at all well that night and when she did manage to drift off sometime before dawn, she dreamt she was anxiously trying to glue a vase back together. The pieces were tiny and the tears she was crying kept blurring her vision. She stood and looked down at the mess and only then did she realise that the vase was heart-shaped.

The realisation only increased the urgency as she was expecting a new delivery of flowers at any minute. Working frantically, Melody managed to piece the heart-shaped vase back together. The doorbell rang and she hurried to open it. There stood George, holding a bunch of roses. Melody stared aghast at the vase. She couldn't accept the flowers from George because the vase was still drying.

She wanted the flowers but where was she going to put them? Anxiousness and fear gripped Melody's heart as George held the flowers out to her. What was she going to do?

She sat bolt upright in bed, her heart pounding fiercely against her ribs. 'Just a dream,' she whispered to herself. She lay back and sighed, breathing deeply. She glanced at the clock and realised it was one minute before her alarm was due to go off. 'So much for a good night's sleep,' she muttered, and clambered out of bed.

She glanced at herself in the mirror. She looked horrible. 'Perhaps a little make-up might be in order today.' Melody finished getting dressed, deciding that she wouldn't chance breakfast as her stomach didn't feel settled.

She arrived at the hospital and went straight to the ward. All through the round, she kept anxiously glancing at the door in case George decided to join them again. He didn't. Feeling a bit flat, she returned to her office, hoping to catch up on paperwork before her theatre list began in half an hour.

Sitting at her desk, it wasn't long before further thoughts of George intruded and, instead of fighting them, she gave in. She was exhausted from fighting her emotions, as well as lack of sleep. She thought about her dream, reflecting on the symbolism of the heart-shaped vase. It was true that Emir had broken her heart but she'd managed to mend it.

With George, her feelings for him were so out of proportion in comparison to what she'd previously felt. She'd been committed to marrying Emir, to spending the rest of her life with him. He'd been a charmer, just like George. He'd been a gentleman, just like George. He'd been a dashingly handsome man, just like George. He'd wooed her, made her feel special, made her feel as though she was valued.

Well, George hadn't wooed her exactly, but he did make her feel special. Melody realised the biggest difference between George and Emir was that George appreciated her intelligence, that he treated her as though she had a brain to talk things out, to be open and honest. Right from the start George had been upfront about the attraction between them, and although she wasn't used to a man treating her in such a caring and thoughtful way, it was very refreshing. Refreshing and scary because it only endeared him to her more. She wanted to spend time with him, talk to him, laugh with him, press her mouth to his and hold him close.

Somehow, in such a short time, George had managed to break down the barriers she'd so carefully erected. Back when she'd split with Emir, she'd told herself she preferred loneliness rather than being used, but loneliness wasn't the greatest thing in the world, not when she went home to an empty apartment after long and exhausting shifts at the hospital.

Whether this thing between them was something temporary or permanent, didn't she owe it to herself to find out? What if George *was* the one for her, the one she would spend the rest of her life with, and she'd let him go? What if—?

A knock at her office door startled her out of her deep reverie and she jumped in her chair, clutching her hand to her chest as Rick sauntered into the room.

'Finished with that file yet?'

'Huh? Oh, sorry.' She looked down at the open file and realised that she hadn't started. So much for getting through her paperwork. 'Not yet.'

'Everything all right?' he asked.

'Yes.'

'Sure? You seem to be...preoccupied.'

She shrugged and looked down, not wanting him to see the tell-tale blush she could feel creeping into her cheeks. 'It's been a busy few days,' she rationalised.

'It certainly has. Today, thankfully, isn't going to be as hectic.' Rick went over her schedule, which included her operating list that morning and time to work on her research project in the afternoon. 'Then there's a dinner this evening.'

Melody groaned. 'Do I have to go?' It wasn't that she didn't want to see George, she did, but she didn't want to see him surrounded by a room full of other people. She wanted to spend time with him one on one, to really talk, to really start to get to know the man better than she did.

'Yes. You do,' Rick told her. 'And now you need to go to Theatre. Starting your list late will not make anyone happy.'

Melody stood. 'What would I do without you, Rick?'

'Fall flat on your face and fail,' he answered with a cheeky grin.

Chuckling, Melody left her office and headed to Elective Theatres. Everything progressed smoothly and she de-gowned just after midday, pleased with what she could accomplish when she pushed thoughts of George aside.

With determination in her step, she headed to the medical research building and walked into her lab. She chatted with the technician who was a collaborator on her research project and spent a good two hours working. Once that was done she headed back to her office determined to tackle her paperwork. So far she'd managed to have a very productive day and she was positive it was because she'd hardly thought about George at all.

Back at her office, she managed a steady half-hour of work before being called to the ED to consult on a case with Dr Okanadu. She was in the doctors' tea room, eating an exceptionally late lunch, studying the X-rays on the computer screen, when the door opened and closed. She didn't break focus to see who had walked in.

'Interesting case?'

A flood of excitement washed over her at the sound of George's voice. She looked up in surprise, right into his deep brown eyes, eyes that were gazing at her with repressed desire. She breathed in and swallowed at the same time, choking on the last mouthful of her sandwich. She coughed violently and George patted her on the back.

'Take it easy,' he said, quickly fetching a glass of water.

'I'm fine,' she whispered, but then coughed again, proving herself wrong.

'You seem to be forever choking,' he jested.

'Only when you're around,' she mumbled as she took a sip. She cleared her throat. 'What brings you to the hospital?' His spicy scent entwined itself around her and she fought hard to resist it.

'Aren't I allowed to call in without an invitation?' He smiled as he leant against the edge of the table. His firm thigh was so close to her arm that she could feel the heat radiating from him. Her breath caught in her throat and her mouth went dry.

Melody took another sip of water. 'No, it's just that... I thought you were lecturing.'

'I was.' He glanced at the computer screen and winced. 'Ouch.' He frowned at the image. 'What on earth happened to your patient?'

'She caught her hand in a conveyor belt. I'll be using this case for my research.' Melody glanced at the clock. 'I want to get to Theatre soon to make a start on it.' Why was she so aware of him? She closed the file on the computer and went to turn the monitor off but accidentally brushed his leg with the back of her hand. An explosion, similar to fireworks, burst through her, and her eyelids fluttered closed for a brief second. When she glanced at him, it was to discover he was gazing down at her with burning desire.

George fought hard for control but it wasn't easy. She set him on fire. With the mildest touch, with the momentary flutter of her eyes, with the perfume that was driving him insane. She set him on fire and he was sick of dousing the flames.

He fought for something to say. 'Er...how many reconstructions have you done like this one?' He couldn't help the huskiness that accompanied his words and as Melody looked away, he feasted his eyes on the slender, smooth skin of her neck. Her hair was clipped back at her nape and he remembered how incredible it had looked flowing freely around her face last night.

'Um...quite a few.' She shifted her chair slightly, trying to put a bit of distance between them without appearing rude.

'Are you operating in the theatre with the viewing gallery?'

'No.'

'Pity.'

'Why?'

'This type of operation should be recorded for future reference.'

'There are already a few in the hospital's library,' she told him as she gathered her notes, and he noticed her hands weren't quite steady.

'Ones you've done?' He could see she was getting ready to take flight and he wanted to stop her. If he edged a little to the side and bent his head, he was positive he'd be able to capture her sweet lips in his. Lips he ached to taste.

'Yes.'

'I'm impressed.'

'Really?' She looked up at him from where she sat, warmed by his praise. Here was a man who had worked with some of the finest surgeons in the world, and he was impressed because some of her operations had been recorded?

'Yes.' He gazed into her eyes and leaned closer. 'I know only the most impressive surgery is recorded.' Unable to resist touching her any longer, he reached out and tenderly ran his fingers down her cheek, bringing them to rest beneath her chin. 'Melody.' As he breathed her name, he lifted her chin slightly, angling her head towards his.

Melody gazed at him, her heart pounding wildly against her ribs. He was going to kiss her. This time, for sure, he was going to kiss her. She watched from beneath her lashes as his head slowly drew closer. She shouldn't be doing this. She had an operation to concentrate on.

'George... I—' She didn't manage to finish her sentence as his mouth finally made contact with hers, and she gasped with anticipatory delight. George groaned as she leaned closer to him. Her lips were soft and pliable, just as he'd known they would be.

Melody sighed and opened her mouth beneath his subtle urging, elated to finally give in to her feelings. He tasted like chocolate and coffee—both sweet and addictive.

Without breaking contact, his hands cupped her face, urging her closer, and she edged from her chair, reaching out for him as she moved to stand in front of him. She was amazed to find her usually wobbly legs were willing to support her.

He shifted to accommodate her, his hands sliding around her back as he deepened the kiss. Never in his wildest dreams had he imagined torture could be so agonisingly delightful. She simply melted into his embrace as though they'd been made for each other. The realisation only increased the overpowering emotions swamping him.

Fireworks like she'd never felt before exploded one after the other throughout her body, each new burst sending her senses spiralling out of control. This was impossible. Never before had she been so overwhelmed by a kiss. Then again, this wasn't any ordinary kiss. The spark that flowed freely between them now, had been repressed for two and a half full days, building and simmering within, only to be unleashed with such intensity.

Her hands were pressed against his chest and she could feel the contours of his firm, muscled torso beneath his cotton shirt. Delighted at being able to touch him at last, she slid her hands up his chest, entwining them about his neck, her fingers plunging into his rich, dark hair. A low guttural sound, primitive, came from him and she revelled in her power.

His hands slid ever so slowly down her sides, his fingers splayed, moulding her ribs. His thumbs lightly brushed the underside of her breasts and she gasped in shock as yet another wave of pleasure coursed through her.

Her excitement was mounting with every passing second and she was having difficulty breathing. What did she care about oxygen when she had George? With a satisfied moan, Melody pulled her mouth from his, dragging air into her lungs, pleased to note that his breathing was just as erratic as hers.

He pressed kisses to her cheek, working his way towards her ear, and she tipped her head to the side, allowing him access. A thousand goose-bumps cascaded over her body, increasing her light-headedness. He was a drug and the more she had of him, the more she knew she'd become addicted.

He brought his hand up and brushed her neck, gently urging her collar aside to make room for his hungry lips. She had the smoothest skin and the most luscious lips. Now that he'd kissed her, the realisation of how incredible they were together only made him want her even more.

His mouth met hers again, their lips mingling together like old friends. Although he wanted nothing more than to deepen the kiss, heightening the intensity, George could feel her starting to withdraw.

He pressed his lips to hers one last time before allowing her to rest her head on his chest, their breathing slowly returning to normal. His arms embraced her, holding her tightly, never wanting to let her go.

As she stood there, listening to his heart gradually return to a steady rhythm, Melody started to feel uncomfortable and awkward. What would happen now? George had kissed her and it had been…mind-blowing. Her frazzled thoughts acknowledged that she would never be the same again. The kisses, the passion, the desire—everything had changed. *Never* had she experienced anything like the onslaught of emotions or the intensity of feeling that had just taken place.

His hands rubbed gently up and down her back. She knew it was supposed to relax her but all it did was increase her anxiety. Why had she let George kiss her? She was due in Theatre. He would leave at the end of the week. He was still in love with the memory of his wife. She eased from his hold and took three giant steps backwards.

Helplessness and confusion were running rampant through her mind and along with it came fatigue. She didn't have the energy for a post-mortem on what had just happened and she hoped George realised that. She tucked a stray curl behind her ear and shook her head.

'We shouldn't have done that.' Her words were a whisper.

'Why not?'

'Well, for starters, someone could have walked in and caught us.' She pointed to the door.

'They didn't.'

'I'm due in Theatre soon. I should be concentrating. Hand reconstruction isn't the same as a knee arthroscopy, you know.' She turned and walked over to the kitchen bench, bracing her hands on the edge.

'I know the difference,' he replied, and she heard him walk towards her. She was so instinctively aware of him it frightened her. George rubbed his hands up and down her arms, making her resent her outburst. 'I apologise for the timing. You're right. You should be concentrating.'

He dropped his hands, although he didn't move back. Melody felt slightly bereft but drew warmth from the nearness of his body.

'We do, however,' he continued, 'need to talk.'

'No, we don't.' She turned to look at him, determination running through her body. 'We don't need to discuss or dissect what just happened, George. It happened. Let's just leave it at that. Now, if you'll excuse me, I need to get my thoughts in order regarding this operation.' With that, she sidestepped him and walked to the table.

She collected her notes, conscious of his gaze on her. When she reached the door, she congratulated herself on not giving in to the urge to throw herself back into his arms. Just before she opened the door, he spoke.

'We do need to talk, Melody, and we will.'

She glanced over her shoulder, to see brown eyes that had not too long ago been filled with desire were now filled with determination. Not trusting herself to say anything, she continued out the door, heading to the emergency theatres, determined to push all thoughts of George Wilmont aside and do her job.

CHAPTER ELEVEN

GEORGE STOOD IN the tea room for a good ten minutes after she'd walked out. His thoughts were completely jumbled and he was having a difficult time making head or tail of them. He'd kissed Melody—he'd kissed another woman!

Guilt swamped him and he closed his eyes. The guilt wasn't only because he felt as though he was cheating on his wife, but the fact that he'd actively pursued Melody, desperate to taste the sweetness of her mouth. He'd *wanted* to kiss her and the guilt from that alone was enough to keep him company for a very long time. What kind of man did that make him? He'd always thought himself honourable, trusting and sincere.

Well, he'd been sincere about kissing Melody. He'd been trusting that his feelings were reciprocated. But honourable? His thoughts had hardly been honourable as he'd held her against him, pressing his mouth to hers, wanting her as close as possible.

What had he been thinking? He had responsibilities. He had a job to do. His behaviour was far from professional yet at the same time it was becoming increasingly difficult to control his desire where Melody was concerned.

She was interfering with his work, his concentration, and it wouldn't do. Right at this moment he was supposed to be working with his staff but he'd needed to see her, needed to touch her, needed to kiss her.

He opened his eyes and paced the room, forcing his thoughts into order. He'd kissed a woman who wasn't Veronique. His wife had died only eighteen months ago and here he was yearning for someone else. He was sure that if their positions had been reversed, Veronique wouldn't have forgotten him so quickly and the knowledge stabbed at his heart.

George grimaced, pushing his fingers roughly through his hair and clenching his jaw. Never before had he allowed any woman to come between him and his work. He'd always separated them into neat little sections. He'd always prided himself on being one hundred percent focused where work was concerned but now he appeared to have no control whatsoever.

He had the responsibilities of the visiting orthopaedic surgeon Fellowship to uphold. He had responsibilities to his staff. He had lectures to write, operations to perform and scheduled deadlines to meet. Even when the tour finished in early December, he was due back at his hospital in Melbourne. They were waiting for him. He had obligations there as well.

Yet one look at Melody and everything had gone! Gone! He shoved his hands in his pockets, thoroughly disgusted with himself and his behaviour. How could a woman make him lose control—over everything? Everything he'd prided himself on being. Reliable, responsible, respectable.

'Ha!' he snorted in self-disgust. He hadn't even treated Melody with respect. She'd been studying and trying to focus on an extremely difficult procedure and he hadn't cared. Hadn't given her the same consideration he was sure she would have given him had the situations been reversed.

He stopped pacing, his jaw clenched tightly. He shouldn't have kissed her. Shouldn't have—but he had. At least he was man enough to accept his actions and take responsibility for them.

George dragged a deep breath into his lungs, the faint traces of her perfume lingering in the air around him. The awareness between them had been almost unbearable yet now—now both knew how incredible they were together. Kissing Melody hadn't solved anything. It had only increased his desire, his yearning, his curiosity—and that made everything worse!

Melody was tired of concentrating. She'd had three long and meticulous hours in Theatre but at last the first stage of her patient's hand reconstruction was completed. Now they needed to wait and see what happened before she could attempt the next stage.

Wearily, she de-gowned and shuffled to the tea room to write up the notes. Once she'd finished, she sipped her coffee and put her feet up on the seat. Closing her eyes, she sighed, glad the day was coming to an end. 'Just the dinner to get through.'

She'd hoped to get out of it altogether but she knew that wasn't professional. 'I hate being Acting Director,' she mumbled out loud as she quickly finished her coffee.

Melody had hoped to be able to go home, enjoy a relaxing bubble bath, but now she would just have to make do with a quick shower before getting dressed and heading to the hotel for yet another event. She was looking forward to George's talk this evening. She was still constantly amazed that with so many dinners and lectures, he still managed to keep every talk fresh and interesting.

'George,' she sighed, as she drove home and headed into her apartment. If she didn't at least make an appearance tonight, she had the strange feeling he'd probably ring to make sure she was all right. She smiled at the thought. That was nice. Attentive and thoughtful. Apart from kissing her right before she'd had to perform an intricate surgical procedure, he'd always been attentive and thoughtful.

Then again, while he'd been kissing her, he'd most definitely been attentive and thoughtful.

She couldn't help but smile and brush a hand across her lips as she remembered just how attentive he'd been. As she finished getting dressed, tonight choosing to wear a white embroidered bustier and a straight, black, silk skirt that came to her ankles, she couldn't help but wonder what George might think of her outfit, especially the split at the back of the skirt, which was not only sexy but practical as it enabled her to walk without shuffling along. She secured her hair up in a high ponytail, letting her curls do their thing. Slipping her stockinged feet into black shoes then picking up her clutch purse, she was finally ready to go.

She couldn't quell her excitement at seeing George again. She was eager to see his reaction to her outfit. To glimpse that smouldering desire in the brown depths of his eyes. To feel her heartbeat increase when he looked at her. To hope for another forbidden kiss.

She drove with care to the function centre and walked through the door at eight o'clock, only half an hour late. She casually walked over to the corner of the room and, holding her breath, searched for George.

'From the back, you look ravishing,' a deep voice said from directly behind her. His breath fanned down her bare neck and Melody couldn't help the shiver of delight that raced through her. 'I don't know if I'm game enough for you to turn around,' he whispered. 'You have the sexiest legs I've ever seen.'

Melody was thankful the room was now swarming with people as waiters brought out trays of food. She had no idea what to say to George. Her mind had gone blank the instant he'd spoken and all she'd been aware of had been the richness of his voice and the emotions he'd stirred up in her.

'Are you purposely trying to drive me insane?' he asked as she slowly turned to face him.

'And if I am?' she challenged, a twinkle of delight in her eyes.

George's smile increased. 'Are you flirting with me, Dr Janeway?'

Melody laughed, amazed at how a few seconds in his company increased her excitement. 'Feels a lot like it, from what I can recall.'

'You are…' he paused, his gaze filled with desire as he looked down into her eyes '…irresistible.'

'I think I'm moving up in the world,' Melody replied, and at George's frown she continued, 'Well, last night you said I was beautiful. The night before you said I was stunning. Tonight it's irresistible.'

He nodded, a slight smile playing on his lips. 'That's because I remember how good you felt in my arms. I'd give anything right now to take you out of here so we can be—' He stopped. 'Ah—yes—hello again, Mr Okanadu.' George quickly changed his tone as he reached over and shook hands with Melody's colleague.

'How did you get on with the surgery, Melody?' Mr Okanadu asked.

George instantly felt like a heel. He'd been so busy admiring Melody that he'd completely forgotten she'd spent the better part of the afternoon performing a difficult piece of surgery. He listened to her reply, glad to hear the patient was doing well.

Moments later, Carmel came over and instructed George it was time for his speech and that they should all return to their tables. George gave his speech, once again adjusting the material to make it fresh and informative. Melody admired him and his professionalism. She also noted that when he sat back down again he moved his chair slightly closer to hers.

In fact, by the time they'd finished their main meal she could feel the warmth emanating from George's leg so close to her own. She tried hard to focus on what Mr Okanadu was saying, nodding and smiling politely, all the while unbearably conscious of George. She could hear her heart thumping wildly against her ribs, could feel the pinpricks of excitement coursing down her spine, could feel her body crying out for his touch. Her reaction was becoming too intrusive and she sternly told herself to stop it.

'Don't you agree?' Mr Okanadu was saying, and Melody hadn't the faintest idea of what he'd been talking about. Once more, she'd been too caught up in thoughts of George that her mind seemed unable to function.

She frowned thoughtfully and said, 'Hmm,' as well as nodding slightly.

'Excuse me,' George said, and Melody quickly turned to give him her attention. He saw an unmistakable hint of passion reflected in her green eyes and for a moment he lost his train of thought. His gut twisted with delight and despair. Things were starting to get way out of hand. 'Ahh…' He frowned and nearly groaned in frustration as her lips parted, her breathing marginally audible. He swallowed, watching as her gaze flicked down to his mouth before returning to his eyes.

It was then his sluggish brain registered that she was waiting for him to speak. Although the looks they'd exchanged seemed to have happened in slow motion, George knew it had only been a few seconds. At least, he hoped it had. Melody had the ability to make him forget all rational thought and in some ways he resented it. No other woman had affected him that way before—not even Veronique.

He cleared his throat. 'Er…you said there were several recordings in the hospital library of other surgeries you've performed, correct?'

'Ye—' Her voice broke and she realised her mouth was dry. She coughed and George immediately held out her water glass. 'Thank you.' She took a quick sip and nodded her head as she replaced her glass. 'Yes.'

'How long ago did you do them?'

She thought for a moment, realising that the person on the other side of George was also listening intently to their conversation. Oh, she hoped and prayed that no one could read the emotions in her eyes when she looked at the visiting surgeon! 'One was in February this year and the other was July. In both cases we've also recorded the follow-up visits, thereby keeping a complete record of any of the after-effects from the surgery.'

'And you're planning to use this case for your research project?'

'This patient will be included, along with the other patients from February and July.'

'Good.' He cleared his throat. 'Uh—I have an evening off tomorrow and I'd be interested in viewing those recordings. Do you think the hospital library will let me borrow them?'

Melody felt the beginning of a smile twitching at her lips. 'Oh, I'm sure they would.'

George watched her lips, noticing she was trying to suppress a smile. He glanced over his shoulder to see that the person next to him was now talking to someone else. He returned his attention to Melody. 'What?' Even as he asked the question, he could feel the tug of his own lips turning upwards. Her eyes were alive with amusement and his gut twisted again at the sight.

'Oh, nothing,' she replied coyly.

'Come on,' he coaxed, his tone dropping to a more intimate level. He was enjoying teasing her a little.

'I'm just in awe of the glamorous life you lead.'

'Meaning?'

'Meaning that on your only night off in Sydney you're choosing to sit in a hotel room and watch a recording on hand reconstruction.' She paused, smothering the laugh. 'What a party animal.'

George's smile increased. 'Who said I was going to be sitting in a hotel room?'

'Oh, you mean you're going to watch it somewhere at the hospital? You certainly know how to have a good time.'

'No. Actually…' he leaned in a little closer '… I was planning to watch it at your place.' As he eased back, George took great delight in watching her amusement slip away, to be replaced by a startled look as the full impact of his words registered.

He shifted slightly and leaned his arm on the back of his chair. As he did so, his serviette slid to the floor. Bending down to retrieve it, he decided to add fuel to the fire and gently brushed a finger on an exposed part of her calf.

The brief contact made Melody jump, her knee hitting the base of the table, jostling the silver- and glassware on top. Conversations stopped. People looked at her. She could feel herself beginning to blush with embarrassment and smiled quickly.

'Sorry. Patellar reflex,' she explained. Everyone returned to what they'd been doing while Melody glanced down at her fingers, which were clenched tightly around her clutch purse. She needed to get control. She needed to get out of there.

Putting her serviette onto the table, she smiled politely at those around her as she stood. 'Excuse me.' With that, she forced herself not to rush but to walk calmly and steadily away from the table. She could feel George's gaze watching her but she forced herself not to care. How could he have put her in such a situation? What had possessed him to touch her in such an intimate manner?

Her head started to hurt. It had been a long day and when she entered the restroom for a moment of peace and quiet, Melody leaned her hands on the bench top and closed her eyes. She was fatigued, and on top of that she was desperately fighting her mounting attraction to George.

After a few minutes she felt more in control and better able to cope with the rest of the evening. Taking a deep breath, she headed back but as she drew closer to the dining room she detoured to the right and through the French doors that led to the balcony.

'How's that patellar reflex?'

There was no mistaking George's deep, sensual tone and she didn't bother to glance over her shoulder.

'Better.' She looked the other way.

'Liar,' he accused softly as she felt his arm brush hers. She shivered involuntarily, instantly responding to the light touch.

'I think I'm a better judge of how my patellar reflexes are doing.' Melody was still finding it hard to look at him. She knew the moment she did, her anger would melt away like snow on a hot summer's day.

'That wasn't what I meant and you know it.'

She could tell he had a smile on that gorgeous mouth of his, even without seeing it. She closed her eyes against the mental image, willing it to go away. It wouldn't. Why was she so in tune with him? Why couldn't she simply switch off her attraction like a light switch?

'Oh?' Melody reluctantly turned to look at him, only to find his face closer than she'd anticipated. 'What was I…' her breath trembled a little but she forced herself to continue. Hold onto the anger, she willed herself. Hold onto the anger '…expected to say? That the visiting orthopaedic surgeon was fondling my leg? That would have gone over brilliantly!'

George chuckled and the sound invaded her heart. She looked away from him but he gently reached over, cupped her chin and urged her face back round. 'Let's get one thing straight.' The taste of his breath held a hint of the red wine they'd been served and Melody savoured it. 'I didn't *fondle* your leg.'

For one blinding second Melody thought he was denying having touched her in the first place. Had he touched her? Had she just imagined it?

'I *caressed* it,' he confessed on a laugh that turned into a groan as he recalled just how perfect she'd felt beneath his touch. 'There's a big difference. One is clumsy but the other is sensual.'

Melody sighed, clinging vainly to her rapidly dissolving anger. 'Well, you still shouldn't have done it.'

'I couldn't help myself.' He shrugged, frowning as he did so.

'Next time try harder!'

'I'm sorry.'

He touched his hand to her shoulder but removed it the instant she glared at him. They were out in public. Anyone might see them talking so intimately together. She edged to the side a little, hoping to put more distance between them.

'I didn't know you were going to react like that. Honestly.'

His tone was so sincere she knew she'd already forgiven him. 'It's all right.' She turned to look out over the city. They were both silent for a few minutes, a comfortable, companionable silence, while they soaked up the beautiful, warm night.

'It's nice here,' he stated. 'In Sydney, I mean.'

'Yeah.'

'How long have you lived here?' Despite the attraction between them, George had to keep reminding himself that he really didn't know Melody all that well.

'In Sydney? About five years now. I attended medical school and did all my training out at Parramatta.'

'Do you like it here? I mean, do you have any plans to leave?'

She shook her head. 'I love it here. I'm close to my brothers, my nieces and nephews and, of course, my parents.'

'Family's important to you?'

'Yes, of course.' Melody paused. 'What about you? Are you close to your sisters?'

'I am. We probably talk about once a month, especially while I've been travelling, but Casey and Rachel talk daily, especially with Rachel in New Zealand.'

'Where does Casey live?'

'She's in Queensland. So are my parents.'

'Oh. Do you have other family in Melbourne?'

He shook his head slowly. 'Veronique's family's in Melbourne. She was born in Sydney but her dad changed jobs and the whole family moved to Melbourne when she was about twelve.'

'Are you close to them?' At the mention of his wife Melody had straightened away from the balcony railing. She kept forgetting he was a widower, a man with experience of what it felt like to be truly loved and accepted by one special person—and that person had been taken from him.

'I'm...' George thought for a moment, as though he was choosing his words carefully. 'They're important to me but... I haven't seen them in almost twelve months.'

'I guess you've had to make a lot of sacrifices this year.' And he'd done it all to carry out his wife's last wishes. Melody took a small step back, starting to realise that, despite what she might be feeling for George, it probably paled in comparison to what he'd shared with his wife. There was no way she'd ever want to compete with his affections for his wife but she had hoped, given the events of this week, that perhaps they were on the verge of a new beginning—for both of them.

'Sacrifices.' He laughed without humour. 'I've made plenty of those.' George looked out at the city lights before them. 'In almost every place I've been I've taken a mental snapshot of the lights, the buildings, the essence of a place, talking to Veronique about what I see and what I'm doing.' He raked a hand through his hair. 'Or at least that's how it started. Then, somewhere along the line, I stopped doing that because I was tired or had to write another lecture or the thousand other things Carmel needs me to do.' His sigh was one mixed with wistfulness and regret. 'I do miss her. So very much.'

'Uh-huh.' Melody wasn't even sure he was aware of her presence as he seemed to be almost talking to himself. He missed his wife, he was lonely and loneliness could make people do desperate things, like kiss a colleague in the heat of the moment. It made her realise she shouldn't read too much into the personal moments she'd shared with George. He'd be gone in a few days and she'd be here, getting on with her life.

She'd known that all along. At the end of the week George would leave and that would be the end of that. However, that wasn't what she wanted any more. Melody wanted to continue to explore where this burgeoning relationship was headed, to see whether George really was *the one* for her. She'd been so unlucky in love in the past, with both Ian and Emir breaking her heart through their cheating and their lies. Now she'd found a hard-working, open and honest man who could make her insides melt with just one desire-filled glance, and kissed her in a way that no one had ever kissed her before.

Still, there was a streak of distrust in her psyche. If they were to pursue this frighteningly natural chemistry that existed between them, would there come a time in her life when she wouldn't question and double-check everything he'd said to her? She'd believed him when he'd said he didn't have a woman in every port, that she was different, unique and special, but who was to say that wouldn't change after he returned to his life in Melbourne?

He would go back to work, find the natural rhythm of his life again, and he would forget all about the crazy red-head in Sydney who had given him a pleasant momentary interlude. She would be cast aside once again, left to pick up the pieces of her life, because from the way he was talking, the way he was reminiscing about Veronique, his tone clearly radiating his love, Melody started to really get it through her thick, emotional skull that George wasn't ready to move on.

'George! There you are.' Carmel opened the door to the balcony. 'I've been looking everywhere for you. Several people are asking after you.' It was then Carmel saw Melody standing back from George and she smiled brightly. 'Oh, hey, Melody. I didn't see you there.'

'I was just about to head inside,' Melody stated.

'OK. I just need to go over a few things with George.'

'No problem.'

Carmel held the door for Melody, then turned her attention to George. 'I know you're tired, George, and I know coming to Sydney has probably been one of the more difficult stops on the tour,' Carmel was saying as Melody left the balcony. 'I know Veronique planned for a full day off so she could show you some of her favourite places but we can cut our time here short and—'

Melody didn't want to hear any more. It was time to face facts, to be honest with herself. George couldn't be part of her life, couldn't be part of her future. She had to view this week as being akin to a holiday romance, one pleasant week of diversions, but soon it would be time to return to reality and her reality was here, at St Aloysius, focusing on running the department, treating her patients and concentrating on her research project.

Did it really matter if she was to never marry, to never find the one person she wanted to spend the rest of her life with? Did it really matter if she never had children?

Even at the thought, tears began to mist her eyes and she quickly sniffed them away.

The exhaustion of Melody's day—in fact, the combined exhaustion of the entire week so far—began to catch up with her, and when she looked towards the dining room she decided she'd had enough. George needed the time to properly grieve for his wife, to come to terms with his loss, and to do that it meant that she needed to completely remove herself from the equation. Being around her, spending time with her, was probably more of a distraction for George than anything else, despite what he'd told her. Right now, she couldn't be certain George knew what he wanted, and it was up to her to be the strong one and to keep whatever was happening between them on a purely platonic level.

Sadness swamped her at the decision. Not bothering to say goodbye to anyone, she returned to her car and wearily drove home. It was too late for her bubble bath. Once inside, she merely stripped off her glamorous clothes, brushed her teeth and pulled on a pair of boxer shorts and a singlet top before climbing between the sheets and crying herself to sleep.

Once again, she was the one to miss out.

CHAPTER TWELVE

MELODY MANAGED TO concentrate during most of Thursday but as the day wore on the more nervous she became. Had George meant what he'd said? Was he still planning to come around to her place that evening to watch the recordings of her hand and microsurgery reconstructions? Had he only been joking?

She checked her phone several times to see if he'd sent her a message or if she'd missed a call but there was nothing. She knew he had a hectic schedule but surely he could have texted to confirm or something? Perhaps that meant he wasn't coming. The knowledge deflated her.

She'd managed ward round and clinic without a problem, as well as getting a debrief from Andy on the status of Rudy Carlew. So far there had been no complications with his surgery and it looked as though he was going to make an uncomplicated recovery.

'Apparently,' Andy told her, 'he's quite impressed with our Evelyn. He's asked her to stay on as his private nurse for the rest of the movie shoot.'

'Good.' Melody nodded sternly. 'That way we can be sure his arm won't be exacerbated. Evelyn knows what to keep an eye out for.'

'Good heavens, Melody. Don't you see the underlying meaning here?'

'What?' Melody frowned at her registrar, focusing on

his face as his words started to sink in. 'What's the underlying meaning?'

'That Rudy Carlew and Evelyn are a couple.'

'Really?' Melody was surprised. 'So soon? They hardly know each other.'

'That doesn't matter. When it's the right person, it's just right,' he pointed out. 'That's how it was with me and my wife. Bam!' He clapped his hands together. 'Like a bolt of lightning. Two months later we were married.'

Melody continued to think about what Andy had said for the rest of the day. She had been trying so hard *not* to think about George but perhaps she should? Perhaps she should consider that she'd been struck by lightning! When her phone rang, she immediately hoped it was George, calling to let her know whether or not he was coming, but instead the image of the caller on her phone screen indicated it was her brother.

'Ethan. How's everything going, big brother?'

'Good. CJ's back at work three and a half days a week and I get two whole days of being Mr Mum to my gorgeous Lizzie-Jean.'

Melody giggled. 'I can't believe you're married with a little girl. After everything you've been through, you finally got your happy ending.' As she was speaking, she felt tears choke her throat.

Before marrying CJ, Ethan had been married to Abigail and expecting his first child, but both his wife and his baby girl had passed away, leaving Ethan almost killing himself with work. Thankfully, Melody's new sister-in-law, who had been left alone and pregnant, had saved her brother. Now the three of them were a family and she couldn't have been happier for them. Everyone was getting their happy ending. Andy had found his wife, even Evelyn had found Rudy Carlew. What about her?

Images of George immediately came to mind and she

gasped a little at how readily her thoughts turned to him. She cared about him and she always would. Closing her eyes, she whimpered as she realised she might have given her heart to a man who might not return her feelings— *again*.

'Mel? Are you OK?' Ethan asked.

'What? Yeah. Why?'

'Because you're whimpering down the phone. What's wrong, sis?'

'Oh…well…everything.'

Ethan chuckled. 'That narrows it down.'

'Uh—I've sort of met someone.'

'Sort of?'

'Remember I told you about the visiting orthopaedic surgeon who was coming?'

'Yeah. A week of lunches, lectures and dinners. You weren't looking—' Ethan stopped. 'You like the VOS?'

'Like? That may be a mild word for the way I feel.'

'What? Wait. What's this guy like? Do Dave and I need to come and meet him? We can come on Saturday and meeting this guy and—'

'Whoa, there, over-protective brother. Steady on.' Melody sighed and told Ethan what had happened over the past few days since George had burst into her life. When she finished, Ethan chuckled.

'It sounds as though you're definitely smitten. I remember feeling like that with CJ. I struggled against it but in the end I came to realise that although we hadn't known each other long, we knew each other deeply. Sometimes, Mel, you just click with people and it sounds as though you've really clicked with George.'

'But what am I supposed to do if he *does* come over tonight to watch these surgeries?'

'If he does come over, Mel, I don't think it's going to be because he wants to watch the surgeries,' Ethan chuckled.

'Why? What does he want to do, then?' She gasped, answering her own question. 'Do you really think he wants to…?' She spoke softly into the phone, a warm blush tingeing her cheeks. She was glad she was alone in her office.

'I think he might just want to spend time with you. From what you've said, he seems to be the gentlemanly type. I should know. I'm one.'

'Ha!' Melody teased her brother. 'Seriously, Ethan, what do I do if he *does* just want to—you know, hang out.' She'd only been telling herself just that morning that she wasn't going to get involved with George on anything other than a professional and platonic level, yet even at the thought of George being in her apartment, Melody's body had ignited with desire. The memory of being held close against him, the way his mouth had melded perfectly with her own, the way he could make her forget about absolutely everything when he stared deeply into her eyes…

'What if I get hurt again, Ethan?' she blurted out before her brother could answer. 'I mean, yeah, it's great that I'm putting myself out there again, but do I really want to? Should I? Can I trust my judgement? Is that actually why I've fallen for George, because I know he's unavailable and therefore it's as though I'm doing a pre-emptive strike on getting hurt? Emir didn't want me, so why should George? What if I'm destined to only fall for unavailable men?'

'Oh, sis,' Ethan empathised. 'You're not doing any of those things and Emir was a fool. So was Ian. Both were idiots because any man would be lucky to have someone as awesome as you.'

'You have to say that. You're my brother!'

'Perhaps but you're actually being much braver than before and it does sound as though this George Wilmont guy—who I'm going to investigate online as soon as we've finished this conversation—is a decent fellow and if there's one thing you definitely deserve, it's someone decent.'

Melody forced herself to calm down. 'You're right. And, besides, he might just want to have a platonic evening of watching surgeries.'

'Because we surgeons are quite boring like that,' he joked. 'Look, you like him so use the opportunity to get to know him better. Ask him the burning questions that are no doubt churning through your mind even now, or just let go and enjoy wherever the evening takes you.'

'But he's still in love with his first wife.'

'And he always will be, but it's not a love that's based in the present. It's a love that's based in the past and sooner or later he'll realise that living with ghosts may be detrimental to his health.' Ethan's tone was soft. She knew he was speaking from experience, that he would always have a love for his first wife, but he adored his present wife.

'OK. So I should just enjoy where the evening takes me.'

'Yep.'

'I think I can do that.'

'And remember—forward is good. You told me that.'

'I did, didn't I?'

'Take your own advice, sis. I'd better go. I can hear Lizzie-Jean grizzling for attention.'

'Ooh. Give her a big kiss from her aunty Mel.'

'Will do. Love you, sis.'

'Love you, too, Ethan.'

After she'd ended the call, she sat at her desk and mumbled, 'Forward is good.' She was still telling herself that as she unlocked her front door a few hours later. She'd heard no word from George, so obviously he'd decided not to keep their—their what? Appointment? Date?

She hurried to her room and kicked off her shoes, pulling the clip out of her hair at the same time. Well, if he wasn't coming round, she might be able to finally get that bubble bath she'd promised herself yesterday evening. At least there was no dinner to attend tonight. Still, she'd give him another hour and if he didn't turn up she'd break out the bubbles. Melody changed out of her work clothes into a loose flowing skirt and top, taking time to brush her hair before heading to the kitchen for a drink. She eyed the choice of soothing herbal teas in her cupboard while she waited for the kettle to boil and eventually chose chamomile. She checked the kitchen clock—seven thirty-seven.

'Oh, stop it,' she told herself as she ran a hand through her hair, but the words were easier said than done. She was anxious and on edge. Would he or wouldn't he come? Perhaps she should call him?

When the doorbell rang she jumped in fright, then remained glued to the spot for a whole ten seconds. Was it him? With her heart pounding rapidly, she smoothed her hands down her skirt, telling herself there was nothing to be concerned about, and forced her legs to carry her towards the door.

She opened the door to see George standing there, holding a bottle of wine. 'Hi.' He was wearing a navy polo shirt and the same denim jeans she'd seen him in the other night—the ones that fitted him to perfection. Melody simply stood and stared at him for a long moment, completely forgetting her manners. He was here. 'Can I come in?' he asked slowly, and she finally snapped out of her trance.

'Of course. Of course.' She stepped back to permit him access to her apartment. 'I wasn't sure if you were coming or not.'

'I left a message on your phone.'

'You did?' She frowned as she grabbed her phone and checked. Sure enough, there was a message from George, the time indicating he'd tried to call her while she'd been talking to Ethan. 'Sorry. I didn't get it.'

'Never mind.' He handed her the wine and she turned to take it into the kitchen and put it onto the bench. She knew she needed to pull herself together, she knew she needed to be professional and platonic. Friendship. That's what she could offer him—for now, or at least until she figured out what was really happening between them. 'Would you like a glass now?' She turned to open the overhead cupboard to retrieve glasses.

'No.'

She jumped at the sound of his soft, deep voice from behind her, not realising he'd followed her into the kitchen. When she turned to face him she gasped in surprise. The look in his eyes was unmistakably raw with repressed desire and she parted her lips, her breathing instantly erratic.

His gaze travelled the length of her body, taking in her clothes. 'You look...' He didn't finish the sentence but instead slowly drew closer to her, causing her insides to heat and spiral with warmth. Nothing could have made her look away from him at that heart-stopping moment, and before she could utter a word George hauled her into his arms, his mouth hungrily capturing her own.

In contrast to the kiss they'd shared yesterday, this one was hot and heavy, leaving Melody in little doubt about just how attracted to her George was. So much for the decision to offer a professional and platonic relationship.

His hands roved over her back as he deepened the kiss. She went with him, eager to keep up, eager to show him just how mutual the desire was. He groaned and urged her backwards and soon she felt the coolness of the wall against her back. He leaned in, his body pressing against her own, and she felt her breasts crushed against the firmness of his chest.

The smell of raw, unleashed craving mingled between them as the need for more rose urgently in both of them. She dug her fingers into his shoulder blades before sliding them firmly down his back, feeling the flexed muscles beneath. Wanting to touch him, she impatiently tugged his shirt from the waistband of his jeans, her fingers now itching to make contact with his skin.

When the task was finally completed, she moaned with delight when she reached her objective. His skin was hot to her touch just as she'd known it would be. Giving in to the itch that had been building within her since early Monday morning, she allowed her hands to explore the solid contours of his torso, committing each one to memory.

George groaned against her mouth, unable to believe how this woman could set him on fire. The sensations he was experiencing were all completely foreign but he was definitely enjoying each new one she discovered. The touch of her hands on his body, the way her mouth was responding to his, giving in to every one of his needs, matching them eagerly.

She lifted one leg slightly and coiled it around the back of his, before sliding it slowly down to the floor. The action caused a stirring deep within him and he could feel himself losing control of the situation.

Breaking his mouth free, they both gasped in air before he pushed her hair aside and smothered the smoothness of her gorgeous neck in hot, feverish kisses. He then changed direction and dipped towards the exposed skin above her breasts. Her hands slid out from his shirt at the same time she murmured his name. 'Mmm,' she sighed, lacing her fingers through his hair. 'George.'

The way she said his name pierced right to his heart and he realised that things were getting out of control. He worked his way up, not wanting to break the contact immediately but knowing he must—and soon. He nipped at her ear lobe and she giggled. The sound was intensely provocative and the last thing he needed right now.

He hadn't meant to lose control like that, to grab her and smother her with kisses almost the first instant after he'd walked into her apartment...but she was all he'd been able to think about for most of the day, especially as he hadn't seen that much of her. He'd missed her and his need for her had increased.

'Melody.' With his breathing still out of control, he looked down at her face. Her eyes were closed, her parted lips were dark pink and swollen from his kisses, her breathing as ragged as his own. She was a vision of loveliness. Unable to resist, he brushed his lips against hers, forcing himself not to deepen the kiss.

'Mmm,' she murmured again, and when he brushed them a third time her hands clamped themselves on either side of his head and held his lips where they belonged. Seductively, she ran her tongue over his lips and was thrilled with the shudder that tore through his body.

Ever so slowly, she kissed him again. Teasing and testing, refusing to deepen the kiss.

'Melody.' This time her name was torn from his lips and she was satisfied with the response.

She kissed him again, not wanting him to speak for she'd already sensed his slow but sure withdrawal. Even though their bodies were still pressed firmly together, George had already mentally distanced himself. She didn't want to think about things rationally and if they stopped completely, then they'd have to talk things through.

Melody just wanted to go on feeling exactly as she was feeling now, not caring about her already bruised heart or the fact that the man in her arms would be leaving within forty-eight hours. She breathed slowly against his mouth before tasting him once again. Now that she knew how incredible they were together, it was something she'd probably crave for the rest of her life.

He didn't break free and he didn't hurry her. Instead, he took what she was offering but held himself under rigid control, still marvelling at how easily he'd lost his perspective. Perhaps the building resistance they'd been employing for the past four days had increased his drive. Whatever this was between them, George knew he'd never experience anything like it again. This was unique for him.

Knowing the moment had come when she couldn't hang onto the physical pull any longer, Melody lowered her hands to his shoulders and slowly opened her eyes. His brown eyes were gazing down into hers, the fire still burning but gradually being doused.

Neither of them spoke but the communication was there. As their breathing steadied to a more normal pace, George reluctantly eased himself away from her. For one fleeting instant he thought Melody might overrule him and drag his body back where it belonged. Instead, she let her hands fall limply to her sides, her gaze dipping briefly to his lips before she looked down at the floor.

He felt awful. How could he have kissed her *again*? He'd already told himself that they would just be friends, colleagues and nothing more. It wasn't fair, to either of them, to torture themselves as they just had. Their lives were running on two completely different tracks. Despite how much he was attracted to her, he also owed her the respect and common decency he would show to other female colleagues. Guilt started to swamp him and he opened his mouth, an apology on his lips.

'Don't.' Melody held up her hand. 'Don't apologise. We both wanted it, we both needed it and we'll both take responsibility for it.'

'You're right, but I was also going to say I never meant it to happen.'

'Liar.' She crossed her arms defensively over her body, rubbing her arms, her body still feeling bereft of his touch. She turned and headed into the living room, leaving him to follow her or stay where he was. She needed to sit down.

'Why am I a liar?' He followed her into the living room. She was sitting with her legs tucked beneath her skirt on a large wingback chair. Her hands were clenched tightly in her lap and her eyes were momentarily closed.

Melody fought for composure before opening her eyes to look at him. 'Because you did mean that kiss to happen. We may not have realised it, but it's been building ever since we met on Monday.' She shrugged, displaying a nonchalance she didn't feel. 'It was…inevitable.'

He registered the truth of her words as he slumped down into the matching chair beside her. 'When you opened the door, I guess everything became too much to control. I was relieved we could see each other without being surrounded by people. I was still trying to resist you because I knew it was the right thing to do, and I was slightly annoyed because you left last night without saying goodbye.' George sighed and shifted in his chair, his gaze intently holding hers.

'Then I had meeting after meeting,' he continued, 'talking to people and presenting information, discussing operating techniques, and the entire time all I could think about was *you*. About seeing you tonight, about being near you, holding you, kissing you.' His gaze dropped to encompass her mouth as he spoke, another thread of desire running through her at such a look. He cleared his throat and eased back in his chair. 'I even snapped at Carmel—twice—and it wasn't even her fault. It was simply because I was behaving like a hormonal, preoccupied teenager.'

'Wow.' She cleared her throat. 'That's, ah, a lot of information to process.'

'We need to be open, to not be afraid to ask questions,' he stated. 'Or answer them.' He reached across, holding out his hand to her, which she accepted. 'Deal?'

Melody felt warmth wash over her at the soft touch from his hand. Open honesty from a man? Was that possible? 'Deal.'

'So…' He gave her hand a little squeeze before releasing it. George settled back in the chair. 'You mentioned you studied in Parramatta?'

'Yes.' Melody smiled. She told him about growing up in that area, about the way her family appreciated vintage cars and her brothers had been over-protective, especially during her teenage years.

George raised his hand and chuckled. 'I understand completely.'

'Hey, you're supposed to be on my side.'

He shook his head. 'As a brother of twin sisters, I'm a card-carrying member of the over-protective brother club.'

'Great. Then you'll get on wonderfully with David and Ethan.'

'I'd like to meet them sometime.' George's words flowed easily from his lips but as he said the words Melody's spine prickled with apprehension.

'Does that mean you're planning on staying in touch after you leave?'

He nodded before shifting in his chair. 'This is why I'm here tonight. To get to know you, to become better friends with you. I don't know what this is, Melody, but I do know it doesn't happen every day.'

'Did it feel that way with—?' She stopped, the question about his wife forming before she'd had time to process it.

'With Veronique?' At her nod, he thought for a moment. 'We were colleagues, then friends, then more than friends, then dating, then engaged, then married.'

'Where are we on that scale?'

'I think we're definitely in the "more than friends" bracket but also in the "friends" and "colleagues" brackets as well.' He stood and walked over to the wall, where there were several pictures of her family as well as framed copies of her medical degrees. 'You and I—we're not doing things in the right order.' He turned to face her.

'I think that's why it's so confusing.'

'Did things happen in the right order with your ex-fiancé?'

'Yes. Colleagues, friends, more than friends. We didn't quite make it to the marriage part.'

'Because he cheated on you?'

'Yes. Several times. With several women, women I still see around the hospital, and there are probably more I still don't know about and don't want to know about.' She sighed heavily.

'It still hurts deeply?'

'Being betrayed? Yes.' Melody angled her head to the side, feeling a wave of emotions she'd thought she'd dealt with rise to the surface. 'With Ian, he flat out lied. He was married, didn't tell me. So that was lying creep number one. A while later, enter lying creep number two who wanted to marry me but with the understanding that he didn't want children.' She sniffed and shook her head slowly from side to side. 'I spent a lot of anxious and soul-searching nights wondering if I could be in a marriage without children and eventually I decided that I could. I could accept that Emir didn't want children, that our careers, the care we had for our patients would be enough.'

'You mentioned he moved to Germany to be with the woman he'd impregnated.'

'Yep.' Tears welled in her eyes. 'It made me realise it wasn't that he didn't want children, it was that he didn't want them with me.' She spread her arms wide then let them drop to her side dejectedly. 'He didn't want me.'

'He really was dead in the head not to want you.' George's words were filled with desire and when she looked at him through her tears she could see by his expression that he meant it.

'Thank you.' She took a tissue from the table and dabbed at her eyes. 'Heartbreak isn't easy but somehow we do survive it.'

'The heart mends. Amazing, eh,' he stated rhetorically.

Melody was quiet for a moment before asking softly, 'How did you feel when you learned of Veronique's death?' George clenched his jaw at the question and Melody quickly held up a hand. 'You don't have to answer th—'

'I felt like dying.'

Melody clutched her hands to her chest, her eyes wide with empathy.

'When I heard the news, I…' He shook his head. 'I wanted to die as well.'

She wanted to go to to him, to hold him, but she stayed where she was. 'I'm very glad you didn't. Think of all the people you've met during the past year. Think of how many lives you've touched, how many people you've helped, how many lives have been improved. *You've* empowered surgeons around the world to be able to save their patient's lives. That's an amazing legacy, George.'

'And one Veronique wanted for me.'

Melody leaned back in the chair and smiled. 'You've done her proud.'

'You don't mind me talking about her?'

She shook her head, once again realising that George had a lot of things he needed to sort out if there was ever going to be anything developing between them in the future. He was still grieving, still…broken. They both were. 'Veronique was a major part of your life,' she continued. 'We've all loved and lost. Sometimes through heartbreak, sometimes through death and sometimes through both.'

'Both?'

She shrugged. 'My brother, Ethan, went through a difficult time. His wife died from eclampsia and his baby girl died almost a day later. Ethan worked himself into a frenzy and it was only after he had a mild heart attack that he confessed his wife had been drinking heavily during her pregnancy and that his daughter had suffered from foetal alcohol syndrome.'

'The poor man.'

'He's good now. He's found happiness again and a new family.'

'And I'll bet you were his rock, the sister who pulled him through the darkest times of his life.'

'We're a close family.'

'That's nice.' George held her close. 'Family is important. I've realised that more and more this year. At first, I couldn't wait to get away, to leave the hospital where both Veronique and I had worked. Now I have such mixed emotions about going back because I'm not going back to my old life. My old life doesn't exist any more. It's gone and I can never get it back.'

It was that, more than any talk about his wife, which pierced Melody's heart. George wanted his old life back, which only reiterated that he wasn't ready to look to the future and the possibility of a *new* life. Which was why his next words threw her completely.

'Melody—I want to spend together whatever free time we have left. It's only going to be an hour here or half an hour there, I know, but what do you think?'

'Do you think that's wise? Especially given what you've just said?'

'I don't know any more. I don't know what's right or wrong, what might happen or won't happen. I just know that when I'm around you I feel calm and I haven't felt calm in a *really* long time. It's very selfish of me, and you have every right to say no.' He looked expectantly into her face.

She was secretly delighted he wanted to spend time with her but was also highly cautious. 'Well, we both have hectic schedules so it would make it difficult.' She was trying hard to choose her words carefully. She didn't want him to think she didn't want to spend time with him because she did, but she also needed to gauge how much time would be enough for her to hold onto her sanity. Self-preservation was a key factor in her life, especially with her track record of relationships. 'I'll be in Theatre tomorrow, doing the second part of that hand reconstruction, while you'll be doing your last theatre stint of show and tell.'

He chuckled at her wording. 'That's exactly how it feels sometimes.'

She smiled at him. 'We could have breakfast together on Saturday morning before your flight to Melbourne.'

'At the hotel?'

She shook her head. 'I know a nice all-day breakfast place I'd like to take you to.' They could say a private goodbye and then she could come home and cry her heart out.

'You'll pick me up?'

'Sure. Then I can take you straight to the airport.' Even as she said the words she wasn't sure it was the best idea but he was right when he'd said they had very little time to spend together.

'It's a date.' The way he looked at her, with a mixture of need, want and desire, left her with little doubt as to how she affected him. He clenched his jaw and shoved his hands into his pockets, as though to keep himself from crossing to her side and gathering her close.

They stared at each other for so long she was about to capitulate and cross to his side, eager to have his mouth on hers once more. George cleared his throat. 'We'd better start watching these brilliant reconstructive surgeries of yours before I lose all control.'

'Wait.' His words took a second or two for her sluggish brain to process. 'You were serious about that?'

'Yeah. I really am interested.' He pulled a USB memory stick from his pocket. 'The library downloaded the files onto this stick for me and told me to keep it.'

'You are really strange if your idea of fun is to sit and watch recordings of surgeries.' She took the stick from him and put it into the USB port at the rear of her television.

Soon they were sitting on the lounge facing the television ready to watch the surgery. 'Are you sure?' she checked one last time as he put his arm down the back of the lounge, his body very close to hers. It was exciting and comforting and sexy to have him so near. If this was her holiday romance, she couldn't think of anything better to do on a date. Watching surgery with another surgeon, someone who really understood her work.

'I want to spend time with you, Melody, and tonight this is all the time I have. I don't think either of us are emotionally ready for the result our attraction could provide, so...' He took the remote from her and pressed 'play'. 'If this is the way I get to spend time with you, then so be it.'

'OK, but it goes for over four hours.'

'If I get bored, which I seriously doubt, I'll fast-forward and you can provide me with a commentary about what I've missed.'

'Oh, joy.' Melody couldn't help but laugh at his seriousness on the issue.

'Also, can we order some food? I'm starved.' He kicked off his shoes and pulled out his phone. 'What do you feel like eating? Noodles? Curry? Pizza?'

'Er...curry?' She marvelled at how relaxed and at home he seemed. He was probably so sick and tired of living out of a hotel that being at a real home was probably something of a novelty. He ordered some food, told her it would be delivered in half an hour, then snuggled closer to watch Melody performing surgery.

They both watched as the operating theatre came into focus and there she was, standing at the operating table, explaining the finer points of what she was about to do. She felt self-conscious watching herself, never having sat through a viewing of the recording before, but with George asking questions she found herself reaching for the remote to pause it while they discussed things in more detail.

It was liberating to be able to sit down with a man and discuss a subject she was passionate about. He seemed to be really interested and the knowledge thrilled her. It was wonderful and exhilarating, as well as desperate and sad. Here she was, bonding with a man who would leave her in forty-eight hours.

CHAPTER THIRTEEN

HER NECK HURT. As the pain sent signals to her brain Melody shifted slightly but the pain continued. It felt as though someone was pinching her neck and she wished they'd stop. It was a mosquito, she realised, and swatted it away. No. The pain was still there.

Slowly, she was drawn out of the dream state to reality. The pain in her neck still there and annoying. She must be sleeping at an odd angle. She shifted slightly, only to come up against a hard obstacle.

Had she left her books on the bed again? She kicked at them with her leg but they didn't fall. She kicked them harder, only to hear them groan. Groan! Books didn't groan! Melody frowned. She felt with her foot and realised with a start that it wasn't a book but a leg!

Her eyes snapped open and she tried desperately to focus. She was in her lounge room, the television still on. She was lying against the back of the lounge suite, her legs entwined with George's, his arm holding her possessively to his body. George! Oh, no. They'd been watching her reconstruction recordings and had fallen asleep.

She scrambled into an upright position, shaking him fiercely. 'Wake up.' She shook him. 'George. Wake up.' With the tiny beams of light peeking from behind her thick curtains, she guessed it to be quite early in the morning.

'Huh?' He slowly moved, stretching languorously. Melody was pierced with longing as she watched him. His body was lean and hard, muscles tensing firmly before relaxing. His leg brushed hers, igniting a spark she'd been trying to repress ever since he'd arrived last night. He shifted to a sitting position beside her and peered blearily into her eyes.

'Mmm.' With his eyes half-closed, he leant over and kissed her soundly on the mouth. 'Hi, there.' His voice was deep and low. 'Guess we must have dozed off.' He reached for her, gathering her into his arms. She resisted him but only slightly. He nuzzled her neck. 'You're a cuddly girl at heart, aren't you?'

Melody smiled. The embarrassment from their impromptu night on the lounge faded a little. How could she resist when he said such nice things?

He pointed to the TV. 'How long did you say that last recording went on for?'

'They're all about four hours and we did watch two—or was it three? We started the second one after we'd finished eating, I remember that.'

George laughed, a deep rumbling sound that warmed her. 'I guess it doesn't really matter. Besides, I think we were both exhausted.'

'It has been an incredibly hectic week,' she replied as she went to move from his arms.

'Where are you going?'

'To grab the remote.' She pointed to where the remote had fallen off the table onto the floor.

'Wait.' He shifted to the right and, sticking his leg out to the side, he managed to bring it closer. 'Almost got it.' He reached over further before crowing triumphantly as he snatched it up into his hand. 'Done.' He pointed it at the set and turned it off.

It was then Melody noticed the clock on the wall. 'What? That can't be right.' She scrambled for her mobile phone and checked the time. 'Ten to eight! I'm due at work in ten minutes.'

Melody sprang from his arms and rushed out the room. Moments later, George could hear the shower running. He shook his head. Carmel must be having a hissy fit. He grimaced as he stood, stretching his cramped muscles again before pulling his phone from his pocket. He'd purposely put it on silent all night, not wanting to be disturbed. Sure enough, there were several missed calls from Carmel and even more text messages.

With a reluctant sigh he called Carmel back. 'Carmel,' he said into the receiver when she answered. A split second later he held the phone away from his ear as Carmel's voice boomed through. 'Calm down,' he tried. It didn't work. He heard the shower stop and realised that Melody was going to be leaving her house very soon. As he'd come in a taxi last night, he had no way of getting back to his hotel—well, no way that wouldn't take another half an hour or more. She'd have to give him a lift.

'Carmel,' he said finally, 'you're wasting time. What's my schedule?' He listened intently, his mind working overtime. 'All right. Bring me a change of clothes and a clean suit. I'll meet you in the theatre block.' He could at least have a shower and change there. He disconnected the call then headed to the kitchen, his stomach grumbling as he checked the contents of Melody's fridge.

A few minutes later she came rushing into the kitchen while he finished his orange juice and bit into an apple. 'Can I get you anything?' he asked.

'Yes. Get out of my apartment!'

'Not a problem. Which way is your car?'

'What?' Melody exploded. 'You can't come to work with me.'

'Why not? I need to go to the hospital. You're going there. What's the problem?'

She looked at him as though he'd grown an extra head. 'The problem, Professor, is that everyone will see you coming to work in my car and as you're dressed in casual clothes, they'll put two and two together and make four!'

'So?'

Melody threw her hands up in exasperation. 'Typical of you. You'll be gone tomorrow and I'll have to live with the rumours and gossip—*again*.' She didn't have time for this. She reached into the fridge and pulled out a banana before storming from the kitchen, George hard on her heels.

'It's not fair,' she continued to mutter. 'Not to my emotions, not to my neurotic thought processes and not to my anxiety, all of which are flaring right now and blending themselves in a fine state.' Her voice broke at the end and she sniffed, doing her best to keep herself under control. She needed to drive. She needed a clear head and yet with George being so close to her, being so insistent, she was finding it difficult to get her thoughts in order. Of course, what he said made perfect, logical sense but emotionally being in the car with him and driving to the hospital first thing in the morning was increasing her irrational levels to maximum.

'This is different and you know it. Nothing happened last night.'

'You know that and I know that but the fact remains that we'll be seen arriving together and you'll be leaving tomorrow.'

'What am I supposed to do?'

'Call a taxi and wait.'

'I can't. I'm lecturing at eight.'

'Then you're going to be late, no matter what you do.' She stormed towards her car, which was located in the communal garage. 'Look, George, I've spent a lot of time picking up the pieces of my life since Emir left and I'm not about to give the people at St Aloysius the chance to give me pitying looks accompanied by not-so-quiet whispers behind my back as I walk past them.'

'Melody, you're overreacting. Besides, what does it matter what people say about you? Surely you're above all that.'

Melody was filled with temper and frustration, and at his comment she wanted to throw something at him. 'You just don't get it, do you? I don't care what people think. They respect me as a surgeon and a professional, but there's only so much gossip and speculation a girl can take, George, and right at the moment I don't choose to take any more.' She'd unlocked her car and noticed that George was determined to get in. He sat beside her as she revved the engine and reversed.

'Drop me a block before the hospital and I'll walk the rest of the way,' he told her quietly, and she started to feel silly about her tirade.

She sighed with resignation. 'Listen, I'm sor—'

'No.' He held up his hand. 'It's fine. You don't need to apologise.'

Although his words sounded sincere, the strained silence that followed made Melody realise that things had just changed—again. She shook her head as she pulled to the kerb a block away from the hospital. His smile was forced when he climbed out and started walking. This week had been a mix of exhaustion and exhilaration and as she drove away from him, glancing at him in her rear-vision mirror, she felt a sense of loss.

'What is *wrong* with you? You're behaving like a complete nut case and all because he needed a lift and you didn't want to be gossiped about.' She reached her designated parking spot. 'It's not as though George is anything special, just a holiday romance, an interlude. Nothing more, yet you're behaving as though you're completely smitten with him.' As she spoke the words out loud to her empty car she gasped. Turning off the engine, she covered her hands with her face and shook her head. 'No. No, no, no, no, no. You are *not*.'

She shoved the thoughts away, but they refused to budge. 'No. You are not in love with him. You are *not*.' But even as she denied it to herself, the truth seemed to slap her in the face. She didn't want to be in love with George Wilmont. 'Nope. I refuse.' She dropped her hands, straightened her shoulders and climbed from the car.

After locking it, she headed towards her office on legs that felt all stiff and uncooperative. *You're in love, you're in love, you're in love*, the rhythm of her steps seemed to state. 'No, I'm not, no, I'm not, no, I'm not,' she mumbled softly to herself, but even when she denied it, she knew it was true.

She was in love with George and not in the way she'd been in love before. Oh, no. This was the *real* thing. With Emir she'd felt secure and safe, yet with George she *needed* him just as she needed oxygen to breathe. He'd become a part of her. A vital, desperate part and one she couldn't bear to be without—yet she had to.

Somehow she managed to pull herself together and concentrate on work. She managed to make it in time for ward round and then headed to Theatre. The second part of the hand reconstruction went extremely well and the success of the operation did much to bolster her failing spirits.

She didn't get time to see George as between an emergency case and a full clinic she was swamped for the rest of the day. That night she dressed carefully in the last outfit she'd bought for her week as host to the visiting orthopaedic surgeon. It was his official farewell dinner and she wanted to look perfect. She was desperate to see that spark of desire in his eyes again, at the same time dreading the thought of seeing that blank, professional look he reserved for people he didn't know well.

Her dress was two-tone, the bodice made from navy velvet and the skirt from pale blue silk. A wide band of navy velvet circled the base of the skirt and Melody had never felt more pretty in a dress than she did in this one. She was glad she'd saved it for last.

She took time with her hair, piling half of it up and leaving the other half to swirl around her shoulders. There was no need for a necklace as the dress had a high neckline. Finally, pleased with her appearance, she drove to the venue. Once again, she noted she was seated at George's table and called on every last ounce of determination she had, knowing she would need it to get through the night.

The instant she saw him across the crowded room her stomach began to churn and her knees went weak. She propped her elbow up on the bar for support and as her mouth went dry she reached, with a not-so-steady hand, for her drink. It was true. It was really true. She hadn't been imagining it after all. She really was in love with George Wilmont.

He spotted her and, just as she'd known, his brown eyes darkened momentarily with repressed desire. He quickly returned his attention to the person talking to him but she could see his impatience in the way he stood, the way he smiled politely and the way his gaze flicked to her another three times in under thirty seconds.

'Wow, boss,' Andy remarked from beside her. 'You look great.'

'Thank you, Andy,' she responded, smiling at her registrar as they were called into dinner. 'As do you.' He offered her his arm and she took it. She wanted to walk in with George, to talk with him, listen to him, soak up everything about him—but at the same time she wanted to keep as far away from him as possible.

It was just too soon. She'd only realised that morning that she was in love with the man and, quite frankly, she needed some time to adjust. Melody wasn't sitting next to George this time, which brought more mixed emotions. She wanted to be next to him, feel his body close to hers, breathe in the irresistible scent of him, fight the pull of his hypnotic gaze, and at the same moment she was glad of the reprieve.

Andy sat on one side of her, with Mr Okanadu on the other, his wife next to him. Mrs Okanadu spoke animatedly about her grandchildren and although Melody smiled and nodded in the right places, she was always conscious of every move George made.

He was seated almost directly opposite her and their gazes clashed several times across the large round table. Just after the main meal Melody excused herself and headed to the rest rooms. Once there, she leaned against the wall for support and closed her eyes. He was gorgeous, sexy and far too close. It pained her that he would leave tomorrow and right now, when she should be making the most of the time they had left together, she was keeping as far away as she possibly could.

'Hi, there.'

Melody's eyes snapped open at the other woman's voice and she found herself face to face with Hilary, one of the theatre nurses. 'Feeling all right?' she asked as she repaired her bright red lipstick.

'Sure,' Melody replied. 'Just a bit tired.'

'I hear the hand reconstruction went well.'

'Yes.' Melody nodded quickly. 'Very well.'

Hilary paused and looked over her shoulder before saying, 'I also hear that you and a certain visiting surgeon have been spending quite a bit of time together.'

Melody didn't need to look in the mirror to know that the colour had just drained from her face. 'Wh-what do you mean?'

'I mean the fact that I saw him get out of your car this

morning a block away from the hospital, and I wasn't the only one.' She grinned wildly at Melody. 'So—what's he like?'

'Like?'

'You know, to kiss? To cuddle? In bed?'

Melody's jaw dropped open in shock. 'That's none of your business.' The instant the words were out of her mouth, she realised she'd incriminated herself.

'So you *are* involved. How romantic! Was I right? Is he divorced or is he just…lonely?'

'Oh, this isn't happening,' Melody mumbled as she turned on the cold tap and ran her hands beneath the water. Taking a deep breath and calling on every ounce of professionalism she could muster, she turned off the tap and dried her hands before answering. 'Look, George is a nice man.'

'No kidding.'

'We're colleagues. *That's all.*'

'Yeah, right. I saw him get out of your car at eight o'clock in the morning. I know which hotel he's staying at, and you were coming from the opposite direction. I was also at his lecture, which started late, and when he finally arrived he was dressed in a suit and his hair was wet, as though he'd just had a shower.'

Melody gulped over the hard lump in her throat. She hated being the subject of hospital gossip and she knew that losing her temper and giving the nurse a piece of her mind would do no good. She was caught between a rock and a hard place—again—and, as usual, the guy walked away with no repercussions. Hilary was waiting for her answer and Melody smiled politely.

'You're a great theatre nurse.'

The other woman frowned. 'As opposed to what?'

'A private eye.' Melody turned on her heel and walked out. Inside, she was shaking like a leaf and thanked her training for making her appear outwardly composed. She tried telling herself she didn't care about the rumours and gossip but it didn't work. She should have made him take a taxi. She should have known that one block from the hospital wouldn't have been sufficient distance for people not to see them together.

'Shoulda, coulda, woulda...' she muttered as she walked over to the now deserted bar and leaned against it. What was she going to do? The pitying glances, the sorrowful looks. They were all going to come again, along with the 'poor Melody' sighs. This time, though, it would tear her heart to shreds and she doubted she'd ever recover.

Tears started to well in her eyes and she willed them away, massaging her temples, trying desperately to get herself under control. She sniffed and realised she was fighting a losing battle. She bit her lip and closed her eyes, tears falling onto her cheeks that she gently brushed away as she concentrated on some deep breaths.

'There you are.' George's deep voice washed over her. 'I've been worried.'

Her heart lunged with happiness at his words, making her feel as though everything would turn out right. He'd been worried about her. He'd been conscious of the time she'd been away from the table. Here was the man she loved, being so—so—darn sweet and yet, as she stared into his face, she couldn't help be swamped with overwhelming anger.

'What's wrong?' he asked when he saw she was upset. George went to place a hand on her shoulder but she quickly stopped him.

'Don't.'

'What's wrong?' he repeated, his tone more cautious than before.

'People saw you getting out of my car this morning.'

'What?' His eyes were wide with shock.

Melody shook her head. 'I knew I should have made you take a taxi.'

'So this is all my fault?'

'Yes.'

'How do you figure that?'

'Because you'll be gone tomorrow.'

'So?'

'So I'm the one who's going to be left with the rumours, gossip and pitying looks.'

'And you think you're the only person who's ever been gossiped about in hospitals?' George shoved both hands into his trouser pockets and looked down at his shoes for a moment. Slowly he lifted his head. 'I had to endure everything and more when Veronique died. She was an admin assistant there, so not only did I get pitying looks and sympathy, left, right and centre, I also had to deal with people avoiding me because they didn't know what to say. For six months, until I left to come away on the VOS, people avoided me. I didn't have normal conversations with my theatre staff except for "Pass me that retractor"!' He spoke in a harsh whisper, one that cut through Melody's self-indulgence like a scalpel.

'In some ways it was a relief to leave. I could concentrate on work, forget my pain and not have to put up with the quiet whispers in the hospital corridors. So, Dr Janeway, you are not the only one to have encountered the horrible hospital grapevine.'

Melody nodded once, acknowledging his words. 'But I can't escape,' she said softly. 'This is where I'm employed and although I plan to focus on my research, I still have to be Acting Director until the hospital appoints a successor. *This* is the hospital where I've been gossiped about before. It may not have been of the magnitude of yours but, still, the words, the looks—they can really hurt and I'm sick of it happening.' Her words were calm as she gazed up at him. She dabbed the tears from her eyes.

'Melody, I—'

'I'm going home now.'

He gazed at her for a long, drawn out moment and the whole world seemed to slip away, leaving the two of them the only people on earth. They'd connected. In five long, hectic days they'd made a dramatic connection and one where Melody had fallen madly in love with the man in front of her.

She wanted him to hold her, to kiss her, to tell her that everything would be all right. She wanted him to comfort her, to tell her she was important to him and that he loved her. She wanted—she wanted things he couldn't give.

George nodded and stepped back. 'I'll make your apologies.'

'I'd appreciate it.' Melody forced her legs to work as she walked past him.

'Can we still meet for breakfast tomorrow morning?' He spread his hands wide, indicating the decision was hers.

'Yes.'

'Good. I want a chance to say a proper goodbye.'

She opened her mouth to speak but closed it again, unsure what she should say. Goodbye? Why did everything seem so final with that word?

'Sleep sweet, Melody.' As much as he wanted to scoop her up and kiss her senseless, George knew he couldn't. He clamped down on the feeling, knowing it wouldn't do him any good. He'd just have to cool his heels until tomorrow. He watched the way she walked, head held high, purse clutched tightly in her hand. Her hips swayed slightly, her shoulders back, and he felt a tightening in his gut. She was dazzling and she'd dazzled him all week long.

Even as he allowed himself to acknowledge these feelings, hard on their heels came ones of guilt and remorse.

He knew he was legally a free man, but mentally and emotionally George wasn't sure if he was ready to move on. No matter what he did, he would end up hurting Melody. He cared about her so much that the thought of causing her pain made him feel physically ill.

If—and it was a big if—there was going to be anything permanent between Melody and himself, he owed it to both of them to deal with his past first, before moving on to the future. For the present? He raked a hand through his hair. For the present he was going to enjoy her company one last time. The consequences, for both of them, would come later. Of that he had little doubt.

CHAPTER FOURTEEN

ON SATURDAY MORNING he met her at the front of the hotel. Carmel would be taking his luggage to the airport so he wouldn't need to worry about it. Instead, he could focus on enjoying Melody's company as she drove them to her favourite café.

'What did you tell Carmel?' she asked him as they sat opposite each other and perused the menus.

'I told her you and I were going out for breakfast.'

'Really? What did she say?'

'She said, "Good."' He shrugged one shoulder. 'She thinks it's good for me to move forward with my life.'

Melody silently thanked Carmel for encouraging George. 'If breakfast is a step forward, then I'm glad to share it with you.' She grinned and reached for his hand.

'This is our last opportunity to be together.' He took her hand in his and raised it to his lips. 'Let's enjoy it.' They ordered food and enjoyed a leisurely meal. 'It's great not having to rush anywhere,' George remarked as he eased back in his chair and sipped his coffee. 'It's great just being with you.'

'I know what you mean.' Melody smiled, holding her coffee cup out to him. He clinked it and they both laughed. She didn't want to talk about their impending separation, about what might happen tomorrow or the next day or the day after that. She needed to savour, memorise, absorb every detail about George.

However, when they could delay their departure no longer, Melody concentrated on the road as she navigated her way towards the frantic Sydney airport, the soothing strains of Mozart filling the car.

George rested his head, eyes closed as the music surrounded them. His internal thoughts were turbulent, his emotions jumbled up and out of control. Meeting Melody had thrown his neatly ordered world into disarray and he wasn't sure how to put it back. He didn't want to leave her but he knew he had to go. He wanted to kiss her, to hold her close, but every time he did so he was later visited by guilt for moving on from his memories of Veronique.

He wanted to tell Melody that she meant a lot to him, that he wanted to be with her, to investigate this attraction, but he couldn't. He couldn't because he wasn't sure. He wasn't sure he wanted to be involved in another serious relationship. He'd loved deeply once before and his world had been blown apart when Veronique had died. Was he ready to put himself out there again? To risk loving another woman?

When Melody pulled into the airport car park she didn't turn the engine off. Instead, she swivelled in her chair and looked at him. His heart skipped a beat as he stared into her gorgeous green eyes. How was it possible she could have such a dramatic effect on him? When he saw tears beginning to gather in her eyes, his heart almost broke at the thought of leaving her.

'Uh—are you OK to go from here?'

'You're not going to walk me in?'

She shook her head. 'I don't know if I can.' Melody gazed into his eyes, her stomach churning with butterflies while her lower lip trembled.

He unbuckled his seat belt then reached out and cupped

her face in his hands. 'Melody.' Her name was a caress on his lips before his mouth met hers in a hungry, fiery and consuming kiss. He never wanted it to end. He wanted to take her with him, for her to be with him for ever. Melody moaned in delight, giving everything she had to him, and, being greedy, he took it.

His phone beeped, indicating he'd received a text message. 'It's Carmel. She says they're calling our flight.' He opened the car door and climbed out, pleased when Melody climbed from the driver's seat and came around to him.

'Will you walk me in?' He just couldn't leave her—not yet. But why? Why was he finding it so difficult to say goodbye?

'I'll walk you to the door but I just— I can't…' She stopped and took his hand in hers. 'I can't watch you walk away from me.'

George shook his head and gathered her close once more. 'I know. I finally understand Shakespeare's "Parting is such sweet sorrow."' He kissed Melody again but when another text message came through, he knew if he didn't hustle, he'd miss the plane. 'I've got to go.'

She held his hand for a moment longer and shook her head, not bothering to choke back the tears. 'George…' She shook her head. 'I—I don't want you to go.' Her words were broken as the emotion burst forth. He clenched his jaw and shook his head before gathering her close and kissing her deeply one last time. 'I—I love you, George.'

He leaned back and looked at her in utter astonishment. She *loved* him? Before he could process her words, his name was called over the PA system.

'I have to go.'

She hiccupped a few times, letting him go and covering her mouth with her hand. He forced himself to turn, to walk away from her, and with each step he felt as though he was walking through a quagmire. He told himself not to look back but just before he was rushed through security he gave in to the impulse and what he saw almost broke his own heart.

There she was. The woman who had just offered him her love, standing alone near the doorway, hands covering her face as she sobbed. She loved him. Melody *loved* him—and he was leaving. He had to. He had to return to Melbourne to find out what his life was all about because right at this moment he really had no clue.

Who was he? How could he let go of the past? What was he supposed to do when the tour ended? He shook his head sadly as he continued through the process of boarding the plane, barely hearing a word Carmel or anyone else said. How had he reached a point in his life where he had no earthly idea what he was doing? Could he ever hope to be happy again, or was he doomed to the loneliness that stretched before him?

Lonely widower George Wilmont. Was that all?

CHAPTER FIFTEEN

WHEN THE DOORBELL RANG, George walked through his house, a slight spring in his step. He opened the door with anticipation and smiled at Carmel. 'I never thought I'd be happy to see you at my door,' he stated, and Carmel laughed. 'Come in.' He beckoned.

'Would it be crazy to say I've missed you?' she asked as she followed him through to the dining room, which was strewn with papers. 'I can't believe it's almost two whole weeks since we finished the tour.'

'I can't believe I've written so many reports and papers in those two weeks.'

'Are they all finished?'

'Ah…there's that Miss Efficient Organiser tone I haven't missed at all.' They both laughed and sat down to chat.

'How are you doing, George?' She gestured to the sparse room. 'I mean, Christmas is two days away and not a decoration in sight.'

He shrugged. 'Not really in the Christmas spirit this year.'

'Are you doing anything on Christmas Day? Seeing Veronique's family?'

He shook his head. 'I'm rostered on at the hospital.'

'I didn't think you were back there until the New Year.'

'I'm just doing a few shifts over the Christmas and New Year period. The acting head of department needs to spend some time with his family.' Even as he said the words 'acting head of department' his thoughts immediately went to a different acting department head, a beautiful redhead with mesmerising green eyes who had captured his heart.

Ever since leaving Sydney to complete the visiting orthopaedic specialist tour, George had been hard pressed to get Melody out of his head. Two days after they'd left he'd received an official email from her, on behalf of the rest of the department, thanking him and his staff for choosing St Aloysius as part of the VOS tour. It had been formal, official and he'd been miserable on reading it. Melody. He couldn't go to sleep without thinking of her smile, without dreaming of being with her, laughing with her, kissing her.

'You're like a bear with a sore head,' Carmel had accused him five days later. 'For heaven's sake, email Melody, call Melody, text her with a plethora of emojis if you're unsure what to say, but do *something*, George. You're making the rest of us miserable.'

And so he'd emailed her, an equally polite message, stating that he and his team had enjoyed their stay. He'd signed off the email asking her what her favourite part had been. He'd received a one-word reply—*You*. Clearly that hadn't been an official email but the reply had made his heart soar with delight, and along with the delight had come the guilt, the guilt that he was moving on from his marriage, that he was moving away from Veronique and everything they'd shared together.

Since then, he'd taken Carmel's advice on board and had sent Melody a text message with emojis. His usual one had been the exhausted or sleeping emoji. She would often reply with emojis of her own, all of them upbeat and encouraging, as though she was eager for him to finish this tour.

Carmel waved a hand in front of his face. 'I know that blank look. You were thinking about Melody, weren't you?'

George sighed, not bothering to deny it. 'She's constantly on my mind. I don't know what to do.'

'Do you love her?'

'I...' He shrugged his shoulders and closed his eyes. 'I don't know. Sometimes I think yes, sometimes I think no. Sometimes I think we had such an intense time together, it must all have been an illusion. Perhaps there's nothing more between us than infatuation?'

'That doesn't sound like fun.'

'It isn't. That's why I was more than happy to pick up a few shifts at the hospital. Work will help.'

'That's what you told me after Veronique's death. Work would help.'

'And it did. It always does.'

'But you also run the risk of working too much, of burying your life in work and then having nothing else to exist for.' Carmel's words held a hint of sadness and nothingness. It helped snap George out of his own self-pity.

'Are you and Diana OK?'

'We're more than OK.' Carmel held up her hand to reveal a lovely engagement ring.

'Wow!' George inspected the ring. 'That's beautiful.'

'Diana chose it. I chose hers. We're very happy, George, but I was so caught up in my work for so long that I didn't see how happy I could be if I just let myself.'

'Are you telling me to let myself be happy? Because if you are, I'm not sure I know how to do that.'

Carmel thought for a moment then changed the subject. 'How's Veronique's family?'

'They're good. Great even. Her parents have travel plans, her sister's pregnant.'

'Good for them.'

'Everybody's moving on.' He shook his head. 'In some ways it's as though we're forgetting Veronique altogether.'

'No.' Carmel shook her head. 'Not *forgetting*, George, but honouring her by not weeping or covering yourself with sackcloth and ashes for the rest of your life. You know she wouldn't have wanted that. She would have wanted you to be happy.'

'That's what her mother told me.'

'It's good advice.'

'But how do I do that?' He spread his arms wide, indicating the house. 'Even this place feels like it belongs to someone else.'

'It did. You're a different man now, George. You're not Veronique's husband any more.'

'No. I'm not that man.'

'You're a new man, with a new world at your command. So the big question is, what do you want? Where do you want to live? Do you want to work at Melbourne General? Who do you choose to share your life with?'

They were definite questions to think on, and after Carmel had collected all the reports and papers and said her farewells, George walked back into his quiet house and sat staring at his phone. Every question he asked himself seemed to lead to one person—and one person only. Melody. He should call her. He should—

His phone beeped. It was a message from Melody. Three emojis—a happy face, a Christmas tree and a heart. He raised his eyebrows at the heart. That was one she'd never sent him before. A heart? Did that mean she still loved him? He hadn't quashed it by not professing his own feelings?

Was it possible that he could be twice blessed in love? First with Veronique and now with the vivacious, intelligent and heart-melting Melody Janeway?

Love? Was he in love with Melody? Even as the question crossed his mind, he couldn't help the large smile that spread across his lips.

Melody put her phone on the table and closed her eyes. She shouldn't have sent him the heart emoji. It was too much. They hadn't even spoken since he'd left, just the initial emails and then text messages consisting of emojis. It was silly but it was better than nothing, and if that's what George needed to do while he figured out what he wanted then she would wait.

It was a decision she'd come to about three days after he'd left Sydney. Her brother Ethan had come to Sydney with a patient and had insisted on having a frank discussion with his little sister.

'You're clearly in love with the man,' Ethan had stated after she'd told him everything.

'I know.'

Ethan had chuckled. 'And yet you don't sound too happy about it.'

'There's nothing I can do, Ethan, but wait. George has a lot to sort out, more emotional baggage than I have, I think. The death of his wife is a far greater loss to deal with than a broken engagement by some jerk I'm better off without.'

'So you're just going to wait?'

'I'm going to *hope*.'

'Hope is good but it'll only get you so far, Mel. One day you'll need to act because if you don't, you risk losing everything. Believe me, I know. I was almost too stubborn to let go of my past so that I could move forward with CJ and now...' he'd grinned '... I'm the happiest man on earth.'

'That's what I want. I want to be happy—*with George*.'

'Does this mean you're thinking about moving to Melbourne?'

She'd sighed and nodded. 'If I have to, yes.'

'Huh. Surprising but good. Or would you prefer George to move to Sydney?'

'I don't care if we both move and end up in Far North Queensland or overseas, I just want to be with him, Ethan. I love him.' Her job was to wait and hope and pray and love George from afar, giving him the space he needed so he could sort out what he wanted. Melody hoped it was her.

Melody spent her Christmas working at the hospital and even though there weren't too many patients in the wards and all the hospital administrative meetings had been cancelled until the new year, she was glad of the opportunity to lose herself. Thinking about George every hour she was awake and then dreaming about him all night was almost becoming exhausting. Almost…

Two days after Christmas, though, the CEO had told her to take time off work. 'Go home, Melody. See your family. Go and see your new niece and spend some time with Ethan in the wine district. You're starting to look as ashen as he used to.'

'But there's so much to do,' she'd protested, but had been overruled.

'And there will be plenty of time to do it,' she'd been told in return. 'This request is not negotiable.'

And so Melody had headed to see Ethan and CJ for the New Year, delighting in spending time with Lizzie-Jean, who was crawling all over the place and starting to pull herself up on furniture. She watched her brother and CJ together, amazed at just how happy Ethan really was, and she yearned to be equally as happy.

She'd received the usual text message emojis from George, the exhausted or sleepy one and—on Christmas Day—a Christmas tree with a smiley face. Had she been wrong to send him the heart emoji? Had she scared him off?

It was only two days into the new year when her phone

rang and she quickly checked the caller identification—her heart plummeting when she realised it was only the hospital's CEO.

'Melody, I'm sorry to call you but we actually need you to come back to the hospital.'

'What's wrong?'

'Nothing's wrong,' the CEO told her. 'We've found the perfect candidate to take over from you as head of department. Isn't that great news?'

'It is. Do you need me to come back and do a handover?'

'That's exactly what we need. If you can have one week with the new head, handing things over while the operating lists and patient numbers are low, that would be helpful. Then, when clinics start up in another week, he'll be ready to take on the full duties and you'll be free to return to your position as resident orthopaedic surgeon and devote as much time to your research project as you'd like.'

Melody breathed in a cleansing breath. It also meant she'd be able to move to Melbourne if she needed to.

'Who's the new head, then?' Ethan asked, as he watched his sister pack.

'I didn't ask and I don't really care.' She laughed with delight. 'I'm free, Ethan. I don't have to worry about letting everyone down and I can move to Melbourne to be near George and—'

'What happened to giving him space?'

'I think he's had enough space. I'm through marking time. I'm going to find that man and make him see sense. I'm going to let him know that I love him and I'll wait for as long as I need to until he can tell me he loves me, too because I'm pretty sure he does...' She frowned. 'At least, I hope he does.'

'Don't go second-guessing yourself,' Ethan encouraged as he zipped up her bag and carried it out to her car. 'It's not that I want you to leave, sis, but, seriously, go and get this whole thing sorted out so I can see you being happy instead of being as miserable as a wet week.'

Melody laughed, not taking offence at her brother's words. It was because he loved her, because he wanted the best for his sister that he was all but pushing her out of his home.

The drive back to Sydney was refreshing as she started making plans for her new future.

She hadn't realised how much of a weight the head of department job had been around her neck until it had been lifted. When she arrived at her apartment, it was to find George standing there, knocking on her door.

Melody closed her eyes and blinked one very long blink as she continued to stare at him. Was she seeing things?

'George?'

He turned to look at her, taking in the bag in her hand and the sunglasses on her head. 'You weren't home.'

'No. I was at Ethan's.'

'Oh. I didn't know.'

'How could you?'

They stood there, so close to each other and yet so far apart, both of them having the most ridiculous conversation as they drank in the sight of each other. 'What are you doing here?'

'I—uh—sent you a text message.'

'You did?' She dug in her bag for her phone. 'I have it off when I drive so I'm not tempted to answer any calls or messages.'

'Good. Safe driving practice,' he stated. 'That's good.'

She found her phone and switched it on, waiting impatiently for the message light to blink so she could look at it. When she opened the text message from George it was to find one single emoji—a red heart.

Melody stared at the emoji, then looked at George, hope filling her heart. 'Really?'

He nodded, then as though the admission had given them both wings they were in each other's arms, their mouths meeting and melding with perfect synchronicity. She kissed him with all the love in her heart, wanting him to feel just how wonderful he made her feel. In return, she felt his own need, his desire and his acceptance of their mutual love.

When one of her neighbours came out into the corridor, seeing the two of them kissing, Melody belatedly realised where they were. She'd been so caught up in everything about him that she hadn't even opened the door to her apartment. She quickly unlocked her door and beckoned him inside. It was then she realised that he, too, had a bag beside him—a large bag.

'You're staying in Sydney?'

'I'm staying wherever you are,' he told her as he gathered her close again, kicking the door shut to the apartment to ensure they had all the privacy they needed.

'I was going to do the same thing. I told Ethan I wanted to be wherever you were and that if you didn't love me I would give you all the time you needed to come to the sane and rational conclusion that we belong together.'

'You were going to leave Sydney?'

'I got a call from the CEO—they've found a new head of department so I'm free, George. I'm free to move to Melbourne or to Timbuktu—I don't care, so long as I'm with *you*.' She pressed a kiss to his lips then shook her head. 'I know we only had one week together but these past ten weeks apart have been absolute torture.' She kissed him again. 'I missed being able to talk to you, to share things with you, to just sit and spend time with you.'

'You could have called me,' he ventured, but she shook her head.

'I knew I had to be patient and to trust you, two things I needed to have more practice with.' She broke free from him for a moment and took his hand, leading him over to the lounge, where they sat down together. 'You needed to sort things out in your own way, in your own time.'

'When I returned to Melbourne—' George stopped and shook his head. 'It was as though I was having an out-of-body experience. I could walk around my house, the place I'd lived with Veronique, and it was as though I was intruding on someone else's life. It wasn't mine. It wasn't where I belonged any more. I felt the same way at the hospital. I did a few shifts over Christmas and New Year, and although everything was familiar it was…out of balance with the man I'd become.'

George shook his head and held her hands in his. 'I'm not the same man I used to be and that's all because of you, Melody.' He held her gaze as he spoke, his tone intense and filled with repressed desire. 'Our week together helped me realise that I'd merely been existing, going through my days one at a time but not really taking anything in. In the beginning the travelling had been good for my grief but it wasn't until I arrived back in Melbourne that I realised I was done.'

'Done with grieving?'

He shook his head. 'Done with the guilt from wanting to move forward.'

'Good, because I don't think you're ever *done* with grieving. It just…changes.'

'It does, and Veronique's mother told me herself that Veronique wouldn't be happy if I was always looking backwards. My wife would want me to be happy and you…' He lifted her hands to his lips and pressed soft kisses to her knuckles. 'You make me happy, Melody. Being with you, laughing with you, working with you.'

'Working with me?'

George gave her a lopsided smile and shrugged one shoulder. 'Didn't you mention St Aloysius had found a new head of the department? That you were now free to do whatever you wanted?'

Melody frowned at him for a moment before dawning realisation crossed her face. '*You're* the new head of department?'

'There was nothing for me in Melbourne any more and everything here in Sydney because Sydney is where *you* are.'

'You took the head of department position?' She laughed with rising incredulity.

'Is that OK?'

'Uh…yeah.' She nodded her head for emphasis. 'Of course it is, but are you sure you'll be happy here?'

'Yes. I like the hospital. I like Rick, who I've insisted remain as my PA, and I like the resident orthopaedic surgeon…very much.' He leaned forward as he said the last few words then captured her lips with his. 'Very much,' he reiterated a few moments later after delighting in the way Melody kissed him back with such uninhibited abandon.

'I love you, George.'

'I love you, too, Melody.'

'You do?' She smiled as though she was still unable to believe it.

'I do, so very much. My life was…incomplete without you.'

'Mine, too.'

'Then be with me for ever, Melody. You complete me and I want to feel like that for ever. Marry me?'

She gasped at his words but before she could answer, he continued.

'Let me show you I'm not like the other dead-heads who broke your heart. I love your intellect, the way we can talk about operating techniques, share the highs and the lows of our jobs. I've never had that with anyone before but when I found it with you it was as though a part of me became complete. Then another part and then another. Be my wife,' he urged. 'Complete me.'

'And children?' she asked hesitantly. 'Do you want children?'

'With you? Absolutely.' His kissed her once more, a kiss that was filled with passion and promise—the promise of a long and devoted life together. 'Say yes,' he ground out as he nibbled his way to her ear lobe. 'Say yes.'

'I will.' She laughed, happier than she'd ever been in her life. 'If you'd give me half a chance.' Goose-bumps shivered down her body as he continued his assault. Giggling, she planted her hand in his hair and gently tugged his head away. 'George!'

'Sorry. It's been so long since I've been able to kiss you like this and all I've dreamed about every day we were apart.'

'Well, we're not apart now.' Her words were filled with love, love for the man who was her soul mate, her other half. 'I'll agree to complete you if you complete me. George, you don't need to show or prove anything to me— because you've already done it. I'm not talking about moving to Sydney but the fact that you accept me just as I am. No man has ever done that before. You're the first—and the last.' She brushed her lips across his. 'Marry me quickly.'

'As you wish.' His mouth met hers in a mutual declaration of love, one they were both willing to contribute to and work at. 'How am I going to be able to keep my hands off you?' he groaned as he buried his face in her neck, unable to resist kissing the soft skin. 'Working with you every day. Sitting next to you in departmental meetings. I don't know if my self-control can take it.'

George raised his head to look at the woman he loved. The woman who had made him the happiest man on the face of the earth. He smiled at her.

'I guess we'd better work out some...' she paused and raised her eyebrows suggestively '...guidelines, then.'

His gaze darkened with desire. 'I look forward to it, Dr Janeway.'

'So do I, Professor!'

EPILOGUE

THE FOLLOWING CHRISTMAS neither George nor Melody was working. Both of them were enjoying spending their holidays with family. Ethan and CJ had decided to host Christmas at their place in Pridham, and with Melody's parents and brother Dave and his family coming to join in the festivities it was most definitely a madcap time for all of them. Donna and her husband Philip were there as well, allowing George to catch up with his old friends.

After they'd all enjoyed a huge barbeque lunch with a plethora of salads, the Australian heat giving them a slight reprieve and only being mildly hot instead of stinking hot, Melody had adjourned inside to relax in the air-conditioning. Sitting in CJ's living room, she put her feet up on the lounge and closed her eyes, a possessive hand on her slightly swollen abdomen.

'Ah, good. I was just coming to see if you were resting,' George stated as he brought her a glass of iced water.

'I am.' Just then she felt the baby move and although she'd been able to feel it shift around for a while, George was yet to feel it. 'Here. Quick.' She reached for his hand and placed it on her abdomen. 'Wait. Just wait a second.'

They both waited, their wedding rings touching as Melody placed her hand over George's. Their wedding day had been a lovely one, nice and quiet but filled with their friends and family beneath a small marquee in one of Sydney's prettiest parks. After the pomp and ceremony of the VOS, neither of them had wanted a lavish affair, preferring to focus on the main aspect, which was the two of them making an open and honest declaration of their love for each other.

Then, only two months later, Melody had announced to her husband that she thought she might be pregnant. George had instantly bought a pregnancy test and they'd waited and watched together as the test had confirmed that Melody's supposition had been correct.

A moment later the baby moved and George's eyes widened in delighted astonishment.

'Did you feel it?'

'I felt it.' He grinned widely and bent down to kiss her abdomen.

'What are you two doing?' CJ asked as she came into the room, Ethan hard on her heels, twenty-month-old Lizzie-Jean wriggling around in her daddy's arms.

'I just felt the baby kick!' George laughed. 'It's the first time.'

'It's a great feeling,' Ethan remarked, coming to stand next to his wife and placing a possessive hand on CJ's very flat stomach. 'And one we're looking forward to enjoying in a few months' time as well.'

'Wait. What?' Melody tried to sit up but found it difficult to move quickly. Thankfully, George was by her side and immediately helped her up. 'You're going to have another baby?'

'Lizzie-Jean's going to have a little brother or sister,' CJ confirmed, and the two women embraced. George and Ethan shook hands then gave each other a brotherly hug.

'We really are becoming one *big* happy family,' Melody stated, and Ethan agreed.

'Come on, CJ. Let's go and break the news to Mum and Dad that they're going to be grandparents again.'

After they'd headed out, George sat on the lounge, his wife in his arms. 'Can you believe it? It's good that all the cousins are going to be close in age.'

'It is.' Melody smiled, tears of happiness starting to prick behind her eyes. 'It's wonderful. Where I thought I'd never find true love, never find the right man for me, into my life you came with a twinkling grin and turned my world upside down.' She kissed her husband. 'Thank you for making me so happy.'

'Right back at you,' he replied, and kissed her soundly, so glad he'd had the courage to take this second chance at love, because now his cup really did runneth over.

* * * * *

MILLS & BOON

Coming next month

REUNITED BY THEIR SECRET SON
Louisa George

Finn walked through to the waiting room and was just about to call out the boy's name when he was struck completely dumb. His heart thudded against his ribcage as he watched the woman reading a story to her child. Her voice quiet and sing-song, dark hair tumbling over one shoulder, ivory skin. A gentle manner. Soft.

His brain rewound, flickering like an old film reel: dark curls on the pillow. Warm caramel eyes. A mouth that tasted so sweet. Laughter in the face of grief. One night.

That night...

A lifetime ago.

He snapped back to reality. He wasn't that man any more; he'd do well to remember that. He cleared his throat and glanced down at the notes file in his hand to remind himself of the name. 'Lachlan Harding?'

She froze, completely taken aback. For a second he saw fear flicker across her eyes then she stood up. The fear gone, she smiled hesitantly and tugged the boy closer to her leg, her voice a little wobbly and a little less soft. 'Wow. Finn, this is a surprise—'

'Sophie. Hello. Yes, I'm Finn. Long time, no see.' Glib, he knew, when there was so much he should say to explain what had happened, why he hadn't called, but telling her his excuses during a professional consultation wasn't the right time. Besides, she had a child now; she'd moved on from their one night together, clearly. He glanced at her left hand, the one that held her boy so close—no wedding ring. But that didn't mean a thing these days; she could be happily unmarried and in a relationship.

And why her marital status pinged into his head he just didn't know. He had no right to wonder after the silence he'd held for well over two years.

They were just two people who'd shared one night a long time ago.

Copyright ©2018 Louisa George

Continue reading
REUNITED BY THEIR SECRET SON
Louisa George

Available next month
www.millsandboon.co.uk

LET'S TALK
Romance

For exclusive extracts, competitions
and special offers, find us online:

📘 facebook.com/millsandboon

📷 @millsandboonuk

🐦 @millsandboon

Or get in touch on 0844 844 1351*

For all the latest titles coming soon, visit
millsandboon.co.uk/nextmonth

*Calls cost 7p per minute plus your phone company's price per minute access charge